UNGRATEFUL

ANGELA CHADWICK

dialogue
books

DIALOGUE BOOKS

First published in Great Britain in 2022 by Dialogue Books

10 9 8 7 6 5 4 3 2 1

A CIP catalogue record for this book
is available from the British Library.

Hardback ISBN 978-0-349-70230-8
C-format ISBN 978-0-349-70229-2

Typeset in Berling by M Rules
Printed and bound in Great Britain by
Clays Ltd, Elcograf S.p.A

Papers used by Dialogue Books are from well-managed forests
and other responsible sources.

MIX
Paper from
responsible sources
FSC
www.fsc.org   FSC® C104740

Dialogue Books
An imprint of
Little, Brown Book Group
Carmelite House
50 Victoria Embankment
London EC4Y 0DZ

An Hachette UK Company
www.hachette.co.uk

www.littlebrown.co.uk

UNGRATEFUL

Also by Angela Chadwick

XX

For Mick, in loving memory

Chapter 1

Catherine Brandon made her way through what must usually be a sports hall, past teenagers hunching their shoulders as parents interrogated university staff. There was a smell of rubber, of feet, that seemed at odds with the corporate banners and tidy piles of brochures laid out for the open day. Could her lack of A-levels be put aside? A no would be a sign, proof her new ambition was misguided. She could already feel the disappointment of it, a toxic residue gathering in her bones. *Do not give up*, she instructed herself, *you'll never do the things you want with your life if you continue being this weak.*

'Cat?'

She turned and saw a man wearing jeans and a blazer leaning against the history stand she'd been looking for. His eyes locked on hers and she felt a jolt of recognition. *Daniel.* In the twenty years since she'd last seen him, he'd broadened out across the shoulders and a short crop had replaced the tentative dreadlocks of his teenage years, but his face still radiated intelligence and interest in the world. She wasn't sure who initiated the hug, but in an instant her chin was resting on his shoulder, his arms were around her.

He broke away first, smiling broadly. 'You look fantastic! What are you doing with yourself these days?'

Cat swallowed. 'Don't laugh, but I'm here to look at courses.'

'Undergraduate courses? You can't mean ...'

She gave him a sad smile. She'd missed the A-level exams she was supposed to do well in. Hadn't been able to take her place at Warwick University. Hadn't made anything of herself.

'Oh,' said Daniel.

Cat braved a look at his face and saw him recalibrating his idea of her. Up until now he probably imagined something so very different. Maybe she was on the ground in Yemen, coordinating food shipments. Or perhaps he pictured her in a suit, preparing policy documents for a think tank. At college, they'd constructed countless grandiose versions of the future, and lying next to him on his single bed, she'd been able to picture everything he described, shivering with anticipation as she dared to believe she might one day become someone important.

She would have done anything to reverse the last few moments, to walk out of this echoing sports hall and let those better Catherines remain intact in his mind.

'What about you? What are you doing here?' she asked.

'Touting courses. I run the history programmes, but they're determined to make a salesman of me. All I seem to do at the moment is hang around answering parents' questions. Hey, have you got time for a coffee?'

Cat was tempted to make her excuses and leave. She was going to be a disappointment – she could already anticipate the embarrassed quality that would appear in his eyes and the swell of mortification she'd feel in response. But this was Daniel. She didn't believe in concepts as trite as fate, but if anyone could help her understand the unsettling feelings that seemed to be overrunning her just lately, the flashes of anger that reminded her of her father, it would be Daniel.

The chatter of parents clutching their free coffees filled the university canteen. It was a vast space with large windows overlooking a busy Portsmouth street, the tables were littered with torn sugar packets and disposable cups, with napkins and crumbs. Cat felt a twinge of empathy for the waitress, rushing around with a blue cloth and bin bag, whispering hasty apologies as she tried to stay on top of the mess.

As Daniel went to order, Cat thought back to their time at sixth-form college on the outskirts of the city. She'd been drawn to him from their very first history class and after a fortnight they'd gone to the pub together and ended up kissing. Like her, Daniel was from a poor, single-parent family. But unlike her, he'd been wholly unembarrassed about his background, often referencing it when lessons touched on class or social unrest. His confidence had been a revelation, encouraging Cat to want more, to believe it possible that council-estate kids could remake themselves into anything they wanted.

Such an insignificant thing she'd been, before Daniel. She'd grown up in Petersfield, a small town half an hour down the railway line from Portsmouth, where she still lived now. People went on about how pretty it was, nestled in the South Downs. But she'd never perceived the beauty. A memory of junior school, so vivid that she could recall the exact shade of golden light pouring through the classroom window, came to her. Outside, there had been a few small shrubs alive with sparrows, jostling and cheeping; tumbling down into the flower beds to flutter their wings in the dirt.

The mascot of the local football team, a man in a chemical-blue puppy costume, had been due to visit and there was to be a photo for the local paper. The headmaster had made everyone not wearing the correct uniform stand up and trudge back to their classrooms before the end of assembly. Cat had been singled out because she didn't have shoes, only plimsolls, so she and Becky Milner, plus a smattering of children from other classes, had to walk back through the empty corridors, while behind them the remainder of the school had chattered with excitement at a grown man pretending to be a puppy.

The thing that really stuck was just how angry Cat's teacher, Miss Jones, had been to see her arriving back. 'Uniform? Of all the petty . . . ' She'd stopped herself, given the girls a smile. But it had been clear to Cat that her teacher felt the injustice more keenly than she did. It should have felt good, but Miss Jones's adult anger somehow deepened Cat's shame. For the first time, she recognised the difference between solidarity and pity. At just eight – a vulnerable, incorrectly dressed eight – Cat had been made to understand that she didn't quite belong.

Daniel placed two cardboard cups down on the table and took the seat opposite her. 'So, what are you planning on studying? Don't tell me history – that would be surreal.'

Cat nodded. 'Yeah. It was always going to be history. I still can't get over you being a lecturer. I was expecting someone in tweed.'

'I'd love having you in my seminar groups.'

'I'd stand out though, right? I mean, I'm old enough to be the kids' mum.'

'Barely. Not that it matters in the slightest.'

'Would I even be let in without A-levels?'

'You weren't able to resit them?' Daniel frowned.

Cat shook her head and looked away. Daniel reached out and laid a hand on her forearm. The sensation of his skin against hers was overpowering, awakening memories that had lain dormant in the cells of her body. How she'd missed him. And now he was here, at the very moment she'd decided to remake herself.

'You must have had a tough time of it,' Daniel said. 'God, I feel so guilty that I didn't get in touch and see how you were doing.'

Cat looked at him, suddenly tired of trying to be glib. 'It's never too late, right? I could educate myself, *do* something with my life?'

Daniel removed his hand from her arm and smiled. 'Of course you can. Our admissions approach is pretty subjective, especially where mature students are concerned. You had a solid reason for not sitting your A-levels and you mustn't be shy about getting the violins out. Just write a killer personal statement talking about how you've developed your interest in the subject. Talk about the reading you've done – drop in a few titles, nothing too mainstream, and you should be fine.'

Cat took a deep breath. She knew she'd be able to write a compelling statement. In her twenties, she'd found the reading lists for Oxford's history modules and ordered several of the books from her local library. As she'd sat next to her mother's bed, or made the painfully slow bus and train journeys to and from hospital, she'd immersed herself in the very same texts Daniel would have been reading.

'What made you decide to do this now?' Daniel asked. 'I mean, it's pretty brave revisiting the idea of uni after so many years.'

Cat sipped the coffee – it was nowhere near strong enough for her taste. 'I've been telling myself – ever since college really – that I'd sort myself out. Mum's recovery took four years. There was no one else to help, so I kind of put everything on hold. Then I got together with this guy, and he gave me a comfortable life. I can't tell you what it felt like, to not have to worry about bills or damp for the first time.'

'Comfortable is a big deal for people like us.' The way Daniel looked at her sent a soothing warmth through Cat's middle.

'This is going to sound really silly, but I had an epiphany a couple of weeks back. I was flicking through the paper, reading about government cuts to libraries and I found myself getting furious. It felt personal. I remember all the afternoons I spent in the library as a girl, staying warm, doing my home-work in the quiet.' She folded her hands in her lap, afraid she might start trembling. 'I want to be the kind of person that *does* shit. Someone who influences things. But I know I need to educate myself if I want to be taken seriously.'

'It's not too late.' Daniel's eyes were suddenly serious. 'I think it's admirable, actually.'

Cat felt strangely close to tears. 'I didn't imagine it, did I? I was doing well at college. If it hadn't been for the accident, I definitely would have gone to uni?'

'Absolutely.'

'Because sometimes I tell myself I was deluded all along. That it was only ever a dream and my dad was right, I was just some small-town tart with ideas above her station.'

Daniel shook his head. 'Christ, if I'm honest, I envied you. The way you'd read something once and know it inside out. I had to study for hours and hours to even come close to keeping up with you.'

Cat tucked a few stray hairs behind her ear. 'Cheers, that's really good to hear. Now, tell me all about you.'

Daniel looked at her and something indefinable passed through his eyes. *Was it regret?* There was definitely something hesitant there and it made Cat ache to see it. Had he thought about her occasionally, in the two decades that had passed?

'I did my master's and PhD, then kind of fell into lecturing. Came back to Portsmouth five years ago to take on the dubious privilege of being the only Black academic in the humanities department. Married a nurse, Elizabeth, and we have three-year-old twins.'

'Congratulations,' Cat said. There was a bitter edge to her tone, even though she hadn't meant to sound that way at all. She was just surprised. What he was describing was so far removed from the international-statesman ambitions he'd harboured when they were younger.

Daniel smiled and drew up his shoulders, as though suddenly self-conscious. It was as though they were both remembering that twenty years ago he'd left her. Daniel had moved on with his life, gone to university like they planned, and Cat had been forced to stay behind. The air between them became charged as they regarded one another without speaking.

'Right then,' Daniel said at last. 'I'd better get back to my stand, before the marketing department snitches on me for disappearing. Can I look forward to receiving an application from you?'

Cat gathered up their empty cups and placed her empty sugar packets inside. 'Definitely. Now I know that you'll be one of my teachers, I'm more determined than ever.'

Chapter 2

When James first met Cat, he'd not long started his new job as web manager at Stewart & Wright, an old English clothing firm known for shockingly priced coats and bags. A couple of the guys had offered to show him the town's nightlife and he'd accepted with relief and gratitude; he was new to the area and keen to establish a social circle.

They gave him directions to a bar named Martin's, where they said they'd meet him at eight on the Friday night. He'd been ridiculously pleased. His decision to move to Petersfield had been made quickly after his break-up with Amy, the girlfriend of his university days. His parents had bought a place in one of the nearby villages after his father's retirement, and it just so happened that there was a suitable job going in the town.

At ten to eight, he found the estate agent's his friends had described and located the somewhat shabby entrance to the bar at the side of the building. The stairwell stank of cigarettes, which struck him as unusual – indoor smoking had recently been banned and he'd become accustomed to the odour's absence.

Upstairs, he made his way along a faded carpet to the bar.

Several faces looked up at once. A bald man, with a tattoo of a tarantula on his neck, quickly whipped the cigarette he'd been smoking behind his back as the murmur of conversation ceased.

James's face became hot. He felt scrutinised as he positioned himself on a bar stool, aware that, at five foot two, he was a great deal shorter than the other men and that they were right now observing this fact.

'What can I get you?' The woman behind the bar had a cloud of long, dark hair and smooth olive skin. She seemed too good-looking, too young, to be working in such a place, yet appeared entirely undaunted by the rather rough-looking men surrounding her.

'Um, what bottled beers do you have?' He was aware of a couple of men sniggering to his right.

The barmaid turned to glare at them and there was instant silence. 'Bud or Beck's,' she said, beaming at James.

'Ah, make it a bottle of Beck's then. And one for yourself.' He tried a confident smile. He'd never bought a drink for a bartender before, but it felt as though maybe this was the kind of thing you ought to do in a smaller town. He wanted to feel at home in this quiet community, to exchange friendly waves and smiles on the street, raise his children in a place where the parks were free of needles.

Across the bar, a white-haired man lit a cigarette with an insolent stare. James sipped his drink nervously. There was an unkemptness to most of the clientele that made him feel self-conscious about his gelled hair and crisply ironed shirt. He looked at his phone. No messages. He hoped the guys would be here soon. The other fellows were still watching him and this felt like the kind of place where fights could break out.

It got to eight fifteen. Still no sign of his colleagues. He wondered whether it was too early to text and decided it was; they might think he was uptight. He'd give them until half past. They'd surely be here by then.

'You're not from here,' a guy on his left ventured.

'No,' James turned to face the man. 'I've just started working at Stewart & Wright.' Another nervous sip from his bottle.

'Tommy works at Wright's, don't you, Tommy?'

The man with the neck tattoo looked him up and down. 'Don't know your face. One of the office lot?'

James nodded. He realised he was running his fingers over the acne scars on his cheek and quickly put his hand down on the bar. 'I manage the website.'

'What you doing here, then?'

'Keep it friendly, gents.' It was the barmaid. She gave James a kindly smile with just a little pity in it. 'Another drink?'

James nodded with relief, watching her bend down to retrieve the bottle from the fridge. She had the tiniest little bottom, and James felt himself flush as he caught the man called Tommy's eye.

Just then, his phone rang and he was greeted by a burst of laughter. 'All right, James, having a lovely time at Martin's? Sorry, mate, it was Tim's idea to send you there. Bloody mean trick if you ask me, but we couldn't resist it. We're in the wine bar over the road. Next one's on me.'

James let out a relieved laugh. He wasn't even angry at the prank that had been played on him, he just wanted to leave. Thank goodness this wasn't where his colleagues spent their weekends.

As he rose from his bar stool, he noticed the barmaid observing him. She was standing perfectly straight and there was something defiant in the set of her mouth. Surely, she hadn't heard the laughter at the other end of the phone? She placed a new beer bottle in front of him and fixed him with a stare. A challenge.

James swallowed. The wine bar was calling. He could already imagine what kind of place it might be: music, wooden floors, younger, prettier people. But the woman's gaze had such power. All at once, he perceived the snobbery and judgement he'd brought to this place and felt a flicker of shame. He sat back down.

If he was honest, James rather enjoyed the surprised reactions whenever he referenced the fact that his partner was a barmaid. He knew he was perceived as bland, on top of being short and nothing much to look at. His colleagues and university friends most likely imagined he'd end up with some mousy type who worked in marketing – attractive, well-spoken – someone whose name you'd keep forgetting. There was a feral beauty to Cat that discomfited everyone.

Ahead of her Friday evening shift, she was eating a donor kebab as they sat on the sofa watching the news, the stink of it was working its way across James' taste buds as he tried to enjoy his own meal of pasta and tuna. She wasn't bothering to use a plate, had simply spread the paper across her knees, dropping fat-sodden strips of meat into her mouth, fingers coated with grease. Amazing how she managed to stay so slender when she paid such disregard to her diet. That waist, those narrow little hips – if she told you she was twenty-five, you'd believe her, even though she was going to be forty the following summer.

On the television, a journalist was interviewing a tearful man outside the shell of a tower block that had burned down a few years back. It was obscene, actually, how the woman persisted in holding the microphone in front of his face, even though the poor fellow could barely get his words out. James looked away and with a jolt noticed Cat observing him. 'Those poor people,' he offered.

Cat tore off a piece of pitta bread and scooped up a mess of oily salad. She wasn't wearing make-up and her dark brown hair was tied back into a scruffy ponytail. 'The government hasn't done anything to help the people who lost their homes,' she said, as she chewed. 'And the managers who shafted the residents with their cost-cutting are still going about their business without a care in the world. It's sickening.'

James took a sip of water before braving another mouthful of pasta. Cat had always been passionate about current affairs, but in recent months it was though a dial had been turned up, as though she was taking each item so very personally.

The next story was about Brexit, which didn't bode well. And sure enough, Cat continued to seethe at the television. 'There are a hundred different ways to leave the EU, but there's only a single way to remain. What were they thinking, boiling it down to a simple yes or no vote?'

'It certainly is a mess,' James ventured.

She looked at him, forehead creased with impatience, then popped the last sliver of meat into her mouth, screwed up the paper and stood. A couple of strands of cabbage fluttered to the carpet, but James pretended not to notice.

'I forgot to mention,' she said. 'I went to Portsmouth University's open day today.'

He looked at her, strangely piqued: he had no idea she'd been considering such things. A whim, no doubt, but surely the kind of thing that warranted discussion first.

She moved the balled-up kebab paper from one hand to the other. 'I should have gone back to education years ago, I'm still not sure why I didn't. I've spent too long observing when I should be *acting*.'

James exhaled slowly. He wasn't quite sure what the connection was, between the notion of her going to university and the idea of her *acting*, whatever that meant. He was careful to maintain a smile as he asked: 'You're thinking of enrolling? As a mature student?'

'Yeah. I mean, it's been bothering me for years, the fact that I didn't get to go first time around.'

James placed his tray on the seat next to him and switched the television off. They'd had this conversation before, back when she was nearing thirty. She'd been insistent and argumentative for a good week or so, her neck flushing red with anger any time James tried to raise a practical concern. But, in the end, she'd given up on the idea, as he'd known she would.

He smiled carefully. 'Wouldn't it be strange for you, sitting in lectures with a bunch of eighteen-year-olds?'

Her breath caught. 'I'm trying not to focus on that.'

James stood up, stroked her cheek with the back of his knuckle. 'I just can't see it benefiting you. Take it from me – uni is all about the nights out, it's a way of delaying getting a job.'

Cat sighed, her eyebrows drawn together. 'Maybe that's the case for some people. But I'm serious about wanting to educate myself. It's important to me, James. I need to prove I can do it.'

'But, Cat, I don't understand. We're comfortable. We're fortunate enough to be able to enjoy the nice things in life. I don't quite—'

'I haven't earned any of this for myself.' Her voice was cold, her face slammed shut.

James felt a stab of fear. He'd always prided himself on the life he offered Cat – her bar money was hers to spend as she pleased, and she normally frittered it away on books and cigarettes. There had never been any talk of rent or contributing to the bills. But increasingly he couldn't help thinking that she didn't value the things he provided as much as she ought to. 'Cat—'

She rested a hand on his shoulder. 'I'm going to do this, James. You might not be able to understand, but I owe it to myself to try to be the person I might have been without the accident.'

He placed his hand over hers. 'Cat, I want to support you, I do. But this is absurd. Take it from me – university won't be anything like you imagine. You'll be frustrated, annoyed at the time and money you're wasting.'

She inspected his face and James felt a wave of nausea. Her eyes were moist, yet there was something so determined, so *final*, in her expression. She opened her mouth, about to speak.

Suddenly, James realised: she'd leave him if he turned it into a simple choice. He wasn't sure how he knew, but his mind raced ahead, seeing her turn away in his mind's eye, watching her gather up her things into a rucksack. He couldn't let her speak, couldn't let her make a fool of him. He pulled her towards him and kissed her on the mouth. She seemed taken aback, almost losing her balance.

'Okay, you know best,' he said at last. He was slightly short of breath and hoped Cat attributed this to the kiss rather than his rising panic. Already, he could feel a tight little kernel of resentment in his core – he was endlessly generous, gave her a life that most women would envy. Yet for a moment he'd glimpsed how easily she might walk away.

Chapter 3

On the afternoon of her interview, Cat waited on a plastic bench in the university's reception area. It was a high-ceilinged space in a Georgian building just off Guildhall Square. She could hear the rumble of trains passing every few minutes and felt that same fizz of excitement she used to experience heading into Portsmouth as a teenager. Maybe it wasn't London, or New York, but to Cat, Portsmouth shared the illumination of these places, possessed of a low hum of importance that seemed to resonate in her chest.

She'd bought a sober black jacket specially for the interview, pairing it with a red summer dress that James had given her for her birthday. It was a little short and she found herself tugging at the hem, conscious of how much thigh was on display. Already, she was desperate for a cigarette.

There were a scattering of other applicants waiting – a boy in a suit flanked by his parents, a pink-haired girl with heavy foundation and dramatic eyeliner. Periodically, a lecturer would stride in and call out a name from a clipboard and everyone would look up in startled unison.

'Catherine Brandon?' she heard Daniel call.

She was careful to project composure as she stood.

Daniel was wearing the same T-shirt and blazer combination from the open day and was giving her a wry smile. 'Since we're old friends, how about we ditch the formalities and get a drink?' he whispered.

'What a good idea,' Cat said. Had Daniel specifically arranged it so that he would be her interviewer? It didn't feel like a coincidence, and this made her slightly uneasy, as though she was somehow cheating by accepting this special treatment.

He led her into the Students' Union bar – a vast, airy space on the top floor of a white, glass-fronted building. There were only a handful of other customers, and the booth Daniel led Cat to felt wonderfully private. She reminded herself once again that she was here as an applicant, someone who hadn't yet been given a place. Yet she felt a flare of possibility. Daniel's vibrancy had such a revelatory impact when she was younger; who better to mentor her as she took her life along a different path? The idea of him being her teacher felt simultaneously wonderful and absurd.

'So, is Malibu still your tipple of choice? My treat,' Daniel said.

'At an *interview*?'

He raised an eyebrow. 'I'm having one, for the nostalgia factor. Might even make it a double.'

'Go on then. I haven't had a Malibu for years, but for old times' sake. Malibu and Coke. Why not? It'll be like we're still seventeen, hanging out in The Centurion.' As soon as she said it, Cat felt her face get hot. The Centurion was the pub they'd go to after class. Intense conversations would lead to frantic kissing, their hands slipping inside each other's jeans beneath the table.

When Daniel put her drink in front of her, his grin told her he was recalling such moments too. She had to look away. This was an interview for goodness' sake. Her job this afternoon was to convince him she was good enough to study alongside a bunch of eighteen-year-olds.

'So, what do you need to ask me?'

'Oh, don't worry about that. Your application was excellent. But since our admissions policy demands we haul you in, I thought we may as well catch up before the start of term.'

Cat felt a surge of happiness as she sipped her sickly-sweet drink. The *start of term*. She was in, she'd really done it. She looked at Daniel and realised he had no idea what he'd just given her, how her very idea of herself had changed in an instant. This was a return to the trajectory her life was always meant to take. She didn't have to be the stagnant, dependent creature she'd come to despise. She exhaled, determined not to be shrill, but rather to muster the cool intelligence of her seventeen-year-old self, the woman Daniel had once loved.

'Sounds good. You know I'm still kind of shocked at you being back in Portsmouth. I assumed you'd base yourself in London, or maybe, I don't know, Jakarta.'

'Jakarta?'

'We were going to be global citizens, remember? Changing the world.'

He threw his head back and chuckled. 'Didn't we have grand ideas of ourselves?'

Cat couldn't bring herself to laugh. 'We meant it though.'

The mirth left Daniel's face. 'As careers go, lecturing isn't so bad. I mean, it's flexible, I can be hands-on with the kids. It's comfortable.'

Cat took another sip. Despite working in a bar, she rarely drank and could feel her inhibitions peeling back. 'Comfortable has been my downfall,' she said. 'James – the man I'm with – comes from money. When we met, he had this three-bedroom house on a nice estate that he lived in all by himself. He was only in his twenties and he owned his own home. I couldn't get my head around it. He had the best of everything, and he was willing to let me share it.'

'You still together now?'

Cat nodded. She felt disloyal, speaking of James. But Daniel was perhaps the only person who could understand how strange it had felt, entering a world of memory-foam mattresses and solid oak cabinets. Even now, when she was alone in the house, she'd have the uncanny feeling that she was an intruder, moving silently, guarding against discovery. 'I thought it would make me happy,' she said.

They were silent for a moment.

'And what does this James think, about you going to university?' Daniel asked.

Cat drained her glass. 'He's not taking it seriously. It's like he thinks I'm some bored housewife looking for a hobby. I've tried explaining just how it feels, looking back over the last twenty years and being appalled at how little I've done. I could have *contributed* instead of being a passive bystander.'

Daniel smiled. 'I think you're being rather hard on yourself.'

'No, not at all. It's like – do you remember in college when we studied Weimar Germany? We couldn't get over how obvious it all seemed, the move towards fascism. We were practically shouting at our textbooks.' Cat looked down at the table. 'Sorry. James always says I sound unhinged when I talk like this.'

'Never apologise,' Daniel said, 'but, you realise that university isn't the only route to a fulfilling career, right? I mean, your application was fantastic; there was so much passion there. And that's great, if you want to study a degree because you love the subject, I'm all for that. But you don't *need* a degree to change your life. And you can be an activist without any qualifications at all.'

'Says the dude who graduated from Oxford.'

Daniel gave a quiet laugh, turning his glass around in his hand. She remembered how it felt, the power and self-belief that emanated from him – she used to feel soaked in it, invincible, alive to the excitement of her own future.

Cat felt her smile fracturing. 'I do know that. But maybe *you* don't understand what an important credential a degree is. It tells people you aren't stupid. It tells them you *deserve* opportunities. After Mum's accident, I thought I'd find some low-paid office job and work my way up. But I barely got any interviews, they wanted graduates; even for reception jobs.'

Daniel bit his lip, then looked away, gathering up their empty glasses. He seemed almost shy with her. 'Let me get another round in.'

The bar had a balcony for smokers, so while Daniel went up to the counter, Cat nipped outside for a quick fag. Her heart was pounding at how much she'd revealed. It felt natural to confide in Daniel, but he wasn't the boy she'd known; she had to keep reminding herself that this older man was a stranger.

He joined her outside, proffering a replenished glass. 'You cannot seriously still smoke? Not now you're a grown-up.'

'You can take the girl out of the council estate ...'

Daniel looked at her curiously. 'You're still letting it define you, aren't you?'

Cat dragged on her cigarette, ready to defend herself. She hadn't clawed her way up and out like he had. She was still hovering above the muck, James's kindness the only thing holding her aloft.

He patted her arm. 'Hey, I'm not attacking you. I just find it interesting. Intellectually you're the equal of anyone I met at Oxford—'

'Mum's accident—'

'I can't believe there wasn't more of a safety net. What a burden to put on an eighteen-year-old.'

Cat smiled as she extinguished her cigarette and led them both inside. Although grateful for his understanding, she'd started to sound self-pitying and berated herself; this kind of wallowing and excuse-making had to stop. 'So why lecturing?' she asked as they returned to their booth. 'I imagined you doing something a little *louder*, I suppose. I half expected you to pop up during the Brexit referendum – maybe the outcome would have been different if you'd worked on the campaign.'

Daniel laughed. 'You're blaming me for Brexit, now?'

'No, I just—'

'I thought I'd become a researcher, one of those public-intellectual types. My PhD was on the US civil rights movement and I planned to write the definitive history – something accessible to a popular readership. Maybe I still will, but these days I've realised how important it is to have balance. Like you were saying – comfortable means a lot to people like us, and pushing yourself upwards can feel exhausting. I mean, I've got years to write my books, but my kids will only be little the once.'

Cat looked at him. His eyes had become clouded and she thought she detected something like regret lurking within. It made her feel less alone, but at the same time deeply sad. Daniel was supposed to be living the life they'd fantasised about, he was supposed to be successful for the both of them. 'Being comfortable has turned me into an onlooker,' she said. 'I'm sick of it. I want to be the kind of person who shapes things, rather than just moaning about them. I don't care if it's exhausting.'

Daniel grinned and clinked glasses with her. To Cat's surprise, he suggested another drink, and then another after that. She was aware of her phone flashing with messages – James, no doubt – but she was happy to stay and reminisce for as long as Daniel wanted. They howled with laughter remembering the time Rachel, their politics teacher, delivered a whole class with her skirt tucked in her knickers. They talked of how worthy they'd felt at signing up to work at a soup kitchen on Christmas day, then both admitted they'd not done anything like it since.

After they'd finished their fourth drinks, Daniel offered to show her around. They'd already taken three hours and the corridors of the history department were deserted, lights off. Cat felt a shiver of excitement: she'd soon be walking these corridors as a student, her mind swelling with new ideas. She'd done it. She was finally going to university.

They walked through an empty lecture theatre and a couple of seminar rooms, then headed over to Daniel's office. It was a small room with two desks crammed inside, each facing a wall. The only light came from a tiny skylight window.

'I share with a World War Two enthusiast,' Daniel said. 'This one's mine.' He gestured to the messier of the two desks. Books were piled high either side of the computer screen. There were pages of notes, in that slanted, scruffy hand that evoked countless memories. Those times in the library, his whole body hunched over the pen as he rushed to capture a thought on the page. Their teacher's eyes widening as he handed in twelve pages of handwritten essay.

She was aware of how close they were to one another in the small room. Daniel cast his eyes downwards. A few seconds ago, he'd been mirthful with drink, but now he appeared in the grip of something strange and powerful.

She reached out and placed a hand on his arm. 'What's wrong?'

'Nothing. Or, well, it's just been so nice, I guess. I remember how much you used to spur me on. You were exactly the person I needed to meet when I was sixteen – I don't think I appreciated it enough at the time.'

She kissed him. She hadn't made a conscious decision to do it, her body simply acted, responding to the pull of remembered feelings. It was as though she were reaching out to that past Daniel, trying to hold the dreadlocked boy of her memories here in this room with her. His lips were warm as they moved against hers for a few precious seconds.

Daniel broke away, jerking his head back awkwardly. He looked startled, and for a moment his face became unfamiliar.

Cat felt a sudden chill. She'd just kissed someone's husband. She'd kissed someone who was going to be her teacher.

How could she have been so impulsive? He'd probably ask her to leave, rescind her offer of a place.

She stared at him, incapable of saying anything as she waited to be ejected. He turned and placed his hand on the door handle. Cat swallowed. Everything ruined through a second of stupidity, just as she'd begun to perceive how good reconnecting with him was going to be. But then the lock clicked and he was kissing her. His hands were on her hips, sliding up her waist. They collapsed onto a narrow sliver of rough grey carpet, a tangle of greedy hands and devouring kisses.

When he entered her, the years fell away. She became the girl he'd loved, the girl who believed she could do anything. Cat cried out, and Daniel placed his finger against her lips. He smiled as they locked eyes and it felt to Cat as though they were both recognising the inevitability of this moment, of finding their way back to one another.

His body was stockier than it used to be, there was more of him to explore with her hands. The hair on his chest was new and he smelled different, a more grown-up aftershave, a lingering tang of detergent. But when he fucked her, it felt exactly as it did before. As though each thrust was adding to an inner store of happiness.

Afterwards, he reached for the box of tissues on his desk, passing her a couple, and the two of them lay still for a moment, catching their breath. This was like before too, an intrinsic comfortableness. No need to speak. No need for Cat to rush to cover herself. She felt calmer than she had in years and strangely rejuvenated.

'That was ... I didn't plan ... ' Daniel's voice was choked

with emotion. He manoeuvred himself up off the floor, reaching for his jeans.

Cat stood too. She'd come here, knowing that today might mark an ending, that she might be told no. But everything had changed. She and Daniel had reconnected, they'd found one another again and she was feeling the same breathless optimism of before. He was giving her a place, she was *going to university*. She'd remake herself, snatching at the life she wanted, dismissing any limitations that were put in front of her. She knew she could do it.

Daniel squeezed her hand. 'I've never done anything like this before. I hope you don't think less of me.'

Cat gave him a gentle kiss on the lips and, with a fingertip, brushed the beads of sweat from his forehead. She was happy. Happy in her blood and in her bones. Happy with each beat of her heart, with each in-breath, with each out-breath. There was no thought for what might come next. There wasn't even any guilt over James, at least not yet.

The two years she'd spent with Daniel were the very happiest of her life and she was revelling in the wondrous feeling that her connection with him had somehow endured. She pictured the two of them here in this office a few months from now. Perhaps he'd be going through an essay she'd been working on, suggesting some additional reading, or helping steer her towards a new idea. A warmth spread through her belly as she imagined him leaning in for a kiss, whispering, *I can't stop thinking about you.*

Enough, she told herself. He was married. What happened here today might just be a one-off, a tribute to their shared past that would cause him endless guilt. That was okay. She would study, get her degree and start doing things that actually made her feel proud. She'd shrug off the wasted years, obliterate the passive, dependent creature she'd allow herself to become. When she looked back on her life, this would be the defining moment. This would be the real beginning.

Chapter 4

From a box in the attic, Laura retrieved a simple black dress. She used to team it with stilettos and a waist-slimming jacket, back when her weeks had been filled with client meetings and presentations. She went to the box marked 'shoes' and took out a pair of pink kitten heels. Fun and flirty, she'd worn them for drinks with the girls a few times. For a moment, she remembered how it used to feel, being the Laura of her old life. She'd been confident, proud, not only of how she had looked, but of how she could build a rapport with just about anyone. Recognising this nostalgic turn of her thoughts, she summoned the image of the young man lying on the road, the asphalt glowing with the reflected headlights of cars forced to brake. He'd been curled in a foetal position and could have been sleeping, were it not for the unatural tilt of his neck.

She'd made a series of promises to herself in the weeks that followed – her atonement pledges. Careless moments of pride would always need to be countered with the vision of the courier's broken body. No exceptions. She'd make sure that every single day contained a moment of suffering, a reminder of the pain she'd caused.

Driving made her chest tighten and her legs tremble, but

she'd forced herself to resume doing it as soon as she was released from prison, concentrating hard as sweat gathered at her forehead. Her favourite food had been pizza, so she'd stopped eating it, going hungry those days it was served in the prison canteen. She'd not touched a drop of alcohol. Not spent a penny on new clothes; after all, the old Laura had accumulated enough to last a lifetime.

A small voice told her that such gestures were meaningless, but this inner speaker was the part of herself Laura hated most. The part of her that, if unchecked, would quickly ensure she slid back to her previous self: a glossy, tittering girl-woman, too absorbed in the shallow pleasures of her own life to consider the consequences of her actions.

Laura's father had once been an accountant. There'd been a big house, private school, riding lessons. But when she was fifteen, he'd been accused of financial misconduct and within a month she and her sisters had been bundled off to the town's comprehensive, moving into a semi that was pointedly in her mother's name.

These days, her father ran a so-called private members club, which functioned as the town's dive bar. It was situated above an estate agent's and Laura was breathing heavily by the time she reached the top of the stairs.

Her father was sat on a bar stool next to Catherine, a girl Laura had known at the comprehensive, and the two of them were deep in conversation, both puffing on cigarettes as she approached. Her father nodded at everything Catherine said, leaning in conspiratorially. Laura felt a pang of envy. Since her arrest, he'd developed a new way of talking to her, the verbal equivalent of hands raised in surrender, an ultra-defensiveness that always made her feel as though she'd been shrieking at him.

'Ah, Laura, welcome to my humble establishment. You've turned yourself out very nicely,' her father said. He was wearing a suit and tie, his belly straining at the waistband of his trousers. He wore his glasses around his neck, secured by thick, black string.

Catherine gave her an appraising glance as she took a long drag from her cigarette. She was beautiful, Laura realised with a jolt of surprise. At school, Catherine had been a scrawny, shrinking thing, even though she'd been in the top set for just about everything. But scrawny had transformed into strikingly slender, and her dark eyes had an arresting confidence.

Laura bit her lip. She'd not kept on top of her highlights since prison. She'd vowed to stop being the shallow person of her old life, yet even as she reminded herself of this, she couldn't help feeling shame at what Catherine must be seeing. Permanent frown lines and dull skin, paired with thinning hair and a slack tummy. She was rapidly approaching the invisibility of middle age, which was just fine, until you saw the shock of the descent register on someone else's face.

Within the first half-hour, Laura's kitten heels were pinching her toes and chafing the backs of her feet. The club started to fill with people, which meant her father thankfully hid the ashtrays away and pretended to uphold the smoking ban. By that point, her eyes were already stinging, and she could feel the stench settling into her hair.

'You're making it too frothy. Tilt the glass.' Cat – as

Catherine was known at the club – towered over Laura as she inducted her into the art of pint pulling. It was harder than it looked. Already, her dress was spattered with beer. She made a mental note to wear something machine-washable next time. Lager slopped over her fingers as she placed the glass down on the counter and she heard Cat give an irritated sigh.

'Take one for yourself, darling,' said the cheerful man she was serving.

'Oh, I'm good, thanks.'

Another of Cat's annoyed exhalations. 'I always accept. You don't have to have a drink, you can just take the money and put it in the tip jar.'

Laura swallowed her embarrassment and turned to Cat with an appeasing smile. 'I must admit, I couldn't quite picture you here, working with my dad. You had this whole child-prodigy thing going on at school, I thought you'd be a writer or a businesswoman or something.'

'Nothing wrong with bar work.'

'No, of course—'

Cat's eyes hardened. 'I had to be Mum's carer for four years. Kind of shat on my plans.'

Laura swallowed. A long-forgotten memory surfaced, hearing a scandalised account of Cat's mother staggering around drunk and getting hit by a car. 'Goodness! You had to look after her? When you were so young?'

Cat's lip twitched. 'Had to wipe her arse and everything.'

'But now – I mean, like you said, there's nothing wrong with bar work – but how can you afford to live around here? There's no way I'm going to be able to rent a flat on these wages.'

Cat fixed her with a cold stare and Laura realised she'd been rude.

'I wasn't trying to—'

One of the regulars held his empty glass aloft and silently, Cat turned to pour a fresh pint of Guinness. Laura found it difficult to take her eyes off her; the outline of her body was so perfect, her hair a silken cloud that invited touch. It suddenly felt so important that Cat should like her.

'Bloody hell. Cheer up, love.' Cat's father was standing at the bar, roll of twenties in his hand. He was wearing a white shirt to show off his deep tan, the outline of his tattoos visible through the fabric. 'Couple of Stellas and a wine for Ri.'

Cat made an effort to smile as she poured the drinks.

Her father gestured to Robbie, one of his sons by his second wife, who'd wandered over to the fruit machines. 'We're celebrating tonight. He's got another little one on the way.'

'Congrats, Terry,' said one of the old duffers propping up the bar. There was a short interlude of cheering. A few backslaps.

Beaming, Cat's father addressed her. 'When's it your turn, then? The old biological clock must be ticking away.'

Cat wrinkled her nose. 'I've opted not to contribute to the global population crisis.'

He narrowed his eyes. 'I've got my suspicions about you. Always had you down as one of them lesbians.'

The others at the bar were all rapt attention and guffaws. For some reason, Terry was a kind of idol to the regulars.

Cat needed a quick retort, perhaps something withering about Robbie and his lack of aspiration. But, instead, she was assailed by a sharp flutter of competitiveness. 'I'm actually going to be starting uni.' She placed the full pint glasses on the bar. 'This September. Degree in history.'

Her father grunted, peeling away one of the twenties and handing it over.

Cat felt hot with indignation. *Let him fuck off to the fruit machines.* He hadn't cared when she was a teenager and her future had been snatched away, so it was ridiculous to expect him to care now. She should have kept her mouth shut, avoided handing him this chance to withhold his interest.

Terry's arrival was shortly followed by the stumbling presence of Cat's mother. They'd divorced when Cat was nine, but in all essential ways, Bernice remained wedded to Terry. At weekends, she was a tragic figure, following him from pub to pub, eagerly anticipating those moments – only occurring once every couple of years – when he'd take her home and shag her, either for old times' sake or just to show everyone he still could.

Her mother always donned the shortest of skirts for these nights out, the scars on her legs concealed with tights, or, as tonight, with a pair of black suede boots that went halfway up her thighs. They were in the midst of a heatwave and Cat was uncomfortably hot even in shorts and flip-flops.

'Hello, love. How you doing?' Even as she addressed her daughter, Bernice was scanning the room, looking for Terry. Her eyes were shining, indicating a state of tipsiness that would soon be followed by cackling laughter and a wobbling, lurching walk. This was how Fridays went.

It was a busy shift and the club was sweaty and airless, punters shouting to one another across the tables. It wasn't until after the flurry of last orders that Cat felt able to take a break. Tucked away in the kitchen, she stood beside the open window and sparked up a fag.

She'd been upset when Martin had told her Laura was returning home and would be working a few shifts until she *got back on her feet.* Cat couldn't help thinking back to school and how very tired she'd become of her loner status and the adversarial relationship she'd had with her classmates. They passed judgement on her for the dilapidated state of her uniform, for her inability to fund school trips, and she'd affected to scorn them in return.

Laura's arrival halfway through year ten had offered a glimmer of promise. A chance to start again, become someone else. As she smoked, Cat picked over a memory from GCSE English class, when Laura had been shedding silent tears over a returned essay for which she'd received a C minus. Her hair had been tied back in a neat plait, and from her blazer pocket she'd produced a little packet of tissues, no doubt placed there by a loving mum.

Cat had been kind. She'd talked Laura through the basics of essay planning, drawing a quick spider diagram of the points she might like to make, then exploring the links between them, finding a logical order, suggesting quotes that might back up her arguments. It was an easy, formulaic process, but Laura seemed to find it revelatory. Cat remembered the pitiful little nod she'd given as she'd wiped her eyes. How she'd appeared almost awestruck as she asked Cat whether she could keep the bit of paper with the diagram.

It had given Cat a happy feeling, having helped in this way. Here Cat was, acting like the kind of friend you saw in Australian soaps. But when Mr Paulson told them to get into pairs for an activity, Laura had turned to Louise Vickers, sitting on her other side, and asked: 'Can I go with you?' And once again Cat had been the only person left without a partner.

I'm not being horrible or anything, but Catherine smells, doesn't she? Cat would never forgive Laura for that comment, whispered to Louise in a later lesson. She hadn't meant for Cat to hear, and that somehow made it all the more humiliating. It wasn't an attack, it was simply an observation. A truth. By that stage, Laura was a well-established part of the popular tribe, featuring girls with ironed shirts, clean hair and beautifully organised pencil cases. They always looked so open and friendly, but when it had come to preserving their place in a group, they could be downright cunty.

Cat could feel the sting of the remark, even now. How casually it had been made, how free from interest in who Cat was, in *why* she often smelled. The world of broken boilers and no hot water, coveting the last sliver of soap and trying to stretch out a single sanitary towel across the whole school day – these things were most likely alien to Laura, even now. It was fitting that Laura should end up here, pulling pints. Yet something about her abject manner prevented Cat from revelling in her downfall, even though she wanted to. Laura had killed someone. What must it be like, living with that guilt? How strange it must be returning to Petersfield, to her father's bar, after a glittering life in London.

The kitchen door opened and Roger, one of the regulars, called through. 'Sorry, love, but your mum's taken a tumble down the stairs.'

Cat stubbed out her fag and headed for the staircase. She had to shove past the gawpers – her customers really did love nothing better than witnessing someone else's humiliation.

Her mother was in the downstairs hallway, leaning against the woodchip wallpaper. She'd laddered her tights and her hair was dishevelled.

'Are you okay? Is anything broken?' Cat asked.

Bernice shook her head. 'I'm fine. Just a clumsy idiot.'

Cat looked up at the crowd forming on the stairs. At least her father had already left and wasn't around to make spiteful comments. 'All right, the rest of you, you can fuck off now. Nothing to see here.'

'Is she all right? Are you all right?' It was Laura, fighting her way through the dispersing crowd.

'She's fine. Just a bit unsteady on her feet.'

Laura placed a hand on Bernice's arm. The gesture felt showy somehow.

Cat picked her up mother's shoulder bag – a cheap and nasty thing, the imitation patent leather crumbling away like old paint – and checked inside. Fags, purse and keys were all present. 'Do you think you can walk?'

'Yes. Yes, I'm fine. I'm so sorry. My leg gave out. I really ought to run through my physio exercises more often.' Bernice took her bag from Cat and started shuffling towards the door. 'I'll be off now. Good night, love.'

Cat patted her mother's arm. 'Text me when you're home safely.' She turned to Laura. 'Shift isn't finished yet. We've got clearing up to do.'

Her face burned as she climbed the stairs. Why did her mother have to make a spectacle on Laura's very first night?

She wished she didn't care. But all Laura's preconceptions about Cat's family had probably just been confirmed. She decided to have another fag in the kitchen before pitching in with the clear-up. Martin kept bustling in and out, loading up the dishwasher, bagging up rubbish and making a performance of being busy. But Cat pretended not to notice. Let his daughter earn her keep, since he'd felt the need to give her a job.

When she was done with her cigarette, Cat filled up two crates with empty beer bottles and headed back downstairs to the yard. The bar had mostly cleared out, just one or two persistent old duffers nursing the dregs of their pints, but when she stepped outside, she heard Laura's voice. 'Don't give yourself a hard time. It's normal to have an emotional response to the person you love being with someone else.'

'It's been thirty years,' Cat's mother replied. 'And yet every day I wake up and it's like he's only just gone through the door.'

They were perched on empty kegs. Laura's head was tilted to one side and she was nodding slowly, with feigned thoughtfulness.

Bernice was the first to spot Cat. She quickly stood up.

Laura stood too. 'We were just—'

Cat stacked the crates in the corner of the yard. 'Your dad's huffing and puffing over being left to clear up,' she said.

'Okay, I better go up then,' Laura replied. 'It was really nice chatting with you, Bernice.'

When they were alone, Cat turned to her mother.

'I—' Bernice tugged at the hem of her skirt.

'Don't.'

'I just—'

In spite of everything, Cat felt a pang of tenderness. Her father's newest wife – his third – had been parading around earlier that evening, and poor Bernice had to watch the two of them tonguing one another like teenagers. Cat pulled her cigarettes from the back pocket of her jeans and handed one to her mother, lighting it for her and taking a seat on a keg. 'I know. But Dad is a shit who doesn't deserve you mooning over him.'

'I ... Okay.'

'And don't go telling things to Laura. I don't know why she's working here. Martin used to go on about how much money she was making in some bullshit marketing job.'

'I think she's lonely. She was asking about you. I think she's in need of a friend.' Bernice's eyes shone with moisture. She seemed so tiny, so fragile – it was a wonder the fall hadn't snapped any bones.

Cat put an arm around her mother. It suddenly felt important to transmit just how much she cared.

'Are you all right, love?' Bernice asked. 'You've been a bit on the quiet side the last couple of weeks.'

For a moment, Cat considered telling her mother about Daniel. Her mind flickered to that kiss in his office, the feel of his older, more masculine body. The only communication she'd had with him since then was an impersonal letter confirming her university place and providing her with a reading list. She ached to see him again, but supposed there was every chance he regretted what they'd done. He was married, a father.

Being with her mother, in amongst the empty beer kegs,

in a yard that stank of piss, Cat had a sense of how difficult everything was going to be. Purpose was elusive, weaving its way into her daydreams and illuminating everything in bursts of silver light that were extinguished all too soon. How easy it was to go on believing that this way of life – James, the club – was the natural way of things.

Cat summoned Daniel's face again, remembered the very specific lightness in her abdomen, the excitement darting up her spine. Perhaps she was going to have to be ruthless, selfish even, if she wanted to guard that feeling, to harness it and let it take her to different places.

'I'm fine,' Cat said. 'Now listen, make sure you have a big glass of water when you get home. Your head's going to hurt tomorrow.'

Chapter 5

Whenever James felt uneasy about Cat, he'd think back to their very first argument and everything it revealed about her. They'd shoehorned three dates into the space of a week, and he'd been driving her back home in the morning on his way to work.

'Here's fine,' she'd said as they reached a row of shabby-looking terraces.

James braked. 'Which one's yours?'

'Oh, it's over there.' She waved her arm, vaguely.

'Which one?'

There was a pause that made James feel uneasy.

'It's in the next road, but it's easy enough to walk from here.' Cat wouldn't look him in the eye.

James remembered laughing. 'I don't think you quite understand the concept of being given a lift home.'

Cat said nothing as she pecked him on the cheek, then opened the door of his Golf.

He felt a sudden wave of irritation. 'Are you ashamed of me or something?'

She'd turned back to face him, a red flush spreading across her neck. 'Of course not.'

'Then why won't you let me see where you live?'

She'd opened her mouth as if to say something, but then thought better of it, turning away and striding along the road, her heeled boots clicking against the asphalt.

Panicked, James had parked the car and hurried after her.

'Cat – wait! Did I do something wrong?' It must be his appearance, his pitted skin, the fact that she was taller than him. And now he was about to face the humiliation of her lying, pretending it was something else.

She'd stopped walking with an anguished frown. 'We come from very different worlds, James.'

'What are you talking about? I thought you liked me.'

'I do.' Her eyes shone, surrounded by smudges of the previous night's mascara.

'I don't understand.'

It was then that she'd confided her fear of him seeing where she lived, her voice choked with emotion. They had an absurd exchange, right there on the pavement. Her insisting that the mere sight of her home would change the way he viewed her, him insulted she could think such a thing.

The expression on her face had been almost hostile when she relented. In silence, she marched them around the corner, to a house with a rotted front gate and small front garden that was overrun with brambles. James had made a conscious effort to maintain a smile as Cat unlocked the door.

'Mum, are you decent? I've got company.'

The cigarette stench had been overpowering as he stepped into the hallway. On the floor was a stained grey carpet which hadn't been fitted and was bunched up in some places, exposing grime-crusted floorboards in others. He began to understand why she hadn't wanted him to see where she lived.

'Suppose I better get you a cup of tea then?' Cat said.

James nodded, even though it would make him late for work. He followed her into the kitchen, where the sink had been filled with dirty pans and most of the paintwork was covered in black mould, thick layers of it gathering near the ceiling. He'd felt like he was on the set of a documentary exposing the squalid living conditions of serial benefit claimants. Not the kind of thing he'd watch, or even believe in, if he was honest.

Cat must have noticed him staring. 'We lost the battle with damp a long time ago,' she'd said.

It was an abominable place. Most of the tiles around the sink had fallen off and were stacked up in a pile on the windowsill. The room was so damp he could see condensation gathering on the floor by the back door. He felt revulsion, true, but it was mixed with a strange fascination. How was Cat enduring such a place? How had she become the beautiful, clever person she was, coming from these surroundings? He felt a warm burst of pride at having discovered someone so unique.

As Cat was putting the kettle on, a woman in a once-white dressing gown came into the kitchen. Her feet were bare, with thick, yellow toenails, and there was a patchwork of scars running up her legs. She hadn't looked old exactly, but she appeared weathered, with smoker's lines around her mouth and scraggly bleached hair reaching down to her shoulders.

'Hello, love.' She'd produced a packet of cigarettes from her dressing gown and offered one to James, who shook his head.

'Give's one, I'm gasping.' Cat snatched the packet and the two women lit up.

The kettle finished boiling and a cloying silence filled the room. James had felt himself reddening as he tried to process everything he'd learnt that morning. Cat was a *chav*, a *stig*, a *skank*. He was barely able to believe it. She lived in filth, her mother reeked of booze. Yet she was funny, razor-sharp, gorgeous. All week he'd been painfully aware of the looks people had given them, pondering the implausibility of him being with someone so flawlessly attractive. Standing in her home, he'd felt his anxiety lifting. He could give her the gift of escaping this place. How grateful she would be.

The weekend before she was due to enrol at university, they attended a barbecue at James's parents' home. James watched Cat puffing on one of his father's cigars, face composed as you like, as she argued with his brother Francis. She was wearing a black camisole top that he'd bought her, emphasising the slenderness of her torso, the pertness of her breasts.

The conversation veered towards Brexit, and one by one the rest of the family vacated the patio as the two of them duelled it out, invoking obscure trade statistics. It was wrong to feel smug, but James couldn't help being pleased by the pinkness of his brother's cheeks, the sweaty tendrils of hair at his temples. Francis wasn't used to having his opinions challenged.

Even better, he kept noticing the glances his father directed Cat's way, starting at the table, then continuing as he re-emerged periodically to top up her glass and make the odd wisecrack. His father didn't have the discipline to resist feasting on her, those legs, that tiny little waist. James could tell it irked him, his son possessing such a beauty. In the beginning, he'd made little jibes about how James mustn't get too attached because a girl like that would inevitably be lured away. It must infuriate him that such a thing had never come to pass.

It was a pleasantly warm September day, so James and his mother Linda were sat on a rug beneath the cedar tree, while Francis's boys kicked a ball about on the lawn. 'More wine, darling?' His mother proffered the bottle of white.

James shook his head. 'Better not.'

She looked over towards Cat on the patio. 'She does rather enjoy going into battle, doesn't she?'

James glanced at his mother. Her forehead was smooth, but her jaw looked unnaturally rigid, as though she might be grinding her teeth. He smiled. He didn't want to argue, not today. As family occasions went, this had been rather okay. Perfect weather for an outdoor barbecue, Francis's two boys being fairly well-behaved. His sister Johanna was here too, and she'd come alone, not like last time when his parents had been in a state of near hysteria at her bringing that butch-looking woman. His father had kept a happy distance from James, hadn't commenced the usual needling. And Cat had agreed to come without making a fuss.

'So, what's this whole becoming a student thing about?' his mother asked.

'Cat's a very intelligent woman. She didn't have the chance to go to uni when she was younger.'

'But she'll be forty soon, won't she? You have to admit, it is all rather peculiar.'

'Not really. She's actually very clever.'

'But what's the endgame, darling? Is she going to start doing internships when she graduates, competing with all the twenty-somethings? Women her age are normally looking after their families. She's left it a bit late to go off discovering herself, or whatever it is she's supposed to be doing.'

James sighed. His mother had such fixed ideas on the trajectories people were supposed to follow. She'd never understand the hidden forces within Cat, the insecurities that constantly plagued her but that drove her to make the best of herself, to find the fun in the dreariest of days. 'Cat doesn't believe in conventional.'

His mother topped up her own glass. Her nails were shaped into perfect ovals and painted a pale pink. 'Well, in all honesty, I couldn't see her being the mother of my grandchildren.'

'Mum—'

She placed a hand on his knee. 'I worry about you, darling. You supporting her is all very noble. But not at the expense of your own life. You'd make a wonderful father. I want you to have that. You deserve to be happy.'

James rested his back against the tree trunk. 'I *am* happy.'

'Darling—'

James looked at his mother, and with his eyes told her the subject was closed. It wouldn't have been right to share his secret belief, that Cat would soon abandon university once she'd sampled the reality of it. Perhaps then she'd change her mind about children. She'd been vehement, angry even, whenever he broached the subject before. But he'd been thinking about it lately, and wondered whether in the past she might have equated having a baby with acceptance that her education really was over, that bar work would be the only career she'd ever know. Who was to say how she might feel after she'd given studying a pop? It wouldn't be too late – you heard all the time these days about women giving birth into their forties, and he could afford fertility treatment if it turned out they needed it.

As Cat and James strolled along the country lanes around his parents' house, Cat felt ill at ease. The Buckles' country pile was truly beautiful, from the cedar tree on the lawn to the polished staircase and the fluffiness of the guest towels. Sometimes she'd imagine the kind of person she might be if this had been her childhood home. Hours of carefree leisure, reading in the garden, would have crafted her mind into a new shape. This was a house she could have brought friends back to – the kind of girl who'd grow up in this place would undoubtedly have friends.

The leaves were showing the first traces of yellow and the hedgerows were teeming with ripening hazelnuts. All around them, birds were singing their final songs of the day as the light dipped. Tomorrow she'd be enrolling at university. James had made a big show of buying her a rail season ticket and had given her his old laptop to use. But something about his manner had grated – his voice had the same quality of inflated interest that he used with his little nephews and she was left feeling as though he wasn't taking her plans seriously at all.

He took her hand. 'This little get-together hasn't been too bad, has it?'

'Your brother is an arrogant piece of shit.'

'True. He takes after our father.'

'No way. Ted is a gentleman through and through. I'm loving the whole country squire thing he's got going on,' Cat said.

James was silent for a moment. It was textbook Freudian really, how being around his father stripped him of his usual self-assurance. It was the only thing that did, Cat had found. Time with his mother made him feel like a king, but there was always something uncertain about James whenever he was in the presence of his father. If she was honest, Cat found it all rather amusing, but she reminded herself just how kind James had been. He might not be taking her return to education seriously, but he was prepared to pay for it.

Her stomach roiled as she considered how she'd betrayed him, how devastated he'd be if he knew just how much she was looking forward to seeing Daniel again. She gave him a sideways glance. She'd serve up the little digs towards his family she could tell he was desperate for. It was the least she could do. 'It is all rather an act though, isn't it?' she said. 'This lord of the manor business.'

James's face brightened. 'Yes! It totally is. I mean, writing a big cheque to pay for the church renovations: he doesn't do stuff like that to be kind, he does it to feel like the big man.'

'Very feudal.'

'Yes, feudal. That's such a good word for it. You always hit these things right on the head. You should have seen him when I was younger, back in Buckinghamshire, doing the rounds at the village fete. I mean, come on, the *village fete*. But he was acting like someone from a period drama. Gracing it with his presence.'

Cat snorted and James gave her a look of such gratitude, it was almost painful. There were times when she'd forget that she was pretending, times when she – for a moment – really did become the woman James wanted her to be.

He squeezed her hand. 'I'll never forget that bloody fete. I must have only been nine or so, and the week before he made me and Francis pick stocks and invest ten pounds each. He'd never give us real pocket money, only theoretical money to invest. Francis did well of course, ending up with fifty quid. My picks bombed and Dad wouldn't let me have a penny, not one penny to spend at the fete.

'Mum tried reasoning with him, but he was like: "Technically, he's in debt to me." I had to look at all the stalls, watch Francis stuffing himself with cakes, buying any old crap he liked the look of. Dad said it was an important lesson.'

Cat was almost on the cusp of laughing, until she caught the wounded expression in James's eyes. Ludicrous as this whole tale was, he still carried the pain. She squeezed his hand in return, playing her part. 'What a cunt.'

At times, Cat almost envied how straightforward James's desires were, how clean the lines between contentment and hurt. The world was run by people like him, schooled to be just about good enough for middle management, their gym habits, their desire for new clothes powering the economy. It was the Jameses of the world who snaffled up all the opportunities, leaving nothing for people like her. And they never paused to recognise what they were doing, failing to appreciate the charmed lives they led.

For a long time, she'd tried so very hard to believe in their life together. Being with James had allowed her to go on foreign holidays for the first time. He was happy to let her arrange them: weekends in Barcelona, Paris and Berlin. She had such a hunger to see the places she'd read about and had worked out detailed itineraries, prioritising the attractions, researching the best places to eat. Once she became less self-conscious about how he paid for everything, they'd started going long haul. A jungle stay in Indonesia, a US trip taking in New York and Washington.

She remembered Vietnam. The aroma of noodle soup hanging in the rain-saturated air. The shouted conversations and constant tooting of moped horns. They'd gone to the war museum in Ho Chi Minh City. Cat had felt energised at the prospect: the Vietnam War had been one of the most vivid units of the history curriculum at college. She and Daniel had felt such fresh outrage at every detail, finding it hard to believe that such atrocities could have occurred in modern times.

She'd been quiet, reverential, as she worked her way through the museum's exhibits. Being in a place she'd spent so much time reading about made her feel intently serious and she wanted to give each exhibit the quiet reflection it deserved.

But James had not stopped yammering. He'd made her take pictures of him posing by a shot-down aeroplane. As they'd read about the punishments prisoners endured, he'd let out theatrical sighs. Inanities along the lines of, 'my oh my'.

It came to a head in the indoor part of the museum. A large section had been devoted to the impact of defoliants and other chemicals on the children of those who'd been exposed. There were photographs of deformities. Embryos preserved in jars.

Right from the outset, James had affected distress. 'Do we really need to see this?' He'd looked like a caricature of a tourist, with his white linen shirt and khaki trousers.

'It's important to bear witness. Women to this day are giving birth to children with terrible disabilities. No one is being held accountable.'

'But this is our *holiday*. I think I might go and get a drink, catch a few rays outside.'

She'd wanted to take hold of his hair, thrust his face into the picture of a girl, howling in agony because – according to the caption – her skin sloughed off at the tiniest contact. *This is a human being*, she'd say. *Imagine if she was your daughter. Imagine if you had to hear her screaming in pain every single day.*

But that spike of indignation had been accompanied by a sensible inner voice, reminding Cat that James had, after all, paid for their trip. She could shout all she wanted, but even if she did, she'd never make him see. He could be kind, he could be generous when it suited, but he lacked the imagination needed for true empathy.

And all at once, Cat found herself thinking what it might have been like if she'd come with Daniel. Tears of fury would have welled up in his eyes. They would have barely spoken, but they wouldn't have needed too. They would have stood next to one another, quietly absorbing everything. She wouldn't need to explain her peculiar mix of emotions, because she knew Daniel would have shared them.

Continuing their walk along the country lane, Cat realised that, for years now, she'd been using James. She felt her breath catch at the ugly truth of it. How absurd that the term – *using* – had never come to her before. It was so obvious, so crass. Playing a part, biting her tongue and all for the sake of comfort. What kind of person did that make her?

She'd have to leave him. This wasn't about Daniel – although spending an afternoon with him had reminded her of the bliss of sharing hopes, of exposing the soft under-belly of her inner life. She hadn't come close to these peaks of feeling with James, even though at the beginning she really had tried. Being with him blunted parts of her. It was unhealthy to share her life with someone who simply couldn't *see* the things that she did. For years, she'd been bending herself into patterns and routines that brought her no joy, that were really only about him.

But worse than that – this *using him* was monstrous. Time and again, she told herself she was devoted to making him happy, yet she'd kissed Daniel, hadn't hesitated to make love to him on the rough grey carpet of his office. It hit Cat then: she didn't love James – she wasn't sure she even liked him.

Chapter 6

Elizabeth had needed extensive stitching after the birth, the day of pushing, followed by an incision to help Kendra enter the world. Daniel had held his firstborn, cradling her wrinkled skin against the warmth of his chest, while his exhausted wife groaned with a fresh set of contractions, weeping at having to embark on the brutality of labour all over again. In the end, Milo had required forceps, and when the pain relief had finally kicked in, Elizabeth had cracked a joke about how her vagina was going to be ruined.

Daniel hadn't taken his wife's subsequent aversion to sex personally. The first few times they'd tried, she'd cried out in pain and he'd had to withdraw, feeling appalled by the tears in her eyes. They persisted for a while, but her tensing, the apprehension on her face, made him feel like a brute.

They were still intimate, spooning in bed, the day punctuated with kisses. If anything, their bond was deeper now; they recognised in one another that same aching love for their children. And with it came an overwhelming feeling of dependency – caring for the twins was a joint enterprise like no other; neither of them could do it alone and so their love was paired with a degree of practical cooperation that turned them into colleagues.

Every morning, Daniel registered fresh shock at having betrayed Elizabeth, at having sullied a marriage that had been marked by its kindness and comfort. It had been a mistake to drink with Cat; he should have recognised the risk and conducted a bland, by-the-book interview.

Seeing her at the open day in the summer triggered a barrage of memories that had lain unexamined for decades. He remembered the uncanny sense he'd had at college of *feeling* her brain responding to things, a kind of low vibration that passed through his body, energising him, making him capable of his best work. As a teenager, he hadn't known how rare it was, to connect with someone so deeply. He hadn't valued it as he ought, he realised that now. For years, he'd been telling himself that the flatness of his subsequent relationships, of his marriage even, was simply a sign of maturity.

Elizabeth didn't deserve to be thought of as second best or in any way disappointing. He argued with himself – chasing his feelings away with calm facts. Their children. The gentle compromises they made whenever they disagreed. The sweet routines of shared tasks and a commitment to one another's well-being. These weren't nothing. They formed the bedrock of a contented life.

Yet, to feel Cat in his arms, her body so little changed through the decades, was to experience a desire so strong it risked unmaking everything he'd come to cherish. It was to step back to a time when he'd demanded more from the world. She made him feel the echo of the boy he'd been, forced him to remember the possibility that resided in his bones and the constant pulse of ambition that had once made every day an excitement.

It was vanity to imagine that Cat might be turning their encounter over in her mind too, returning to the carpet of his office as often as he was. He had no way of knowing what she thought. He didn't dare message her. If she regretted the experience, then lifting her phone number from her application form would constitute harassment. She might be appalled, perhaps even angry, at how the interview had gone. Maybe anger would be best – she could speak of making a complaint and he'd have to placate her, apologising profusely. Their encounter could be chalked up to a drunken mistake, no risk of it happening again.

But he couldn't resist the belief that she'd delighted in it too. The look in her eyes had been transcendent – that wasn't booze, that was memory, connection. He'd felt it, a temporal shift as the boy he'd once been rose up and clung to the girl within her.

What if she thought they were about to embark on an affair? She surely wouldn't. The two of them had both despised their own fathers for leaving when they were young.

All Daniel could do was wait to read her reaction when he next saw her, then work out how to respond. The prospect was like a weight pressing against his chest. He could think of nothing harder than seeing expectation in those dark eyes of hers, and having to let her down. But there was no other option.

From the podium, he scanned the lecture theatre on the first day of term, seeking her out. There she was, in one of the middle rows, chatting to the girl sitting next to her. She was wearing a maroon hoodie and her hair was tied back in a simple ponytail. A pad of A4 paper and a pencil case were lain out in front of her, even though this was a generic welcome talk and Daniel wouldn't be saying anything worth writing down.

Cat smiled when she met his eye and he found himself uncharacteristically nervous as he began his usual spiel about study skills, stressing the fact that students would need to devote at least ten hours a week to supplementary reading. Too often now he spoke from notes, or from memory, trotting out the same lines each year. He knew he should be putting more in, trying harder to spark those moments of engagement that could change the trajectory of someone's life. But it was so damned hard to find enthusiasm, confronted as he was by dreamy eyes and constant phone checking.

He waited for Cat in the corridor afterwards, saying a few individual words of welcome to the other new students as they filed past. It was his smallest cohort yet; he experienced a prickle of unease every time he thought of it. Humanities programmes across the country were laying off staff.

Cat gave a wry smile as she saw him waiting. 'Hello.'

He walked alongside her, hoping he appeared natural to the other students. 'Do you have time to get a coffee?' he whispered.

'Yeah, that would be good. Certainly better than getting a Malibu, at any rate.'

Daniel laughed nervously. He didn't recognise the sound, it was so artificial, loaded with embarrassment and regret.

They took a table by the window in the second-floor refectory. You could see the tower block where he'd grown up

from here; the balconies dotted with laundry, with knack-
ered old sofas and potted plants. It was the scene of so many
feverish afternoons, he and Cat together in his single bed,
evenings working side by side at the kitchen countertop while
his mother watched *EastEnders* in the living room.

'You made it,' Daniel said. 'You're a student.'

Cat searched his face. 'I hope I really did deserve my place.'

Daniel swallowed. 'Of course you did. I should have let one
of my colleagues interview you, I see that now. You would
have wowed their socks off, Cat. There's no question, you
belong here.'

She took a sip of her coffee. 'I have to do it now. Remake
myself. If this doesn't push me towards the kind of life I want,
then I don't know what will. It's kind of intimidating. I'm so
desperate to make a success of it.'

Daniel touched her arm, feeling a tremor beneath her
sleeve. 'You have to believe you will. If you only knew how
rarely I come across students with your level of talent.'

Cat looked him in the eye. Such a penetrating gaze,
Daniel felt she could read just how often he thought of their
interview encounter, replaying all the details, making sure
he remembered the urgency of her cry, the frankness of her
gaze as they came in quick succession. He had to look away,
down at the table. *I love her,* he thought to himself. His chest
tightened in surprise. He barely knew her. But that wasn't
true. He saw her opposite him and felt a thread of intimacy,
running all the way back to their teenage years. He batted
the sentiment away, angry at his own weakness. It wouldn't
come to any good.

'I'm sorry I kissed you,' she said. 'I was very drunk.'

Daniel felt his heart fracturing at those words. But they were saving him, freeing him from obligation. He wanted to clasp her hands. To kiss her and somehow explain the effect she was having on him, the memories that were surfacing. Instead, he thought of the twins. Kendra's pride in her braids, how she would swish her head from side to side to make the beads clack. The dimples on Milo's cheeks when he smiled. They were always so happy to see him, running into the hallway the moment he arrived home.

He braved eye contact once more. 'I'm the one to blame. I'm not sure why I thought drinking with an ex-girlfriend was a good idea.'

She laughed, but it was a choked, strangled sound. He was hurting her, he could tell. *Ex-girlfriend* felt unnecessarily callous. She was so much more than that. They'd shared something profound, impossible to replicate with others, or at least so he'd found.

'I'd like very much to be friends,' he said. 'I want to make it up to you, for swanning off to Oxford after your mum got run over. I was a shit.'

'You were eighteen, Daniel. You needed to get away, I understood that. If it had been the other way around, I would have gone too.'

They were both silent. Daniel was suddenly certain that Cat would in fact have supported him, visiting every weekend, talking on the phone as often as he needed. He felt the full weight of his treachery. If they'd stayed in touch, he would have encouraged her to resit her A levels, to go to uni the very next year. He would have insisted on it. Her whole life could have been different. His too.

He remembered A-level results day. How, despite the fact that there would be no grade envelope waiting for her, she'd met him at the college bus stop and gone with him to collect his results. He'd let her squeeze his hand and reassure him that four As would be waiting for him. On that anxious walk, he hadn't once asked her about her mother.

'I did try to call,' he said, as if trying to absolve himself. 'Your phone was disconnected.'

Cat nodded. 'We had to do without for a couple of years.'

'And I have to own up to searching the internet for you a few times. But there was nothing, no social media, not a trace. I figured you maybe got married, changed your name.'

She smiled, but there was sadness in her eyes. 'Funny, I never felt the need to try to look you up. I kind of knew, deep inside, that you'd be thriving, doing the things you were supposed to. I didn't need to see it, just believing it was enough.'

He felt the most delicious sensation spiralling through his veins. He'd been a presence in her life, all these years, she'd treasured their time together. For a moment, he felt *believed in*, in an entirely new and exciting way.

'We can be good for each other,' he said, newly energised. 'I want to make sure you get the most out of being here. And, selfishly, I like being around you. I wish more people our age gave some thought as to the direction their lives have taken. You're a good influence.'

'Hardly,' Cat snorted.

'Don't belittle yourself. I know how much strength it must have taken to come along to that open day; I know how hard it is to remake your life when your patterns and routines are fixed. I've certainly not been brave enough to try it.'

Her face softened. It almost broke him to see how grateful she looked. 'Friends then,' she said.

And Daniel wanted to feel relieved, he really did. But those words, *I love her*, were carved inside him now. He could behave well, care for his family exactly as he ought, but it would never feel like it used to. He'd always be preoccupied with what might have been.

Cat had been so determined to maintain a cool rationality where Daniel was concerned. It was absurd to think they could pick up their former relationship after a twenty-year hiatus – she knew this. Yet, the moment Daniel confirmed it, she felt a wave of dismay. She wanted him. It wasn't just physical – although sitting opposite him, she felt the pull of his body, the desire to touch, to kiss, to lick. It heated her skin, she was sure she must appear flushed, wanton. No – she wanted the energetic pulse of his mind, to feel known and understood. As a teenager, he'd made her feel secure for the first time in her life.

She remembered the day she brought him home. No one was allowed to see her house – not the boys she'd shagged at school, nor the handful of girls who'd been sort of friends in the years before puberty set them at odds with her. The dilapidated furniture, the damp, her mother's boozy naps on the sofa – she could be someone else while these things remained unknown.

But Daniel was different. Daniel lived in a tower block. Daniel blamed policies not people. She decided to test him, watching his reaction closely as he stepped into the hallway of the old council house. Bernice had been on the sofa, fag in hand, all panda eyes and voddie fumes.

'You brought a fella home?' Her mother had been open-mouthed, slurring.

But Daniel hadn't flinched. He strode towards her. 'Daniel Simmonds. Nice to meet you.'

As she shook his hand, Bernice's eyes had been on Cat. 'Your father won't like you taking up with a Black fella.'

Bile had burned the back of her throat. All along, Cat had known that her mother would say something like this – how stupid to create the opportunity. Daniel was wonderful – interesting, clever – so why was Cat doing everything she could to make him despise her?

But Daniel had only laughed. 'In that case, I can't wait to meet him.'

'She drinks?' he asked later, in Cat's bedroom.

'Yep. Every night until she passes out. She blames Dad leaving, but I remember her being pissed all the time, even before that.' She maintained a spiteful edge to her voice, her way of assuring Daniel it was all right to be disgusted.

'Poor woman,' Daniel said.

Cat looked at him, surprised.

'She was a teenager when she had you?'

Cat nodded and Daniel shook his head.

'Can you imagine it, having a baby thrust on you now? It must have been tough. I wonder what she wanted to be when she was our age.' There was an intensity to his eyes that told Cat he really was considering these things, he wasn't faking compassion to make her feel less humiliated. Bernice was a *person* to this sixteen-year-old boy, in a way that she'd never been for Cat.

*

Back in the refectory as she drained her coffee cup, Cat looked at Daniel and said, 'I'm going to try my best, be a good student.' He'd been such a catalyst before, broadening her aspirations, steering her towards compassion. He could be so again. Even if he went home to another woman each night.

He smiled, looking relieved. 'It's so wonderful that you're doing this, now. And I want to help you. Anything you're unsure about, anything you want to discuss, you should get in touch.'

Cat returned his smile and Daniel lowered his gaze, picking at his thumbnail.

'We could have coffee every so often,' he said. 'I mean, now that we ... we're friends, and that's what friends do.'

Cat nodded. She realised that she had been prepared to leave James at the very first sign that Daniel might want more than friendship. How much harder it would be now, knowing there was nowhere to jump to.

Chapter 7

She wasn't looking too bad, Bernice thought. Black skirt and top, push-up bra. Say what you wanted about her, she still had a tiny waist, still scrubbed up all right. Her hip had been giving her grief lately, the old injuries resurfacing, pain coming in sharp stabs. She tried her best to walk normally, but the stairs defeated her, and she had to grip the banister as she climbed slowly, leading with her good side.

She heard Terry before she saw him, his bellowing laugh carrying down the stairwell. When she made it upstairs, she clocked him at a table with a few of his workmates and their wives, white shirt showing off his tan. Rhiannon was in the seat next to him, looking all adoring, which probably meant Cat was going to be in a foul mood. Hardly surprising. Her father's third wife was only a year older than Cat, and the two of them had been at school together.

Bernice headed for the bar, doing her best not to limp. A few of the regulars were laughing at something Cat was saying, and the new barmaid, Laura, was grasping the pumps, looking uncomfortable. Bernice took a bar stool near Cat's crowd.

'All right, love.'

Cat's expression was pinched. 'All right, Mum.' She reached for a glass and poured a vodka without Bernice having to ask. Just a splash of Coke, not drowning it like Laura did.

'So, how's life as a student?'

'Good. Busy. I'm sorry I haven't been round.'

Bernice caught the glance her daughter directed towards Terry's table as she took the money. Poor thing. Whenever she caught those furtive looks, Bernice remembered those Saturdays when Cat had waited by the window, chin resting on her hands. Promises of zoo trips, ice-skating. Most of the time, Terry hadn't even called to tell his daughter he wasn't coming. And so, little Cat had waited. Getting furious whenever Bernice suggested they watch a bit of telly or pop to the shops instead.

'Never mind that, love. What's it like?' Bernice asked. 'Are you learning lots of new things?' As she waited for her daughter to respond, Bernice was aware of Laura, inching closer. She was a pleasant enough lass, but Bernice wished she'd stop hovering around. Opportunities to catch up with Cat were too few, especially now she'd started uni and wasn't doing the lunchtime shifts any more.

'Yeah,' Cat said. 'I'm having to work really hard to keep up, to be honest.'

Old Roger Hampton held up his empty glass and Cat rushed over to serve him.

Laura gave Bernice a smile and she smiled back to be polite. She couldn't think of anything to say. She was tired. In truth, it had been an effort to drag herself out for the evening.

All her life, Bernice had envied those who could be funny and interesting without seeming to try. Terry was one of life's naturals. The life and soul, they called it. His arrival would kick-start a night out. Everyone leaned in whenever he told a story, squawking with laughter in all the right places. Even in his quieter moods, just the fact of him being there, sitting in the corner, provided reassurance, acted as a seal of approval somehow. When others spoke, braving banter of their own, they would keep looking over at Terry, waiting desperately for a laugh, or even just a smile.

Bernice used to have to get the drinks down her neck to keep up, to work up the nerve to try a joke here and there. She'd felt him starting to slip away long before he left. The one-word answers. The way he stopped looking at her. It was like he'd suddenly realised she was no kind of company at all.

Laura had learned from her mistake with the kitten heels and over the past few weeks she'd been wearing the same ballet flats and machine-washable dresses to work. She'd experimented with jeans, but where Cat managed to imbue her habitual denim and vest combo with the elegance of an off-duty model, Laura looked like she was about to embark on a weekly Tesco shop. Her prison weight was still sitting around her middle, padding out her hips; nothing looked good on her, and she was annoyed with herself for noticing.

She watched as Bernice tried to engage her daughter in conversation yet again, asking this time about the train journey to university. Cat seemed determined to answer as briefly as possible, as though she couldn't see the hurt in her mother's eyes. Yet something about Cat's deliberate brisk-ness didn't quite ring true, it was as if she were acting a part, making a performance of surliness to try to conceal a deeper unhappiness. Several times Laura found herself considering whether she might put a hand on Cat's shoulder, look her in the eye and ask her whether she was really okay. But she held back, wary of Cat's cutting remarks, her disdainful stares.

As the night progressed, a tall man wearing glasses and a striped T-shirt sidled up to Bernice. She accepted his offer of a drink with a flirtatious smile and the two of them fell into light conversation.

'Make it a double,' he told Laura when she served them the next time.

Laura looked at Bernice. 'Is that okay with you?'

Bernice looked at the man and the two of them barked with laughter. 'I'll have a triple, love, if he's paying.'

With each drink, Bernice's eyes became ever more glazed and dreamy. She soon gave up trying to talk to Cat and sank into a kind of stupor, nodding vaguely here and there whenever her companion seemed to expect it. Laura remembered all too well this kind of slow-motion night, the point where confident hilarity abruptly withdrew, and time seemed to slow. Simply being, breathing, remembering to blink, required unthinkable energy and concentration.

When the man took himself off to the loo, Laura leaned over the bar to ask Bernice whether she was all right.

'Fine thanks, love.'

'Can I get you a glass of water?'

Bernice gave a little snort.

'Let me get you one. You'll thank me tomorrow.'

As she placed the glass on the bar, Laura felt the sudden chilliness of Cat's attention. She smiled nervously, but, to her surprise, Cat whispered a thank you.

They both got caught up in other orders, but when she next had a free moment, Laura felt emboldened to whisper: 'That man – he's bought your mum five or six drinks. He's being rather methodical about it.'

Cat pressed her lips tightly together. 'Dirty bastard. Wife left him a month ago. He's been on a mission ever since.'

'Do you think we should step in?'

Cat sighed. 'I never know what Mum really wants. Maybe she's enjoying herself, I don't know. She's an adult. She knows what these men expect of her.'

Laura took Cat's forearm and squeezed it. 'I'll keep an eye, don't worry.'

For the remainder of the shift, Laura felt energised, adrenaline flooding her body with new life and purpose. She'd offer Bernice a lift home, she decided. Bernice could have a seat in the kitchen while she and Cat cleared everything away, and once they'd locked up, Laura would ensure that Bernice got home safely. Perhaps Cat would come for the ride too; they could all have a cup of tea and wind down companionably.

Shortly after ringing the bell to call time, Laura approached Bernice with her offer. The man had an arm around Bernice's waist – it looked affectionate, but, in truth, Laura could see he was holding her upright.

'No need,' the man snapped at Laura. 'We're having a sleepover, aren't we, gorgeous?' He kissed Bernice on the mouth, a full-on snog.

Laura put a hand on Bernice's back. 'Bernice? You don't have to go home with him if you'd prefer not to. I thought we could have a nice girly chat. Save your legs the walk. You can rest in the kitchen while I finish up. You can smoke in there, if you like.'

The man's face puckered in anger. 'What are you, the bloody fun police?'

Bernice reached over and pinched Laura's cheek. 'I'm grand, love. Don't you worry yourself about me.'

Laura walked away then, doing her glass-collecting run, furious with herself for not being more authoritative. Cat joined her, wiping down the tables as Laura cleared them. 'I tried,' Laura said. 'Should I have pushed a bit harder? I mean, maybe we should have got the police involved.'

Cat gave a bitter laugh. 'They're not going to give a shit. This is just what she does.'

Laura bit her lip. She wanted to comfort Cat; the vigour she was applying to cleaning the tables suggested a deep rage. She imagined hugging her, pulling that angular body into her own, but at that moment Cat looked up and Laura's courage failed her. Balancing a stack of pint glasses, she returned to the kitchen, just in time to catch sight of the man shepherding Bernice down the stairs.

She loaded the glasses into the dishwasher and started tidying the bar area. She was close to tears and had to focus on her breathing to avoid drawing attention to herself. These desolate feelings were her companions, her education. She had to inhabit them fully – this was how she remembered, this was how she avoided slipping back to that old careless Laura.

'You all right, flower?' It was Roger, a retired chap, neatly dressed as always in a shirt and tie. He had thinning white hair and a pleated forehead which gave him the appearance of a thinker.

Laura nodded.

Roger sighed. 'Suppose I better make a move. Always hate heading back. House feels so empty since Pam passed.'

Laura blinked away her tears and studied his face. He looked resigned, unhappy, but in a gentle way, which was unusual for Martin's customers. In most cases, the sadness of the men who propped up the bar was bound up with an anger that left Laura feeling too afraid to offer anything other than small talk.

She drew herself up. She conjured the courier. Recalled precisely the icy dread that spiked through her as she approached his lifeless form. Thankfully, she could still do it, creating the kind of memory she could step into, remembering with her body, smelling the burning rubber and metallic tang of blood.

'If you don't mind hanging on five minutes or so, I'll give you a lift,' she said to Roger. There. Something useful she could do. Today's act of kindness.

It was inevitable that when they pulled up outside Roger's house, he would invite her in, and Laura would say yes. She was tired and her legs and back ached, but if he wanted company for a little while, then this was something she could provide.

His kitchen smelled of digestive biscuits and was remarkably clean and ordered. A single plate, single knife and fork were laid out on his draining board.

'You take sugar?'

Laura shook her head.

There were two dishcloths hanging on the rail, pink, floral

things, probably purchased by the deceased Pam. Poor Roger mustn't have any respite from his grief; every inch of this house seemed to offer up memories of a life lived as part of a couple.

He placed a pristine white teapot and two matching cups and saucers onto the breakfast counter. He'd even gone to the trouble of filling a tiny jug with milk, which slopped over the side and pooled at the base. Laura heard him swallow and felt an unfamiliar panic at having no idea what to say next. She thought she was being kind, but for all she knew, the poor man probably wanted to curl up and go to sleep.

'So, what was it you used to do? When you were in London, I mean?' Roger inspected the ragged edge of one of his fingernails as he spoke. His hands reminded her of her grandfather's, red with swollen fingers.

'I was a new business manager. For a marketing agency.' Her dismissive feelings towards that old life must have seeped into her tone, because Roger bowed his head, as if he'd been reprimanded. She hadn't meant to be unkind, but any talk of work, of London, sucked Laura back into the night of the accident.

One of the agency's clients had hosted drinks to mark their tenth year of trading, and Laura had been dispatched to work the room, collecting business cards. How proud she'd been of the beaded clutch tucked beneath her arm, of the flattering black dress she'd worn. She'd glided between clusters of suits, taking such delight in the dropping of shoulders, the smiles that greeted her overtures. People were at ease with her within a matter of minutes. She hadn't really understood until later how much of that skill came from the glass of white in her hand.

She rested a hand on Roger's arm. 'Tell me about you.'

'Nothing to tell.'

'You have a lovely home.'

'That's down to Pam. She did like things neat and tidy.'

Laura felt a twinge of awkwardness, but quickly pushed it aside. Her feelings didn't matter. Confronting grief, keeping her eyes trained on its white-hot embers, was what she was destined to do, how she would atone. 'You don't have to talk about it. But it must be hard – living here without her?'

She saw Roger swallow. But then he managed to muster a brave little smile that broke her heart. 'Got used to it after a while. It's been three years.'

She reached out and held his hand. His eyes widened. She sensed the pain, simmering beneath his skin. It made his unassuming manner, his attempts at being chipper, all the more tragic.

'It's okay.' She tried to project control. To, just for a moment, deploy some of that old Laura's charm and authority.

The man stared at her hand encasing his own. She wanted – needed – to provide the comfort he so clearly ached for. But how? The moment was slipping away. She was failing yet again. Failing to deliver on her atonement pledges, failing to make any impact at all. Any moment now, he'd say something about being tired and Laura would be expected to take her leave, her failure cemented. Roger would go to bed lonely and disappointed, perhaps more so than ever, now he'd had this short brush with connection.

There was another thing she could try. She lifted his hand and placed it against her breast. Roger snatched his arm back, stumbling up from his stool. His eyes were alarmed as they met hers, but then a look of understanding settled on his face. He put his hand back on her chest, tentatively at first, then gaining confidence, kneading the flesh with an unschooled enthusiasm. He stepped towards her, delivering a wet, beery kiss.

'Shall we go upstairs?' Laura whispered. *She could do this.* Perform one of the few deeds that added to the happiness in the world rather than depleting it. It would be distasteful to her, but she didn't deserve any better.

She followed him into his bedroom. He was silent and Laura was afraid that any minute now the spell would be broken. She had to go through with it. She was certain. This was the only way, the only thing she could do. Scanning the room, she saw that the bed was neatly made with a tartan cover. There was a woman's dressing table beneath the window and it was covered in framed photographs, many of a lady Laura assumed must be Pam, slim with permed auburn hair.

Laura heard Roger's breath catch as he hovered uncertainly by the bed, so she took the lead, cradling his head as she kissed him. She removed her dress, unhooked her bra and the sight of her breasts seemed – finally – to shatter his inhibitions. He stepped forward, squeezing and kissing them with the fervour of a teenage boy. Laura looked down and the sight of a tender pink bald spot at the crown of his head made her feel an unbearable sadness. She pushed the feeling away. She was providing comfort. The world may laugh at her, but what did such things matter? As she unzipped his trousers, she was sure of the rightness of what she was doing and felt almost triumphant.

He was still soft, so she started with gentle strokes. As they lay on the bed, he continued fussing at her breasts, then placed an experimental finger inside her knickers. She made her strokes a little firmer, but as the minutes passed, he remained unable to achieve an erection.

She was prepared to be patient, but without warning, Roger abruptly pulled away and started tugging at himself. 'Just let me—' He grew red in the face as he pumped away with his hand. The sight of his fat fingers wrapped around his cock was so very appalling. Laura had to look away as beneath her the bed rocked with Roger's furious motion.

He growled. 'I never used to . . . This has never . . .'

What was she doing? She'd offered herself as an act of kindness, but Roger's face was now wild with humiliation and anger.

'Just give me another couple of minutes.'

'It's okay.' Laura got up from the bed.

'If you . . . just stand there – let me look at your boobs while I—'

She gathered up her clothes. 'It's okay. Really. Let's pretend this never happened. It's my fault.' Every moment in this room intensified her feelings of degradation.

He stopped his tugging, finally, thankfully.

She braved a look at his face as she threw her dress back on. He looked disappointed, yes, but it seemed to Laura that there was something of hatred in his expression too. No doubt she deserved it. She'd only wanted to make him feel better, but it seemed as though her efforts had left them both feeling far worse than before.

Chapter 8

Six weeks into the first semester, Cat was due to receive her first set of marks back for an essay on the origins of World War One. She was enjoying this module, finding the complex web of alliances and tangled ideologies endlessly fascinating. She admired the boldness with which some writers put forward their theories, purporting to demonstrate a clear lineage between events.

It felt like such a luxury to prioritise reading and thinking, to spend time refining her own ideas. She'd loved working on the essay. The long afternoons stretching into evenings in the library, picking through a multitude of accounts and drawing on sources outside of the core reading list. The library would slowly thin out as her fellow students went home, later re-emerging in sparkly tops and bright shirts. She forgot to eat, sometimes even forgot to smoke, such was her absorption.

But it worried her that she didn't have a clear sense of how she was doing, or whether she was reaching the required depths of understanding. She found herself speculating, imagining marks that fell short of a pass, lecturers having a *quiet word* about whether she might be struggling. What would she do then? Not everyone had it in them to work at this level and failure was a very real possibility. *There's no shame in deciding it's not for you*, James kept telling her.

From their earliest coffees, Daniel had offered to give her essays a read before she submitted them, but it felt wrong to take him up on the offer. He didn't provide this service to other students and to avail herself of it would feel like cheating.

'Why are you so committed to helping me?' she'd asked him earlier that week. They'd sat at their usual table in the canteen, and he'd gazed out the window for a moment before answering.

'Because you helped me, back in the day,' he said. 'Seeing how your mind worked, how you'd find patterns and hidden motivations that weren't obvious to others – it inspired me to push myself even harder. I envied you, if I'm honest. The way you could read something once and really *know* it. I don't think I'd have got into Oxford if I wasn't, on some level, competing with you.'

Cat laughed. 'And now look at us. The professor and the barmaid.'

'Don't do that.' Daniel drew his shoulders back.

'Well, it's true. Nothing to envy now, is there?' She wasn't sure why she was suddenly so angry. It just seemed unendurable to have him rhapsodise about their former connection when he was married to someone else, when he'd been clear they could be no more than friends.

He held her gaze without speaking. She could feel her eyes starting to water as her breath quickened and she became certain she was about to cry.

'I haven't done half the things I wanted to do,' he said quietly.

'Oxford made me timid, more concerned about fitting in than changing the world. I find myself wondering sometimes – if you and I had stayed together, would things have been different? Would I have held on to the things we both believed in? I never set out to be a lecturer – it was never a *dream*.'

Cat had swallowed. She could feel the heat radiating off his body and nothing would have been more natural than to walk over to his side of the table and take him in her arms. Her own thoughts had pondered the same questions; her daydreams had meandered through an array of different lives where the two of them had gone on encouraging one another, believing in one another.

At that moment, another lecturer had come over to their table to talk to Daniel about rescheduling one of his seminars. It gave Cat a moment to catch her breath, but she was more disappointed than relieved. What might she have said if the moment had stretched out? Everything she wanted to be, everything she wanted to feel in her life, seemed to flow from the two years she had spent with Daniel at college. Could it be possible that he felt the same way?

Cat's phone pinged when she was on the train heading towards university the following morning, sodden umbrella at her feet. Her marks had been uploaded to an online portal and with trembling fingers she logged on to retrieve her own results. Ninety-one per cent. A first. She slumped back in her seat, closing her eyes for a moment. The relief of it left her strangely emotional, her breath catching in her throat, eyes stinging. A degree was within her reach. The transformation she wanted for herself wasn't a fantasy. Here was proof.

Once she'd steadied herself, she read through the lecturer's comments. This particular unit was led by a white-haired man named Anthony. He was quietly spoken in lectures, but Cat appreciated how he managed to be clear without repeating himself or waffling as a couple of the other staff were prone to do. His comments were complimentary. *I'm particularly impressed with how you interrogate each of the sources you draw on, reaching intelligent conclusions around their reliability in a systematic manner,* he wrote. *You have an engaging writing style and make your points clearly and effectively. My only constructive comment would be to look at your introduction and consider how you might frame your arguments with more confidence. It felt just a smidge tentative when compared to the substance of your essay.*

In the box titled 'other comments', he'd written: *Catherine, this really is an outstanding start and one of the best first-year essays I've ever read. It left me wondering why you're always so quiet in the seminar sessions? You're obviously articulate and opinionated, so it would be wonderful for us all if you were to plunge yourself into the classroom debate a little more.*

Cat stared at this for some time, smarting. Had she been noticeably withdrawn? A couple of weeks back, Daniel had joked about it, asking her when she was going to start *putting the young 'uns back in their box.* But the truth was she already felt so conspicuous, so grateful for being tolerated. She didn't expect to make friends with people young enough to be her children. Cat was already older than Bernice had been when Cat herself was eighteen. But it felt unnecessarily boorish to disagree with her classmates in a public setting, to put forward her own views as though this was a shift at Martin's and they were the old duffers, relying on her to perform for them, to fill the silence. But she'd try, find a way to engage that felt natural to her.

Today, Cat just had the one lecture on the Russian Revolution, followed by a seminar on the Bolsheviks' consolidation of power. She felt a deep unease as she headed towards the classroom. She'd started gravitating towards the same group of girls – Chloe, Grace and Sophia – who seemed slightly more mature than some of the others. They all had long, shiny hair that was either aggressively straightened or, on a rainy day like today, pulled back into messy buns. Their jeans were tight, their make-up minimalist but applied with care. A couple of times they'd extended invitations, to a student night at a club, to a party in their halls, but Cat had joked about being too old for such things.

When she joined them after a quick cigarette, they were all eagerly comparing marks. 'I got fifty-two per cent. But a pass is a pass, right?' Chloe was leaning back in her chair, but Cat could see the anxiety in her eyes.

'That's right,' Cat said. 'Our first-year marks don't count towards our final grade. All we have to do is pass.'

'Thank fuck for that,' Grace said. 'I got a sixty-one. What about you, Soph? I bet you got a first.'

Sophia reddened and Cat felt unexpectedly protective. There was a ruthlessness to the act of comparison that reminded her of school. Everyone was smiling, but she remembered all too clearly the resentment, the hostile whispers, that followed another person's success. This generation was no different, she feared; she could feel the air around her becoming taut.

'I got seventy-nine,' Sophia said.

The others whistled. Chloe reached over and tousled Sophia's hair.

'What did you get, Cat?' Sophia asked.

Cat felt the group's collective attention settle on her and her stomach flipped. She smiled, trying to bat away her awkward feelings. She was almost forty years old, it was ridiculous that she should feel so exposed. 'Ninety-one per cent,' she said, not making eye contact with any of them.

She heard Sophia's breath catch, but the others were silent. Their lecturer came into the room and there was a shuffling of chairs as everyone got ready to begin.

'Fuck! You're a dark horse, aren't you?' Grace whispered.

Cat smiled, unsure whether she was proud or ashamed. She vowed to herself, as the discussion themes were divvied out between groups, that today she would participate. She'd share her views and question the arguments of others. Because she was good enough. The mark had proven it and she felt a little more convinced of her own right to be there.

After the seminar, Sophia leaned over and asked whether Cat wanted to join the rest of the group for lunch in a café. She declined; her bar money didn't stretch to such things, so she'd got into the habit of making sandwiches every morning, not wanting to ask James for any more money. But for the first time, she felt a little wistful about not accompanying them. She'd expended so much energy on studying, on doing her very best work, and it struck her that she was still very unsure who she wanted to *be* in her classes. Preparing herself for the kind of activist career she wanted wasn't just a matter of getting the right grades; her graduation wouldn't mark an instant transformation. She needed to work on herself, she knew that. She just wasn't quite sure how such things were done.

She headed to the library, smoking two fags en route and securing her favourite desk on the second floor, by a window overlooking the park. This afternoon, she was going to be working on an essay for Daniel on the earliest slave rebellions in the Americas, knowing that it was a special interest of his. She'd chosen to explore why alliances with disgruntled white settlers had only ever been short-lived, why there was no unified uprising against a landowning class who'd been vastly outnumbered. Her grade had encouraged her, letting her believe that she might just write something that would impress him.

She piled her desk with reference books and unwrapped her cheese-and-pickle sandwiches as she started to read. *I'm happy*, she thought. *This is what it feels like to be happy.*

James finished up with the design agency earlier than planned. He'd half expected the account manager to suggest lunch, given that he'd driven to their offices in Portsmouth for this meeting, but an offer wasn't forthcoming, and James found himself dashing back to his car in pouring rain.

Once inside the Golf, he thought of Cat. He didn't know her timetable, but she'd be somewhere in the city right now, perhaps due a break. He fired off a quick text, asking what she was up to. He had a notion that he might surprise her; whisk her off for a fancy lunch before he had to go back to the office.

She did appear to be sticking to university, which was

rather unexpected. He still didn't fully understand the purpose of the enterprise. She said it was all about starting again, having a career. But James imagined what he'd do if the CV of a forty- or thirty-something who'd only just graduated landed on his desk. He'd discard it, convinced there was something wrong with the person, sure that someone whose life fell so outside the normal order of things could only bring chaos and problems. And maybe he'd be right to do so.

Cat was magnificent in so many ways, but he couldn't imagine her blending into an office. She wasn't the type to nod politely in meetings, or witness others' incompetence with quietly gritted teeth. What they never taught you at uni was that success at work really came down to an ability to tolerate things quietly. To show enthusiasm when it was required and agree with the right people.

He was just about to give up and drive off, when she returned the text. *In the library working on an essay. About to put my phone in aeroplane mode, so I'll see you at dinner x*

James had driven past the university's library before now. It was an ugly concrete building right in the centre of the city and he remembered it because of the students spilling into the road, not paying attention to the traffic. It wasn't far from here, and if he remembered correctly, there was a car park close by. Checking he had his umbrella in the back of the car, he headed off, strangely excited at the idea of observing Cat in this new setting. Had she made friends at university? Perhaps he might meet one or two of her classmates.

She'd all but barred him from Martin's. Not that it gave him any pleasure, sitting in that grimy, smoky bar waiting for her to wrest empty glasses from filthy old men. But they'd rowed when she'd first suggested he stop coming.

He'd given her an opening, true, because he hadn't been able to disguise his distaste for the place and was complaining about the length of time he had to wait for her to finish her shifts.

'There's no need to hang around. I always used to walk home on my own before,' she said.

He'd drawn himself up. 'I thought you might like to see me. I didn't realise I was becoming a nuisance.'

He'd seen a moment of panic pass through her eyes. But she regained control of herself quickly, she always did. 'I'm not saying that at all. It's lovely having you keep me company. But I know it's wretched for you, sitting there listening to the regulars blather on.'

He'd only been half appeased by that, but he did give himself permission to reclaim his evenings, returning to the gym and visiting his mother. He'd told himself the arrangement was working, that none of the unkempt fellows at that godawful place were anything resembling a threat.

But a feeling had been born that day. It was a low-level suspicion, barely perceptible most of the time, at others manifesting itself as a burning deep within his gut. Could it be possible that she was using him? His mother seemed constantly riled by Cat and her perceived lack of gratitude for everything James provided. But this only served to make him feel worse. What if the house was the real draw? Just thinking it was enough to fill his stomach with something sour. Yet he returned to the idea, time and again. Any time Cat seemed to prefer her own company to his, he would come back to this: *Why was she with him, really?*

The library spanned three levels and had a spiral staircase running through the centre. James walked a full circuit of the ground floor, largely dominated with banks of computers. He could sense the glances being directed his way and was aware how out of place he must look in his suit, carrying his golfing umbrella. The students all looked painfully young, and just like when he'd been at university, there was a persistent hum of chatter that didn't sound very much like study.

He made his way up the staircase and scouted the first floor. Already his heart was pounding, not from the exercise, but from anticipation. There was a tiny part of him that was getting ready for a confrontation, for the discovery that she wasn't where she said she was.

But at last, he spotted her on the top floor, sitting alone in a row of desks. Her hair was in a messy ponytail and she was scrawling into a notebook, deep in concentration, surrounded by books.

James found himself suddenly reluctant to approach. He intuited the fact that his presence wouldn't be welcome, that Cat wouldn't trouble to mask her irritation at being interrupted. People would stare, wondering who he was.

In his mind, he had heard the sharp voice of his mother: *a pleasant lunch isn't too much to ask for, not when you're paying for this odd little hobby of hers.*

He walked towards her. She was wearing a bobbled old hoodie and he noted how seldom she wore the cashmere jumper he'd bought her the previous Christmas.

'Surprise,' he whispered as he neared.

Her body jolted and, as she turned to him, she couldn't conceal her dismay at him being here. She corrected herself instantly, parting her lips as she gave him a warm smile. 'This *is* a surprise, what brings you to rainy old Portsmouth?'

James recounted the agency visit. Raised the prospect of lunch.

Cat looked wistfully at the pile of books on her table, swallowed. 'I've actually eaten my sandwiches already.'

'I just thought it would be nice. That's all. I don't get to see much of you these days.' She was embarrassed to be seen with him. Didn't want her classmates laughing about how short he was, commenting on his pitted skin.

Cat swallowed, then smiled again. 'Fuck it. Let's go. I'm going to pick somewhere expensive and order a whopping great big dessert.'

James felt his body unclenching. He felt better. She knew she needed him.

Chapter 9

The marks kept rolling in, Cat kept doing well. She loved every aspect of her new life: the coffees with Daniel, the feeling that she was embarking on a deep exploration of subjects that fascinated her. So much of what used to make her unhappy now felt diminished in significance. She was working fewer bar shifts now, and spending less time with her Martin's customers led to a strange new fondness for them. It was happening: she was remaking herself into someone better.

One grey afternoon, Cat looked at her phone and saw that Laura had been trying to get hold of her. She called her back as she walked from the library to the station – they weren't friends as such, so she supposed Laura must want her to cover a shift.

'Thank God! Where are you?' Laura sounded breathless.

'In Portsmouth, about to get the train home.'

'Don't get on. I found your mum in the toilets when I was closing up this afternoon. It's okay – she was breathing, but I couldn't wake her, so I called an ambulance. They've taken her to St Luke's. I didn't know what to do. I thought someone should be at the hospital, so I'm driving down the A27 now. I can pick you up from the station and take you there.'

'Fuck!'

'Wait for me by the front of the station.'

Cat took a deep breath. 'I will. Thank you. Is she . . . What did the paramedics say?'

'Not much. Listen, I'll be with you in ten minutes. I hate using the phone when I'm driving, but I'll be with you soon.'

Heart thudding, Cat waited near the station taxi rank, scanning the stream of traffic passing by. Pigeons gathered hopefully by her feet, inspecting her fag ash as it fell to the ground. She'd always known her mother drank too much, but it was one of those facts that sat quietly in the background of her life, unsettling, but easy enough to ignore. The moment Cat became riled up and said something about the drinking and the stumbling, collapsing behaviour that went with it, things would escalate and the two of them would end up sniping at one another. Or, rather, Cat would be sniping, becoming increasingly infuriated as Bernice started wailing, snot and tears running down her face. Cat's whole life had been dominated by these same cycles of escalating drinking and bitter recrimination; it was far easier to cope if she detached herself, trying not to react to slurred speech and drunken pairings, swooping in only when she felt her mother was in real danger.

The years before she first got together with Daniel had been the worst. Too many times, Cat had been surprised by the presence of some strange man rooting through the kitchen in the morning, stinking of beer. It was no way to live. She took up smoking at fourteen to help with the anxiety, steeling herself against whatever unpleasant surprise might come next. She hated being at home, stayed in the town library each evening, until it closed. She could never shake the feeling that whatever sluttish behaviour her mother had indulged in, however often she drank the money meant to feed them both, Cat was the one in the wrong for getting angry. Bernice would always lower her eyes and apologise. She'd agree with whatever insults were flung at her and cry with remorse, but she'd never change.

Laura pulled up in a blue Fiesta, red-faced and breathing heavily.

Cat climbed inside the car. She felt her stomach twist with embarrassment – of all the people to find her mother, it had to be Laura. She of the swishy hair and neat handwriting, the *Catherine smells* comments. 'Thanks so much for coming to get me.'

'It's no trouble.' Laura signalled and pulled away. 'I needed to do something useful.' And she looked as though she meant it. She wasn't that same schoolgirl any more, Cat had to keep reminding herself of that.

'She was unconscious? In the toilets?'

'I thought she'd left. Thank goodness I needed a wee before heading home, I wouldn't have found her, otherwise.'

Cat closed her eyes for a second. She could imagine it, all too clearly. There had probably been vomit, maybe even shit. Had Laura attempted to clean it, or had she left it there for Martin to deal with? She rested her head against the window.

Laura wiped her eyes with the back of her hand. 'I should have noticed she'd had too much and stopped serving her.'

'It's not your fault. You can't always tell how drunk she is. Anyway, she normally has a bottle stashed in her bag. She thinks she's being ultra-discreet when she tops up her drinks.'

'Goodness!' Laura looked astonished, as though she really had no idea that such things went on. Under normal circumstances, Cat would perhaps be scornful; and she'd welcome the feeling, letting it harden her against the pain. But Laura was the first person in a long time who'd shown any kind of interest in, or concern for, Bernice.

After a long wait in A&E, an Eastern European nurse led Cat past rows of occupied beds. Laura insisted on waiting around, but thankfully seemed to know that Cat would want to see her mother alone and didn't insist on accompanying her. There were groaning patients, harried-seeming relatives, and one old man who appeared so defeated it chilled Cat to look at him. Bernice was propped up, attached to a drip. Her eyes flickered open as Cat stepped inside the blue curtained cubicle. 'Oh, darling, what are you doing here? Get yourself home,' the words were slurred, but Cat was flooded with relief. At least she was conscious; it couldn't be that bad this time.

Cat sat in the plastic chair next to the bed, folding her hands in her lap. The clamour of buzzers going off at the nurses' station, trolleys being wheeled over hard floors, put her right back to the aftermath of the accident. She felt a tightening at the base of her throat, a sting across her eyes. The desolation at being her mother's only visitor, at never knowing how to lessen the pain, still lived inside her. None of it had dulled with time.

'Is there anything I can get you?' Cat was trying to sound brave, optimistic, but it came out sounding gruff.

'No, love. I just need to have me a nice little sleep. You get yourself home. Or off to that university. No need to be here. You go and do your studying.'

Cat's mouth felt dry. A tiny part of her was embracing Bernice's insistence that she leave – it was exoneration; she could escape this place knowing the drip would do its work. But this was the fifth time in two years that alcohol poisoning had led to a hospital admission. And those were the times Cat knew about; she suspected Bernice might have concealed others.

'What can I do, Mum?' she asked. 'How can I make it better?' Since starting university she'd spent less time with her mother than ever before. She'd cut back her hours at the club, so they weren't having their midweek chats. For weeks now, Cat had been aware of owing her mum a visit, or a phone call at least – there just was always something else to do.

Bernice reached out a hand, placed it on Cat's knee. A cannula was inserted into a vein, taped in place. It was all too familiar. Too much like before.

'Don't worry about me,' Bernice started to cry. 'I'm big enough and ugly enough to make my own way.'

'Mum, stop.' Cat wiped her mother's tears with the sleeve of her hoodie. 'You get yourself to sleep. I'll just sit here for a little while. It's no bother. I want to stay.'

Would she ever be free from guilt? Cat's young classmates spoke of their mothers so differently, talking of shopping trips and lunches they looked forward to. Recounting sound advice, often with derision, but each time giving Cat a little pang as she heard the tenderness echoing through the generations. How wonderful it must be to know such normality, such ease. Cat wondered what it must feel like, to roll your eyes indulgently as you complained about how your parents fussed over you. For love to take the form of care, of protection and ruthless advocacy.

She remembered creeping down the stairs one night as a child, shivering in her thin nightie after hearing her father shouting in the kitchen.

'Stupid slut! You always have to spoil everything, don't you? Always have to go too far.' He transformed words into hard points that pierced and stabbed.

Cat had approached the open door and seen her mother on all fours, a puddle of sick on the floor in front of her. She'd clutched the door frame. Even though she couldn't have been more than eight, she'd known she was witnessing something terrible, something nice little girls never had to see.

'I should make you lick it up like a dog,' Terry had yelled. 'You always fucking embarrass me.' With that, he'd aimed a kick at Bernice's ribs, knocking her down, her hair landing in the sick.

Cat's mother had started to cry. Not the restrained tears you saw quietly sliding down the noses of adults on TV. This was more like the inconsolable sobs of an injured toddler. It was wrong for her mother to be crying like that, Cat had known. Very wrong. She'd frozen, unable to avert her eyes as her mother's terrible keening seemed to resonate, to connect with something deep inside her belly.

When Bernice had spotted her, she'd quickly drawn herself up, brushing at her face with her palms, smearing mascara everywhere. 'It's all right, Cat, sweetie. Get yourself back to bed. Mummy's just got a poorly tummy, that's all.'

Cat's father had flashed her a grin. He'd been wearing a

white shirt that still looked pristine, and his dark brown hair remained gelled in place. 'Good evening, Kitty Cat.' He'd opened his arms and Cat ran to him.

'You should be fast asleep,' her mother had said. 'Get yourself back to bed, sweetheart. Everything's all right.'

'Your mum's been making a mess of the kitchen. She should clean it up, shouldn't she?'

Cat nodded, knowing that's what her father had expected of her.

'You tell her, then. Tell her to clean it up.' His smile had been warm, showing off the chipped front tooth that served to make him look all the more genial. Cat wanted, more than anything, to make him happy, to ensure he carried on smiling. But she couldn't speak. Even though her mother had stopped wailing, Cat could still feel the horror of the sound vibrating inside her.

'Terry, please—'

Her father had kicked at Bernice again and she landed hard on her side.

'Oh, for Christ's sake, woman! Look at her, Cat, look at the state of her. You'll never end up like that, will you?'

Cat had shaken her head resolutely. Her father patted her shoulder and she'd felt a rising pride. He'd seen that she was different, seen that she had nothing in common with that abject woman on the floor. Even at eight, it had seemed vitally important to Cat to disassociate herself from everything her mother stood for.

Once Bernice had drifted off, Cat managed to catch the doctor doing his rounds. He was a dark-haired young man, well-spoken, but with a look of consternation around his eyebrows. Cat asked him about a referral to rehab and he nodded vaguely, shifting his weight from foot to foot, clearly desperate to be on his way. 'She's definitely a candidate for that, but waiting lists are currently nine months.' Something in his tone made Cat want to shout in his face. He wasn't dismissive as such, but he managed to convey such weariness, such an absence of hope.

She was on the cusp of making a scornful comment but stopped herself just in time. This doctor wasn't responsible for the waiting list, she reminded herself. It was the politicians who really deserved her anger. Privately educated men who believed passing out in pub toilets was something that the likes of Bernice were simply expected to do. Give them their intravenous fluids, and send them on their way, expecting them back at A&E within a month or so.

This was why she was at university, Cat told herself as she strode towards the exit. She didn't have to accept this dismissive thinking. She was educating herself in order to push and push against the lazy stereotypes. She'd do something, find a way to change things. Stand for Parliament, maybe.

Cat stopped walking. Her stomach lurched, but in a not-unpleasant way. It was a feeling of rightness, of inevitability. *Parliament.* Why shouldn't she try it? It was perhaps the most direct way to bring about change. Just a few months ago, she couldn't see a future beyond pulling pints – now she was contemplating standing as an MP. It was hilarious. Absurd. But the idea inhabited her completely and, within a few short paces, it made her into someone else, someone who was going to fight for people like her mother.

*

Laura had overridden Cat's objections and waited at the hospital to give Cat a lift home. As it was now long past dinner time and her stomach was growling, she'd suggested they stop at a KFC on the way back. To her surprise, Cat had agreed.

'It was really bloody kind of you to come and get me,' Cat said. She was attacking her food, fingers gleaming with oil.

Laura was still deeply shaken by the afternoon's events. There had been watery vomit over the washbasins and on the floor; Bernice's skirt had been hitched up, her tights and knickers halfway down her thighs. For several moments, Laura had been unable to move, her breath coming in heavy rasps, part of her longing for someone else to come along and take command. Such energy it had taken to break the spell of inaction and call for an ambulance. 'No trouble at all,' she said quietly.

'To be honest, I'm relieved I didn't have to ask James to come and get me. He'd be bending my ear the whole way back about *willpower* and *individual responsibility*.' Cat shook her head as she slotted another handful of chips into her mouth.

Laura was intrigued; this was the first time Cat had alluded to the man she lived with. Their shared hospital dash seemed to have fractured Cat's usual reserve. 'Does James not get along with Bernice, then?' Laura asked.

Cat snorted, but her eyes remained sad. 'He never had to deal with people like Mum, not 'til he met me. Whenever he says two words to her, I can see his chest puffing out over how open-minded and compassionate he is. But he isn't, not really. He'll lend Mum a hundred quid to stop her gas being disconnected, but if she tries to have a conversation with him, I can see him recoiling. Patronising cunt.'

Laura straightened her back.

Cat laughed. 'Bitter old bitch, aren't I?'

'I'm fascinated,' Laura said. 'I mean, why—'

'Why am I with him?'

Laura nodded. She was aware she'd overstepped. This candour was very unlike Cat, and it struck Laura that maybe she was taking advantage.

'He took me into his life when I was at rock bottom. I'd wanted out of my mum's world for so long, and there he was, dangling a shiny key. It sounds so mercenary when I say it out loud. But it didn't feel that way at the time. I wanted to be in love. I kept telling myself I was.'

They ate in silence for a few moments. Laura wondered if maybe the most generous thing she could do would be to tell Cat about her own drinking. Describe the thud of the courier's body. She knew Cat would be shocked, and for a moment Laura craved that reaction, she wanted to see the disgust and disbelief on Cat's face. But that wasn't support. It was the old Laura, trying to make everything about her.

'Are the two of you married?' Laura asked, after a while.

'No. Never interested me, the whole wedding thing. And it's just as well, because James has never asked. His mum would never allow it, it'd give me a claim on his assets.' Cat grinned and Laura felt something tighten inside her. Sometimes Cat seemed to almost demean herself.

'So, what are the next steps with Bernice?' Laura asked.

Cat cracked her knuckles. 'She's on the list for a drying-out programme. Nine months is the expected wait. It makes me sick. Mum does get in the right frame of mind to sort herself out every once in a while, but they're never ready for her.'

'Will she stay with you, when she comes out?'

Cat stared at Laura, mouth open in surprise. But then her shoulders stiffened, her eyebrows pinched together. 'That wouldn't help anyone.'

Laura swallowed. 'No. Maybe not. I'm just wondering how we might be able to help her. I mean, a rehab programme would be great, but there must be things we can do in the meantime? Has she tried AA?'

'Many times,' Cat's eyes darkened. 'Never sticks with it.'

'I could offer to go with her?' Laura said.

Cat shook her head, oblivious to the confession concealed within that offer. 'She's an adult. She knows what she has to do if she wants to sort herself out. If you really want to help her, don't vote Tory. They've made it so that there's fuck all for people like her.' She began scooping her meal packaging, impatient to leave.

There was so much that Laura wanted to convey. A phone call here and there. A shopping trip. Sometimes it was the small things; just ensuring someone felt loved might be enough. Bernice's disease wasn't alcoholism, it was loneliness. Laura saw as much every time Bernice tried to engage Cat in conversation and her daughter appeared distracted.

'I might just nip out for a quick fag before we get in the car.' Cat stood up.

'If there's ever anything I can do . . .'

Cat didn't trouble to acknowledge the comment as she moved away from the table.

Laura considered holding her back, trying to persuade her that one or two visits a week might provide the solace Bernice needed to straighten herself out. But Cat radiated impatience.

Their earlier camaraderie had fled and Laura sensed that pressing the issue would lead to the kind of verbal sparring from which Cat always emerged the winner. Even when she was wrong.

Chapter 10

Sunday lunchtime was the most predictable of Cat's bar shifts. There was a cohort of around ten or so regulars who'd hover round the bar, having a fixed number of pints, talking about the same damn things, week in, week out. Today, Daniel was going to be visiting her at Martin's with the rough beginnings of a book proposal. It felt risky, bringing him here, but James always went to his mother for Sunday lunch and tended to stay there until late afternoon, knowing that Cat often kept the bar open to claim an hour or two of overtime.

The plan was for Daniel to arrive as she was closing up, then they could lock the doors and spend an hour in quiet conversation, treating Martin's as Cat's own private living room. Daniel would be driving half an hour each way, giving up time with his family. It was his suggestion and Cat tried not to think too hard about what it might mean. It would be so easy to develop hopes, to believe that this hunger for her company meant more than it really did. They'd done well at redefining their relationship as a friendship, falling into a pattern of meeting for coffee Tuesday and Thursday afternoons. They acted as though this wasn't significant and were careful how they spoke about it, even with one another. But Cat was coming to depend on these meetings – being with Daniel made her ambitions feel plausible.

She was anxious as the time for calling last orders approached. There were just four customers left: the skinhead twins at the fruit machines, old Roger sat at the bar staring at his pint glass, and Cat's mother. Since being discharged from hospital, Bernice had slowed down her drinking, taking four times as much Coke with the vodka and sipping each drink slowly. Cat wanted to be encouraged by this, but she'd been here so many times before, stuck in a continual cycle of hope and disappointment.

'So, have you broken up for Christmas now?' Bernice asked. She was wearing a low-cut sparkly jumper, her bleached hair scraped back into a tight ponytail.

Cat nodded.

Her mother lit a cigarette. There was a nasty purple bruise on her hand, from where the drip had gone in. 'That's nice. You deserve a chance to let your hair down a bit.'

To Cat's dismay, Roger ordered another pint and bought Bernice another vodka. She was determined that everyone should leave promptly, that she and Daniel should have privacy without her having to waste precious minutes explaining his presence to the regulars.

As she rang the bell, calling time at two o'clock sharp, she looked up to see him arriving, wearing jeans and a white jumper that looked new and expensive. She'd not seen him in his weekend clothes before and he gave the sense of having been dressed by a woman. He sat on a stool at the bar and grinned. 'Am I too late for a drink?'

'Make it a quick one. Bar's closing.' Cat flashed a smile, but her insides felt liquid.

Her mother was studying Daniel's face with a puzzled expression. She'd adored him before – all through college, he'd remained respectful of Bernice, asking her about her day, treating her with dignity even when she'd been drunk. After a moment, Bernice's eyes lit with excited recognition. 'I know you!' She turned to Cat. 'It's Daniel!'

Cat gave her mother a vague nod.

Bernice smiled, reaching out and touching Daniel's shoulder. 'How've you been? It's been ages, hasn't it? You probably don't recognise me, I'm a broken-down old thing these days. You were going to Oxford. Oh, you and Cat, such a couple of bright sparks. I've never known anything like it. You're the kind of people they make films about.'

Daniel put a hand on Bernice's arm. 'Really lovely to see you again, Mrs Brandon. I was so sorry to hear about your accident. It must have been a tough few years for you.'

'Oh, never mind all that. What are you doing with yourself? Look at you – still a handsome devil, I see.'

Daniel beamed at Bernice, and Cat felt such warmth towards him. 'I'm an academic at Portsmouth University. One of Cat's lecturers as it happens.'

Bernice gave Cat a questioning glance. Roger had snapped out of his drowsy state and appeared to be observing the conversation. And the skinhead twins – racist and proud of it – kept turning around, staring hard at Daniel to convey he wasn't welcome. Cat glared back at them.

'Right, can we start drinking up please, everyone?'

She wondered whether Daniel was aware of a hostile note

to the atmosphere. He must be, even though he continued chatting warmly with her mother. The regulars seemed to be sipping their drinks far more slowly than usual, as though waiting for a confrontation. Bernice seemed oblivious, barraging Daniel with questions, affecting delight at his job and the pictures of his children he ended up showing her.

At eighteen minutes past, Cat put her foot down, warning Roger she was going to take his pint away regardless of whether he was finished and telling the twins that the fruit machines were going to be turned off in thirty seconds, final warning.

Bernice continued to hang around even after the others left. She gathered up her things and stood expectantly, perhaps thinking Cat would accompany her out of the building like she often did, locking up as she went. Cat saw a smile creep across her mother's face as she took in Daniel continuing to sit on his bar stool, advertising the fact that he was staying behind. Cat was about to mumble something, but Bernice gave her a gentle pat on the arm. 'I'll be off then, love. You have a lovely afternoon.'

After she'd locked the front door, Cat returned to the bar and poured Cokes for herself and Daniel. She was aware of the stale beer smell, clinging to her clothes, of the shabbiness of the patterned carpet and heavy velvet curtains. What must Daniel be thinking, now he'd had this glimpse of her world? It was absurd that they were both pretending their meeting was innocent, that it was natural to meet in a closed bar rather than in either of their homes. The hours they shared at university were never enough. Cat was already dreading the long expanse of Christmas holiday.

'Talk me through this book proposal then,' she said.

He took his laptop out of his rucksack and placed it on the bar. 'I've been trying to distil what I really want to write about. I think there's a definite need for an accessible overview of the US civil rights struggle; but what I'm particularly interested in is how Black activism has intersected with, and influenced, other protest movements over the decades.' He pulled up a document, lines in various colours linking historical figures, rebellions and movements together in a complex timeline stretching from the earliest plantation rebellions to recent Black Lives Matter protests.

Cat nodded encouragingly. She could visualise a thick tome sitting in bookshop windows – a collage of archive images across the cover, Daniel's name in large type. She felt a shiver of delight that he was involving her, that in many ways they were picking up threads of conversations that began twenty years ago.

Daniel sighed. 'I really should have got on and written it in my twenties. I'm so irritated that I didn't. I look back now and I couldn't tell you what I did with the time instead. Commented on pictures on social media. Went to the gym. Watched box sets.'

Cat smiled. 'You always tell me off for looking back and finding fault with myself.'

He picked up a beermat, turned it over in his hands. 'I was midway through my PhD when Mum died, and – I know it sounds silly – but after I'd cleared out our old flat, it felt like I didn't have a home any more. It changed my priorities. More than anything, I wanted to settle down and make a family of my own. I guess that's what grief does – alters your perspective, makes you crave unexpected things.'

Cat and Daniel had both been through so much as young people. It would have been the most natural thing in the world to reach out and comfort him. How easily she'd kissed him on the day of the interview. She could blame drink, but really it was the physical presence of him, the way his lips called to her memories, just as they were doing now. She was certain that if she touched him, he'd respond, but he'd regret doing so and would perhaps come to resent her.

She kept her palms face down on her knees. 'Do you not like teaching?' she asked.

Daniel winced. 'I should like it, shouldn't I? And some days I do – when a student turns in work that shows they're really thinking about things, that they've listened to your feedback, you feel like you've done some good in the world.'

'And it's true. You're reaching so many people, making them question what they think they know.'

'Perhaps. But those moments are kind of rare. It feels like so many of my students are just going through the motions. Maybe that's my fault. Maybe I just don't have it in me to make them care.'

Cat sparked up a fag. She had become aware of a certain jadedness emanating from Daniel during his lectures. They were always well-structured, but perhaps reading from notes constrained his natural passion. She'd felt herself wincing at how different he was behind the lectern, how unlike himself. 'It must be hard,' she said. 'Kids these days seem to have such short attention spans – I know I sound like an old fart for saying it.'

He gazed at the row of spirits behind the bar. 'We were so alive at college, weren't we? I remember how furious we were with the older generation for simply accepting things, for not fighting. We swore that would never be us.' He sipped his Coke. 'Seventeen-year-old me would be appalled with the person I am now. He'd demand to know why I'm not *louder* in opposing the things that are happening in our country. I mean, I know I should be more engaged with Black Lives Matters – I'm a civil rights historian for goodness' sake.'

Cat sucked on her cigarette. 'Why aren't you doing more? I mean, it's something you're passionate about.'

He dropped the bar mat he'd been fiddling with down onto the bar. 'Perhaps I'm afraid.' He looked up at her. 'I've never admitted that to anyone. But the truth is, I'm not sure I want the life that comes with being a spokesperson for a cause. That sounds awful, doesn't it?'

'No, it doesn't. At seventeen, we couldn't possibly under-stand the personal sacrifices people have to make. We didn't have anything to lose back then, and we couldn't imagine ourselves into the shoes of people that did.'

Daniel shook his head. 'The thing is, I have so much admiration for the Black historians who are prepared to talk publicly about discrimination. But I see the abuse they get, and I think of the twins and . . . '

'Hey,' Cat put a hand on his arm. 'It's a lot to ask of anyone, to step into a torrent of abuse just for being who you are and daring to have opinions.'

'But isn't that exactly what you plan to do? Live an activist life after you graduate. Dive into battle. Get Brexit reversed.'

Cat smiled. 'Maybe. This may sound silly, but I've actually been giving some serious thought to standing for election as an MP.'

She saw Daniel's breath catch and found herself watching his reaction even more closely. Sometimes the smallest twitch of his mouth could keep her buoyed up for days.

His eyes widened, just slightly, then Cat saw a private smile move through his face. 'You should. I can absolutely see you doing it. You'd be magnificent.'

The relief of those words. She felt caressed by his belief in her, moved almost to tears. 'I've been thinking about this town and how so many people who oppose the Tories don't even bother to vote,' she said. 'If I could mobilise the council estates, organise mass turnout, the Conservatives would never see it coming. They're so used to thinking of this area as a safe seat. They barely bother campaigning, pompous fuckers.'

Daniel nodded. 'You could join a party now, start volunteering and build some experience.'

They held each other's gaze for a moment, then both looked away, suddenly self-conscious. How wonderful it would be to have Daniel hold her, to close her eyes and feel his breath against her neck. *Be with me*, she wanted to say. *We'll map out a campaign together and it will bring us both joy and purpose. I'll champion your book, do everything I can to support you, because no one wants to see it published more than I do.* But she knew she'd never say these things aloud. Daniel was a father, part of a family. And with his Oxford education, his PhD, it was absurd for her to consider him her equal, even for a moment.

Chapter 11

When James arrived back from the Indian restaurant, he served up their curries, balancing side dishes of naan, papadum and spicy dips on their trays so they could eat on the sofa in the living room. In recent weeks, Cat had become absorbed in her studies to the point of obsession, avoiding conversation, refusing to accompany him to a colleague's pre-Christmas drinks. Even when she interrupted her reading to step outside and smoke a cigarette, she'd put her headphones in, listening to political podcasts that only served to make her even more irritable. It sounded so innocuous – he knew no one else would detect these odd, sinister notes in the way she was behaving – but she'd gone far beyond what could be considered a healthy immersion in her course.

'Ta.' Cat took her tray and immediately set upon her meal. Little splinters of papadum exploded over the sofa with each mouthful.

'I thought we could watch a film after.'

'You can. I was going to go upstairs to read.'

'You're working yourself very hard with all this studying,' he said. 'Are you taking on too much?'

Cat shrugged, attention firmly on her food. She was wearing one of his old sweatshirts and the smell of cigarette smoke clung to her hair. He tried not to be wounded by her refusal to engage – there were moments when she seemed on the cusp of some sort of breakdown.

'Your time at uni will go by so quickly,' he added. 'I suppose you'll be thinking over your plans for after?' He knew there must be a way, some trick of rhetoric, to reintroduce the idea of children, perhaps making her feel just a fraction of his own longing. He'd tried so hard to reconcile himself with doing without, to revel in the picture he painted for colleagues of the carefree life they were living, three holidays a year, spontaneous trips to London. But increasingly he was becoming aware of his deep sorrow, an absence that stripped all else of significance.

Cat laid down her fork and reached across to the coffee table, to the Coke can James had placed on a coaster. She snapped it open and glugged. 'I have started making plans, actually,' Cat said. 'I'm going to stand for election as an MP.'

James looked at her. Was she joking? Since the Tory landslide of the previous week, she'd been spouting all kinds of things about the inadequacy of the opposition. Did she really think she was the person to wade in and fix things?

She laughed. 'You look like a gaping fish, James. I know it's a bit out there, but think about it – I've lived in this town all my life, I could turn that into an asset, turn the years spent behind the bar at Martin's into a supporter base.'

James knew he had to tread carefully. He tried to smile. It was absurd. *Cat, an MP!* He wanted her to imagine great things for herself, of course he did, but this had such an air of the ridiculous about it. It was as if he'd asked one of his little nephews what they wanted to be when they grew up, and they'd replied with 'king' or 'superhero'.

He looked down at his plate. 'Don't you need loads of money behind you for that sort of thing?'

'Not necessarily. I've been mulling it over. This area has always been diehard conservative. People who hate the Tories can't even be arsed to vote because they think it's pointless. But what if I were to create an upsurge in turnout from the most deprived parts of town?' She spoke rapidly, her eyes alive with frenetic energy. It was unsettling. Her connection with reality seemed to have slipped. Yet she looked more beautiful than ever; even without make-up, her skin was flawless and she looked so implausibly young.

He took a mouthful of curry and rice. Forced himself to chew and swallow. 'It sounds very much like a lot of commitment, without any guarantee of success.'

Cat turned to face him, her cheeks flushed. 'That's exactly the kind of thinking that stops people getting involved in their democracy. Things only change when someone has the courage to put themselves out there. To give it a go because they believe in something.'

'And that's wonderful. But it's asking a lot of yourself, isn't it? To devote hours and hours to canvassing with only a slim chance of securing an MP's salary as a result.' It seemed absurd to be arguing about this – it would never happen, and he wasn't sure Cat even wanted it to.

'Why are you being so dismissive?' her voice was cold.

'I'm not, Cat. Or at least I'm not intending to be.' He put a hand on her knee. 'I'm thinking about you. I mean, politicians are fair game, aren't they? The media would come after your family. They'd have a field day printing pictures of your mum falling over drunk, or reporting on your dad brawling in pubs. Do you really want that?'

Cat said nothing. Her body was strangely rigid as she mechanically forked pieces of chicken into her mouth. James knew that he'd been unkind, but he'd coddled her for too long. He shouldn't be made to feel like the bad guy for simply bringing the conversation back to reality.

He took a deep breath. 'I can't help wondering whether once you've given university a try, your feelings around children and starting a family might change. You'd still be young enough.'

She took another swig from her can. 'I don't even *like* children.'

He was taken aback by her dismissive tone, by the two deep lines emerging between her eyebrows. He'd misjudged. 'I'm just saying that life doesn't have to be one battle after another. You should find something that makes you happy.'

'And that something would be babies, would it? I'd take the trouble to educate myself after all this time, so I can stay indoors changing nappies?'

'It wouldn't have to be like that.'

She sighed.

It was impossible for James to go on with his meal. He wanted to explain the happy warmth that could be hers once she stopped feeling she had things to prove. A baby could represent roots, a future filled with love and happiness. They'd be a family in a way that had so far eluded them, and perhaps then he'd be free from the twisting fear he'd felt ever since he mustered the courage to ask her out all those years ago. However much he did for her, however much she'd come to rely on him, she had it in her power to turn around one day and laugh in his face. *And who else would have him?*

'Cat, I'm on your side here. I'm happy to go on supporting you in whatever you do. There's no harm in having another think about children, while you still can. Not saying you'll definitely change your mind. It's just worth having a think over, that's all.'

She gave a bitter laugh. 'I'm very aware how much you support me.'

James was about to respond, but Cat was gazing at him with such intense dislike, he felt his stomach tightening.

'I hate you making me feel like there are hidden terms,' she said. 'If you're supporting me through university to make me even more beholden—'

'Cat, no, it's not like that—' He put his tray down on the coffee table. He had to regain control of this conversation.

'If you're expecting me to pay for the roof over my head by getting pregnant, then tell me now.' She was clutching her knife and fork mid-air, her hands balled into tight fists.

'There's nothing weak about changing your mind. And you're nothing like your own parents, you know that right?'

'Fuck you, James!' She slammed her cutlery, her tray, down onto the coffee table and got up to leave the room.

James sprang up and followed her, placing a hand on her shoulder. She wheeled around. For a terrible moment, James thought she might hit him, her eyes were lit with naked rage and, in that moment, her similarity to Terry was striking.

He took a deep breath. 'Are you all right, Cat? I'm worried.'

Her hands dropped to her sides and she bowed her head. 'I don't know ...'

He held her by the waist.

She sighed. 'Sometimes I feel like you can't resist reminding me how much I owe you.'

'Cat—'

'You should throw me out.'

His stomach lurched. *Where on earth had that come from?* 'I'd never do that. You're my world.'

'I'm sorry, I get so angry—' her voice cracked.

'It's okay.' He ran a finger along her cheek.

She closed her eyes and bowed her head.

'Tell me what's wrong,' he said.

He heard her breath catch. 'Sometimes I feel as though I'm just a big joke. I may as well join my mum in her bedsit, buy a bottle of vodka and accept the life I was born into.'

He stroked her hair. Perhaps he was weak, feeling such tenderness. 'You'll do no such thing. But you don't have to stick at uni if it's making you unwell.' The words *throw me out* were still echoing in his ears. Was that what she really wanted? He couldn't bear the idea that the words had contained a plea.

Cat was silent, and they stayed where they were, holding one another. James was the only person who fully perceived her vulnerabilities, who saw the fragile woman behind all the smoking, swearing bravado. At times, the responsibility was overwhelming and he became afraid, so afraid, of misinterpreting things and ruining everything they had. So he remained still, not speaking, simply waiting for the moment when Cat's body would relax and he'd know that everything was once again okay.

Chapter 12

Laura almost didn't answer the call. She was sitting in her old room, on her single bed, holding the phone aloft with her one-time best friend's name emblazoned across the screen. But if she didn't pick up, Karolina would leave a message and Laura would be expected to call back.

'Laura? Happy New Year! How've you been?' Karolina chirped as soon as Laura accepted the call.

'You know. Getting settled back home.'

'It must be lovely being with your family.'

Laura mumbled something that sounded like assent. She was forty and sleeping in a single bed made up with hot pink sheets. Her parents were terrified of being alone with her, giving a start if they wandered into the living room and found her there.

'I miss you,' Karolina said.

'Me too.' Already, Laura's throat was tightening, her eyes stung. She should have let the call go to voicemail. Karolina was one of the few people from her old life who'd tried to visit her in prison; who'd been extending all kinds of social invitations since, even though Laura always declined. How could she explain the disgust that engulfed her with each reminder of her old life? She didn't want to hurt people, but she couldn't endure these fragments from the time before.

She heard Karolina swallow at the other end of the line. 'Listen – I don't know who you're still in touch with, but there's something I think you should know. In case you hear by accident.'

Laura looked at her nails. They were brittle, ragged things these days. 'Go on.'

'It's Abdul. His girlfriend is pregnant and they've started announcing it. I thought you'd rather hear it straight up. It's so unfair, I'm really sorry.'

Laura took a deep breath. She and Abdul had been trying for a baby for three years prior to the accident. They'd had tests. Nothing wrong, their lack of success had no clear medical basis. Abdul had hinted a few times that maybe she should ease off the wine, but he'd never pressed the issue, unaware of the extent of her problem. Karolina was one of the few people who'd known they'd been on the waiting list for IVF.

'Are you okay?'

Laura scrunched her eyes shut. 'Fine. I'm pleased for him. I am.'

'There's still time for you,' Karolina offered.

Laura said nothing. She felt skewered by misery, even as she insisted to herself that Abdul deserved to be happy.

'We should catch up properly,' Karolina ventured. 'I could come down. Be nice to get out of London and see you.'

'Maybe. Listen, I'm really sorry but I'm late for something. I've got to go.'

*

There was still an hour before she needed to leave and open up the bar for one of the dull weekday lunch shifts, but Laura craved movement, escape from the confines of the house. Without saying goodbye to her parents, she stepped out into the misty January morning and set off towards the town centre at a brisk pace. Wet leaves stuck to the pavement and the air was heavy with the dank, earthy scent of deep winter.

Remembering her atonement pledges, she steered her imagination to the thing she least wanted to see. Abdul – his forehead creased with emotion, eyes welling with joy at what she hadn't been able to give. His arm around a faceless woman: a younger, more fertile woman. His large hands, the knuckles lightly dusted with hair, carefully supporting the head of a newborn.

Laura didn't deserve such things. It was her own habits, her own carelessness with her body, that had squandered away every monthly opportunity. She believed she could have it all back then. Parties. A job that required her to wear tailored clothes and good shoes. The crispness of a nice, tart Pino Grigio. She was just having fun, she'd told herself, she wasn't harming anybody. But how could a baby have made a home in such a woman? Nightly she poisoned her blood. She killed her chances. Her womb was most likely a shrivelled, desiccated thing. It was only right that Abdul should get to create a family without her.

She crossed the main road. Returned the wave of a neighbour out with his Labrador. Walking fast made her out of breath and helped her control the pain. She tried to concentrate. *The past is gone. Unchangeable. All I have control of is now. The person I can be today, tomorrow. The mark I can make. I didn't deserve a baby.*

She paused outside a cake shop, gazing at the window display without really seeing the contents. She'd been resolute when she left prison. Her life would be gently led; she'd take care never to harm anyone again, not through so much as a carelessly uttered word. She'd devote herself to those small, unshowy acts of kindness that could soothe troubled souls.

She'd had such a clear vision of herself working at her father's bar. Providing companionship for the lonely, being a listening ear for anyone who needed it. She imagined herself putting customers into taxis. Calling to check they'd got home safely. Nothing grandiose.

Laura rested her head against the cool glass of the shop window, not caring how odd she must look. These imagined kindnesses of hers were entirely unwanted. Christ, it was almost funny remembering the sudden straightening of backs, the widening of eyes that greeted her early overtures at friendship. When the punters noticed her at all, they could barely mask their disappointment that she wasn't Cat.

Of course, Roger was different. Not long after their first encounter, he'd asked her for a lift home, and as she pulled up outside his house, stomach roiling with dread, he'd announced that he'd been and got some Viagra.

She'd been expecting an awkward exchange. A stuttered excuse about his previous difficulty in performing. She'd reassure him, and they'd both laugh nervously. Perhaps she'd pop inside for a quick sip of tea, a few comments on the weather, and she'd be able to leave, having gone some way to restoring dignity for both of them.

But Viagra. The poor man had obviously seen their awkward encounter as a beginning – how could he be expected to know the strange impulses behind Laura's reckless behaviour? She'd been cruel, letting him believe she was interested. Those hands at her breast. White chest hair, slack flesh and wrinkled skin. It was repulsive and her body tensed at the memory. But she'd started this. She couldn't bring herself to reject him and hurt him all over again.

The triumph on his face as he pounded away at her had let Laura believe she was offering comfort of a sort. She'd screwed her eyes shut, trying to suppress the rebellion of her body, the instinct to push him away from her, to scream in his face. Afterwards, he'd seemed defeated, keen for her to be gone. He'd kept his eyes averted from her body, as though she'd morphed into something shameful. She always left his house with the sensation that the two of them had actually deepened their misery. As though the act, and Roger's success in performing it, widened the chasm between them.

Laura stepped away from the window and forced herself to carry on walking. Here she was, for all her pledges to help others, feeling sorry for herself. It wouldn't do. She mustn't stand for it.

Life had always been far too easy for her, she'd come to recognise. She'd gone to uni back when the fees were only a token gesture and she'd been lucky to graduate into the final years of a healthy job market. Things had changed so rapidly that if she were to start again now, she'd probably be perpetually unemployed.

She remembered advertising for an assistant the month before the accident and receiving over three hundred applications. Whittling down the list had felt impossible – she had to make all kinds of arbitrary decisions, like only seeing people who graduated with a first, who had more than six months of internships under their belts. The procession of intelligent young people who'd sat in front of her in the board-room came with unsolicited campaign plans they'd prepared, with original ideas and articulate answers to each and every question. She remembered the guilty realisation: *these kids are so much better and brighter than I ever was. If I'd been born just a few years later, I wouldn't have this job.* But, being the old Laura, she'd allowed the insight to dissipate almost immediately.

She reached the supermarket. She hadn't planned on going in, but it was still too early to open up the bar and she couldn't think of anything better to do with herself. Automatically, she went to the wine section. She wouldn't weaken. She was past all that. But still, she browsed. Reading the descriptions on the labels. *Top notes of cherry and blackcurrant, under-pinned by oak. An ideal accompaniment for venison.*

This wasn't the first time she'd come here. Making theoret-ical selections. Imagining cooking for Abdul and their friends, the menu she'd plan, the wines she'd pair with each dish.

'You all right, love?' It was Bernice, wearing the supermar-ket's blue uniform and pushing a stock trolley loaded up with nappies. Laura had seen Bernice at the bar a couple of times since her hospitalisation and hadn't known whether to allude to it or not. When she'd asked Bernice how she was doing, Bernice had replied with a cheery *fine* that made Laura feel further questions might be impertinent.

Laura couldn't speak. A tear rolled down her face but she didn't wipe it away.

'What's the matter?' Bernice stepped in and placed a bony arm around her shoulder. She smelled of cigarettes and cheap perfume.

'I'm sorry. I . . . '

'All right, love, don't you worry. Let it all out.'

Laura took a step back. 'You're working. I didn't mean . . . ' There was so much sympathy in Bernice's face that she almost broke down anew. 'I just found out my ex-husband's going to have a baby.'

Bernice reached out and squeezed her arm. What had Laura done to be worthy of such compassion? In years gone by, people like Bernice would have been invisible to her. Or, no, actually it was worse than that, she would have wrinkled her nose, finding the miniskirts and bleached hair distasteful.

She pulled her hand free from Bernice's grasp. 'I'm an alcoholic, do you know that?'

Bernice gave her a gentle smile. 'Well, this ain't the best place for you to be standing, is it? Come with me into the baby aisle. Oh – fuck me, I'm always putting my foot in it.'

Laura smiled. 'It's fine. The baby section is fine.'

Bernice led the way, pushing the stock trolley, Laura trailing behind her. Already, Laura felt embarrassed. She'd said too much. Imposed the weight of her confidences onto a stranger, someone who'd been hospitalised the previous month, who clearly had her own problems. She ought to shift the conversation onto safer ground, salvage what dignity she still had before scurrying off to work.

Bernice began restocking the nappies with surprising speed. 'The thing about men is, they will go around making babies. You just have to put it to one side, love, shut it out.'

'Your ex has other children, doesn't he? That must have been hard.'

'It was Cat I was worried about. Terry barely bothered with her once the boys were born. But that's all in the past. They're handsome enough lads, take after their father in that respect, but neither of them are a patch on Cat. Terry's got a little girl with his newest woman. Lily. Only eleven. Poor Cat. Knocking on forty, with a little sister who's only just started senior school.'

Laura smiled. 'Cat's lucky to have you, worrying about her.'

'But that's not the point, love. Men will be men. You have to just toughen up to it. You've done bloody well to keep off the drink. How long's it been?'

'Three years. But I was in prison for most of that, so it doesn't really count.'

Bernice's eyes widened. 'Martin never let on that you were in prison.'

'No. I'm sure he didn't.' Laura laughed bitterly. In spite of her parents' mortification, she'd vowed never to hide what she'd done. 'I killed a young man. Drink driving.'

'Oh, love.' Bernice gave her a look of such compassion that Laura wanted to press her head into her shoulder and close her eyes.

'We should go for coffee one day, when you have time,' Laura said. 'I know what stopping drinking is like, how hard it is. I've been through it.'

Bernice looked puzzled for a moment, then turned her attention back to her stock trolley, hoisting the packets onto the shelves. 'Ah, life's tough enough, sweetheart. Each to their own and all that, but if you ask me, a little drink never did no harm.'

Remember the pledges, Laura told herself. *Never shy away from what's uncomfortable.* 'I used to feel like that. But the truth was, I was completely dependent. It sounds silly, but I absolutely couldn't get through a work function without a drink. I used to suggest we do client meetings over lunch, just so I could have a glass of wine.'

Bernice laughed. 'Sounds like you were a long way off passing out in pub toilets.'

'I was closer than I ever knew. But anyway – if we went for coffee, I wouldn't go on about it. I'm here to listen, but I wouldn't get preachy or anything like that. Go on. My treat.'

Bernice smiled, but didn't meet Laura's eye. 'I'll be propping up the bar at Martin's regular enough. Plenty of time for a good old chat there. No need to go out of your way for me.'

Laura looked down at the tiled flooring. She'd overstepped. For all she knew, Bernice was perfectly happy with how much she drank. It was right that she should reject interference. But it stung all the same.

After leaving the supermarket and heading over to Martin's, it struck Laura that she was lonely. She couldn't remember a time in her life when she'd felt this way, wrapped in longing to just sit and chatter aimlessly to someone who wasn't being awkward with her. She'd suggested to Cat that the two of them do lunch one weekend, but Cat pleaded a lack of money and time. Laura had actually been excited by the idea of meeting up with Bernice, sitting down in a coffee shop and having a slice of cake. With Bernice, she'd be able talk about prison, about the accident, without witnessing the inner recoiling she'd seen in her old friends, within her own family.

She was done with suits, with empty banter and false hilarity. She'd looked down on her father's bar once, slightly embarrassed at the unseemly way he was forced to make a living. But she was no better than the very coarsest punters. A young life had been extinguished because of her. Because she'd been pissed and her reactions hadn't been fast enough. Because she'd been so arrogant about the clean, ordered life she was living, the money she was making, the ease with which she could navigate a party.

She was so clear on the parts of her old life that she was renouncing, so definite about it, that it never occurred her to ask herself what was left. Who was she without the trappings of that former life? She realised now that she didn't even know who she *wanted* to be.

Chapter 13

As more essays came back, Cat continued receiving high grades and became aware of a ripple passing through the classroom whenever she was asked about her marks. But her long sessions in the library hadn't gone unnoticed either, and the gasps of disbelief seemed free from envy and resentment. She ought to be thrilled; she hadn't dared hope for this level of success, yet she was aware of a creeping dissatisfaction.

It was James. Being forced to spend so much time with him over the Christmas break made her confront ugly truths she'd been avoiding for months, years. She was using him, there was no denying it now. She was too cowardly to abandon a comfortable home, lying with her every gesture to avoid sudden destitution. Worse than that, sometimes an ill-chosen word of his would be enough to send her into a feverish rage. Like when he tried to talk to her about children; there had been a split second when she experienced a desire to hit him, so surprising and yet so strong.

She imagined herself doing it, swinging her fist into his mouth, making him bleed, making him experience, just for a moment, what it was to be an abject thing, stripped from the power of his money. She'd never been more aware of her father's blood in her veins and it terrified her, this idea that there was something brutish inside her, something no amount of essay-writing or high marks could purge. University was supposed to act on her, to expunge the crassness from her mind, bleach every dirty, stained part of who she was. But she could feel herself getting impatient, intolerant of the pretences she had to maintain.

The Christmas break had also driven home her increasing attachment to Daniel. How frequently her thoughts turned to him, indulging secret hopes that he might want more than friendship, that between them they'd find a way to tumble back into old ways of being.

She needed to make more of an effort to open herself to university life beyond the curriculum, she decided. Give the experience of being a student every opportunity to transform her. University had never meant to be about Daniel. She wouldn't simply wait to be disappointed. She was doing this for herself, desperate to believe the second half of her life could be more meaningful than the first.

The group of girls she gravitated towards in seminars had kept urging her to go to yoga class with them, and at the start of the new term, Cat decided to try to cement her new friendships by giving it a try.

Throughout the lesson, she struggled to get into the poses, finding herself close to giggling at the tide of ostentatious breathing filling the sports hall. It was shocking to confront the stiffness of her body. When attempting to touch her toes, her hands barely passed her knees, and when they had to hold something called 'boat pose', what abdominal muscles Cat possessed juddered wildly and she kept collapsing onto her mat.

At the end of the class, she lay on her back with closed eyes as the instructor encouraged everyone to visualise a beautiful beach at sunset. Almost reflexively, Cat laughed to herself at such hippy nonsense – everyone here took themselves so seriously, treating relaxation as though it were a solemn task, as important as making a living. As they were encouraged to exhale out their preoccupations and worries, Cat wondered how many of the participants had ever known real care. There was an assurance about them that told Cat they'd never struggled to feed themselves, never had to put an inebriated parent in the recovery position. Yet even as she acknowledged this, she became suffused with sadness – what must it feel like to be free from this snide inner commentary? To not be compelled to analyse someone the moment you met them, reading their family histories through their clothes, the condition of their hair and the way they held their body when they spoke.

After the class, she joined Chloe, Grace and Sophia at a coffee shop. They'd chosen a snug little place, with bright yellow walls and stripy tablecloths. The counter was piled with big slabs of home-baked cakes, and even though James was always on at her about her sugar intake, Cat couldn't resist ordering a slice of chocolate cake to go with her coffee.

The young women were busy comparing the modules they'd opted to study this semester. The second part of Daniel's unit on American history was mandatory, but for the optional units, her classmates had chosen an array of different subjects. Cat had selected classes on the Cold War and Mao's China and had already made good inroads into the reading. As she sipped her coffee, the conversation veered towards their lecturers and their various teaching styles. She felt a strange combination of intrigue and anxiety as she waited to hear everyone's thoughts on Daniel.

'He gives the impression of being a little bored,' Grace said. 'I mean, he covers interesting stuff, but he looks like he'd rather be somewhere else the whole time.'

Cat nodded along, but she felt a defensive prickle moving across her scalp. These women couldn't begin to under- stand the complexities of Daniel's relationship with his job. Suddenly, she wished she hadn't come. It was hard to endure hearing the others speak of him.

'He's kind of hot though,' Chloe ventured.

The others laughed, and Cat realised that they were all looking at her, waiting for a reaction.

'I've seen you hanging out with him,' Grace said. 'Are you, like, friends or something?'

Cat nodded.

There was a moment of silence, and she became aware that she was expected to elaborate. Her coffees with Daniel must appear curious; she could sense they'd discussed it as a group before now. This was the kind of attention she'd feared, for Daniel's sake more than her own.

'I knew him at sixth form,' she offered. 'A long time ago.'

'He's gorgeous,' Chloe gave a wry smile. 'And you know what they say about Black men.'

Cat stared at the woman. 'No. Tell me.'

Chloe reddened. 'Well, you know—'

Cat shook her head, taking in the other women. They all looked embarrassed, yet somehow complicit; ready to reassure one another that Cat was being oversensitive. How quickly the mood had soured. It was so tempting to laugh, to try to re-establish the former light-hearted tone. Cat wasn't spoiled for friends, and she knew that nothing could incur dislike quicker than questioning someone's behaviour.

'It was just a joke.' Chloe's voice was quiet, containing a crackle of latent tears. This angered Cat even more, the way the woman had transformed herself into a victim just moments after making a racist comment.

'Stereotyping is offensive and ugly,' Cat said.

'I don't think she meant it that way,' Grace offered.

Cat raised an eyebrow. 'Maybe not. But let's try to do better, okay?'

The lull in conversation continued beyond the point of being comfortable, then Grace executed a pivot, talking about the virus dominating the news. It was a topic the others latched onto, speculating and sharing snippets of things they'd read, giving Cat an opportunity to catch her breath. She hadn't liked taking that scolding tone with Chloe but was indignant at how casually these educated young women felt they could demean others.

When she'd first got together with Daniel as a teenager, she'd told herself she didn't notice his race, but quickly realised it wasn't true.

'I never really know,' Daniel had said one time, 'whether people are making an effort to get along with me because they like me, or because they like the idea of themselves having Black friends.' They'd been in his flat, in bed, taking advantage of the long hours his mother worked as a cleaner.

'Your personality is what draws people in,' Cat replied. 'It's got nothing to do with you being Black.' Yet even as she uttered the words, Cat had known she was skirting over complexities. If she'd been asked what attracted her to Daniel, she would have cited his forthrightness, the agility of his mind and power of his empathy. It would have been true. Yet she had to acknowledge that there had been an unmistakable frisson at the sight of her fingers against his dark skin. There hadn't been any Black students in her year group at secondary school, and although she resisted admitting it to herself, Daniel represented something cosmopolitan and exciting. It was appalling to look back at just how crass she'd been.

In the earliest weeks of their relationship, she'd taken him back to Petersfield and they'd walked around the shops hand in hand, stopping for a drink in one of the pubs just off the square. At the back of her mind, she'd harboured the strange hope that her father might encounter them. He'd be furious, uneducated bigot that he was, and Cat would have taken great delight in countering any stupid thing he said. She saw herself standing up, shielding Daniel with her own body as she commenced a verbal tear-down.

But how humiliating such an encounter would have been. She'd been appalled with herself for wishing such a thing, at the vanity of her desire to use Daniel's race as an opportunity to make a hero of herself. From that moment, their relationship had deepened. She'd had a glimpse, just for a second, of what it must be like for Daniel – he'd always be a kind of symbol to others, in a way that Cat never would be. Although they were both from poor families, her white skin conferred a kind of ease that was denied to him. She was so used to thinking of herself as being at the very bottom of the pile and it had been a shock to confront an advantage she'd never perceived before.

The conversation had broken off. One of her classmates had just asked her a question. 'Sorry?' she said.

The third woman, Sophia, smiled at her. She had blonde hair, pulled back into the standardised messy bun. 'I was just wondering why you didn't go to university straight after college?'

Cat felt a heaviness inside her as she prepared to recount her mother being hit by a car, the missed A-levels, the four years of rehabilitation. But at the last moment, she stopped herself. Why was it necessary to share a glimpse of those sordid years? She was so very tired of being defined by that awful time in her life, by her own cause-and-effect narrative that placed her failure to get a degree firmly in the lap of the government and its inadequate social-care provision. Every part of the story was true. But it was becoming a kind of fable; bearing less and less relation to the pain and confusion she'd felt at the time. Some days, it felt as though the story belonged to another girl entirely.

'Maybe I just wasn't ready,' she said.

With the exception of Chloe, who still appeared to be sulking, the others nodded sympathetically.

How glorious it could have been, if it had been true. If she'd had the luxury of being too immature. If she'd had parents who coddled her, keeping her in a state of suspended adolescence. If she'd had a gap year, visiting a succession of beaches, smoking weed with other young people, dancing in her bikini.

Cat had never had the chance to be fragile or vulnerable like these girls. She envied them and pitied them all at once. The lewd comments of a Martin's shift, the brushes against her bottom that marked most glass-collecting runs – they'd never be able to handle such things. Yet, wasn't there something beautiful in that? To not be ignorant, or naïve necessarily, just certain you deserved better.

She couldn't help thinking of the Cat she'd wanted to be, the Cat who could have gone to Warwick at eighteen, who would have been established in a career for years by now. This unformed version of her was a shadow, accompanying her everywhere, reminding her daily of everything that might have been. She had no way of knowing whether she and Daniel would have maintained a distance-relationship. But she knew she'd never have sought out a James figure. She would have clawed her way out of her parents' world on her own terms and would certainly have been the richer for it.

Chapter 14

Bernice had considered not turning up for Maureen's wedding reception. Terry was good mates with the groom and would be there with that new wife of his. He'd probably bought her something nice to wear, and she'd be parading around, curly hair extensions trailing down her back, enjoying the jealous glances of the older wives.

Bernice on the other hand would have to wear her usual Friday night denim mini. She looked as rough as anything at the moment, with grey skin and roots that badly needed doing. But she was sure there'd be free drinks. The more Bernice thought of it, the more certain she became. The groom was in the building trade, like Terry, and always had a roll of twenties in his back pocket. It would be a point of pride for someone like him to have plenty of free booze sloshing around at his wedding party.

Bernice had been serious about cutting back. She wasn't one of those sad bastards who woke up with the shakes, who needed a drink first thing in the morning. It was just that after her first sip, she'd start to feel happy and interesting, brave enough for a bit of banter. There was always a voice inside her that told her to keep going. To drink until she fell down, until she entered a deep, dreamless sleep.

But she didn't have to make a recluse of herself while she got a handle on things. And she needn't do any of that cold turkey business, she'd just slow things down a bit, take a good half glass of Coke with every shot. The young doctor had frightened her, no doubt about that. Cirrhosis of the liver and a stomach ulcer to boot. Thank goodness Cat hadn't been there to hear. No wonder her hangovers had been getting worse. Bernice had felt overwhelmingly tired when the doctor tried explaining her scans, and he must have taken it for boredom because he'd suddenly stopped and sighed: 'Listen – if you don't stop drinking, you'll be measuring your life expectancy in months, not years. Sorry to be blunt, but that's the truth of it.'

After that, he appeared to simply give up on her, walking away, not lingering to check she'd understood or to offer her the chance to ask questions. And, strangely, it was that moment of dismissal which fed her determination. She was so used to being a nobody, a joke, and most of the time she didn't even mind. But this chap was being paid to help her. It would have cost nothing for him to have spoken kindly.

Stepping though her front door the afternoon she was discharged, she'd been assailed by the stench of unemptied bins. The teenager in the flat above had his heavy metal up loud and she knew she wouldn't be able to sleep, even though it was the thing she needed most. When she'd put her phone on charge, a voicemail from the supermarket informed her she was on her very final warning.

Why reject the small comforts life had to offer people like her? She'd never have a car or wear expensive clothes; but a nice voddie was generous with its gifts, sharing its happy warmth with celebrities and kings as well as the likes of her.

Arriving at Martin's, her expectations were met – free house wine until ten. It was Laura who rushed over to serve her. The girl meant well, but she was always getting in the way of Bernice being able to catch up with her daughter.

'Large glass of white, please. The free stuff. I'm a wedding guest.'

'How are you feeling?'

'Fine and dandy,' Bernice said.

Cat was nearby, pouring a round of whiskies for Terry. Trust him to be the flash one ordering expensive drinks when there was free wine on offer.

Laura handed her the wine, alongside an unasked-for glass of water.

Bernice nodded, taking the wine glass by the stem, pretending not to see the water. She was grateful when a chap on the other side of the bar called Laura over for a refill. Bernice drank her wine in two long gulps but held off asking for another until Cat was free.

'How are you doing, darling?' she asked her daughter. 'University still going well?'

Cat smiled as she topped up her mother's glass, but it didn't reach her eyes. 'Yeah, it's good.'

'It must be lovely, getting to know that Daniel again. I had no idea he was still living in this neck of the woods.'

'Me neither.'

'To think of him in Portsmouth, only half an hour's train ride away.'

Cat shrugged, her mouth tightening, and Bernice became

certain her daughter was upset. She was trying her best to conceal it, but that's the kind of girl she was – Cat would hobble home on a broken leg rather than admit something was wrong.

'You were such a sweet couple, you and him. Is there any chance—'

Her daughter met her eye and for a moment Bernice glimpsed how much she yearned for that man. 'He's married,' Cat said, scanning the bar, desperate for someone to serve, someone to extract her from this conversation. The fact that she hadn't mentioned James was telling.

'I really did like Daniel,' Bernice ventured. 'The two of you were so mature. Encouraging each other, being all disciplined with your books and your studying. And, Christ, your bedsprings never stopped creaking.'

'Mum!'

'It's what a woman needs, love, to be wanted like that.'

Cat shook her head and started wiping down the bar.

Bernice had been taken with Daniel from the very first time she saw him, but she'd never liked that James fella. At first, she supposed it was down to how quickly Cat had left home. She'd known she ought to be pleased that her daughter had moved out of the council shithole she'd been raised in. And she was. But whenever she thought of losing Cat, she'd imagined the girl buggering off travelling perhaps, or going away to university like she always planned.

It had felt like Cat was cheating somehow, moving into a house provided by a man. This was what Bernice expected from other young women, but not from Cat. Experience had taught her that nothing in life was ever truly free. And it was this that unsettled Bernice the most.

The first time Bernice had seen James and Cat together, she'd thought to herself, *That man wants to be Cat's mum.* He'd fawned over her, bringing her drinks, making a fuss about her smoking, acting all horrified at the food she chose to eat. And Cat had seemed to act up to it: grateful at times, at others behaving like a stroppy teenager. It was a dynamic that riled Bernice in a way she couldn't quite pin down with words. She felt her daughter had made a pact to be someone she wasn't, and all because she'd been so desperate to stop being poor. Bernice could understand that, she could, but she knew Cat was capable of more.

Ordinarily, Cat would have said *no bloody thanks* to this extra shift. She loathed the false hilarity of weddings, the conspicuous drinking that led to exuberant dancing, followed by fist fights in the early hours. The fact that both of her parents had been invited was an extra incentive to stay away. But she needed the cash. Having coffee with Daniel a couple of times a week devoured a big chunk of her bar money. He'd paid the first few times, joking about her being a poor student. But after she arrived early one time and ordered for them both, they'd fallen into the habit of taking turns. Only fair, Cat supposed, but it didn't leave quite enough for books and fags.

After making a show of buying her rail ticket for the first quarter, James hadn't offered to help out when it was time to renew. Cat seemed to remember him implying he'd cover the train costs, but she didn't feel she could ask him for the money straight up. She dropped a few hints, but they weren't fruitful and she ended up having to borrow ninety pounds from Martin. It shouldn't irk her, given she was living rent-free and eating James's food every evening. But it struck her that James wasn't really generous. He was just thoughtless with money, which was something altogether different. He was so accustomed to wealth that he never knew how much was in his wallet; he treated cash like the paper it was, withdrawing money in two-hundred-pound batches to *save doing it again later.*

She remembered her shock at coming home from university at the end of the Christmas term and finding a profusion of high-end perfume gift sets laid out across the dining table ready to be wrapped.

'These can't all be for your mum and your sister?' There was surely several hundred pounds' worth of cosmetics lying on their table.

James had laughed and named a handful of his friends' wives, plus the woman who worked for him. These were acquaintances, not even people he was close to. Cat felt something inside her harden at this whimsy, this ostentation. The price of one of those sets would exceed her mother's weekly food bill and it had struck Cat that so-called generosity could in fact be something quite ugly if it were exercised with so little care.

There were shrieks of excitement as the DJ played an eighties pop hit, a surge towards the dance floor. Everyone was drunk by now and there were a few theatrical displays of reluctance. Women cackled as they dragged their partners from their chairs. *God, weddings were awful.*

It was a hard-drinking crowd and the bar remained busy throughout the evening. Bernice disappeared once they stopped serving free wine, but most of the others hung around, ordering large rounds of top-shelf spirits, novelty liquors in all kinds of garish combinations.

'Where's your mum gone?' Laura was slightly breathless, standing next to Cat as she pulled a pint. Her ponytail was coming loose and Cat realised with a jolt just how different the woman looked from the prim schoolgirl she'd known.

'She's gone. She's taking things a bit easier at the moment, you know, after hospital.'

Laura scratched at her scalp. 'Do you think she can get home safely?'

'Yeah. Or she might have gone to The Bell. I don't know.'

Laura's eyes darted around. Her jaw twitched. Cat found she was bracing herself for judgement. *Just you try keeping tabs on a grown woman like my mother*, she wanted to say.

'She's been looking run-down. Do you know what the doctors told her?' Laura ventured at last. There was a burst of cheering as the DJ played *Sweet Caroline*.

Cat shook her head as she placed the pint glass on the bar and took the money. 'I can hazard a guess that they told her to stop drinking. Or at least to scale back.' She needed to carve out more time for her mother, she knew that, it was just so hard with the commuting to university and the hours she needed to put in to do her best work.

They'd been so close in the years following the accident – they hadn't a choice, the needs of Bernice's broken body forced intimacy on them. Cat showed love by stifling her disgust at the oozing, stinking infections. By navigating the convoluted bus routes to get to their appointments with surgeons and physiotherapists. It was sad to remember such things, but at least Bernice had stopped drinking for a time. She resumed the very moment Cat left home.

'I think she gets lonely,' Laura said.

Cat turned to pour a round of shots for one of her father's mates. When she was done, she turned to Laura, having to shout over the din. 'I don't think you can imagine what her life has been like. My dad used to beat the shit out of her. He brought on a miscarriage one time; she almost died on the bathroom floor.'

'Goodness, that's terrible.' Laura's cheeks flared pink.

'There are no structures in place to give people like her dignity any more. Next to no mental health provision. Piss-poor addiction treatment. Think about *that* next time you vote.'

'But, Cat – we don't have to wait until the next general election to help her. Did you broach AA?'

Cat snorted. 'AA is all well and good, but it doesn't change the fact that she's living hand to mouth, that a full-time wage barely covers her rent and food. It's no wonder she turns to drink.'

'You can help someone without having to fix the whole system.'

Cat gave a bitter laugh. 'Your daddy's livelihood depends on my mother and people like her not *fixing* themselves. Don't take food from your own table.'

Laura shook her head. 'What happened to you?'

Before Cat could come up with something stinging in response, Laura huffed off to do a glass-collecting run.

Cat knew she stopped making sense when she was this angry; in such moments, she became needlessly horrible. But the one thing she couldn't abide was when people pretended to understand, to speak to her with authority, when really they couldn't have any idea of what things had been like. No teenager should be tasked with helping a parent take a shit, with wiping their backside.

After calling time, Cat lit a cigarette in the kitchen and made a conscious effort to try to cheer herself up. She revisited dreams of the House of Commons, of sitting at a kitchen table somewhere with Daniel, the two of them working on her election campaign plan. But she couldn't lose herself, couldn't make the images feel like they were anything more than fantasies. Her life was following some kind of predestined trail, it seemed, sticking to a template prepared for her by her parents. The instincts and traits she'd inherited from both of them never felt closer to the surface.

Martin came into the kitchen, carrying a stack of dirty glasses. He pointed at her cigarette. 'My turn next.'

Cat flicked her ash, nostalgic for the years when it had just been the two of them working the bar. 'What are we doing here, Martin?'

'Not making enough money.' He plonked the crate down and started loading the dishwasher.

She smiled at him, enjoying the way his face lit up with pleasure. 'We're better than this,' she said.

He fished his fags and lighter from his pocket. 'One day, we'll have a bar in the Caribbean.'

'The Med would do me,' she replied.

Once the bar emptied out and Martin had cashed up, Laura put a hand on her father's shoulder. 'You go on home, Cat and I are going to have a drink,' she said.

Martin's eyes widened in surprise. He looked at Cat and she raised an eyebrow in response. This was news to her. Another lecture, she supposed.

Laura waited as the sound of Martin's footsteps retreated down the stairs. 'I didn't mean to overstep earlier,' she said at last. 'I'm going to pour myself a lemonade. Can I get you anything?'

Cat shook her head.

'I just want to be useful,' Laura said, returning with her glass. 'I can't tell you what a shock it was, finding your mum in the toilets like that. I was terrified.'

Cat picked up her cigarette packet. Only two left. She'd be gasping tomorrow if she smoked one of them now. 'The thing is, I'm kind of used to it,' Cat said. 'Drinking until she passes out is normal for her. I know it shouldn't be – I just don't know what I can do.' Even as she said it, she knew it wasn't true. She could visit more, at the very least pop into the supermarket to say hello on her walk back from the station.

'I can't imagine what it must be like – living with that kind of stress.'

Cat looked down at the bar. She wasn't used to talking like this. She never hid anything from Daniel, but it was so much easier to speak of larger themes, to talk of policies, speaking of deprivation in terms of statistics rather than examining her own pain.

She looked up at Laura and saw nothing but concern on her face and somehow this provided the calm she needed to order her thoughts. 'I've been close to breaking ties so many times. Nothing I do ever makes a difference – it's exhausting. And I'm sick of being reminded where I come from all the fucking time.'

'Cat—' there was sympathy in Laura's voice, but Cat wasn't ready to listen to platitudes.

'I can't escape it,' Cat pressed on. 'I might be clever, I know I can talk nicely, give a good impersonation of a nice middle-class lady when I want to. But there's something thuggish in me. I get so *angry*. I'm worried that I'll get my degree – absolutely breeze it – but when I graduate, I'll just be the same person I always was.' To her horror, her voice broke.

She lit her second to last cigarette. To hell with it.

'Cat—' Laura put a hand on her arm.

Cat stiffened. Was this what having friends was like? She felt exposed, ashamed of the rawness of her pain. At this precise moment, she'd rather be at one of the dinner parties James insisted they went to, nodding while some bore rattled on about property values.

'You're not your parents,' Laura said. 'And you're not a saint, either, so there's no shame in finding it hard.'

Cat turned to face the bar, exhaled smoke.

'Do you want to hear something funny?' Laura said after a while.

'Yes. I really would.'

'I'm having sex with Roger Hampton.'

Cat stared at her.

Laura's mouth twitched. 'Ridiculous, isn't it?'

'Why on earth are you doing that?'

Laura closed her eyes for a moment. 'I wanted to be nice, I suppose. Then he expected it again and letting him down would have meant undoing that original moment of kindness. And so, I suppose the answer is I'm sleeping with him to be polite.'

Cat burst out laughing. Laura looked embarrassed for a second, then they were both keeling over, eyes streaming as the giggles rose up from their bellies.

'Fuck me, I was not expecting that,' Cat said. 'He's like, seventy. Please don't offer to sleep with my mum – you know that won't fix her, right?'

Laura's laughter trailed off, leaving sadness in her eyes. Cat felt an unexpected moment of pity. Laura had killed a man. Cat remembered telling herself it was kind of great that everything had unravelled for snotty Laura Turner. Her nice handwriting and perfect manners wouldn't get her very far in prison. And she certainly wouldn't be telling people they smelled in there. But that had been before they started working together.

Tragedy had branded the woman in front of her, Cat could see that now. It was etched into Laura's face. Even when she laughed, you could still see the traces. How moving it was, that, in her own small way, Laura was trying to help others, to avoid retreating from the world and basking in her own bitterness as Cat had done for so many years.

Feeling unexpectedly tender, she clasped Laura by the hand. 'It's going to be okay,' she said.

She wasn't sure whether she believed it, but Laura looked grateful and Cat felt a surge of optimism. Perhaps all lives needed to be remade at some point. Perhaps that was simply the way of things.

Chapter 15

As Daniel approached her in the café, Cat could see from his furrowed brow and restless eyes that he was as unsettled as she was. The university had announced that teaching was going to be moved online in response to the virus sweeping the country. The canteen itself was noticeably quieter, as though people were deciding not to linger in public spaces.

'Well,' said Daniel. He took the seat opposite and she passed him the cappuccino she'd ordered for him.

'I guess we won't be able to meet up for a while.' Instantly, Cat regretted saying it; she hadn't been able to disguise just how bereft she felt.

'We'll see one another on screen,' Daniel said. 'It's going to be strange, sitting in my study, talking to a computer all day long.'

Cat gave a little laugh, but really she wanted to cry. The virus had been dominating the news. Watching the steady escalation was overwhelming: footage of deserted streets in China, the rapid construction of field hospitals, frantic emergency wards in Italy, corridors filled with coughing patients. And since the weekend, hazmat-suited staff cleaning doctors' surgeries in the UK. The previous night, James had taken delivery of several packets of surgical face masks and bottles of hand sanitiser, despite nationwide pleas to leave supplies for medical staff. As recently as last week, the situation had seemed dismissible, far away. Now James barked at her the moment she came through the door, insisting she wash her hands, keeping a close eye to ensure she didn't touch anything before she scrubbed herself in the downstairs toilet.

Daniel placed a hand on her forearm. When she looked up, she could see he recognised her unsettled feelings.

'I can't believe that after twenty years of wanting to go to university, I finally get here and *this* happens.' Her eyes stung. She knew she sounded self-indulgent – people were dying – but the routines of university life had brought such joy. Her quiet afternoons in the library, coffees with Daniel, even the weekly yoga class – it was going to be so hard to give these things up, especially since James's firm was now encouraging office staff to work remotely. Just the thought of trying to study with him in the house made her feel exhausted. The state of absorption she entered when she read was incomprehensible to him; he always felt he could interrupt her.

'It won't be for long,' Daniel said. 'I reckon the government will announce a lockdown, like they've done in Italy. Three weeks of staying indoors, then the virus will be wiped out and life will get back to normal.'

'I can't be shut in a house with James,' Cat said. 'Even for three weeks.'

'I'm sure you're not the only person thinking that about your partner.'

'You don't understand – I've made up my mind to leave him. I've kept putting it off, but how can I go on pretending everything's fine if we're under the same roof twenty-four hours a day? Fuck!' She put her head in her hands.

She was imagining it clearly. Hearing James's voice all day long. Having him monitor how many cigarettes she smoked, how many coffees she drank. She felt a pressure at her temples. If there were a lockdown, she'd have no way to make money. She'd be completely dependent. She had no savings; there was just enough in her purse for a fortnight's worth of fags and a few chocolate bars.

'It's over between you?' Daniel asked in a quiet voice. His eyes were wide, his body very still as he inspected her face. There was no trace of a smile.

Cat couldn't answer straightaway. Daniel looked frightened. She'd let herself believe that they were true friends, that they'd resurrected part of what they'd had before, albeit without the sex. But she realised in this moment that she'd always be *the other woman* in his eyes. Someone to feel guilty about. Someone slightly dangerous. She could see the rapid calculations he was making, wondering how he was going to handle whatever obligations Cat tried to place on him.

She drew herself up. 'Yes. I haven't told him yet – which I know is awful. But, as soon as I can support myself, I'm going to live on my own.'

She noticed Daniel's shoulders drop. She wasn't going to turn up at his door, wasn't going to be a problem.

'With your grades, you'd most likely be eligible for a scholarship next year,' he said. 'I've got a leaflet in my office. We can swing by in a bit.'

Cat nodded. She was planning to take out a student loan so that she could rent her own bedsit in the autumn. Her body felt lighter as her mind conjured it – freedom from the need to make conversation about tedious things, from having to devote Saturday nights to dinners with James's boring friends who talked about property – always property – and the quality of local schools.

Ever since she'd embarked on university, she'd accessed a store of bravery she hadn't known existed. She could feel it swelling and growing with each day. It was going to transform her, she vowed, she was going to become the person she was always meant to be.

Daniel had never known the humanities block be this quiet during term time. On the short walk from the cafeteria, he and Cat had passed a handful of people wearing face coverings – scarves, decorators' masks. The world had changed over the course of a few short weeks. The corridors of the history department were deserted and when they arrived at Daniel's office, they saw that his colleague, Sarah, had already taken away her files and a significant portion of her books. Thankfully, there hadn't been any cases of the virus at the hospital where Elizabeth worked, but he knew it was only a matter of time. He and Elizabeth had talked about how Daniel would have to distract Kendra and Milo whenever she arrived home so that she could go straight into the shower, bagging up and sealing the clothes she'd worn to work that day. He dreaded the idea that nurseries might soon have to close – he wouldn't be able to give lectures whilst caring for the twins, and their daytime sleeps were becoming increasingly unreliable.

He looked at Cat, standing in his office, and everything

else fell away. She was wearing tight blue jeans and a simple parka over a hoodie. Her trainers had seen better days, but she stood tall, regal, her dark eyes suggesting she had the measure of him, of everyone. Sometimes in bed, as his wife slept next to him, he'd lay awake, thinking ahead to the next time he would see Cat, itemising all the things he wanted to discuss with her. She understood him better than anyone, there was never any need to repeat himself or clarify his meaning. Sometimes he felt they were thinking as one being, their emotions dipping and rising in unison.

'Here,' he picked up the scholarships leaflet. 'This is the one I was thinking of, the "excellence scholarship", designed to "support outstanding undergraduate students during years two and three of their course".'

'Yeah, but I wouldn't exactly say I'm outstanding.'

'I probably shouldn't say this, but you have the highest grade average of your year. If any history students are going to qualify, it'll be you. You just need to complete the form. I'll write your reference and add your grades.'

'Thank you.' She tucked the leaflet into her coat pocket and, although she smiled, her face was tense with anxiety.

'It's going to be okay,' he said.

'I'll miss you.' She held his gaze, her brow pinched, as though she was trying not to cry.

He felt something inside of him, a kind of tugging sensation that stole the air from his lungs. They had an unspoken agreement not to send text messages, or call. She'd told him once that her partner looked at her phone sometimes. Daniel found the idea preposterous, but it wasn't his place to challenge it.

'I'll miss you too,' he said. And he was aware his tone

conveyed something that had no right to be there. It was unfair to let her see his feelings; he was a married man. Yet the idea of her walking away right now was intolerable. He'd come to need her. Her enthusiasm for her studies had rekindled his own; he was driven to work on his book by a desire to impress her.

There was a simplicity to her MP dream, to her planned journey through education and into activism. Many times during their conversations, he was aware that she hadn't been exposed to the same mundane workplace routines as most people their age. She'd been able to retain an idealism, unsullied by hierarchies and reporting structures. At times, this tipped into naivety, but it was always beautiful. It felt like she was taking him by the hand, leading him away from all the things that left him jaded.

'Okay. I'll hope to see you soon,' she said, giving him a sad smile. 'I'm going to go and max out my library card. Make sure I've got a good book haul at home.'

Daniel was aware of the rise and fall of her chest, the graceful arc of her neck. He wanted to bury his head in her hair and for a moment pretend he'd never married, that she could be his.

She walked out the door. Daniel tried to focus on his desk. He needed to find a box from somewhere and work out what needed to come home with him. He looked up at her retreating back and saw her stop. She turned around and their eyes locked. She stepped towards him and he towards her. Once she was back inside the room, he closed the door and locked it.

'Daniel—'

'Cat—' He placed his hands on either side of her ribcage. She closed her eyes and they kissed. It was slow and tender, and he realised she'd been longing for it, just as he had. She tethered her dreams to him in a way that was unhealthy. He'd gone on letting her, and now he was perhaps fuelling hopes that she was always so careful never to speak aloud. The right thing to do was to stop. To send her away, make her understand that she didn't need him the way she thought she did. But this nearness was ecstasy. And it struck him: why did staying apart have to be inevitable? Would his children really be any happier if he denied himself this?

They made their way to his chair and she sat in his lap, straddling him, her fingers pressing into the flesh around his shoulder blades. There was none of the fevered fumbling of before, when perhaps they'd both worried the other might suddenly sober up and put a stop to what they were doing. This time, there was no pretence; they knew they both wanted exactly this. Deep kisses. Exploring her skin, the tendons in her ankles, her jutting hip bones and taut thighs. Once he was inside her, they maintained a slow rhythm, looking one another in the eye and feeling so completely known, so understood.

After, they stayed on his chair, wrapped in one another's arms.

'If things had been different—' he began.

'I know.' She kissed him. 'You don't have to explain.'

'But I want you. I've never wanted anything as much as this.' If he were to die during this pandemic, he'd cling to this moment. It seemed suddenly so absurd to turn away from a bond that could bring him such happiness, such fulfilment.

'You've already helped me so much,' she said.

He clasped her hand. 'No. It's you – you've helped *me*. Cat, you have to look after yourself. We'll get through this funny old time and we'll work out what to do. I promise. We'll find a way.'

He saw her breath catch. Then, her eyes seemed to take on a hopeful radiance as she inspected his face and saw that he was serious. They'd find a way to be together. They had to.

Chapter 16

Before she even got to morning tea break, Bernice had several dust-ups on the shop floor. They were stripping the place bare. Loo rolls were the first to go, which would have made sense if this new illness gave you the shits, but it didn't, and she couldn't for the life of her understand why people were loading up their trolleys with nine-packs.

She was restocking the medicine aisle as best she could when some snooty so-and-so with a fur collar, ears dripping with gold, demanded that she run out the back and get her some toilet roll, preferably quilted.

'We're completely out,' Bernice had said. 'But we've got a few kitchen rolls left, if you're desperate.'

She'd thought she was being helpful, but the woman erupted with a 'How dare you!' and carried on for five minutes straight, shouting about how disgusting it all was. People stopped to gawp. A few of them muttered agreement as the woman told Bernice she ought to have wrestled toilet paper out of people's hands.

Soaps were the next item to vanish; even those ridiculous herbal ones at sixteen pounds a pop. This made Bernice chuckle to herself, because surely if you were worried about this virus, you'd want to leave some soap for your neighbours, give them a chance to wash their hands too? This time, it was an old fella who felt he needed to shout at her. In the end, she'd pretended to go out the back to search, just to be rid of him. Angry he was, one of those red-faced types who stood too close, jabbing a finger towards her chest.

When tea break came around, she nipped outside to the loading bay for a ciggie and gave Cat a call.

'The whole world's gone mad,' she said when her daughter answered. 'Are you all right for bog roll? I can filch one from the staff lav if you're short?'

'We're well-stocked, Mum. James was one of the first to start shelf stripping, I'm ashamed to say. We've got a bit of a toilet-roll tower going on in the spare room.'

'Ah, that sounds about right. What about your food shop though, love? People are getting a bit grabby over the tins. Do you want me to get you anything, before they all go?'

'Nah, we're good. Thanks though.'

'It's bloody murder here. Still, there might be a bit of overtime later in the week. Keep the wolves from the door.'

'They're saying there's going to be a lockdown.' Cat's voice was suddenly serious. 'Martin's is going to have to close for a bit.'

'I better go and panic buy meself a few voddie bottles then.'

'Not funny.'

'I know, sweetheart, but we mustn't let ourselves be glum.'

'I could come and stay, if you liked?'

Bernice extinguished her cigarette, then, after checking how many she had in her packet, lit another. 'You pop over whenever takes your fancy. About time we had a nice girly night in.'

'No – I meant, if we were ordered to stay indoors, I could move in with you for a bit.'

Bernice felt a flutter in her belly. What a joy it would be to have Cat living alongside her again. They could top and tail in the bed. Watch a bit of telly in the evenings. Have a good old cackle. But was this what Cat really wanted? Or was it charity? Bernice refused to let herself be a burden. 'Are you and James having problems, then?' she asked, carefully.

'Oh no, it's nothing like that,' Cat said, too quickly, Bernice thought. 'I was thinking about you. I mean, you ended up in hospital, Mum. I thought you might need someone to keep an eye. I hate the idea of you sitting indoors alone.'

'Kitty Cat, there's always a bed for you at my place if you ever want to kick that fella to the kerb. I mean it, any time, night or day. But I don't need anyone to look after me. Bless you for offering. But I'm a big girl. I'll be fine.'

There was a pause. Every part of her longed for Cat to admit that, yes, she did want to get away from that toff she'd taken up with. She knew her daughter was proud, but she was strong too. Ditching him could be the making of her – a girl like Cat should never feel beholden.

'Well, okay. I mean, me and James are fine, so I guess I'll be staying here then. But call me if you need anything. And stay safe.'

That's what people were saying now instead of goodbye, *stay safe*. So bloody sombre, it gave Bernice the giggles normally, but this time she felt troubled. What if Cat really did want to get away from James but was too proud to admit it? Bernice had just robbed her of an opportunity.

Chapter 17

The weeks passed with a strange new rhythm and it became apparent that the lockdown was likely to extend throughout the spring at least. It would be many more weeks before Cat could meet Daniel in person, or speak to him privately. Once a week, she'd see him on screen, amongst a gallery of her classmate's faces. She'd look into his eyes and tell herself that he was returning her gaze, that something was being transmitted between them. Perhaps, like her, he was remembering that moment in his office. Her straddling him as they moved slowly, as one. *I've never wanted anything as much as this,* he'd told her, luminous words she could hold within herself, getting her through this time of rising death tolls and harrowing footage of people struggling to breathe.

Sometimes she'd hear a toddler squealing in the background as Daniel was speaking, see him glance over his shoulder, startled. He blurred his background on all his video lectures, so she couldn't get a proper look at the room he worked in. She would have liked to have surveyed the books, the pictures, she was so hungry for traces of him.

But as the weeks passed, she couldn't fail to notice a kind of deterioration. He was often unshaven, and tiredness set in around his eyes. He'd lose his place several times in the course of a lecture and stopped monitoring the seminar discussions – something her classmates bitched about incessantly. More than anything, Cat wanted to hold him, absorb some of his cares and provide the consolation he needed.

I've never wanted anything as much as this. There'd come a time when she'd be worthy of such a sentiment, when she would show him just how much help and support they could offer one another. But for now, she didn't dare send him a single message; they were both locked down with other people, their feelings would have to be deferred.

She'd followed his advice and applied for a scholarship, and he'd blind-copied her when he emailed a reference to the university's disbursement committee. In many ways, it had felt like receiving a love letter.

Catherine Brandon is one of the most intellectually engaged students I've ever had the pleasure of teaching. A mature student who has returned to education after several years of caring responsibilities, she has a fine mind and has demonstrated time and again the ability to develop and support unique new narratives around historical events. She utilises an incredibly diverse range of sources, subjecting them to proper scrutiny and contextual analysis . . .

The language grew increasingly pompous, but she was touched by how strongly he made the case for her. She reread the document, several times a day, whenever the doubts came. Daniel believed in her. She could remake her life.

When this was all over, they would find a way. If snatched encounters were to be Cat's lot, then fine, she'd be grateful for each and every one of them. There would be no demands on her side. She'd never stop him from being the father he wanted to be, even if that meant they could never be a couple in the conventional sense. But their connection was too profound to disregard.

Because Martin had always paid her cash in hand, Cat wasn't entitled to any government support whilst the bar was closed. The rail ticket she'd got into debt for was now worthless and the cash in her purse diminished to almost nothing as she struggled to navigate the refund process. After the first week of lockdown, as James wrote out a list for the weekly shop, she'd swallowed her pride and asked whether he might buy her a couple of packs of cigarettes.

'Absolutely not,' James had said. 'I'm happy to cover most things, but I'm not contributing to you destroying own lungs.'

'I'll pay you back, once Martin's reopens.'

'I don't think that's likely, the way you burn through your money. But that's not the point. If this pandemic has taught us anything, it's that health should come first. Take this opportunity to give up.'

He wouldn't budge. Cat was so irritable that she had to take herself away into another room, before she said something he wouldn't be able to forgive. Later, she raided the house, rummaging through all his drawers, his coat pockets, in search of any cash he might have forgotten about. But there was nothing. He'd made her completely dependent on his whims, on his views on what she should eat, what treats she deserved. In the empty house, she screamed, as loud as she could, until her throat felt torn.

When he returned from the shopping trip, grumbling at

the length of time he'd had to queue outside the supermarket, he presented her with a packet of nicotine gum. 'See, you can't say I'm not compassionate,' he said with a smile.

She'd stared with disdain at his outstretched hand. It was childish not to accept this balm for the misery that awaited her, but his smugness was intolerable. She strode from the room without saying a word. Never had she paid less regard to keeping James placated, to performing the version of herself that he wanted to see. It was as though a tiny part of her wanted him to throw her out.

She gave up the fags, cold turkey. The first three days, she remained in a state of fist-clenching anger. She had a persistent headache, coupled with what she could only describe as an itch at the base of her brain. Everything annoyed her.

James's unending video calls were a particular source of rage. His days followed a steady pattern. His boss would call and list some things he wanted to see on the website – James had a special tone for these calls, sounding overconfident and taking every opportunity to agree with, and repeat, what had just been said. He'd then speak to one of his subordinates and pass the request to them, being overly pally, occasionally confiding a belief that he didn't even agree with what was being asked. There couldn't be a clearer embodiment of a middle manager as James played his part in passing instructions along a chain. It was maddening for Cat, having this soundtrack to her days. Wherever she was in the house, she could still hear him, his voice intruding into her thoughts.

Worse still, James felt that the two of them being at home should mean daytime sex, as it sometimes did at weekends. This was particularly loathsome whilst the memory of her tender encounter with Daniel was so fresh in her mind. Sex with James was the very antithesis of that connection; she never truly inhabited her body when she was with him, her mind always looked forward to it being over, to sleep or to reading.

Such strange games they played. Early in their relationship, James had given her a slight hint that he enjoyed feeling used by her – not financially, but sexually. It was framed as a joke, something about her *having her wicked way*, but she detected a serious note, an almost painful longing. Eager to please in those fresh, uncertain days, she'd indulged him, engaging in a kind of role play where she was this insatiable, wild woman, ordering him around, using him for her pleasure.

It had been fun, to start with. Sometimes he'd call her a slut and she'd put a hand over his mouth, grinding herself against him still harder, acting out the contempt that, as the months passed, she really started to feel. It wasn't domination as such, she knew he would hate that, but it was only ever performance. She was oversexed council-estate scum; he was her object, who never failed to satisfy her in the end. She despised herself. But she knew how quickly his disappointment could morph into hurt silences that lasted for days.

So, when he came down to the sitting room where she worked, giving her a certain look as he pretended to be interested in what she was writing, she knew what she had to do. It was this, or Bernice's bedsit. Sex or the food bank. 'Come here,' she said, a chill sweeping through her body. She snatched at his belt buckle, pulled him to her. 'Let's see what you've got for me.'

He feigned hesitancy, but as she unzipped his jeans, she saw he was already hard.

With a wave of dismay, she stood and shoved him backwards onto the sofa, climbing on top. 'Touch me,' she said.

As he complied, she thought again of Daniel. How frankly they'd gazed into one another's eyes, neither of them concealing their naked longing. But she pushed the memory from her mind. Daniel had no place in this moment. How saddened he'd be if he could see her now, putting on a show for the man who was refusing to buy her cigarettes.

Chapter 18

A spasm in her stomach wrenched her awake. Bernice raised herself up onto her hands and heaved up a stream of bile. It burned the back of her throat as it spattered onto the asphalt. She shivered, looking around, trying to work out where she was. There was the sound of water flowing. A stream. She was on the footpath that ran through the posh end of town where Cat lived. The windows of nearby houses were all dark, a lamp post further down the path the only source of light. It must be very late.

She wasn't ready to stand; she was too dizzy for that. She retched again, but this time nothing came up. There was a sharp pain in her belly. Insistent, like nothing she'd known before. She pulled herself into a sitting position, hugged her knees to her chest and breathed deeply to stop herself from crying out. When at last the pain subsided, she tried to piece together the evening.

She didn't have her phone any more, she remembered that. Someone had filched it from the staffroom at work. They were in the midst of a thieving spate, with purses and fags going missing, one of the girls even had her perfume and lippie nicked – the staff lockers were so easy to pick. Low.

That's what it was. Pinching the odd chocolate bar from the storeroom was one thing, but taking from hard-working people was truly despicable. Bernice would put money on it being that Sara Benson. She started a month ago. Hubby liked a drink.

The misery of not being able to ring Cat, of not being able to go to the bar and have a good old chat, Bernice remembered fretting about it earlier that night. Having a few drinks back at the flat. Eating a Pot Noodle. Watching a bit of telly. She'd gone to check on Cat. That was it. A daily walk was allowed, no rule to say you couldn't take it in the night-time.

She remembered setting out, hoping she might see her daughter at a window, maybe she could shout up and let her know she didn't have her phone, just in case Cat had been trying to call her. Bernice was worried about her daughter. She'd come into the supermarket with that chap of hers last week, and something hadn't been right. Bernice hadn't been able to put her finger on it. There were no black eyes, nothing like that, but Cat didn't seem to have any fight in her any more, she seemed flattened out. Bernice could tell the fella was getting impatient while she and Cat had a bit of a chat; he'd been grasping the handles of his shopping trolley, staring straight ahead and somehow conveying a fury that frightened Bernice.

So, Bernice had obviously set out for a walk tonight, but she couldn't remember a damned thing about it. Given how late it seemed to be, it was most likely that she'd passed Cat's house already and was looping back home. But nope. All blank. Had she tried shouting up to Cat, or had she made do with a little peep? Surely, Bernice would have remembered if she'd seen her daughter.

Her mouth was dry. She didn't have a bag with her. No ciggies. Keys in the pocket of her jeans though, thank fuck. Had there been a bottle? She scanned the ground all around her. No sign of one now at any rate.

Slowly, she eased herself up. Her head swam. Out of sheer cruelty, her mind remembered that Pot Noodle. The wet slop of it. Tiny slithers of carrot. Her mouth filled with water, she could smell the deposit she'd left on the ground and it prompted her to retch again. Nothing coming up, but each time she heaved, it felt like she was opening up a wound inside her. How it burned! Must be that ulcer the doctor told her about.

She'd just pop back to Cat's house. Take a little look to check that everything was okay, then she'd get herself home. How many hours to go until work? No idea. She'd make it though. One foot after another. That was all she had to do.

Bernice got there at last. Car on the drive. Tubs of flowers by the front door. All very nice and civilised. There was an outside tap at the side of the house and Bernice hurried towards it, cupping water in her hands and slurping up big mouthfuls. Her stomach felt twisted up, like an old dishcloth. She splashed water over her face and looked up at the house. The bedroom curtains were drawn, lights off. Her daughter was obviously asleep in bed like the other respectable people on this street. There was nothing untoward. No cause for worry. But still, this subtle feeling of dread continued to grip her.

She steadied herself against the side of the house. Enough of this nonsense. Home to bed. She shuffled along their drive, past James's car, and something caught her eye. She leaned closer. The car had been keyed. C.U.N.T, she could make out, carved into the dark paintwork of the passenger door.

Bernice froze. *That couldn't have been me*, she thought. *I only went out for a little walk, I wouldn't have done that, I'm not the type.* She searched her memory. But everything between setting out and waking up on the path was a blank.

She had the sudden feeling of being watched and glanced up at Cat's window. No one there, the room was still dark. All around her the streets were deserted, filled with an eerie silence. She wasn't sure how much more she could take of this lockdown, of the aching loneliness and unrelenting worry. She was losing control, drinking far too often, letting her mind dwell on past miseries when she ought to know better. She looked at the letters on the car one more time, then hurried away, trying her best to ignore her roiling stomach.

Chapter 19

The snarling faces, beer bellies and wide stances; biceps, baseball caps and tattoos. The braying, barely concealed aggression. Never had Daniel been more afraid for his children than when he beheld those so-called counter-protesters on the news. They'd come out in strength, presenting themselves as preservers of law and order – playing on stereotypes of Black protest. From the safety of his living room, Daniel could imagine himself in that crowd, inhaling the stench of sweat, feeling the heat emanating from angry bodies. His bowels turned to water as he considered the plight of anyone with dark skin who might need to walk past that mob.

These protests were *against* Black Lives Matters, a denial of the rage people felt at police brutality, at discrimination that put you at greater risk of dying. Never had he expected to see such naked bigotry out in the open like this. He'd told himself things were getting better, that his children would have the opportunity to navigate the world on their own terms, having an equal chance at landing a plum job, no more likely to be arrested than the next person. He was a bloody fool.

He thought of Cat and how, as they'd sipped coffee, he'd berated her for her pessimistic view of human nature. 'I work in a bar. I hear what people are saying,' she'd told him. 'My Martin's customers are only too happy to believe it's someone else stopping them from climbing the ladder, whether that's immigrants or EU legislators.'

He'd teased her, accused her of patronising the very class of people she aspired to help, and she'd given him a knowing smile. When the country showed its continued appetite for Brexit by giving the Tories a landslide election victory, she'd refrained from telling him 'I told you so'. But he'd seen something harden in her eyes – she was channelling her rage into hard work, determined to play her part in creating a better future. It left him feeling humbled and slightly ashamed that he wasn't doing the same.

Ever since reconnecting with Cat, Daniel had been picking over his life; trying to define the moments that shaped him into the unexceptional man he now was. Growing up, he'd encountered daily abuse in the playground and on the streets. He was spat on, set upon by other children – his day could take a sinister turn at any moment, sometimes the sweetest-looking old pensioner might shout an appalling slur.

The combination of puberty and the discovery of James Baldwin and Toni Morrison had helped him cultivate a kind of defiance as he entered his teenage years. He'd tried his damnedest to take pride in his brown skin, grew his hair and wore it in twists. He weaponised his grades, working into the night out of a visceral need to be the best in his class, to outperform those who sought to mock or dismiss him. Meeting Cat for the first time had been revelatory – she was clever, but far less confident and certainly less disciplined than he had been. The act of helping her seemed to confirm the existence of some new aspect of himself, something loveable and pure. It had been a wonderful two years, and often he asked himself who he might have become if their time together had continued.

When he arrived at Oxford, the only Black student in his class, he'd felt scrutinised in an entirely new way. He and Cat had been fawned on at college for their high marks, their heated contributions to classroom debate. But Oxford took every opportunity to tell him how lucky he was to be there. He spent less time developing his own aspirations and more on simply fitting in, trying to belong to a world that for so long had represented the pinnacle of success. And perhaps that feeling had stayed with him, ensuring he prioritised his own comfort, leaving it to others to call out injustices.

Daniel's lockdown hadn't been filled with the bread-making and yoga that his colleagues chatted about at their departmental meetings. Elizabeth worked three twelve-hour stints in the hospital per week, so during office hours he often had sole charge of the twins. They couldn't be left unsupervised for prolonged periods while he talked into his computer camera, something he tried to convey to his boss whenever he put unscheduled calls in at short notice.

His days were comprised of a litany of tasks: meal preparations, emptying potties and pleading with the twins to get dressed. Thank goodness they were able to run off their energy in the garden. Daniel thought often of the tower block he'd lived in as a child. He imagined being trapped in the old flat with Kendra and Milo, having to confine their games to the tiny sitting room, always unbearably hot in summer, no garden to escape to for fresh air and sunlight. The headache of doors slamming all around them, heels clonking on the concrete staircases. He felt a twist of compassion for all the families living there now. Lockdown was profoundly unequal in the sacrifices it was asking of people.

He was undoubtedly overworked, yet as the weeks passed, the time took on a golden quality Daniel hadn't expected. His children's laughter, their unalloyed joy at bombing around on their balance bikes, and the absolute trust they showed in him were sources of simple delight. He'd always prided himself on being a hands-on father, but really he'd parented in small slithers of time – the hour between returning home and putting them to bed, small parcels of weekend. He found himself working harder than he'd ever worked before, but he understood his children better now. He laughed with them, comforted them when they cried, sometimes he even joined them for their afternoon nap, the three of them snuggled in his bed. But this contentment was easily undone, he only had to think of the news, remember the footage, to know that the twins would soon be exposed to countless injustices and cruelties. He couldn't tolerate it. He needed to do more, do whatever he could to challenge the systems that would devalue their lives.

He agreed to do an interview on the Black Lives Matter protests for his local radio station. He must have done a decent job, because it was followed by a request from Radio 4. He spoke of arrest statistics, of the white supremacist culture that systematically denies Black people opportunities. Would his words change minds? He didn't know. But the very act of trying to reach others eased something in his chest; a knot of guilt he hadn't known was there. It was high time he made progress on his book. Perhaps then he could stop reproaching himself for having sought comfort, for embracing the kind of ordered-middle-class existence that had obsessed him as a child.

'How did it go?' Elizabeth asked as she wheeled the double buggy through the back door. She'd taken the twins to the seafront to give him a quiet house for the Radio 4 interview. She was technically part-time, but her shifts were gruelling and throughout the pandemic her patients were dying faster than ever before. She lost someone most days, holding a phone to their ear so that families could say their final good-byes. Daniel knew that if their places were reversed, he'd be surly and withdrawn.

'Okay, I think.' Daniel bent down and unclipped Kendra, swooping her into the air as he lifted her from the pushchair.

'I want to ride my bike,' Kendra announced, and Daniel followed her back outside, helping her clip her helmet on.

Elizabeth followed with Milo and as their children played, she wrapped an arm around his waist. 'I'm proud of you,' she said. 'I had a sneaky listen on my phone. You did brilliantly.'

Daniel smiled. But already the treacherous thought was rising: had Cat listened, what did Cat think?

He and Elizabeth were silent, watching the twins chase one another in wide circles around the garden, screaming with pleasure. He wanted this moment to etch itself into his memory: the afternoon light, the unspoken pride and delight he shared with his wife.

He hoped Cat realised their encounter in his office had

been an aberration – the urgency of the television news, the fear, the sense they were living through a landmark time had all conspired to give that day a dreamlike quality. It was another one-off. Even though it had felt like more. Even though he'd been careless enough to voice his desires. *We'll find a way*, he'd told her. But Cat would surely know it was impossible. They couldn't be together without betraying his children.

Each time he saw her on his screen, he felt a kind of bereavement, an aching awareness of physical distance. She joined his lectures from a very tastefully decorated room: a big screen TV on the wall, houseplants in the corners. It was very different from her mother's old council house and he felt a wave of indignation towards the man who'd provided it, who slept with her beside him, able to reach out and touch her whenever he pleased.

Daniel knew Cat loved him; he'd known for some time, if he was honest. Yet he'd continued to meet up with her for the sheer pleasure of having her listen, of hearing her careful reflections. It was only now he realised how unfair he'd been: perhaps all these months she'd been waiting for him to say a word, or perhaps simply to touch her in a way that said *yes*. He could have stepped into a new life with her at any moment. And what a life it would have been.

But to embrace that life would shape him into something detestable.

Once things got back to normal, he'd do the right thing. Cat needed to throw herself into university life, abandon their meetings and find her own way. And he had to let her.

Chapter 20

On the final night pubs were allowed to remain open, Roger had been sat at the bar at Martin's, sinking Guinness as he spoke of his terror of the virus and the prospect of a lockdown.

'I'd be all on my own. Not seeing a soul from one day to the next,' he'd said.

Laura had tried to stay detached, vowing to herself that tonight would be the night she'd plead tiredness and decline to accompany him home. But she couldn't help feeling pity each time she looked into his frightened eyes.

'It'll only be for a little while,' she'd said.

Roger had extinguished his cigarette. 'You could come and stay with me. Temporary like, just for the lockdown, if we have one.'

Laura had been about to reject him, but then it'd struck her: would being confined at home with her parents actually be any less miserable? She had felt instantly guilty, they both meant well. But their unease with her, their continual references to her getting *back on her feet*, prevented intimacy. She couldn't be the daughter they'd once known, and neither of them had accepted it.

And so, minutes after the Prime Minister addressed the

nation, Laura had gathered up a selection of clothes and toiletries into a suitcase and gone to break the news to her parents. They'd been in the living room together, looking stunned as a newsreader recapped the rules that were to underpin the lockdown.

'I'll be giving you a little space,' Laura had announced. 'I made a pact with one of the regulars at the bar. He's all alone and I promised to keep him company if we went into lockdown.'

'Which regular?' her father demanded.

'Roger Hampton.'

'What on earth are you thinking? You can't stay with that old fool. Goodness me. No. This has gone too far.' Martin had turned to his wife. 'He's a pensioner, Miriam. A boozy old bore.'

'This is an opportunity to help someone who needs it,' Laura had said. 'I want to be kind.'

'Stay and keep us company, darling,' her mother had replied. 'That'd be kind.'

'You have each other. Roger has no one. I promised him.' Laura had been able to tell from the way her father regarded her that he had suspicions. Had a rumour reached him? She was sure Roger had bragged to a couple of the other regulars and, in certain moments, it was an effort not to hate him for it. But she swallowed down her embarrassment. Atoning wasn't meant to be easy. She was supposed to suffer. And she could, with some certainty, tell herself she'd make Roger's lockdown less lonely, less harrowing, than it otherwise would have been.

*

As the days passed, she became less sure of her decision. Thankfully, there was no suggestion of her sleeping next to Roger; he'd allocated her the spare room. But aside from the distasteful fumblings that followed his Saturday night Viagra, her presence didn't seem to bring him any joy. He spent hours watching news coverage of the pandemic, along with repeats of *Only Fools and Horses*, the volume turned up so loud that she could hear it in every room of the house. He wrinkled his nose at the curries and tagines that Laura prepared in his kitchen, steadfastly refusing to try them, sticking to his usual diet of supermarket ready meals.

They made a few attempts at board games, but, if anything, this seemed to make the time go more slowly as Roger forgot the rules and became bad-tempered. Indeed, most of the time, he seemed petulant and irritated. Laura felt a spike of possibility as she asked him whether he might prefer having his house to himself after all. His face crumpled. 'Oh no. You mustn't leave me.'

And so she stayed, reminding herself of the harm she'd done in her former life, refusing to feel sorry for herself.

Once a week, while Roger spoke with his nephew, who was, thankfully, unaware of Laura's presence in the family home, she'd go up to her room and video-chat with Cat. She'd been nervous when she first suggested it – they'd been making tentative steps towards friendship prior to lockdown, with Laura on the cusp of repeating her invitation to have lunch or coffee – but it was still a new friendship that hadn't yet found a natural rhythm.

Still, one April afternoon, while Roger sat in his armchair clipping his toenails, Laura had composed a text. *I hope you're keeping well? Let me know if you fancy a video chat sometime. I could do with seeing some different faces! This whole situation is so weird.*

The wait was uncomfortable. As soon as Laura had sent the message, she worried she sounded needy. Cat must be interacting with her university classmates all the time; she wouldn't feel the same desperation to connect. But Laura missed her – more than she expected – Cat's funny one-liners, the way she demolished anyone who dared to make a bigoted or ignorant comment, made Friday nights go by so quickly. Something about her physical presence, the grace of her figure, the sweep of her hair, was pleasant to be around.

Happily, Cat had texted back after a couple of hours. *Different faces? Yes please! I'm free this afternoon if you want to send a Zoom link?*

After that first time, they made a regular appointment of it, sometimes talking for over an hour. A couple of times, Laura had seen Cat's chap wander into the room and peer over Cat's shoulder to look at her screen. He was short with a muscular upper body, but largely forgettable, and in truth, Laura was more interested in seeing inside Cat's home. The old Laura would have envied Cat for the apparent perfection of her domestic set-up, the Farrow & Ball paint, the beautiful ferns in their wicker pots. New Laura was simply delighted to have a weekly chat to look forward to.

Today, sunlight flooded in through the open window of Roger's spare room. There was a family of sparrows nesting in the eaves and she could hear frantic cheeping each time a parent returned.

'I still can't believe you're shacked up with Roger Hampton,' Cat said with a cackle.

Laura shrugged. 'Where's your other half today?'

Cat's face tightened. 'Working upstairs in his office.'

A silence stretched between them. Laura could tell Cat was unhappy, but it wasn't something she felt able to probe, knowing that Cat's partner might walk in on them at any point.

'Please show me what Martin's face looked like when you told him,' Cat said.

Laura opened her mouth, trying to simulate the precise combination of shock, concern and distaste.

Cat's shoulders heaved with laughter. 'God, I miss the club,' she said. 'Does that make me a sad fuck?'

'Of course not. You were a queen holding court behind that bar most nights. I don't blame you for missing that.'

Cat snorted. 'I'm trying to make the best use of the time. Reading as much as I can, doing prep for next term. I'm thinking of starting my dissertation mega early.'

Laura smiled. 'I wish I had something like that to focus on. I've volunteered to work at the food bank, but they haven't got back to me yet. I think they might be inundated with offers.'

'That's a really lovely thing to do. Why didn't I think of doing something like that?'

'You're busy—'

Cat shook her head, eyes shining with angry tears. 'No, it's more than that – I always get stuck on the big problems while you roll your sleeves up and actually make yourself useful.'

Laura tried to protest, even though she felt a twinge of pleasure at how Cat had characterised her.

'You've changed so much. I'm not sure if you realised, but I felt kind of bullied by you at school,' Cat said.

Laura stared into the screen of her phone, shocked at the starkness of this statement.

Cat lowered her eyes. 'Maybe bullied is the wrong word, but you were part of a group of girls, all clean and – I don't know – it seemed like you enjoyed excluding me.'

'Cat – goodness – I had no idea. I certainly don't remember—'

'I expect a lot of it was me. I didn't feel like I belonged and was maybe more standoffish than I needed to be. I heard you tell someone I smelled once.'

Laura could feel the heat rising in her face. She could believe it, that was the sad thing; the old Laura was more than capable of saying such hurtful things without even recognising the potential to wound. 'Gosh. Cat, I'm so sorry—'

'No. I'm not after sympathy. I just wanted you to understand why I was a bit of a bitch when you first came back to Martin's. I didn't want you there.' Cat sighed. She looked uncertain and a little upset.

'What's brought this on?' Laura asked. 'Is everything okay?' She saw Cat's eyes flick to the corner of the room.

'I'm in love with a married man,' she whispered. 'One of my lecturers. I can't see him or even talk to him. I miss him so much.'

'Oh, Cat.'

'He feels the same way. We should be making plans, deciding what to do, but I'm stuck here with a man I'm really starting to hate.'

'Goodness. I can't imagine what that must be like.' Through

the months they'd worked together, Laura had sensed that Cat was dissatisfied with her relationship. But hate was a strong word, and Cat was always so precise with language.

Cat shook her head. 'A few times I've thought of just going to him, to Daniel. Fuck the consequences. But he has kids – I can't . . . I have to let him do things his way.'

'Tell me about him. What's he like?'

Cat looked up towards the ceiling and let out a sigh of frustration. 'He really *gets* who I want to be, what I want to do with my life, you know?'

'But – you can talk to other people? I mean, it's lovely that you share so much with this man – but you can confide in others too, surely?'

Cat closed her eyes for a second, as though blinking back tears. 'Yeah. I suppose. Anyway, it's really nice to talk to you. You must say hello to Roger for me.'

'You can ring me any time,' Laura said, disappointed the call was ending so abruptly.

Cat nodded as she waved goodbye. For a long time afterwards, Laura sat on the single bed, cradling her phone, trying to remember the things she might have said to Cat back at school. Her memories of schoolgirl Cat were dim: hunched shoulders, greasy hair, a general air of grubbiness, coupled with pique at the improbable straight As. She remembered others bandying about the terms *slut* and *slag* in their final year, once it became apparent that Cat had slept with at least three of the best-looking boys in their class. None of those boys had become Cat's boyfriend, Laura remembered that, but they were happy enough to brag about what they'd been up to with her.

Laying down on her side, Laura ached with the weight of shame. How often in her life she'd brushed against suffering, completely unaware. Would a few shifts at the food bank ever reverse that? Would sex and board games with Roger? She remained still for several moments, picking over her memories as she fought a growing sense of futility.

Chapter 21

'I suppose you're outgrowing me.'

Cat blinked her eyes open. Light was flooding through the curtains and James was already dressed, kneeling on the floor by her side of the bed, his face so close she could feel his breath against her cheek. She propped herself up on her elbow, dazed and sleepy. 'What?'

His eyes were cold, his face strangely still. 'You got a scholarship. You didn't even tell me you were applying for one. Why would you keep that a secret?'

Her email. He must have been looking through her laptop while she slept. For a moment, Cat felt her muscles loosen with relief – she'd made a good call, agreeing with Daniel not to exchange personal messages, an agreement she'd stuck to, even though she'd been tempted to break it many times.

She sat up. 'You've been reading my emails.'

'It was *my* laptop not so long ago. I didn't think it would be a big deal to pick it up and check the headlines. I didn't realise you had so many secrets.'

Cat sighed. 'The scholarship isn't a secret. I just hadn't got round to telling you about it. Why are you acting like this? It's exciting news.'

'But you're not poor, Cat. I'm paying for everything. Why would they think you needed a scholarship?'

She threw the covers off and climbed out of bed. 'It's not about need. This is the university recognising that I'm talented, that I'm doing well.' She picked yesterday's vest and shorts off the floor, put them on, trying not to look at James. Just a few more months, that's all she had to tolerate, then she'd be in her own bedsit.

Fuck, her inbox contained an acknowledgement of her student loan application. Had he seen that too? A loan would be so much harder to explain.

Out of the corner of her eye, she was aware of James stepping towards her. 'So, what are you going to spend the money on? Cigarettes?'

'There's a long list of books—'

'Or maybe you're planning to pitch in with the bills? Pay for your half of the groceries.'

He was standing too close. His eyes were alive with an anger she'd never seen before. If she hadn't just woken up, if she had a moment on her own to think things through, she might be able to work out why he was so enraged and how best to respond.

'Yeah,' she lied. 'I'd like to contribute.' She'd make sure she was out the door the moment her first loan instalment was paid.

James placed his hands on her shoulders and she tried not to wince. 'I just don't understand why you've been deceitful.'

'Oh, for fuck's sake, James, stop making a drama out of it. Anyone else would be happy for me. And while we're at it, I don't quite understand why you were rooting through my inbox – that's not where you'll find the headlines.'

'You don't get to make me the bad guy. I put up with a lot.'

This was clearly an allusion to the previous week, when they'd been woken to the sound of Cat's mother shouting outside the window. Cat had opened the curtains to find Bernice propping herself up against the side of James's car.

'Kitty Cat, is everything all right, love?' she'd slurred.

'You've come here at one in the morning to ask if I'm all right?'

Her mother had staggered. Almost fallen over. 'Got a spare ciggie?'

'No, I've given up. Hang on, I'll come down.' But she'd felt James seize her arm. He'd joined her at the window.

'Stop shouting,' he'd hissed. 'And, Bernice, go home, we're in lockdown for goodness' sake.'

At that, Bernice had started screeching. *Keeping my daughter under lock and key*, Cat heard. *Too good for you. Acting like your shit don't stink.*

James had shut the window and Cat had grabbed her clothes and gone running downstairs, planning to go outside and calm her mother. This was all her fault. She should have called more often, shown that she cared.

James caught up with her in the hallway. 'You have to stop enabling her,' he'd said, taking her arm again.

'Let me go to her,' Cat had insisted, trying to pull herself free. She'd been livid with him for presuming to interfere, for his lack of compassion. Her mother was still outside, alone in the dark and clearly off her tits.

'Cat, I'm only thinking of what's best.'

She tried again to shake herself free, but his grip was strong.

'Listen, Cat—'

'Hey!' Something about being restrained in this way fuelled an instinctual panic. Cat had flailed and tussled, aware of his strength and how powerless she was in contrast. How easily he could contain her. He wasn't even exerting himself as he turned her into something ridiculous, a screaming, shouting harpy.

She drove her knee into his groin. She hadn't made a conscious decision to do it, the need to fight him off had been animal, fierce, all thoughts of placating him forgotten. And there he was sinking to the floor, gasping for breath. She'd stepped back, stunned.

'You . . . you kicked me,' he'd panted.

Cat had switched the light on. James was red-faced, crumpled. She'd only been trying to free herself. He'd left her no choice, keeping hold of her arm like that. But she was trembling as she recognised her own capacity for violence.

'James? Shit! I'm sorry.' She crouched down next to him, cradling his head as a spasm of fear passed through her. Had she been justified in kneeing him? Surely James was only trying to help, to prevent her rushing outside half-clothed when her mother was making a scene? There was no way he'd continue feeding her, letting her live rent-free in his home after this.

But, unexpectedly, James started to cry. 'I only want what's best for you,' he'd said, wiping a tear from his cheek.

Cat felt the full force of her treachery. She'd been unfaithful, was planning to leave, yet James could forgive her for behaving like her father, for giving in to the rages that simmered in the background of her mind more often than she cared to admit.

The two of them remained locked in a shuddering embrace for some time. Guilt kept her there. How much she'd taken from him. How callous and unfeeling she'd been. When Cat finally broke away and opened the front door, her mother had gone. She tried calling, but it went straight to voicemail. *She must be sleeping it off,* Cat had hoped. They didn't discover James's car had been keyed until the following morning.

Standing in their bedroom, Cat felt an unexpected pang of guilt. Every month she stayed, she delayed the process of James moving on with his life. He was denying himself the opportunity of fatherhood for her sake, under the illusion that she loved him, believing the two of them would grow old together enjoying three holidays a year, restaurant meals and regular cinema trips.

It wasn't his fault that he didn't really know her – she'd never given him the opportunity. She'd lied to him every day, curating her very personality in order to keep life comfortable. For a moment, she was tempted to confess. To tell him everything in a single burst of compassion. But then she thought of the squalor of Bernice's flat, of the long wait until the scholarship and loan payments reached her bank account.

Inspecting James's face, she tried to calculate the quickest and most effective way to shed the atmosphere of suspicion. She decided sex.

'Right,' she said, steering him to the bed. 'I think it's about time you stop all this sniping and show me how sorry you are for waking me up.'

Chapter 22

As the year crept into summer, the government slowly eased restrictions. People were granted the freedom to leave the house multiple times a day, so Cat opted to take walks when James was at work, sometimes meeting up with Laura to do a few loops around the town's lake, sometimes enjoying being alone, free to roam across her own thoughts rather than being barraged by James's stream of consciousness.

The university announced that it would begin a careful reopening from July, meaning Cat would finally be able to go to the library and select new books. The prospect delighted her. It wasn't simply escaping James; the idea of returning to those places where she'd taken such definitive steps towards her new life felt essential. Something about the city bolstered her faith in her own future. The scholarship money and her student loan would both arrive in her bank account come September and she'd be able to find somewhere of her own to live; a place to work quietly, accountable to no one. Somewhere Daniel could visit.

It was outside of term time, so she wouldn't be seeing Daniel at lectures. She did, however, break her own embargo on texting, being very careful with her wording: *I'm going to visit the university library next week when it opens. What books do you think would be most helpful for next term?*

He seemed to understand her, because he responded, asking her the day and time she planned to visit, and not actually suggesting any books. After she replied, she deleted the entire thread and waited, in gleeful anticipation. It had been more than three months since they'd made love in his office, since they'd been able to speak intimately. She was hungry for his presence. All throughout lockdown, she'd wanted nothing more than to feel the heat of his body, the vibrations of his mind.

'You're taking the train. To Portsmouth?' James was incredulous, but his voice carried an angry undertone. They were in the kitchen, Cat making coffee whilst James prepared an overly complicated breakfast of granola, fruit and yoghurt.

'I have my mask and my hand sanitiser.'

James stopped what he was doing and turned to face her. 'What could be so important that you need to go and expose yourself – expose both of us – to infection?'

'I need to change my library books.' She spooned sugar into her cup, unable to look at him.

He sighed. 'I'll have to take you in my lunch break. Drive to Portsmouth and wait while you run in and out. You can't use public transport.'

She couldn't let him spoil this for her. She was careful not to react; to maintain what she hoped was a gentle expression. 'That's really kind of you. I was going to spend a couple of hours searching out journal articles. Would your work be okay with you taking a whole afternoon?'

James laughed, but his eyes were cold and serious. 'Your first proper job is going to be quite the wake-up call.'

Cat smiled nervously, hating him. But he didn't raise any further objections to the train.

It was a bright day, with sunlight streaming in through the library windows. How good it felt, returning to her usual desk, freeing herself from the confines of James's home. Cat was there ahead of Daniel and spent a leisurely half-hour selecting new books to borrow. It was eerily quiet. She was the only student on the second floor, which meant she and Daniel would have the privacy to really talk. What had lockdown been like for him? She longed to believe he relived their moments together as often as she had. Had he made any headway on his book? Perhaps he'd let her read his chapter drafts. She'd tell him how wretched the past months had been for her, how she was more resolved than ever to leave.

Today they would reach their understanding. The parameters of their relationship would be redrawn and finally she'd know how much of him was available to her. She wouldn't call it an affair – this was so very different from her father's rutting with lonely women – but she was pragmatic enough to know that a few encounters a week might be all Daniel could offer. It hurt, yes, but she took comfort in the idea that while there may be a need for sneaking around, for him to head home at certain times, their connection was unique. Perhaps she could look forward to a day, at some undefined point in the future, when Daniel moving out wouldn't feel like such a terrible upheaval for his children.

She heard his footsteps on the stairs and her body felt

strangely light as she looked up to watch him approach. He was wearing denim cut-offs and brown leather sandals paired with a simple white T-shirt. His eyebrows were drawn together as he scanned the space, checking they were alone.

She stood up, planning to greet him with a hug, but he stopped a metre or so away from her desk, showing scrupulous respect for the social-distancing guidelines still in force. They were in public, after all, Cat told herself. She smiled, her body unfurling with relief at the sight of him.

'You look well,' he said, through his black fabric mask.

She couldn't quite return the compliment; Daniel appeared tired, his eyes seemed to be withdrawing into his skull, even the way he stood seemed to convey a deep exhaustion. She longed to touch him, to place her hand against his cheek, caress the muscles of his shoulders. 'It's been too long,' she said. 'I've missed you.'

Daniel said nothing. It was intolerable not being able to see his mouth, only having half a face to read. Why was he being so guarded? Yes, they were in a public place, but they were alone.

She sat back down and Daniel took a chair from one of the other desks, positioning it so that he was facing her but still two metres away, still keeping his mask on, even though Cat had removed hers. It wasn't a set-up that lent itself to intimacy – they'd have to speak loudly if they were to be heard. But she rallied her courage and looked him square in the eye.

'I'm leaving James this autumn, as soon as my first student loan instalment hits the bank. I'll get my own place – it'll probably be a shithole, but it'll be mine.'

His eyes widened with alarm, but she needed to continue,

to force him to understand how accommodating she was prepared to be.

'I know you have a family, and I don't want to influence the choices you make,' she said. 'But I've realised that comfortable is a curse – it's so unimportant, so irrelevant, compared to true understanding, encouragement and purpose.'

Daniel opened his mouth, ready to interrupt, but she went on: 'I'm ready to be poor with you, if that's ever an option. But if not, I'm here anyway. Even the crumbs of what you have to offer will make me happier than I am now.'

'Cat—' His eyes seemed to convey an intense pain. She hadn't done a good enough job, he wasn't understanding her. She shouldn't have spoken of *crumbs*, it sounded too desperate, something her mother would say.

'I mean it,' she said. 'You do so much for me. You always did – just talking to you activates the better parts of me—'

He got up from his chair and approached, kneeling beside her. His whole bearing was one of apology, of pity. 'Cat, I'm so sorry. I know I've given you hope. But this has to stop. I can't betray my family.'

'But—' The pity in his eyes was too painful. There was a tightness in Cat's throat and she had to look away. All these months, he'd been building the courage to let her go, to dismiss her. How stupid she'd been. Just like her mother, believing that sex equated to love.

She braved another look at Daniel. His eyes were welling up and it was impossible not to remember the feel of him in his office, the urgency with which he'd held her. She refused to believe he didn't love her. Yet here he was, dumping her – that was the brutal truth of it.

'I—' She couldn't go on. She wasn't sure that she could continue at university without him. All the things he'd encouraged her to believe about herself and her future were dissolving, right here in this library.

Daniel watched the colour drain from Cat's face. She placed a hand down on the desk to steady herself and he saw her chest heave as she caught her breath. How natural it would be to place an arm around her, to feel the warmth of her body as he held and comforted her. He hadn't treated her well, he knew that. It had been selfish of him to seek her company for so many months, suspecting the complex feelings she harboured.

Telling Cat how much he wanted her in that final, passionate encounter had been unforgivable. His judgement had been clouded by the strange atmosphere of that time, the terror of death palpable in every news broadcast. It had felt important to say something. But it had been a mistake.

He'd created a feeling of dependency in Cat, even before that last encounter. It wasn't that she was needy, far from it; the ugly truth was he'd inserted himself into her life because of how it made him feel, every time she looked at him. He felt seen, he felt adored, and it had shattered his judgement.

'Cat – you're a wonderful woman—'

He became aware of a librarian at the top of the stairs. She bustled past them, carrying a handful of books, very deliberately not looking in their direction. He needed to be careful. One of his departmental colleagues could appear at any moment.

'You'll graduate and start doing the wonderful things you're planning. I know you will.'

'Stop it,' she whispered. 'You've told me it's over; you've been nice and clear. You don't need to baby me.'

He stood up, knees creaking. He was desperate for this exchange to be over, but he returned to his chair. If she needed to cry, if she wanted to shout at him in rage, he had to let her.

She raised her head and inspected his face. Her neck was flushed, her eyes watery. Even as a rational inner voice screamed at him not to backtrack, to be sure she understood their parting was final, he found himself longing for their coffees to resume. Was it impossible to go back to being friends? He wanted to show her the first three chapters of his book – he felt he'd done a good job, but hearing it from her would bring the most exquisite pleasure.

She swallowed. 'Thanks for being straight with me,' she said. 'That's decent of you.'

'I'm sorry it has to be this way.'

She silenced him with a wave of her hand and looked down at her desk, picking up the journal in front of her, trying her hardest to appear calm. Her breath gave her away. Daniel could see her chest rise and fall, could hear the air moving through her throat as she tried to master herself.

He was convinced there was more he ought to say. He wanted to plead for forgiveness – a selfish part of him perhaps hoped to hear a response that would absolve him somehow. He thought of the twins, now back at nursery, how uncertain they'd been on the day they returned, grasping his hand tightly, Kendra whispering that she'd prefer to stay at home with him. But then he found himself thinking of all the meetings he and Cat enjoyed in their first term, the unmistakable camaraderie, the encouragement she'd given him, simply by having such high expectations.

'I really am sorry,' he said, after a while.

She looked up, giving him a sad smile. 'You don't have to stay any longer,' she said. 'I know it's awkward. I appreciate you coming here and putting yourself through it.'

It seemed too cowardly to leave; yet he rose from his chair, feeling unsteady on his feet. He'd done it. Ended a hope he'd cruelly nurtured. His family would be everything to him now. He hesitated for a moment, wondering whether there was anything he might say to salvage her esteem for him. But he felt spent, inadequate to the task of making things better.

'Goodbye then,' he said.

Cat didn't look up. 'Bye, Daniel.' There was a strangled quality to her voice he knew he'd never forget.

Chapter 23

Once lockdown restrictions eased, Laura repacked her suitcase and headed back to her parents' home. Roger didn't object – they were in truth so very tired of one another by that point.

Like Cat, Laura found herself relieved and even a little excited when Martin's reopened in July. Here was structure, an opportunity to begin again with her atonement pledges. People would need comfort and support more than ever before, and she was ready. She'd be that listening ear.

Operating a cash business meant that for years very little of her father's income had gone through the books, a tactic that left him unable to qualify for a grant to make up lost earnings. He was itching to reopen and start filling the till. He and Laura flung the windows open, aired the place and rearranged the tables and chairs to ensure everything was adequately spaced, in case they were inspected.

'Bloody nonsense,' her father murmured. He often worked without a face covering, grumbling to the regulars about the extra burdens placed on pubs and restaurants. But Laura was more cautious, wearing a visor even though the regulars teased her about it relentlessly. They were almost uniformly older men, many of them smokers, several of them over-weight. She lived with a constant terror of inadvertently contracting the virus and passing it to one of them. Her hands were chapped from repeated washing, and it stung every time she applied antibacterial gel.

Roger had let it be widely known that Laura had *shacked up* with him during lockdown. There had been sniggering at the bar and Tommy Dickinson, who must be in his fifties, who was obese and breathless, had grabbed hold of her hand and asked her whether she wanted to try 'all shapes and sizes'. His three companions – bunched too closely together, despite her pleas – had all laughed, a swell of deep, resonant contempt that left her fighting tears. Thank goodness she'd been working the shift alone and her father hadn't been around to hear.

She'd only wanted to make Roger feel good about himself. She believed she'd been doing something kind, yet she'd attracted such derision, from him and everyone he talked to. She couldn't help feeling spikes of resentment, which she had to atone for by repeatedly putting herself back in the night of the accident. The explosive bang as her car smashed into the motorbike. The body on the asphalt. Parents in Portugal learning they'd lost their only son.

'Hello, hello.' It was Cat's father, Terry. Something about him always put Laura on edge. He was well-built, solid but not paunchy like her other customers. And he was hand-some, too handsome really for a place like Martin's. His hair was thick and dark like Cat's, and he shared her olive skin and brown eyes. In a suit, he'd look truly magnificent, but he tended to stick with worn jeans and heavy work shirts, the sleeves rolled up to show off strong forearms covered in tattoos.

Yet in spite of so much that was outwardly pleasant, the impression Terry created was feral and mean. Maybe it was down to how alert he always seemed, eyes roving over the place. He always spoke just a little louder than he needed to, something that struck Laura as calculated to command attention, or even to intimidate.

Laura greeted him with what she hoped was a friendly smile. 'Pint of Stella?'

Already, his presence had affected the atmosphere. The skinhead twins broke away from the fruit machines to deliver an enthusiastic welcome. There was backslapping. A male energy that left Laura feeling slightly cowed and nervous about having to remind everyone of the distancing regulations, which they kept ignoring.

By the time she'd poured Terry's pint and taken his money, things had calmed down and the twins resumed their gambling. Laura swallowed, aware of her own reluctance to start a conversation. Snobbery. Classism. That was what her reaction amounted to. Old Laura creeping through, yet again.

'I've been hearing all sorts of things about you.' Terry smiled; his teeth were perfectly straight and surprisingly white. He lit a cigarette without asking whether it was okay. Her father let people smoke, but they had to engage in a mini-performance, whispering a request and looking grateful when an ashtray was placed in front of them.

Laura said nothing as she started tidying up the spirits, straightening the already-neat line of bottles.

'What brought you here, anyway? You seem like a nice

girl. Too nice to be getting pawed at by the old fellas that drink here.'

She felt a pressure building at her temples. Her face became hot, but she tried to take a defiant tone. 'Your daughter works behind the bar. Don't you worry about her?'

'Cat's a funny one. Likes being queen bee. Always was a little madam.'

Although Laura recognised Cat in the description, she still felt indignant. A cleverer woman would retaliate, but something about Terry left Laura feeling uneasy and stupid.

'But we're talking about you,' Terry added. 'You're nothing like Cat – you always struck me as having a bit of class.'

'Hardly. I went to prison for drink driving.'

'I heard.'

'There's nothing classy about that.'

Terry gave another of his eyebrow raises and took a hearty drink from his glass. 'So. What's a man got to do to get the Roger treatment, then?'

'What?' She sounded shrill. The twins both turned around.

'Calm down. It's just a friendly question.'

'That was ... a mistake ... '

'A mistake that happened rather more than once, if dear old Rog is to be believed.'

'Can we talk about something different?'

He grinned at her, then sauntered over to the twins.

Laura hurried into the kitchen. She needed to breathe. It felt as though she was going to burst into loud, unrestrained tears. She bit down on her knuckle.

Again, the meditation. Picturing the curled-up form. The strange angle of the biker's head. Abdul collecting her from the police station, folding her into him and gripping her tightly. In the weeks following the accident, he'd become increasingly impatient. 'He was driving the wrong way! Without lights! Why are you behaving like this? Do you actually *want* to go to prison?'

'Yes!' She deserved punishment. Why was that so difficult for the people she loved to understand? She'd taken a life. She told her husband of the function room, the soft, flattering light. How she'd accepted glass after glass from silent waitresses in starched shirts; not even interrupting her conversation to say thank you. She described how she'd listened to a succession of middle managers, so smilingly calculated, tilting her head in sympathy, giving encouraging nods. She always had a follow-up question at the ready if the conversation lulled.

At first, Abdul looked puzzled. But it hadn't taken long for him to become impatient. 'You were just doing your job.'

'I had the car with me. I'd planned to drive all along. I kept taking drinks. I lost count. I thought just not feeling drunk was good enough.'

'Your reactions were probably just fine. He was driving the wrong way, Laura.'

She'd groaned in frustration. Why couldn't Abdul see that her pain, her disgust, transcended the accident itself? She despised the Laura she'd been on the night of the accident. So glib, so inflated with pride at the leads she was generating, at her silhouette in that black dress.

A shout brought her back to the moment. 'Need some change!'

She stepped back into the bar area. One of the skinheads

was brandishing a twenty and she managed to smile as she changed it into coins.

After the skinheads' departure, Terry planted himself on a bar stool. It seemed to Laura inevitable that he'd hang back, casting an imposing shadow over the bar. Throughout her shift, she'd felt his eyes on her, been aware of his leering grin. She wouldn't let her apprehension show; he didn't have the right to make her feel afraid. There was only five minutes to go before she could ring the bell and insist he finish his drink.

'Shouldn't you be getting back to work?' she asked.

Terry gestured to rain-patterned window. 'Not in this weather.'

'Well, I'll need to be locking up and getting home soon.'

He patted the bar stool next to him. 'Have a drink with me.'

'I don't drink.'

Terry snorted. 'You're an enigma, you are. Working in a bar, but not drinking. Classy girl, educated, but letting dirty old pensioners fuck you.'

Her hand gripped the side of the bar. 'I think you should leave.'

'I get lonely too, you know. Just like poor old Rog.' He said this in a fake voice, deliberately wheedling as he screwed his face into a parody of neediness. Yet still, there was an air of menace in the way he was holding his body, taking up space.

Laura shook her head. She turned the bar lights off, then headed out into the seating area, straightening chairs, being deliberately brisk.

Terry seized her by the waist, gripping her with a strong forearm.

'What are you doing?'

'Come on,' Terry said. 'Why not have a little fun?'

She tried to pull away. 'You're a married man. Jesus!'

He wrenched her visor off, flinging it to the floor. Laura lurched forwards, trying to prise his arm away, but he wrapped his other arm around her neck, pulling her face towards his. 'Playing hard to get?' He hissed the words, his breath hot and moist against her cheek.

Something inside Laura snapped. The sobs she'd been holding back for years came all at once. What was she doing here? Why wouldn't Terry just leave? Nobody listened to her. 'Please. Leave me alone,' she managed to say.

He turned her around, seeming to embrace her as she shuddered, drenching her face with tears and snot. The humiliation of it, being held by such a man, unable to control herself. Did he think he was comforting her? Or did they both know he was restraining her? Knowledge of what was going to happen next pooled in her stomach, an acid burn of fear. She knew she needed to act, but he was so much stronger. And they were completely alone.

'Come now, enough tears.' He spun her around. There was no trace of compassion on his face. He was focussed, intent.

'I— Please don't—'

'This will make you feel better.' His tone was so gentle; it almost came out as a whisper, as though they really were lovers.

When he lifted up her dress, confirming what she knew and dreaded, she was paralysed, unable to react, even though every cell of her body wanted to flee. She started to panic, her throat became tight and she couldn't get enough air in her lungs. *It will be over quicker, if I don't move*, she told herself, still fighting for breath. *Picture him leaving, picture him walking down the stairs, leaving you here alone. It will be over soon.*

He pushed her backwards, against one of the tables, hoisting her onto its cold, sticky surface. He didn't try to kiss her. She was thankful for that. As he pounded into her, she tried to cultivate a sense of detachment. She felt the *no* inside her chest, imagining screaming it as she tried to shove him away. But what then? It was easier to simply let Terry take what he wanted than to fight him and lose. He wouldn't hesitate to hurt her.

It didn't last long. She carried on sitting there, naked backside against the table, knickers midway down her calf as Terry adjusted himself and zipped his jeans. He cupped her chin in one of his palms, forcing her to look at him. 'This didn't happen, all right?' He sounded so calm, so in control. 'Like you say, I *am* a married man.'

Laura said nothing. She wanted him gone, needed to be alone and quiet for a long, long time. There was a stinging feeling between her legs and she was certain he'd torn her.

He cupped her chin. 'Let me hear you say it. This didn't happen.'

She kept her gaze downwards. 'This didn't happen.'

'Good girl.' He slapped her bare thigh.

At last, he was gone. Laura sank to the floor, hugging her knees closely to her body. Why hadn't she been firmer? She could have at least articulated that *no*, loudly and clearly. In London, she'd carried a rape alarm in her bag. She imagined herself to be the kind of woman who would kick an assailant in the balls, file a coherent police report with her head held high. How could she have comprehended this paralysing fear? Feeling the power in his arms, the strength of his hands had been enough to secure her silence.

She gave up trying to make sense of it all, letting her mind empty completely. She'd spent hours in prison in this kind of semi-catatonic state, looking up at the ceiling. And it was nearly time for the evening shift when she finally got round to lifting herself up and wiping herself clean.

Chapter 24

Cat lay in bed next to James, trying to focus on her breathing like they taught her in yoga, trying to quieten her mind as she drew the air in deep. It had been a fortnight since she'd met Daniel in the library. She'd not read any of the books she'd brought home with her that day. Her passion for study was gone, her dream of becoming an MP felt laughable. She was a barmaid. Partner of the man snoring gently next to her. She ought to be grateful for the home he provided. For the Egyptian cotton sheet she lay upon. Grateful to have left the squalor of her childhood behind her.

But she felt bereft. Humiliated. Such belief she'd had in her connection with Daniel, it was unfathomable that he could walk away from such a thing. Which meant it couldn't have been real in the first place. It had been a delicious hallucination, altering her blood chemistry, tricking her into happiness, into optimism.

She passed most days in her bed. Grateful for those moments when she was able to slip into a light sleep. Occasionally allowing herself the relief of tears when she remembered the Daniel of long ago, pressing against her on the bus, becoming increasingly passionate as they talked about Kosovo, or the mendaciousness of Tony Blair.

For nearly a year, she'd believed she could again be the girl at his side. The girl who believed talent and hard work gave her relevance, a destiny. Life had taught her otherwise, but during their time together she'd surrendered herself to the bliss of disregarding her own experience.

Shortly after three in the morning, somewhere between sleep and wakefulness, the landline started beeping. Cat hurried downstairs, certain it must be something bad.

'Could I please speak to Catherine Brandon?' It was a female voice. Official and practised.

'Yeah. That's me.'

'Hello there. Sorry to disturb you at this hour. I'm calling from St Luke's. Your mother was brought to us this evening in a very serious condition.'

Cat became aware of James stepping into the room in his boxers. Standing over her.

'What happened?' Cat asked.

'She was brought in by ambulance. We're treating her for alcohol poisoning and felt we needed to notify next of kin. I'm afraid she's very unwell.'

Cat was familiar with the way nurses spoke. She knew the sinister connotations of *very unwell*. 'Are we talking life-threatening?'

There was a pause at the other end of the line. 'I'm sorry to say she's in a critical condition. If you're able, I would suggest you make your way here. I can let you spend an hour with her.'

Cat could feel the thudding of her heart as she stood perfectly still, listening to the nurse talk through the protocols, telling her she'd have to visit alone and wear a face covering.

She'd be able to hold her mother's hand, but wouldn't be able to hug her.

'Cat? What's happened?' James's hand was on her shoulder as she replaced the telephone receiver. 'Cat?'

For several minutes, she was folded into her shock and misery, unable to speak. Here came the barrage of memories from before: the interminable wait for news, the cautiously worded assessments of doctors and, above all, the feeling of utter powerlessness.

James drove her to the hospital, dropping her outside the main entrance. Cat trudged to the Medical Assessment Unit, past the specially designated 'quiet room' with its box of tissues and poster for bereavement counselling, then navigating her way along a row of patients, some groaning, some in an uneasy slumber. With a jolt, she recognised her mother – how had Cat not noticed how thin she'd become? Her curled form under the sheet suggested the fragility of terminal illness, of impending death. Cat felt a moment of sheer indignation – this was wrong, her mother couldn't die, she'd rally, look sheepish as Cat scolded her. Dying was something that happened to other people. Bernice always pulled through, always survived.

A nurse, wearing a surgical mask and visor, was making some adjustments to the drip stand and nodded at Cat as she approached. 'Hello. You must be the daughter. We spoke on the phone. I'm Jenny.'

'What's happening?' Cat asked.

'Your mother has acute alcohol poisoning. Her potassium and sodium levels are low and we haven't been able to rouse her yet. We're giving her drugs to support her heart.'

Cat stood there, transfixed by the rise and fall of her mother's ribs. This was the only movement; Bernice was otherwise perfectly still, in a state far beyond mere slumber. Cat steeled herself with a deep breath. 'Is she ... is she dying?' Even now, part of her believed in the fairness of the universe. Her mother couldn't die. She wasn't even sixty years old.

'I'll ask the doctor to pop along and go through everything with you,' the nurse said. She gestured towards Bernice. 'You should talk to her. It helps.'

Cat moved closer to the bed. All traces of expression were gone from her mother's face and there was a dreadful vacancy to it, as though her brain was shutting down, leaving her in a dream-free darkness. Those bony arms and sunken cheeks – why hadn't they terrified Cat into action?

She sat on the plastic visitor's chair and waited. The doctor came and spoke of rehydration, of damage to her mother's organs. He lifted her mother's eyelids, shone a torch into her unseeing eyes.

Bernice had always meant well; that was the thing that really broke Cat's heart. She remembered the summer her father left, her mother sitting her in the beer garden out the back of The Oak, looking so proud and expectant as she presented her daughter with a glass of weak shandy. She'd viewed these outings as a treat for Cat, planning them excitedly, looking slightly crestfallen when her eleven-year-old daughter showed no interest in trying out a dab of lippy. If Cat could have those afternoons again, she wouldn't be such a sullen, grumpy thing. She wouldn't demand to know, hundreds of times, *what time did Dad say he'd pick me up?*

How often had her mum patted the sofa and declared

happily that *EastEnders* was about to start? She'd never given up, never been defeated by Cat's sneers. And Cat had been a shit, all through her teenage years, taking every opportunity to show her mother how she despised her, how she viewed ending up like her as the very worst thing that could happen.

Why was it only now that Cat was realising how much she loved the woman? Those mascara-caked lashes. The look of contentment every time she lit a cigarette and took her first drag. The unflinching interest in whatever her daughter had to say, even on those days when Cat was feeling morose and was, in truth, being a little ranty and boring.

All night, Cat held the essence of her mother tightly inside her. It was too late. Far too late. Where had she been in the months of lockdown? Time and again, she'd reminded herself that her mother was alone, that really she should talk to her more, see how she was doing. But their exchanges had been cursory: a few words in the supermarket, calls where all Cat really wanted to do was quickly reassure herself that her mother was fine so that she had one less thing to worry about. She'd secretly enjoyed the month when her mother was without a phone and Cat could skip the calls guilt-free.

Cat's preoccupations over the previous months seemed perverse now. The solemnity with which she planned her own future, the devotion she applied to her own intellect. What would these things matter if Bernice were to die? What did anything matter in the face of such pain?

'I'm sorry, I'm going to have to ask you to leave now,' the nurse said at last. 'We need to cap how long visitors can stay, given the situation. I know it's tough, but I promise we'll call if there's any change.'

Chapter 25

The sharp pain as her bottom collided with the table. The lager on his breath, combined with a surprisingly sweet scent emanating from his hair. He could crush her throat on a whim; her arms and legs were feeble sticks. What a terrible thing not to be able to protect yourself. To feel muscular bulk pressing against you and recognise the inadequacy of your own strength. Countless times each day, in quivering moments, Laura would be there once again. The *no* she wanted to say, to shout, held tight within her chest. Frozen indecision. *Stupid little girl. Silly bitch.* She deserved the pounding, shunting brutality of it.

Seeing him again, having to serve him, her hands had trembled, beer slopping onto the bar. A couple of the other customers gave her a hard time, annoyed when she didn't laugh at the quips they made, when she appeared distracted midway through their stories. With each shift, she felt fresh terror at the idea of Terry being the last person to leave. She'd be the same frightened creature as before, she knew she would. He seemed to sense it, to know what she was afraid of. And he smirked. He leered. Told her with his eyes that she wanted it really, that she should be so lucky to have him do it again.

Quit! old Laura shrieked. *You don't have to be here, you don't have to see him. He should be locked up. This was rape.*

But was it? She'd asked him to leave her alone, true. But surely she could have been more forceful? The 'no' she'd wanted to scream, but hadn't physically been able to, was eating her from the inside out, gnawing at her confidence. She'd wanted it over with; had known that the fastest way to make him leave was to screw her eyes shut and breathe through the pain as he tore his way inside her. She hadn't fought. She'd let him do it. Could he have taken that as consent?

No. He'd known she hadn't wanted it. He'd known it was only terror preventing her from kicking, biting, doing any-thing she could to get away. These things were palpable with every brutish thrust. It was rape. He'd raped her. But it was his word against hers.

More than once, she'd asked Roger to wait with her until it was time to lock up. And back at his house, under the gaze of dead Pam, looking out from multiple picture frames, she'd screwed him with a desperate lunacy. Better that than to be alone. She didn't have to let the encounter with Terry define who she was. Her body could be a tool, an instrument, a gift. Offering it up of her own volition could leave her exhilarated; this was action, choice. She was choosing to make others happy. Roger thought her to be in love, and spoke of her with derision. He could brag, he could boast, but he knew she'd keep coming back. He'd just never know why.

So, it was with a now-familiar nausea that Laura parked her-self behind the bar for her Friday night shift. She felt ready to face Cat now, but it had been difficult to start with – holding the secret of what happened felt like a betrayal of their new friendship. She'd never be able to describe what happened, would never speak her humiliation out loud.

Laura rested her elbow on the bar and wondered, guiltily – how much misery did she have to endure before she could once again think of herself as a good person? There were moments when she thought she might simply walk away from this life of penance. Call her London friends. Have a drink. At such times, she felt she might be able to leave her unhappiness here in this smoky bar. It shocked her, imagining the relief of it.

Something Fat Al was saying made her to pay attention. '... in St Luke's. Skirt up and knickers down when she was found. Shat herself, is what I heard.'

'Like when I found her in the yard that time. Puke all in her hair,' Roger said.

'You're talking about Bernice?' Laura asked. 'Has something happened?'

'Sparko on Borough Road.' Fat Al gave a sanctimonious headshake. 'Just lying there on the pavement, had to be carted off in an ambulance.'

Roger took a sip of his Guinness. 'Had a hard time of it, that one.'

Fat Al nodded. 'All those years it took to sort her legs out. Shame. She was a stunner before.'

'The way Terry used to knock her about,' Roger whispered. 'Me and Pam saw him drag her out of The Bell by her hair once. Didn't care who saw. Laid into her right there and then in the car park.'

Fat Al and Roger both stiffened, and Laura could tell

without turning to look that Cat must have arrived. Unbidden, she remembered the scrawny girl that walked the corridors of their old school. The other girls used to recoil from her, making a deliberate performance of it – *stay away, she'll give you AIDS*. They called her all manner of filthy names. *Ho. Slut. Slag. Stig. Stigger. Skank.* How had Laura failed to recognise such things as bullying? She'd not revisited the memories until very recently, because they hadn't seemed important, it was just kids being kids. At the time, she'd chosen to believe Cat was somehow complicit, that it was a game she could have stepped away from at any time.

Bernice as a mother. Terry as a father. How it ached to revisit her memories of Cat with this new understanding. What pain those dead eyes must have been concealing. It seemed as though her whole life Laura had been guilty of a failure of imagination. She hadn't been able to comprehend the lives that Cat, that Bernice, had lived. By choosing not to see certain things, she'd inhabited a world of comfort and calm, while all around her people suffered.

'I'm going to have a fag while it's quiet.' Cat sat on the stool next to Roger, who immediately offered his packet.

'You're smoking again?' Laura asked.

Cat nodded. Her hair was swept over one shoulder, a luxurious mass. And it was incredible to Laura to see the woman she was now, to know that she had survived and that she remained defiant.

'I heard about your mum,' Laura whispered, when Cat joined her behind the bar. 'You don't have to be here, if you don't want. Me and Dad'll manage.'

'I need the money.'

'How's Bernice doing?'

Cat lowered her eyes. Up close, there were signs of tiredness on her face, her skin lacked its usual glow. 'She's improving slowly. They had to operate on a gastric ulcer and her liver is damaged.'

'I'm so sorry. If you ever need a lift to the hospital, do let me know. I'm happy to take you, any time.'

Cat smiled her thanks at this offer and looked as though she was going to withdraw from the conversation, to perhaps wipe down the bar so that she didn't have to continue talking. But then she seemed to change her mind. She looked Laura in the eye. 'I let her get this bad.'

'No, Cat, you're not responsible for her.'

'But I could have been kinder.'

Laura touched Cat's shoulder. She wasn't supposed to, they technically ought to be standing further apart, but there was such vulnerability on Cat's face, even though Laura knew that if the customers dared say anything, Cat would be more than capable of turning and giving them a withering takedown.

'I've been preoccupied, I neglected her.' Cat was managing to keep her voice unnaturally even.

'It's going to be okay,' Laura said. 'Think in small steps. Do one thing at a time. Otherwise you'll be overwhelmed.'

Cat sighed. 'Do you mind if I tap your lover boy up for another fag? I'll get to work after that, I promise.'

Laura nodded. 'Of course. But I mean it – we'll work out a plan. We can find her an AA meeting. And I can pop along and visit her whenever your tied up with uni.'

Cat bit her lip. 'That's kind of you. But this is for me to sort out.'

It was a newly established habit that Martin would leave Laura and Cat to close up Friday nights, once the empties had been gathered and the tables wiped down. They'd lock up and have a private drink, just the two of them, and after that, Laura would run Cat home in her Fiesta. Cat could sense that Martin was deeply wounded at being displaced, but, in truth, she preferred conversation with Laura. She didn't have to *perform* for Laura, now that she'd learned to separate her from the girl of her memories.

'Here you go,' Laura handed her a glass of Coke and joined her at the bar.

It had been a quiet night, the hours stretching out as Cat answered eager enquiries about her mother's health. A surprising chunk of their regulars were opting to stay away. A couple of them had died.

'How are things going with that married man?' Laura asked. 'You don't have to talk about it if you don't want. I just hope you're being supported, that's all.'

Cat lit a cigarette, even though she'd overdone the smoking out of boredom and was feeling a little nauseous. 'He ended it with me.'

'Oh, goodness. I'm so sorry.' Laura tilted her head, obviously hoping Cat would say more. She had to fight a rising sense of humiliation – being the other woman, an affair ending ambiguously – these all sounded so pedestrian to Cat, when what she'd had with Daniel had been anything but.

'I wasn't expecting it.' Cat was aware of her voice starting to crack and paused to take a deep breath. 'I thought he *needed* me. Which, with hindsight, is bloody ridiculous, because he has a career, a family.'

Laura reached across and patted her arm.

'But I believed in what we had. And I believed in the way he made me feel – like I could do all the things I wanted. Like I was worth something and could actually make a difference if I tried. But it was all illusions.' Cat looked down at the carpet. 'Sorry.'

'Do you not think – maybe – that it was a little inappropriate for him to become so intimate with you? He was your teacher.'

Cat looked up. 'It wasn't like that. He's not some kind of *student shagger.*'

Laura took a sip of her fizzy water. 'I'm sure he's not. It's just, he should be encouraging you to feel capable in your own right. That's his job. What you're describing sounds like dependency.'

Cat straightened up on her stool and lit a cigarette. 'I don't expect anyone else to understand. He didn't make me dependent. He made me feel capable, actually. Capable of doing the things I really wanted.'

Laura opened her mouth to say something else, but then seemed to think better of it. She folded her hands in her lap and gave Cat a gentle smile. 'I don't think you've ever told me what it is you want from university.'

Cat flicked her ash. 'I need to do something about inequality. I say that fully aware that it's a grandiose, selfish thing to come out with – more about my own ego than helping others. But I have to believe that I can make some kind of difference, that I can make things easier for girls born into the kind of life I had.'

'Wow.'

'I know, right? Fucking ridiculous.'

'Not at all. But it sounds kind of scary, setting your sights on something so big.'

'It *is* scary. But then I think of Mum. She could so easily be dead. And no one besides me would care. All the pain and suffering, a life getting by on just the scraps. I can't live an apologetic life like that. The insignificance of it makes me want to scream.'

'I think you're doing Bernice a disservice. She's brilliant. She's always been kind to me, and I'd be devastated if any-thing happened to her. Perhaps in her own way, she's making the world a better place.'

This was almost too hard to hear. Cat stubbed out her fag and put her face in her hands. She wanted to believe that Laura was lying, speaking the kind of polite, hypocritical nonsense that teenage Cat and Daniel used to scorn the middle classes for. But her tone was free from the sugariness of platitude. It sounded to Cat like there had been real love in those words.

'Hey.' Laura was off her bar stool, wrapping Cat in a hug. 'I'm just—'

'Cat, you can cry. It's okay.'

And she did want to surrender to it, she really did. She wanted to believe that people like Laura were genuine, alive to the humanity of others in the same way that Cat was alive to their faults. But ever since she was a teenager, she hadn't been able to shake the belief that well-off people, girls like

Laura who had *nice things*, lived in a kind of collective illusion. A storybook world where even the baddies had hidden good qualities. Cat could only believe in the world she saw. A life of bruises. Of long shifts on your feet that still didn't prevent the phone getting cut off.

She needed Daniel. Maybe that was dependency after all. But it wasn't as straightforward as craving his touch – she needed the hot, angry certainties of her teenage self, something only Daniel seemed able to bring forth.

'Shall I run you home?' Laura asked.

Cat nodded. She knew she needed to stop wallowing. Perhaps tomorrow she'd wake up and find she'd recovered a fragment of her former drive. Perhaps she'd be compelled to look at her books and would feel some of her old excitement. She hoped so.

Chapter 26

Bernice smoothed the sheet covering her as she saw Cat approach. She wasn't quite sure how long she'd been in hospital, but it felt like weeks. After her stomach op, she'd been moved onto a ward and the racket was doing her headache no favours. The woman opposite had been coughing her guts up for hours. Some crazy bitch further down the row kept shouting for a nurse, then forgetting why. Bernice felt like shit. Her whole body was heavy and every time she thought of food, her mouth filled with watery spit that announced the imminent danger of vomit.

Cat arrived, eyes roving across the drip, the plastic curtain, the doctors' notes attached to a clipboard. Even though there was so much Bernice ought to say, she felt strangely subdued by her daughter's presence. She wasn't sure how much the doctors would have told her. Did Cat know what a mess she'd made of her body? She hoped that she could spare her at least some of the knowledge – the poor girl had enough to worry about.

Her daughter plonked herself down in the visitors' chair, she was wearing a mask, but her eyes were crinkled, as though she was attempting a smile. 'How are you doing today?'

'I'm right as rain, love. Thank goodness they let you visit – they're barely letting anyone in at the moment.'

'I've been in a couple of times before, but you weren't awake.'

'It was lovely of you to come though.'

'Do you remember how you ended up here?'

'I . . . ' In truth, Bernice remembered very little about that night. She'd had a few drinks in the afternoon, while getting ready – a small bottle, filched from the supermarket. She hadn't had a single clean skirt, so she'd worn her work trousers, drenched herself in perfume because the boiler was on the blink and she hadn't fancied a cold shower.

She remembered Laura telling her she'd had too much, refusing to serve her anything other than tap water. After that, Fat Al had bought her a couple at The Bell. Then nothing. Nothing until some doctor was murmuring away about God knows what and she just wanted everybody to shut up so that she could sleep.

Cat proffered a carrier bag. 'I had to go to your flat to get you some clothes. I'm not sure if they'll let me visit again, so I wanted to be sure you have everything you need.'

Bernice felt her body pinch with shame. Memories of the flat were hazy, but she knew it must be in a right state. 'Oh, Cat.'

'Don't worry. I'm not going to lecture you. I took a load of laundry to do at James's, and in the meantime, I've brought you a few things of mine you can borrow.'

'Thanks, darling. I'm sorry to be such a nuisance – I know you must be busy with the studying and everything.'

'They're talking about sending you to rehab,' Cat said. 'But the wait is going to be a joke.'

By the hollow, frightened look she glimpsed, Bernice could tell that it hurt her daughter to even say *rehab*, to have the feel of it in her mouth.

'I could give it a go, I suppose,' Bernice offered.

Cat leaned forward, her voice little more than a whisper that barely penetrated the mask. 'You agree with them? You think you're an alcoholic?' She was trying, so hard, to be matter of fact, but Bernice could see the terror in her eyes. The thing was, Bernice really didn't know whether her daughter was more afraid of an admission or a denial.

She swallowed the saliva pooling in her mouth. Breathed deeply to try to stave off the feeling that she was about to puke. It took a few moments to get herself back under control. 'I don't wake up with the shakes or anything. I just take it too far, I suppose. Always have. Once I get going, there's no off switch.'

'I should have done something sooner.'

'Don't be silly, love. It's not down to you to look after me. You should be cracking on with the studying, making new friends.'

Cat sighed. Her gaze on the drip stand; Bernice found it so hard not being able to see the rest of her face.

'What is it?' Bernice asked.

Cat shook her head. 'It's nothing. I'm just relieved, that's all.'

'No, something's bothering you. Tell me,' Bernice said. Headache be damned, if Cat needed to vent her frustration, then the very least Bernice could do was lie here and take it. She'd manage somehow.

Cat made several false starts – about to speak, then changing her mind. Bernice waited. When she finally began, her daughter's voice was low, controlled. 'It's just, being able to walk again, recovering from the accident, took such a long time.'

Bernice nodded. The months she'd spent in this place still haunted her – the hours lying completely still, her legs, her back, seized with pain.

Cat adjusted her mask, took a big lungful of air. 'I was happy to be there for you. I know I went on about university, exams and all the things I was missing. But you were my mum. Things couldn't have been any other way.'

Bernice felt her eyes sting. 'You were an angel. Poor darling.'

'But it seems like you're going out of your way to try to undo all that work, every single night of the week.' Cat's voice was quiet, disappointed, and this was somehow far worse than if she'd opted to shout, to give Bernice the angry mouthful she deserved. 'And I just don't understand why. I wish I could, because then, maybe, I'd know how to help you.'

Tears slid down Bernice's nose as Cat looked away, down at the floor. Back when she was a teenager, Cat had come to the hospital every day, even though the bus ride was a right pain in the arse. There had been days when Bernice felt unable to talk – when every breath was focussed on withstanding the pain – but Cat had simply curled up in the chair and read her book. Never any complaint about coming all this way for a few wasted hours.

Bernice must have been a right sight, bandages everywhere. Operation after operation. And she'd been grouchy, she remembered that, too caught up in her own discomfort to thank her daughter for the trouble she was taking, or to apologise for the exams she'd missed.

Now she wanted nothing more than to sleep. Even a week of bed wouldn't be enough to overcome this tiredness of hers. But she needed Cat to believe everything was going to be okay. She'd do anything to put a stop to the embarrassment and misery she'd inflicted on her daughter.

'I'm just passing the time,' Bernice said. 'I try not to be a nuisance. I won't give you any more trouble, I promise.'

Cat's body tightened. Her fingers, resting on her lap, pressed into the flesh of her thighs. 'But why don't you want *more*? Why aren't you grateful for the extra years of life the doctors gave you? Four years of hard work, for you and for me. Then, the minute I move out, you're back propping up the bar.'

'Cat—' She reached for her daughter's hand.

'I'm sorry.' Cat jerked her arm away. She shook her head. 'Don't listen to me. I'm not blaming you. I know I've been self-involved. Too busy to pay attention to what was really happening.'

'That's enough, darling. You've got nothing to blame yourself for.'

Cat sighed, pinched her eyes closed for a moment. 'I know you don't mean it. But sometimes, when I see you pissing it up, it's like you're sticking two fingers up at me. All those years I gave to your recovery – you seem so willing to throw them away, to undo all the good work.'

'Darling. I never—'

'And the way you hover round Dad, after everything—'

'I don't—'

'You *do*, Mum. Every Friday, following him to Martin's—'

'I come to Martin's to see you, sweetheart.'

Cat was silent, the uncertain expression on her face so very like those times as a girl when she'd sit at the window waiting for Terry's van to arrive, to be taken away. Bernice wanted to scoop up this older incarnation of her daughter. To somehow transmit with her body just how much she loved her.

If she could only make Cat understand that when everything else blurred into grey insignificance, her daughter remained, her outline bright and clear in the fug of Bernice's mind. She was the single thing in Bernice's whole sorry life that felt worthwhile. Bringing her into the world, sticking by her, doing the best she could – these were the only things Bernice had to feel proud of.

She reached for her daughter's hand. 'I come to Martin's to see you.'

Chapter 27

'I hope you didn't think it was wrong of me, suggesting this,' Daniel said, once Cat had locked the club's front door and re-joined him at the bar.

'You shouldn't text me. I told you, James snoops,' she said. Something about her expression conveyed distance, but she was trying to maintain her smile.

'I know,' he said. 'But I didn't like leaving things as they were. I mean, we're adults. We don't have to break off contact completely, we can still be friends.' He hoped it was true, but already he could feel desire wrapping around his spine. He felt strangely broken every time he looked at her.

She sipped her Coke. 'I read the chapters you sent me.'

He felt a familiar jolt of excitement. 'And?'

'They seem timid compared to some of the conversations we've had. I know you're writing about the early years, but you could really draw out the themes that are still relevant today. I mean, we know the white underclass very rarely found common cause with slave rebellions, but I don't think we've even begun to understand why. There would have been so many benefits to these two groups engaging with, and supporting, one another, so I'd I think you could go a bit further in interrogating the systems that kept them apart.'

Daniel nodded, even though he was stung. In truth, he'd imagined Cat praising the chapter. He'd weaved in quite the range of primary sources and at times he thought it almost read like a thriller. But she was right – he needed to find a unifying thread that would give the work contemporary resonance. For a moment, he recognised the absurdity of having a student critique his work, but this was swiftly replaced by an aching sense of nostalgia, memories of working at the kitchen table in his mother's council flat. As maddening as it was to hold back, to refrain from touching, Cat's presence brought with it a strange reassurance.

'Do you have your computer with you?' Cat asked.

Daniel nodded, removing it from his rucksack and opening the file. She went through the text with him, suggesting additions and proposing one or two areas he might cut.

Fixing their gaze on the screen protected them from the intensity of eye contact and he felt his heartbeat slowing, his breath returning to its normal rhythm. Braving a side-glance, he saw that Cat's shoulders had relaxed and her face was animated with real engagement and interest. Her hair was loose, a thick curtain flowing down her back, and her olive skin had darkened in the summer sunshine. She had no idea how attractive she was. It was one of the things he'd loved about her.

'I can't wait to start reading your work again next term,' he said. Her essays the previous year had reminded him why he got into teaching in the first place. The perspective was always so different from the well-worn arguments normally trotted out by undergraduates.

Cat turned to face him, her eyes hard. 'I am going to do it,' she said. 'I'm going to graduate.' She continued to stare at him, a challenge in her gaze.

'Of course,' Daniel said. Although strangely, her fierce tone made it feel less plausible.

She gave him a curt nod and reached for her cigarette packet. He felt something inside him unfold itself, and for a moment experienced pure rage at the unfairness of it all. Why couldn't he have her? Why did duty have to mean denial, suppression?

'I've really missed you,' he said.

She looked surprised, but hopeful too. And seeing that struck a blow, deep inside his guts. He could sense her desire – it sent ripples through his body. He reached out and touched the side of her face.

And then he was kissing her. The bliss of giving in. He snatched at her clothes, almost brute-like, but she was kissing him back. She wanted him. Nothing else mattered. He lifted her from the bar stool and carried her over to the battered old sofa next to the fruit machines.

After they'd had sex, the exhilaration quickly dissipated for Cat. Just one month ago, she'd been heading into Portsmouth, full of excitement at the understanding she expected to reach with Daniel. She'd been offering herself, without attaching terms, and she expected to see joy and relief. *I've never wanted anything as much as this,* he'd told her.

But then he'd rejected her – that was the stark truth. He'd turned away from the intensity of their connection at the very moment Cat had chosen to embrace it. It left her doubting everything, flattened by loss. In the weeks that followed, she'd picked over her memories – the unprecedented ease with which she'd been able to speak of her family; the depth and range of their coffee conversations.

She remembered one of their early dates, him asking what she planned to do after her A-levels. He'd been so appalled when she shrugged and suggested 'an office job'.

'You're the brightest person in our class,' he'd said. 'Imagine yourself on your deathbed, seventy years from now. What kind of life would you have wanted to live? What things would you hope to be proud of? Don't leave all the opportunities for mediocre fuckers.'

It had been revelatory, thinking of her life as something to be occupied and savoured. Until that point, she always thought in terms of *getting by*, *making a living*. Enduring, rather than enjoying. She'd always feel grateful to Daniel for helping her shed the downtrodden mindset gifted to those with upbringings like hers.

But she'd been strict with herself since the library dumping – shouting down every whisper of hope that he might change his mind, that he'd realise how essential she was to him. She refused to engage in delusions, refused to behave like her mother – and then he'd texted her, suggesting a get-together. *Was* this a relenting? Had he decided he wanted an affair after all? Much as she craved clarity, she was too afraid to ask, and this left her feeling debased. Really, he should explain what he wanted without her having to prompt him.

He smiled as he returned from the toilets, handing her a wad of toilet paper to wipe herself. 'It's been so wonderful seeing you,' he said.

Cat stood up, putting her knickers and shorts back on. 'You too.' She meant it. She'd felt such creeping desolation after their last meeting; even this uncertainty was better than that.

She locked up the building and parted ways with Daniel in the car park across the road. Again, she considered asking what this encounter meant, but couldn't muster the courage to frame the question. If she tried to extract some kind of pledge from Daniel, to seek assurance that he was committed to her, he might retreat. So she avoided the question, accepting the ambiguity he'd created with a cheerful demeanour, even if that meant she was debasing herself.

James met her in the hallway when she arrived home. He'd recently resumed his Sunday lunches at his parents' house and she was startled to see him back so early. 'I brought back some leftover apple pie, would you like a piece?' he asked.

'No, ta. Maybe later.'

He hovered over her as she sat on the stairs and removed her sandals, flexing her toes and inspecting a blister.

'I thought we might do something this afternoon. Maybe a walk along the Downs?'

Cat sighed. She really didn't feel like it. It was getting so hard to play her part, to act as though she believed in her life with James.

'What have I done, Cat?'

'What do you mean?' She looked up at him, starting to feel uneasy. She'd been uniformly declining the social invitations put forward by his friends, perhaps knowing that this was bringing a confrontation ever closer.

James's forehead was creased as he gave her an appraising stare. 'It seems like you're in a snit with me all the time at the moment.'

She felt a coldness in her belly. Over the years, she'd constructed an array of narratives to try to assuage her guilt over taking so much from James without truly loving him. She did at least try to make him happy, instigating sex whenever she sensed he wanted her to, biting her tongue and listening as he blathered on about his work. But all these self-deceptions crumbled away to nothing. She was using him for his money and that made her a shit.

She put her head in her hands, unsure of what she might say, what she ought to do next. She wasn't sure she had the energy to go on pretending.

'I work so hard to support you,' James said. 'Anyone else would be so grateful for the life you have, for the opportunities I'm giving you.'

And there it was. *Grateful*. Just as she had started to feel remorse, he'd undone it in a single breath. *Grateful*. The word implied so much about the gulf between them and how he saw her.

She stood up. 'Grateful?'

He sighed. 'Not many men would pay for their forty-year-old girlfriend to play student.'

'*Play student?* Are you fucking kidding me?'

He put a hand on her arm, his jaw set, eyes cool and unrepentant. 'Okay. Bad choice of words. But you know what I mean. I don't think it's fair to shut me out like this. Not when I'm doing so much to help you.'

'Right.' She reached into the back pocket of her shorts,

pulling out the wages she'd taken from Martin's after cashing up. 'Here.' She thrust the money, two tens, towards him.

'Cat—'

'Go on, take it. We'll have to agree a repayment plan for the remainder.'

'I don't want your money.'

'But that's what it all comes down to, doesn't it? Take it.'

'Cat, calm down, please.'

She stepped in closer, pressing the notes against his chest. They fluttered down to the carpet and Cat stared at them, feeling indignant, yet somehow ridiculous.

'What the hell's the matter with you?' There were two deep lines between James's eyebrows.

She lifted her arm, imagined the satisfaction of slapping his face, anticipated the look of shock that would appear on his face.

'Seriously, Cat.'

She pictured her mother, the wild light that filled her eyes some evenings. The spittle that gathered in the corners of Terry's mouth as he ranted, growing in volume, gesticulating as he warmed himself up for his first punch. Standing over her mother as she lay prone on the floor. Delivering a sharp kick to the ribs. Spitting in her hair. *See, Cat. This is what stupid whores get.*

'I'm sorry,' she said. And she meant it. She couldn't justify going on living with James, it was cruel to him and her dependency was damaging her in ways she'd only just begun to understand. The moment the scholarship and loan payments landed in her bank account, she would leave. No more excuses.

Chapter 28

The first thing Cat noticed, was how much healthier her mother looked. Her hospital stay had lasted almost three weeks, and during that time she'd gained a little weight, enough to soften the gaunt angles of her face. When she walked, it was with purposeful strides and she was noticeably more upright, as though her spine were a string that had suddenly been pulled taut. It shocked Cat to realise just how she'd come to accept the drunk version of her mother. How crumpled posture and dreamy detachment had become expected and familiar.

Bernice was wearing the jeans and T-shirt Cat had loaned her as the two of them attempted a gentle walk around the estate. It was August and the car park outside her mother's block was chaotic, with children chasing one another and yelling, careening around on bikes, while unattended younger siblings whined for attention. They headed to an older street of privet hedges and flower beds, escaping the shadows of the flats.

Without her usual heavy foundation and thick eyeliner, Bernice looked like a much younger woman. 'Got the sack, finally,' she said. 'Nice of them to do it while I was in hospital.'

'Bastards.'

'I'll have to see about that Universal Credit, while I look for something else. Gonna be tricky without a reference.'

Cat nodded. She was trying, so very hard, to give her mother her full attention, but her chest was tight with apprehension. James had been distant and snappy that morning – punishing her for yesterday's outburst. Should she put an end to things by confessing to not loving him? Pack her things and move in with Bernice? She looked at her mother and tried to weigh up whether a houseguest would make things better or worse. It would complicate Bernice's benefits claim, Cat realised. And it might deprioritise her on the waiting list for therapy.

'You all right, love?' Bernice asked.

'Me? Yes, fine. Just wondering what I can do to help.' She took two cigarettes from her packet and offered one to her mother.

They both stopped walking for a moment as they lit up.

'A cup of tea here and there, maybe,' Bernice said. 'Bit of company, that's all I need.'

Cat exhaled smoke, the stark simplicity of her mother's wants shaming her. If she'd been more attentive, this most recent hospitalisation might not have happened. Not for the first time, she asked herself why it was so hard to spend time with Bernice. She spent her evenings talking to an array of different people at the bar. When she was being paid to do it, she could be expert at filling silences, at creating an atmosphere of warmth and fun. Yet these skills always deserted her in Bernice's presence. Why? There was an aversion there – she tried to suppress it, to argue with it, but it was a heavy stone inside her.

The thing was, she really did love her mother, feeling an

almost animal devotion that defied logic. Bernice was toler-
ant, gentle, so it was entirely irrational for Cat to feel such
unease in her presence.

'I will be your bit of company,' Cat said, smiling even
though she felt her body rebelling at the idea of long, uncomfortable hours in the bedsit; the joyless duty of it.

'I'm not going to fuck up this time,' Bernice said. 'I'm going
to be like you. Starting again. I'm gonna remake myself into
one of those sexy but dignified older-woman types. Maybe
I'll even come and join you at uni.'

Cat must have shown some of her surprise on her face,
because her mother erupted into deep, throaty laughter.

'Your face. I'm only joking, darling.'

Cat laughed too, did her best to make it sound convincing.
It occurred to her that she'd never be able to view Bernice
objectively, to see her as a woman with her own possibilities,
her own wants, desires and needs. It was impossible for Cat to
separate the woman in front of her from images of Terry kicking her on the floor, from drunken wailing and the months
in hospital that had so brutally ended Cat's adolescence. For
so much of Cat's life, Bernice had personified everything she
didn't want to be.

'Can I ask you something? It's about Dad, so you don't have
to answer. Why did you stay with him? I don't mean at the
beginning, but later, when he was shagging around. Why put
up with his bullshit, his violence?'

Her mother winced. 'Difficult to answer, darling. There
was a time when he made me feel like I was everything.
Stepping into a pub, on his arm, I was somebody. Little me,
not a word to say for myself, but people envied me.'

'But when he hit you – surely the magic left then?'

'I was young, darling. And things were different in them days.'

Cat knew she should stop. There was a cruelty to her questioning; it was the wrong time to be delving backwards. 'But once I was old enough to realise what was happening – did you not worry, about how it might impact me?'

Bernice sighed, taking a long drag on her fag and flicking the butt into the road. 'I don't know what to say. Maybe I was frightened of being on my own, I don't know. I just thought our lives would be better if he was with us, that's all. What's brought all this on? That James hasn't laid a finger on you, has he?'

Cat shook her head. He may have restrained her a handful of times, but in those moments she'd been frantic, a snarling animal perhaps only seconds away from violence.

'What about that Daniel fella? Seen much of him?'

'No.' Instantly, Cat conjured Daniel's face. It struck her now how guilty he'd looked when he told her he missed her. The sex had taken on a mechanical, joyless quality, as though Daniel hadn't celebrated the act, but rather despised himself, despised her.

For a moment, Cat anticipated the relief of confessing what had happened. Of giving voice to the growing realisation that she'd been used, and perhaps would allow herself to go on being used. But she couldn't bear the idea that it gave her something in common with her mother. How sternly she'd resisted it – her whole life. The idea that her greatest worth lay in her body, that she was part of an economy trading in fuckability.

For years, she told herself that she offered James something unique, that she provided a kind of happiness. *This is what grown-up relationships are*, she'd insisted to herself. Anything, rather than believe the ugly truth, that she paid for her bed and board with sex and compliance. She used James and he used her in return. The idea that things might one day become so transactional with Daniel was truly abhorrent.

They reached a crossroads and started looping back towards the flats. Cat tried to forgive herself for how little she was enjoying her mother's company. She wasn't rushing the encounter, was doing her best to be interested and warm. It used up unfathomable amounts of energy, but she was doing it all the same.

When they reached the flats, she hugged Bernice goodbye and insisted she take her half-full fag packet. 'I'll pop by and see you tomorrow,' she said.

'Only if it's not too much bother.' Bernice's eyebrows were pinched, but Cat saw fear skittering through her eyes. Her mother was terrified of slipping back.

Chapter 29

When Daniel arrived at Martin's a week later, Cat realised she'd been watching out for him all along. He hadn't told her he planned to visit; there was no reason to expect him to randomly turn up.

For a moment, his appearance felt like a gift, a reprieve from the oppressive weight of the past fortnight. She felt as though she might cry. Conversation at the bar quickly petered out as the regulars searched her face, curious about what was written there, perhaps alerted to the presence of secrets.

'Sorry to show up unannounced,' Daniel whispered. 'It was kind of a spur-of-the-moment thing.' He took a seat on a bar stool and removed his mask. He looked so pleased to see her. How easy it would be to believe he was devoted to her, unable to stay away. She'd indulged in countless daydreams. *I've reconsidered. It's not fair to my wife to stay with her, loving you the way I do.*

But still there was an uneasiness in Cat's stomach – she remembered the charm her father could put on for her mother, those nights when it suited him to claim her. Every time, the most tender joy would light Bernice's face as she rushed towards her own humiliation. *This is it*, she seemed to be saying to herself, every single time. *This will be the night he comes to love me again.*

Cat poured Daniel a lime and soda. She hadn't told him about Bernice's most recent hospitalisation, she realised. They'd sat together the previous week, going through his book, and her own mother's near-death experience hadn't come up. She felt a sudden urge to share it all. A tiny part of her wanted to shock, to see some trace of disgust on Daniel's face. But she couldn't say anything in front of the regulars. They were all so hungry for details. It was universal among heavy drinkers, this desire for degradation, to hear tales of passings out and shittings of pants. Only then could they reassure themselves that they were different, their own problem didn't compare.

Ignoring their grumbles, Cat was ruthless in shooing away the others and locking up at two on the dot. Climbing back up the stairs, she felt apprehensive. *Why was Daniel here?* She wanted to believe her friendship was the draw, that he wanted to laugh with her, hear her opinions and be the person who consoled her. But she was no fool. And if she really believed he was trying to use her, it would sour her memories and she'd be undone.

'I know it was wrong of me to just turn up,' Daniel said. His eyes searched her face a little too intently, seeking out some sign that she was pleased to see him. 'How are you?'

She'd do her best. She would try to be just friends, because if it worked, their conversations could continue and she wouldn't have to deny herself his encouragement, the energy that he alone fuelled in her. 'It's been a rough month. My mum basically drank herself into a coma. There's liver damage, plus an ulcer that's eaten its way through her stomach lining. But even after all that, she still doesn't have a place in rehab. They sent her back to her flat, to the same life she was living before.'

'Oh, Cat, come here.'

As he embraced her, she rested her head against his chest and inhaled. Beneath the woody notes of his aftershave, there was the softer, more familiar smell of his skin. Whenever she was this close, she could be sixteen again – absorbing his ideas, his outlook, with a teenage urgency. She was the girl who believed hard work and talent would be rewarded.

Memories of their time together were the bedrock of all her desires for the future; she wanted to shield them from any souring, from taking on a sordid quality that even now she could feel rising up and polluting everything. But where had he been, these past few weeks? If he was a real friend, she'd have felt able to call him, to confide in him without the sense that she was transgressing, breaking one of many unspoken rules.

'They only let me visit her in hospital because they thought she was dying.'

He pulled away from her, two deep grooves between his eyebrows. 'That's outrageous. Why do their policies need to be so inhumane? Honestly, it's like the government are using this pandemic to make cutbacks and introduce control by stealth.'

She felt a wave of sadness as she took a seat on the bar stool next to him. Perhaps he was right, but he was missing the point. She needed empathy for everything she'd been forced to confront and feel, for her pain to be seen and soothed. The memory of her mother's curled form, skeletally thin on the hospital bed, was still so close to the surface of her mind. She kept returning to it, and every time, she felt the horror anew. Yet she could tell that Daniel was on the cusp of a diatribe about the government's mishandling of the pandemic, and couldn't help feeling an aching disappointment that he didn't realise how unhelpful it would be for her to hear.

'It really is so unfair, isn't it?' he continued. 'Everyone is being impacted in different ways. I know I'm one of the lucky ones, able to work from home. When I think of the army of delivery drivers out there on zero-hours contracts—'

She couldn't endure it. Couldn't enact this parody of their former relations. 'Why are you here, Daniel?'

His eyes widened as he stopped talking and regarded her. 'I wanted to see you.' He sounded almost hurt, and something about this annoyed her.

'So, we're not working up to rutting on the sofa again?'

For a moment, he looked as though he'd protest; then he dropped his gaze. 'Look, Cat, I miss you. I know it's wrong. I know I shouldn't have come here. I didn't plan it. But I couldn't help myself. I can't stop thinking about you.' He looked up, reached across and tucked a strand of her hair behind her ear.

How easy it would be to surrender. To take the comfort of his skin against hers, losing herself in memory, in dreams. But there was the image again: her mother's fragile body, suspended between life and death. Sunken cheeks. It was the antithesis of all her fantasies. It was real.

'I assume you didn't tell your wife you were coming to

spend an hour with an ex? You made up some bullshit excuse, right?'

He swallowed. 'It's for me to face that guilt. You don't have to worry.'

'But you're betraying me too. You decided you didn't want a relationship with me, but here you are, a second time. What am I supposed to think? I mean, are you changing your mind? Do you want us to be together?' Even as she said the words, she felt a jolt of electric possibility. *Might he say yes?* For the briefest second, she was able to imagine it. The joy of no longer needing to hide. Lie-ins at the weekend. Reading the papers in bed. Conversations beginning at breakfast being resumed over dinner. And what dinners they'd have: sitting opposite one another, talking non-stop. It could have been so good, that's what hurt the most.

Daniel broke eye contact, looking over at the row of spirits. This was the truth of where they were now. They could only find joy when they evaded confronting certain things. She would be left waiting for those moments when Daniel found his way to pretending, to self-justification.

She could lean forward and kiss him. She knew he'd respond, embracing his own immorality for a few precious minutes. Part of her wanted it to happen. She ached to surrender herself to his words, to delight in the idea of him missing her.

She slid from her stool and took a step towards him. Heard him gasp as she kissed the side of his neck. Already, his hand was at her waist. She lifted his chin and kissed him on the mouth. He responded with his whole body, pressing himself towards her, abandoning himself to the urgency of the moment. She savoured the heat of his mouth, the sound of his quickening breath.

She pulled away. 'Have you changed your mind?' she asked.

'What do you—'

'Or is this just sex? Here and there. Whenever the urge takes you. Is that the pattern we're establishing? I'd like to know.'

He took her hand and squeezed it. 'No, Cat, you know it's not like that. God, you know how much I respect you.'

'But not so long ago, you were telling me we couldn't see each other any more. And I accepted it, Daniel, even though it devastated me.'

'I didn't mean for anyone to get hurt.'

'Then why did you *use* me?' Her voice crackled. 'You must have known how easy it would have been to tell myself you were changing your mind. You left me feeling stupid and cheap.'

His took his lower lip between his teeth. 'I just ... It feels so wrong turning away from something so perfect.'

She sighed. 'But it can't be perfect, Daniel. Not when you have a wife and kids. I understand it's complicated for you. But I can't be here, waiting for those occasional moments when you manage to tell yourself it's okay.'

He looked at the floor, his shoulders rising and falling with each breath. 'You're just so bloody hard to give up.'

She raised an eyebrow. 'I'm a person, Daniel, with my own wants and needs that don't suddenly disappear whenever you feel guilty.'

Even now, she felt little pinpricks of doubt. Need she really deny herself the pleasure of seeing him? What was her second year at university going to feel like, now they were simply lecturer and student?

She looked him square in the face. 'Come on. I need to lock up. I'll walk you to your car.'

Chapter 30

When James returned from Sunday lunch with his parents, Cat still wasn't home. It may have been on the early side, but an uneasy feeling crept across his skin. He remembered her coming back the previous week, the split second of shock that passed through her eyes at him being home earlier than expected. Whenever James inspected the memory, he became riled by Cat's obvious lack of pleasure. She'd averted her eyes from him, holding her face in a carefully neutral expression, almost as though she was guilty about something.

He poured himself a glass of coconut water and considered whether he might make the most of the sunshine by lying out in the garden. Shops and cafés were open once again; yet he had a strange listless feeling, aware that for the past few months he hadn't really done anything memorable. There had been walks, interminable walks. He started each morning with a weights session in the garage and put in solid half-hours on his stationary bike. But when people asked what he'd been up to, he had nothing to say.

Cat was leaving him to his own devices more and more. It was something his colleagues would most likely envy; yet there seemed to be a disengagement behind it that riled

James. It felt too much like contempt, as though she was indifferent to what he might need or deserve.

Enough, he told himself. They should go out. A trip to the seaside perhaps. Maybe have afternoon tea somewhere quaint. He needed to reassure himself they were still a couple – the urgency of the feeling shocked him, and it struck him that all this time he'd been lonely. Ironic, when they'd been spending more time together than ever before.

He loaded up the car with beach towels, sunscreen and bottled water. He went through Cat's drawers and found her bikini – it must have been over a year since she'd last worn it. He remembered their Cyprus trip with fondness. They'd hired a villa and had swum naked in the pool. Things could be good again. He'd make it so. He'd chase these unsettling feelings away.

James made the short drive into town with the air conditioning pelting full blast. There was a car park just around the corner from Martin's and he parked the Golf and walked over to meet her. If she still had customers, he'd maybe look up a few places to eat on his phone while she got rid of them.

When he reached the club, the gate leading from the street into the small yard was closed. He pulled at it but found it was locked.

He sent her a text. *Where have you got to? I've decided to whisk us off to the beach.*

She responded quickly. *I'm still working. There are a few stubborn buggers at the bar, but I should be home soonish.*

He put his face to the bars of the gate and looked up at the top floor. The windows were closed, the heavy velvet curtains drawn – it looked as though she'd locked up already. His body stiffened as he reread the message on his phone. She was lying to him. For several moments, he stood there on the pavement. The sun seared the crown of his head and he felt sweat trickling down the side of his face. She was lying.

He started typing out a text. *I'm outside the building and you're not here.* His finger hovered over send. But he decided it might be better to wait for her at the house. Text messages wouldn't cut it, he needed to look into her eyes as he asked about her whereabouts. He didn't like this sensation of doubt, but he'd know, as soon as he looked at her, whether she was telling the truth.

Striding back to his car, he was aware of a restless energy rising up through him. He felt as though he could break into a run, shout at the top of his voice. Why pretend to be at work when she wasn't? He longed to hear something that felt true. To laugh at what a huge, silly misunderstanding it had all been. But there was a cold feeling in his middle. If a friend had told him their partner was lying about their whereabouts, James would pity the poor bugger, assuming an affair was to blame.

He reached his car, but for the moment felt unable to drive. Had one of Cat's filthy customers taken her home? Was she fucking them in some scuzzy little bedsit? Or – the thought occurred to him – could she still be inside Martin's? The fact that the curtains were drawn struck him as a little odd, now he thought of it. He could see the gate from here, so he opened the car windows and sunroof and waited.

As soon as he let his mind explore the possibility of infidelity, things began to click into place. How apt the phrase was; he almost heard a click inside his head as everything he knew and suspected solidified. It would make so much sense. The volatility of Cat's moods wasn't down to anything he'd done. It hadn't been his fault. All along, there had been a third party in the shadows, manipulating her feelings. It felt like being kicked, this idea that she should care for someone else. Care enough that her mood was brought low. Most of the time, he could suppress it, but every once in a while, he'd feel a creeping certainty that her innermost places remained just out of his reach.

He couldn't think like this. It *wasn't* his fault. After everything he'd done for her – rescuing her from that council dump, putting a roof over her head – she was letting another man fuck her.

And suddenly, there she was, a man at her side. He was tall and well built, wearing denim cut-offs and a plain white T-shirt. James couldn't be certain, but he was pretty sure he'd seen this man on Cat's computer screen during one of her online lessons.

Cat and the man crossed the road, walking side by side. All she had to do was shift her gaze to the right and she'd spot his car, but she was deep in conversation and didn't look his way. Once they reached a blue people carrier, they stopped walking. Cat's companion put a hand on her bare shoulder and the two of them were still for several moments, speaking in low voices. The man kept his hand on Cat, as though touching her was his right, as though he was staking a claim somehow.

Then, he leaned in to kiss her. James was transfixed, watching their lips draw closer, but at the last moment, Cat turned her head. She did so slowly, more in sadness than in anger.

The man said something, and she rested her cheek against his chest as he wrapped his arms around her.

James exhaled. This man was Cat's lover. Even though she'd rejected his kiss, something in her bearing seemed entirely new and strange – there was a suggestion of intimacy, of pliability, that James had never seen before. His Cat, his majestic Cat, almost looked needy.

The man got in the car and drove away, and Cat lit a cigarette, walking straight past without seeing James or noticing his car. He could have called out to her, but opted not to, simply watching her cut through the car park, joining the footpath that led to their estate.

She'd been cheating on him. With one of her lecturers. It perfectly explained the change in her behaviour. What a fool James had made of himself, trying to understand what had been upsetting her. She must have seen how worried he was, yet she let him continue wasting his time, trying to unravel possible reasons for her unhappiness. James was almost shaking at the ingratitude of it, the sheer nerve. She'd lived in his home, had accepted his food and his money, yet she'd been sneaking off to sleep with this other man. She hadn't troubled to keep any of her old fun or enthusiasm back for James; it was as though he meant nothing to her.

It took several minutes before he was able to start the engine and drive home. His mind was filled with visions of the man's hand over Cat's breast. Of him penetrating her. He didn't spare himself. He let the pictures keep coming, feeling a nauseating sense of confirmation. She was so beautiful, so alive. He remembered how proud he'd been in the early days of their courtship, but how his happiness contained a splinter of fear that he could never measure up to such a woman, that one day she'd be stolen away by someone brighter, someone as beautiful as she was. Now that day had come.

She arrived home minutes after James had backed the car onto the drive and positioned himself in the hallway, ready to confront her.

'So, the seaside. I suppose I could take an afternoon off from studying, enjoy the sun.' She sounded cheerful, there was no trace of the emotion he'd witnessed in the car park.

His heart was thudding. The life he'd made with her had collapsed within a single afternoon. The moment he opened his mouth, there would no longer be a future together. No changing her mind about children. No more holidays or excursions to look forward to. He'd be back to living in this house alone. He hesitated as he glimpsed the sorrow that would await him, but it was only for a moment; his anger was strong enough to carry him through.

He drew closer, looked her in the eye. 'You were with a man. I saw you. The two of you were shut in Martin's together.'

He saw a flicker of uncertainty pass over her face as she returned his stare.

'He's one of your lecturers, isn't he? You're fucking one of your teachers, that's why you're so bloody obsessed with university.'

Was she going to have the gall to deny it? He wouldn't stand for that. He wouldn't let her make any more of a fool of him. He'd march her through that door right here and now. He'd shove her belongings into bin bags and throw them out into the garden.

She said nothing and her eyes became shiny with unshed tears. James folded his arms and waited.

'We're friends. He was helping me with—'

'Do not lie to me, Cat. You can pack your bags right now if you think you can insult my intelligence by coming up with some kind of tall tale.'

He saw her breath catch. 'Okay.'

'You're admitting it? You're having an affair?'

She lowered her head, tried to rest it on his shoulder, but he moved away.

'Answer me,' he demanded. 'I need to hear you say it.'

Cat's face drained of colour; her voice was almost a whisper. 'It happened at my interview. I'd pinned so much on university—'

'You've been living in my house, fucking another man for a *year*?'

He saw her swallow as she braved eye contact. 'Daniel had the power to decide whether I was let in or not. I thought I had to go along with it. It was stupid. I don't know what I was thinking. But I was scared that if I—'

'Having sex with him? That's how you got your place?' James's voice was fierce. Almost inhuman. He was glad of the rage inside him, of how it was holding him up, giving him strength.

Cat winced. Her neck was flushed, her eyes screwed shut as a tear slid down her nose. 'It sounds so transactional. But I didn't know what would happen if I said no and I supposed I panicked. I'm so sorry.'

James stood very still. His mind was still taunting him with images of Cat groaning beneath the other man. His hands running along her skin. Did James believe her account of coercion? Or was this abject manner nothing more than an act? Was she, in fact, laughing at him?

'And now?' he demanded. 'You've got your place. Why are you still seeing him? Why is he coming to that god-awful bar to meet you?' He recognised an urge to grab her by the shoulders. To shove her. It scared him, how much he longed to hurt her, to make her feel some of his own suffering. She'd reduced him to something quite pathetic.

She looked up and he saw something righteous burning behind her eyes. 'I didn't ask him to come. I've been trying to put a stop to it. I think he's finally got the message.'

James rested a hand against the wall. This was all too much. An hour ago, he'd been imagining the fun afternoon and evening they'd have at the beach. He knew he should be unpicking things, making a cold assessment of what was true and what was lies. But his mind was consumed by images of the man's hands on Cat's body. 'The absolute bastard,' he said.

Cat wrapped her arms around his middle and looked down at him. Her eyelashes were still damp and when she spoke, her voice was little more than a whisper. 'I've felt so dirty, so worthless. I thought about telling you, hundreds of times, but I knew you'd be upset. I wanted to spare you and deal with it on my own. Please – don't end it with me, not over a stupid lack of judgement. Please.'

'I'm not upset, I'm angry. Angrier than I've ever been in my life.' He was shouting, something he never did.

Cat sighed and squeezed him tighter. 'I'm so sorry. It's just – you know how much getting a degree meant to me. I've been paying the price for a stupid moment of panic.'

James broke free from Cat's embrace and went into the kitchen, pacing across the wooden floor. If Cat was telling the truth, the man was an absolute shit. To abuse his power in that way. To manipulate Cat into offering up her body. *His* Cat! The calculation of it, to play on her fears, dangling what she wanted in front of her until she gave herself to him. James sank down onto the floor, resting his back against the cleaning cupboard.

'Are you okay?' Cat asked. She was wearing a plain black vest and denim shorts, hair up in a simple ponytail. Her face was blotchy and she'd never looked more vulnerable. Christ. If she was telling the truth, then she'd been harassed within the last hour, that man thinking he could lay his hands on her.

He rubbed at his face. Tried to get a grip. 'We'll end this. Get him sacked, like he deserves.'

Cat swallowed. Shook her head. 'We mustn't do anything rash – they could kick me out, for going along with it. And I'm sure I've got through to him now. I made him understand that nothing can happen. It's finished. He won't try anything again. Honestly, it's finished.'

James stood up, feeling he'd regained his perspective. At long last, he'd discovered what was wrong with Cat. It was nothing he'd done. No shortcoming of his. He rested a hand on the small of her back. 'They wouldn't dare,' he reassured her. 'We'd create such a stink. If it got out that lecturers were trading places for sex, there'd be an outcry.'

Cat looked down at the floor. 'Honestly, James, I've handled it. I laid down the law with him, he's not going to attempt to see me again.'

He placed his hands either side of her face, forced her to

meet his gaze. 'You're the victim here. You've been taken advantage of and we're going to make it stop. That bastard is going to pay.'

Her eyes were still watery. She looked frightened in a way he'd never seen before – it was unexpectedly arousing. She was his, still his.

He pulled her close. Kissed her neck. 'My beautiful, beautiful Cat.' He had a vision of her laying on a bed, her hair splayed out across the pillow, closing her eyes in disgust as this other man explored her body with his hands. It was wrong of James to find the image so compelling, but he needed to touch her, to reclaim every part of her for himself.

Although she didn't respond to his kisses, Cat didn't push him away either. He was behaving like a brute of a man, tugging her shorts down, hoisting her up onto the worktop. He made love to her subsumed by images of the other man doing the same. It was wrong. It was disgusting. And after his powerful climax he felt so overwhelmed with guilt that it was a torment to have her look at him.

He cleaned himself with kitchen roll. Buttoned his flies. He felt strangely close to weeping. He could just about manage to give her a consolatory pat on the arm before fleeing to the bathroom.

Chapter 31

At Bernice's first therapy session, they talked about the habits inside your head. The way you sabotage yourself by believing things that simply aren't true. *Not drinking means you have to stay at home, bored and alone. The only way you'll have a bit of a laugh is by loosening up with a few voddies.* They'd warned it would be hard, clearing your mind of these lies. And they were right. She was dealing with something far trickier than thoughts; they were more like truths, deep inside her bones. Ignoring them felt like those unbearable seconds walking out of a shop, one or two things she hadn't paid for inside her coat, her insides gripped with terror.

But binning off old habits was possible. That's what they told her, anyway. She tried to imagine herself as one of those older women you saw in coffee shops, expensive-looking haircuts, laughing with their grown-up daughters as they nibbled overpriced cakes. It felt such a long way from who she was now, and there was part of her – the sensible part, perhaps – that knew she'd never be that kind of sophisticated, *together* woman.

She took the staircase at Martin's slowly, breathing deeply to try to silence the voices inside her own head. *Why are you bothering? Name one person besides Cat who'd even give a shit if you drank yourself to death.* She'd have a glass of water. Hopefully one of the regulars would know their way around the benefits system and might be able to help her make sense of it all. If she was really lucky, someone might take a shine and offer to do the application for her. She was already two months behind with her rent and the gas company was threatening disconnection.

There were two of them at the bar: Pete and Ian. She smiled, hoping they might ask if she'd like a drink, or at the very least offer her a ciggie. But they drew themselves up awkwardly, sharing a quick glance, and Bernice found that she didn't have the heart to try to flirt. News must have got out about her hospital stay. If she was in a better mood, she might have been able to laugh at how uncomfortable these fellas looked. There was perhaps nothing they feared more than a self-confessed alkie, here to spoil their fun, to kill the atmosphere by reminding everyone of what they might one day become.

It was Laura behind the bar. The girl looked surprised, but managed to pull herself together more quickly than the other two. 'Bernice, it's good to see you. What can I get you?'

'Just a tap water, please.'

She saw Pete and Ian exchange another of their snide looks. Ian's fag packet was right there on the bar. In fact, he had two of them, stacked one on top of the other. 'Spare a ciggie, Ian?' She looked him directly in the eye and smiled, making it almost impossible to say no. He deserved that. She was going to be sure to smoke at least three before she left here. The packet Cat had insisted she take was long gone, and the support group leader told her she needed to search for small things in her day that she could be grateful for. Today, Ian's fags would have to do.

Laura placed a glass on the bar. Instead of water, it was full to the brim with Coke, but she didn't ask for money.

'Thank you,' Bernice whispered. As she lit the cigarette Ian had grudgingly handed over, she felt her eyes welling up. The truth was, she hadn't felt ready to leave hospital. She'd been looked after there. Meals arrived on trays and there were no dishes to wash. It sounded ridiculous – she was a grown woman – but it made her feel the way her grandparents had, when she was a young girl visiting their calm, ordered home that smelled of lavender. She needed just a bit longer. To get her energy back. To be sure she wouldn't slip.

There had been one moment in her whole life when she'd been brave, when she'd felt like she'd be able to handle whatever nasty things might happen. It was when she'd made a stand over Gary, the man her mum moved in to their crowded flat when Bernice had been sixteen. He'd been far too eager to wallop Bernice and her brothers, seeing the tiniest things, even a look sometimes, as *damned cheek*. 'It's him or me,' Bernice had said, and her mother had simply laughed and told her, 'Gary puts food on the table.'

Her friend Janet said she could stay, and Bernice had lived two glorious nights in that calm house of hers, until Janet's mum put her foot down. After that, she worked her way round friends' sofas for months, lugging every item of clothing she owned in a bin bag, aware of the eye-rolls of parents whenever she asked in her politest voice whether she might use the washing machine. Later, she'd had to turn to men.

Older men, with their own houses, who never let her have anything for free.

'How've you been?' Laura asked Bernice. She realised the bar was silent. Pete and Ian hadn't resumed the conversation they'd previously been having about football; they kept staring at Bernice and exchanging glances loaded with derision. There was no sign of Terry; she'd heard he was working on a job in the next county, which thankfully meant he wouldn't be popping in for lunchtime drinks for a while.

Bernice picked at a nail. 'Giving myself a headache trying to work out what this Universal Credit is all about. It's all different since last time. Any of you know anything about it?' She looked hopefully at the others.

Pete drew himself up. 'Never claimed benefits in my life.'

Bernice looked stung and Laura felt a surge of anger on her behalf. 'Aren't there advisors who can help you with that sort of thing?'

A weak smile. 'They make you do everything online these days. Fat lot of good that does me. I don't know the first thing about computers.'

'But there must be somewhere you can go to ask questions, get help?'

Bernice shook her head. 'There used to be a Job Centre in town, but they closed it.'

'Well, if you like, we can go to the library after my shift and use the computers there. I'll see if I can help.'

'Oh, would you, darling? That's ever so nice of you. I don't want to be a nuisance.' Bernice's eyes were wet, and Laura felt a stab of sadness. Such gratitude over a bit of googling.

It was the very least Laura could do. Unbidden, she felt the sensation of Terry's breath against her neck, heard his raspy breaths building to a crescendo of grunts. She tried to suppress it, before it made her tearful.

'No problem. And my dad left the *Post* in the kitchen, if you wanted to have a look at job ads?'

'That'd be a massive help. Thanks, love.'

By the time Laura had kicked the others out and locked up, she felt thoroughly exhausted. She'd been feeling unwell on and off, and if she hadn't offered to help Bernice, she would have curled up in bed the very moment she got home. Her muscles were longing for it; she could imagine doing it, getting beneath her hot pink duvet without even pausing to remove her smoke-infused clothes.

'Can we pop into the newsagents on the way?' Laura asked as she locked the club's outer gate and she and Bernice stepped out onto the street.

'Of course, love.'

'I've got a weird kind of bug or something. I feel sick all the time, but if I get hungry, it's so much worse. I can only control it by grazing on biscuits, which isn't doing my hips any good.'

'Not preggers, are you, darling?'

'What? No!' Laura stopped walking for a second. She and Abdul had been trying for years; it wasn't possible. She tried to do a calculation, but her periods had been so irregular since prison that she couldn't be sure how late she was. Three weeks maybe? Nothing unusual, these days. In her old life, she used to write a little 'p' in her diary, then skip ahead fourteen days and draw a small heart to indicate her most fertile day. Now, she never bothered keeping track.

Bernice smiled and patted her on the shoulder. 'It's just that was always a sure-fire sign with me. Those first few weeks I'd be nibbling away. I'd have to get up in the night and eat bits of cheese, like a little mouse.'

'It's just a bug.'

'Got sore boobs by any chance?'

Laura inhaled. Her breasts had become unbearably tender. Just wearing a seat belt was uncomfortable.

As she stepped into the newsagent's to buy the much-needed chocolate digestives, Laura felt pressure building in her skull and was grateful to focus on the mechanics of selecting the biscuits, queuing and paying.

She felt the pull of Boots, just over the road, and longed to abandon her plans with Bernice to go and buy a test. She needed to know, needed to eliminate the possibility at the earliest opportunity, because what a torment it was to believe even for a moment that such a miracle could be true if it wasn't.

If it was true – and it couldn't be – but if it *was*, she wouldn't know who the father was. All her life she'd longed for a tiny baby to care for, to love. Yet if the wondrous, unlikely event had come to pass it would be Roger's baby, or Terry's. Which, of course, meant it was going to be fatherless.

'You all right, love?' Bernice laid a hand on her elbow.

Laura forced herself to smile. 'Yep. Let's head on over to the library and get cracking.'

'Get one of them biscuits down your neck first.'

Laura nodded, opening the packet right there on the street

and taking the small, slow bites that the last few days had taught her were necessary to avoid retching.

She'd never noticed before how libraries had at some point taken on a destitute, unkempt air. The place didn't look like it had been decorated since she'd come here as a girl, her mother leading her by the hand and gently pressing upon her stories that always seemed just a little beyond her reading level, her breath catching with impatience whenever Laura struggled. There was a man parked on the sofa who was clearly mentally ill, muttering to himself, wearing a blazer with food stains spattered across his lapels. And most of the people sitting at the computers had a desperate air about them, something in their movements, in their strained concentration, suggesting they were looking for hope and not finding it.

'Right,' she said. 'Let's find the application form.'

To start with, Bernice was meek, answering the questions Laura needed to ask her in a quiet voice. There were some details she didn't have to hand, so Laura started compiling a list of extra information they'd need before the application could be submitted. She was glad of the task, the need for concentration that distracted her from speculating about a possible pregnancy.

After a while, Bernice appeared to grow in confidence, asking questions of her own. 'How long until I get the first payment?'

Laura did a quick search. 'They say to expect it to take six weeks.'

Bernice's face was ashen. 'Six weeks? What do they expect me to live on until then?'

Laura looked at the screen. 'It says here about food banks . . .'

'Six weeks? I'm fucked.'

'Have you got any savings?'

Bernice snorted.

'I could lend you some money. Cover the necessities.'

'That wasn't what I was getting at, darling.'

'I know you weren't.'

Bernice's head was bowed, two spots of pink spreading out across her cheek.

'Let me lend you something,' Laura said. Maybe for a moment she was proud of her own generosity. But as soon as she noticed the feeling, she was back in the club, Terry's pelvis shunting into her, her backside bruising against the table. This was the man Bernice loved, how preposterous for Laura to pretend to be her friend. 'Honestly,' Laura added, 'I can afford it. Let me give you five hundred. It's right there, sitting in my account. My mother won't even take rent off me.'

Bernice's back appeared to shudder as she took a breath. When she looked up, her eyes were brimming with tears. 'I *will* pay you back.'

'There's no hurry at all.'

'But I will. I don't want to take it, I really don't. But I don't know what else to do.'

Laura swallowed, picking up her shoulder bag and logging off the library computer. She found herself unable to look at Bernice. She couldn't witness the degradation that she was somehow contributing to. As much as she liked and pitied the woman, she wanted her gone; she couldn't endure this unearned gratitude a moment longer.

'You're a wonderful person,' Bernice said. 'And if you *are* preggers – well – that's one lucky, lucky baby. I think you'd make a fantastic mum.'

Chapter 32

For a couple of days, Cat thought she'd got away with the preposterous lie. James was subdued, pulling his face into a hurt expression every time she met his eye. But he didn't allude to her betrayal, and so neither did she. She wasn't sure what had possessed her in the moment of discovery – she was a mere three weeks away from the start of term and her first loan payment. *Why lie?* For the past year, she'd been telling herself she was going to abandon her relationship with James, imagining the relief of casting off her dependency. No more boring dinner parties or having to pretend to be interested while he wittered on about his work. No more sex for the sake of appeasement, or having to smile patiently when he interrupted her thoughts.

But she was faltering. She told herself it was down to the pandemic – there was talk of a second wave of infections and her bar money might abruptly stop at any point. Yet beneath this very real concern, she was aware of a deeper fear. She'd never set out on her own before – she despised women who were afraid of such things, but as she contemplated an irrecoverable break, she felt panic bubbling in her throat. A broken boiler. The theft of a purse. Annoyances to some, but catastrophic for the likes of her. Experience had taught her there was no romance in poverty, no satisfaction to be had in carefully parsing what little money was left after rent payments, visiting the supermarket at the end of the day in search of the heaviest discounts.

If she were to stay with James until she graduated, she wouldn't have to worry about such things. It was only two more years, and they would pass so quickly, she knew they would.

Towards the end of the first post-discovery week, while she was still vacillating, she received an email from the university marked 'private and confidential'.

Dear Catherine,

We have received a troubling allegation about the behaviour of one of our lecturers, Daniel Simmonds, in relation to yourself. We'd welcome the opportunity to discuss this with you further, as part of our investigation. Please advise whether you are available to attend a meeting via Zoom next Tuesday at 3 p.m. It will be with myself and a member of the HR team. You are very welcome to arrange for someone to accompany you in this meeting, should you wish to do so.

I very much look forward to hearing from you.

Best wishes
Professor Louis Richardson
Dean, School of Humanities

James must have formally complained to the university. Amidst the dismay, she felt a glimmer of admiration – it was a bold step. She still wasn't entirely sure whether he believed her version of the affair, so perhaps this was his way of calling her bluff and forcing the truth to the surface.

But it meant Daniel was now going to discover she'd implied manipulation, that she'd framed herself as a victim. How could she possibly explain it? Her face burned as she imagined owning up to the lie, having to describe her cowardice. How he'd despise her, and he'd be right to do so. Her fabrication could cost him his job if she didn't immediately rebut everything James had said.

She'd handle things. She'd attend the interview and make sure that she left Daniel's boss in no doubt that his behaviour had been beyond reproach.

She fired off a quick response, expressing surprise and consternation at the idea of a complaint – because, certainly, she had no grievances at all, Daniel had been entirely professional – but confirming she'd join the meeting so they could clear everything up.

She said nothing to James, but in the days that followed, she had the sense that he was watching her closely.

On the day of the appointment, James was participating in one of his online team meetings upstairs – he was still working at home three days a week, an arrangement that looked set to continue into the new university term. Cat could hear the odd burst of forced laughter from the spare room and felt an unexpected pang of affection – James tried so hard to make others like him and sometimes this made him appear so desperately vulnerable. He had the capacity to keep looking away from the truth, to retreat into the myth of their life together. Sometimes it was hard to tell whether staying or leaving would be the worse cruelty.

She opened her laptop and clicked the link, joining a man and a woman on screen.

'Aha – Catherine. May I call you Catherine?' The Dean was a white-haired man, wearing a beige jacket and tie, sitting in a book-lined study.

Cat nodded.

'Excellent, excellent. I'm Louis. We're joined by Michelle, one of my HR colleagues. Are you okay if we start? Maybe you're waiting for someone to join you at your end?'

'It's just me,' Cat said in a quiet voice. She had wondered whether it might be better to conduct the meeting from a coffee shop, but knew from the many tedious Tuesdays gone by that the team meeting James hosted normally ran to ninety minutes. Better to stick to their normal routine to avoid him asking questions.

'Okay, well, we're meeting today because I received a rather concerning email from a man claiming to be your partner,' said the Dean, fiddling with an expensive-looking pen. 'He alleges that you've been somewhat coerced into an intimate relationship with one of our lecturers.'

Cat said nothing.

The HR woman, youngish with glasses, inclined her head towards her webcam. 'No one's in trouble at this stage,' she said. 'But I'm sure you'll understand, we do have to formally investigate. I wonder if you might be able to tell us about your relations with Daniel Simmonds? Help us build a picture.'

Cat folded her hands in her lap, smiled. 'There's not been any coercion at all. He's a good friend. We've known each other a long time, we actually went to sixth-form college together.'

Both faces on the screen nodded sympathetically.

After a short pause, the Dean cleared his throat. 'I understand that Mr Simmonds conducted your admissions interview. Is that correct?'

Cat nodded.

'I'm sorry to ask what may seem like an impertinent question, but was this interview followed by something more intimate?'

Cat swallowed. To deny that anything at all had happened would seem implausible. They might feel the need to go back to James and explore what had sparked his complaint.

'It's not like it sounds,' Cat said, trying to sound as casual and unembarrassed as she could. 'Daniel didn't do anything wrong. We were overdue a catch-up. Like I said, we're old friends – I used to be his girlfriend actually – and so after the interview we had a few drinks. I mean, I would say by that point he wasn't even on the clock, he'd finished for the day. It was an out-of-work social thing.'

There was a collective silence.

Cat's body was alive with adrenaline – she was managing to sound convincing. It wasn't quite the truth, but it wasn't a lie either. 'Look, my current partner is a little on the jealous side. I'm not sure what he said to you, but from my side, there are no complaints. None at all. Daniel is a good teacher and he's been entirely professional. It's not his fault that James feels threatened. I'm sorry James involved you, I didn't ask him to and I'd like to be clear that he doesn't speak for me in any way.'

'I'm sorry to press the point,' the HR woman said, 'but did you have a sexual encounter with Dr Simmonds at your interview?'

'It was *after* the interview,' Cat replied, turning down the volume on her computer's speakers. 'We were catching up. Two consenting adults who knew each other twenty years ago. There's honestly nothing here to investigate.' She remembered that leather booth, the taste of Malibu and the roughness of the grey carpet against her backside. If she had been led to a standard interview room by a stranger, sat opposite them and answered their questions, would she have managed to impress them? The idea that her place at university was somehow reliant on Daniel's compassion prickled beneath her skin.

'Just so that I'm clear, after the interview, you had ... physical contact?' The woman's forehead was furrowed as she asked the question. Cat felt riled by her evident distaste – she seemed like the kind of person who would have joined in shouting the *slag* taunts across school corridors.

'We had consensual sex, at my instigation,' Cat said, her eyes flicking to the living-room door. She could no longer hear James upstairs and her stomach lurched at the thought that his meeting may have finished early, that he might have crept downstairs.

Another pained silence. Still no noise from elsewhere in the house.

'And, throughout your first year with us – did you continue to have relations?' the dean asked. 'I appreciate it's difficult, but we do need to build a thorough picture.'

'We were good friends.' Cat folded her arms, thinking of the coffees that had often been the highlight of her week.

'By that, you mean you met socially?' he pressed.

Cat nodded. 'Here and there. In the canteen, never for more than an hour at a time.'

Another agonised silence. Were they relieved she didn't have an appetite to push this further? Or angry that James's email had forced them to invest time in an unwanted investigation? She willed the meeting to finish, before James looked in on her. If he was done with his team meeting, he was sure to do so.

'Okay, I think we need to circle back and focus on the interview itself,' the HR woman said. 'As you can imagine, we have strict policies around staff conduct, so perhaps you could tell us in your own words exactly what happened.'

Cat quickly rattled off an account of the day. She implied that Daniel had asked her the appropriate questions and conducted the interview formally. She ended with them leaving together, but omitted the after-hours tour – they didn't need to know that Daniel had used his office for sex. 'I just want to stress that I didn't feel coerced in any way. We were both clear that everything after the interview was entirely separate from the university.'

The Dean exhaled audibly. 'Thank you for being so candid with us. Of course, we do have strict policies in place prohibiting romantic or sexual relationships between students and lecturers.'

Cat stared at the screen, a chill spreading through her body. 'But we were a couple previously. I'm not some impressionable thing that was manipulated into it. It's a completely unique situation. There's no complaint. I didn't ask you to investigate *anything*.'

The dean drew himself up straight, adjusted the knot of his tie. 'Be that as it may, we're very keen to maintain a culture of professionalism. All our staff are aware of the policy and the expectations it places on them.'

Cat smiled, even though she was breathless with dread. She had to get this right. 'We're ex-partners – we knew each other as teenagers, long before Daniel would have been subject to any of your policies. Sometimes there are grey areas that require a bit of discretion.'

The silence took on a loaded quality as her interviewers both looked at the screen, perhaps waiting for the other to speak.

'Well,' the HR lady eventually said, 'is there anything else you'd like to add before we conclude this meeting?

Cat shook her head. She thought suddenly of her scholarship – would the fact that Daniel wrote her recommendation invalidate it in any way? She needed the money.

'In that case, thank you for your time.'

Cat closed her laptop at the very moment James walked through the door. 'Who were you talking to?' he asked.

She considered saying Laura, but at the last moment changed her mind. Perhaps here was an opportunity for closure. To put James's mind at rest while she was still uncertain what her living arrangements were going to be.

'The dean at the university. About ... you know ...'

'You didn't tell me you had an appointment.' His eyes burned with indignation, but his voice was cold.

'It was kind of a last-minute thing. But you would have

been proud of me. I gave a really clear account. And thank you – by the way – for contacting them and having my back.'

'Are they going to fire him?'

'They said their investigation might take several weeks. But reading between the lines, I think that's a likely outcome. They kept talking about the policies he violated.'

James didn't quite smile, but he drew closer and put an arm around Cat's shoulders. She was thankful that he couldn't see her face as she contemplated the call she needed to make. If news of the investigation hadn't already reached Daniel, then it was her duty to warn him.

Chapter 33

'Can I top up your water?' Cat asked her mother.

Bernice raised an eyebrow and slid her glass across the bar. 'Good job Martin isn't here to see me taking up a bar stool without spending anything.'

Cat snorted.

'I'm going shopping in a bit. They've got a few jobs going at the petrol station, so I thought I might pop in and ask about work. I was going to see if I could pick up something half decent to wear from one of the charity shops.'

'I'll come with you,' Cat said. 'If you don't mind waiting for me to close up.' She knew her tone was artificially bright, but the gratitude on her mother's face twisted at Cat's insides. So little it took to make her happy. Always so little. She took out her phone and texted the plan to James. He'd become rather insistent about being kept up to date with her movements.

'That'd be nice, darling. My work trousers are ruined and I don't think I ought to turn up in a going-out skirt. A fiver should be enough for something, do you think?'

'We'll sort you out, don't worry.'

Again, a beam of happiness. Cat was only just coming to realise the extent of the power she had over her mother and was, in truth, a little intimidated by it. She couldn't undo the impatient sighs with which she'd greeted Bernice's overtures in the past; couldn't expunge cutting comments she'd previously made. Being with her mother might always feel like an effort, but Cat was doing her best to see her with fresh eyes, to be alive to the woman instead of all the things she symbolised.

'Will they make you wear one of those funny hat things, when you graduate?' her mother asked.

'It's a long way off. I have to earn my degree first.'

'What about when you finish? Have you thought about what you'll do?'

It was just Cat and Bernice at the bar, the handful of other customers had taken tables. Why not confide in her mother? 'I'm going to try to get into politics. I'd like to one day stand as an MP.'

'Darling! That's wonderful.'

Cat couldn't help but smile. 'There'll be a lot of work involved. No guarantees I'd even be nominated. But I want to try. I feel as though it's the one thing I care enough to be good at.'

Bernice proffered her fag packet, but Cat shook her head, knowing her mother probably couldn't afford to spare one.

Her mother lit up and inhaled with relish. 'You know, the more I think about it, James is the perfect politician's husband. He can trot along behind you, carrying your handbag.'

Cat laughed. 'If we were ever interviewed for one of those cringy magazine spreads, he'd be divine.'

'I can see it now, love. They'd have a picture of him gazing at you all adoring. And one of him in the kitchen looking very pleased with himself as he dries the dishes.'

Cat grinned, a little surprised by how accurately Bernice conjured a politician-at-home spread. How easy it was to go on thinking of James in her life, to forget her treacherous plans to leave him.

'What about that lovely Daniel?' Bernice asked.

Although one of Martin's few rules was no smoking behind the bar – that and always accepting any drinks that were offered – Cat took her fags out of her back pocket and lit one. It was quiet and no one would tell on her. 'All in the past,' she said.

Bernice pressed her lips together. 'I'm sorry to hear that, love. I can't help thinking how good the two of you were for one another.'

'We were. But we were children, really. And he's different now. A nice middle-class husband who wants to do the right thing.'

Bernice sighed. 'They all turn out different in the end.'

As Cat took another drag of her cigarette, she registered the persistent unease in her belly. She'd called Daniel on the afternoon of her meeting with the dean, but he hadn't picked up. She followed up with a brisk, *I need to talk to you*, text. But again, no reply. He must be furious with her.

'I guess James has always been predictable,' Cat said. 'I've been lucky, I suppose.'

Bernice wrinkled her nose and Cat felt a pang of protectiveness.

'Well, he's certainly more dependable than Dad ever was.'

'Terry is far from perfect, but I don't regret a minute of the time we had together. I'd do it all over again, because he gave me you.'

Cat paused, not quite sure how to respond. Would it ever get easier, talking to her mother? She felt relieved when she saw one of the other customers approaching with empties in his hands.

Once Cat had called time and prised pint glasses from the hands of a few stragglers, she and Bernice prepared to get going before the shops closed. She stepped out of the kitchen, bag looped over her shoulder just as Daniel arrived at the top of the stairs. He was wearing a green T-shirt, his eyes loaded with anxiety.

'Can we talk?' he said.

Cat looked at her mother.

'It's okay, love, I'll be on my way.' Bernice wore a hopeful smile.

'I'll come and join you. Start off in the hospice shop, then if I'm still not there, go to Cancer Research – they always have the best stuff.'

Bernice patted Cat's arm. 'Take your time.'

Cat stood next to Daniel as the two of them watched Bernice disappear down the stairs. She was aware of his breathing, a barely contained rage rippling through his body.

'Daniel, I—'

'What did you do?'

'It wasn't me. James contacted the university. He saw us, that last Sunday.'

Daniel stared at her, as though he was meeting a stranger for the first time, someone he'd heard unsavoury things about. 'Have they interviewed you about it?'

Cat nodded. 'I tried calling you, but you didn't answer.'

'What did you tell them?'

'They were focussing on my admission interview. I couldn't deny that we had sex. I thought they might want to talk to James, if I did that. But I made out that we only caught up socially *after* the formalities. And I kept telling them we go way back.'

Daniel pinched the bridge of his nose. 'Is this revenge?' he asked. 'Your way of punishing me for not wanting to leave my wife and kids?'

The spite of his words was more devastating than any physical blow. Yet perhaps she deserved it. It hadn't been James's discovery that set things in motion, it was the stupid lie she'd told. She'd painted Daniel as a villain to save herself.

She swallowed, met Daniel's eye. 'I'd never set out to hurt you, you know that.'

He looked down at the carpet and shook his head. 'This is ... I'm screwed.'

Cat didn't know what to say. She considered reaching out and putting a hand on his shoulder, but felt newly shy. Ashamed.

After a prolonged silence, Daniel looked up. 'I have something to ask of you. I know it's unfair, but you could save my career.'

'Go on.'

'Tell them you lied. Say we never had sex. Maybe you and James were arguing and you made it up to hurt him. Or maybe you had a crush and concocted a bit of a fantasy.'

'What?' Cat was appalled. In the meeting with the dean, she'd taken great pains to make Daniel's behaviour appear more professional than it was, and on some level, she'd been expecting recognition for that.

He reached for her arm, but she flinched. Should James feel the need to check on her whereabouts and see them together, things would unravel even further. 'It's black and white, Cat. If I slept with you, I've breached the student relationships policy. I could be sacked.'

Cat sank down onto one of the bar stools. She hadn't known about the policy, about the risk Daniel had been taking. But *he* must have. All along, he'd known what the consequences could have been.

'Daniel, I really want to help, but I can't present myself as some kind of deluded liar.' Even as she said it, she remembered the lie she'd told to preserve her place in James's home. How she'd betrayed Daniel in that moment, depicting him as a predator offering her a university place in exchange for sex. Her breath caught at the idea of him one day finding out, at there being an angry email from James in an evidence file Daniel might have the opportunity to read.

But if she took the fateful step and tried to protect Daniel, would she even be believed? Her classmates had noted how close she was to him. The two of them had been so keen to uphold the innocence of their relationship, they'd never tried to conceal the coffees and lunches they had together. They'd been right there in the canteen for everyone to see.

'I know it's a lot to ask. But trust me – allude to stress, to depression, and everything will be forgiven. As a student, you'll be given a second chance. I won't be.' Daniel's brow was puckered, his impatience breaking through.

Cat felt something harden in her. 'But we're both responsible. You wanted it too. And you never told me it could get you sacked.'

He sighed. 'We're both facing very different consequences. Don't you understand how hard I've worked, how easily everything can be undone?'

Cat lit a cigarette. Daniel hadn't asked her about James's discovery – how he'd reacted, whether she still had a home. This indifference added another layer to her grief, but strangely it also made her feel a little better about not helping him. 'You're asking too much,' she said.

He drew closer. 'Just do this one thing for me. Please, Cat.'

She turned away from him, resting her forearms on the bar. 'Will you at least recognise that you've not treated me well? That maybe you ought to have given me a fair and above-board interview.' If he conceded this much, she'd relent. She imagined the conversation she'd need to have with the dean, picturing his lip twitch in distaste as she told him she'd made everything up. She screwed her eyes shut.

'Cat, can you not imagine the absolute luxury of a stable job for someone like me? Owning a house. Having a garden. Mock all you want, but I worked my way out of that tower block. And now everything is going to be ruined. Not just for me, but for my kids too.'

'But things aren't exactly easy for me either. If James throws me out before my loan payment comes in, I'll be homeless.'

Daniel placed a hand to his temple. And Cat did pity him, in that moment. It would have been better for both of them if they'd never reconnected, if Daniel had never come back to Portsmouth and was working at a university far away from here.

She swallowed. 'I'll talk to them again. Make them understand our situation is unique—'

'It doesn't work like that! You're not going to *persuade* them to overlook this. Cat, come on – please. I don't deserve this. My kids don't deserve this.'

Cat searched his face. She wanted to make him happy. And maybe she deserved to be branded a troublemaker and a liar. If only he'd shown some form of care for her, some empathy for her own situation. Cat could hear the gentle hum of the fridges behind the bar. She realised she was waiting, perhaps for a hand on her shoulder, or a softly worded apology. That's all it would take to topple her resolution. But Daniel just looked at her, holding his body unnaturally still. She was a *problem* to him.

'Daniel, I'm sorry we were found out. But I'm not prepared to tell any more lies. I think I've been very fair to you.'

When he turned and left, Cat realised she was shaking. She was doing the right thing. She'd countered the allegations of coercion that James had made, and now Daniel's bosses had the truth, nothing more. She waited in the bar for a moment, lighting another cigarette, hoping to feel certainty inching up her spine, a sense of rightness. It didn't come. She couldn't escape the feeling that she'd dragged Daniel into something sordid and dirty, that she was to blame, for everything.

Chapter 34

Laura was now the proud owner of a black and white ultrasound image. She hadn't let herself believe in the baby, had steeled herself to be told there was nothing there, but the very moment the technician put the probe to her abdomen, she'd seen a curled form on the screen, a perfect little head, a belly, a spine.

Within seconds, the woman – experienced at allaying fears – had assured Laura there was a heartbeat, zooming in so she could see the rhythmic squeezing for herself. Tears had leaked from Laura's eyes as she watched. She'd even forgotten her pledges for a time, allowing herself to bask in happiness.

The pregnancy had been dated at seven weeks and six days, but when the technician heard about Laura's irregular cycle, she warned against trying to pinpoint a specific conception date. Roger, Terry – the being inside her was too precious to have either one of them as a father. She didn't need to know.

She hadn't told anyone besides Bernice, who squealed with such unaffected joy that Laura was able to believe everything might just be okay. She was angry with herself for her reluctance to tell her parents, for the archaic, un-feminist impulse that made her ashamed to present herself as a single mother.

She'd announce it to them when she had a plan; when she'd decided where they were going to live; when she'd contemplated what kind of mother she was going to be.

She winced as her father blew cigarette smoke in her face. Very soon, this week, she promised herself, she'd start planning her future life. She couldn't endure the idea of a return to marketing, but she knew she couldn't continue working at the bar with everyone puffing on cigarettes, with the jostling that went on Friday and Saturday nights.

She remembered thinking Cat's decision to return to education had been curious, but now Laura found herself looking at teacher training. It was helping others and would certainly be more meaningful than her former career. And because she already had a degree it would only take a year to get the qualification she needed. There might even be grants for single mums. *Single mums.* It felt shocking to think of herself as such, but nothing would dampen her happiness.

She poured her father a glass of red. It was a quiet start to the Friday night shift and his mood was morose.

'Bitch didn't even give me any notice. Just stopped turning up.' He was talking about the cleaner, who Laura had never met, but whose efforts appeared uneven at best. There had been a bogie smeared on the wall of one of the toilet cubicles for over a fortnight now, just thinking about it was enough to make Laura retch.

'Bernice is looking for work,' Laura offered.

'Don't be silly, darling.'

'I'm serious. She's stopped drinking. She'd be reliable.'

Martin looked annoyed. 'What's this sudden fixation all about?'

'What do you mean?'

'This mission you seem to be on, saving the town's dregs one by one.'

Laura swallowed. 'There's nothing wrong with wanting to help people.'

'Well, we're not going to be helping Bernice by letting her guzzle away my profits.'

'I told you. She's stopped drinking.'

Laura noticed a ripple of fear pass over her father's face. She looked over her shoulder and saw Cat arriving for work.

'You talking about my mother, by any chance?' Cat perched on the bar stool next to Martin and helped herself to one of his cigarettes. Laura felt a kind of ache in her centre; the two of them were so relaxed with one another.

'I was suggesting that Dad hire her, to replace the wayward Moira,' Laura said. She didn't dare to meet her father's eye, but she could feel the look of absolute loathing he was giving her.

Cat shrugged. 'She'd be grateful. And – hell – if she does start drinking again, just sack her.'

'We'll see,' her father said. 'I'm not looking for grateful, I'm after someone who can clean.'

Cat responded with a wry smile that left Laura feeling annoyed. Why did Cat always make light of her mother's pain? Laura wanted to shock her with details of the five hundred pounds she'd had to loan Bernice, with the fact that the poor woman hadn't yet received a single benefit payment.

But she said nothing. Of the three people clustered around the bar, she was the outsider and she knew it. She turned away, resting a hand on her stomach. The wonderful thought came to her: she wasn't alone any more.

Although the shift was quiet, trade did pick up as the evening drew on. Her father was busy doing his rounds. He liked to join people at their tables for the length of time it took to tell an anecdote, acting as though he still believed himself to be the wealthy accountant of the past, as though these were guests at a party in his home and he was the beneficent host, dividing his attention equally, making sure no one felt left out. It was so very sad to watch.

'Two pints of Stella, a Guinness and a blow job, please miss.' It was fat Al, guffawing with one of his mates.

'Wash your fucking mouth out.' Cat emerged from the kitchen, bringing his laughter to an abrupt halt.

Laura was frozen, one hand on a fresh pint glass. She hadn't realised Cat was in earshot.

'Just having a laugh, Cat,' Al quickly mumbled. 'No harm meant.'

'Thanks,' Laura whispered, once she'd poured the drinks.

Cat angled her head. 'Are you and Roger still—'

'It's come to a natural end,' Laura said. She hadn't been able to face the thought of sex with him once she'd learned about the baby.

'Thank goodness for that,' Cat chuckled.

Later, as she cleared up, it struck Cat that while always willing to listen to others, Laura never revealed much about herself. Recognising this made her feel strangely disappointed, because she'd come to consider Laura a kind of friend. How she'd looked forward to their calls during lockdown, the walks that had followed, when people had been able to once again meet outside. But could it be a true friendship without reciprocity? Friendship had never come easily to Cat. In fact, the only time she'd had any social circle to speak of had been back at sixth-form college.

'You looking forward to being back at uni?' Laura asked as Cat loaded up the dishwasher with sticky glasses.

'Yeah. Only a couple of weeks to go.' She shut the door and switched it on.

'Is everything okay?' Laura placed a hand on Cat's elbow. 'You've been kind of subdued.'

Cat lit a cigarette. 'Daniel – the lecturer I was seeing – is kind of in the shit. I didn't realise his work has a zero-tolerance approach to staff-student relationships. I mean, I'm the same age as him – it wasn't exploitative or anything. His bosses don't have the right to pass judgement.'

Laura gave her a weak smile.

'Go on. Out with it,' Cat said.

'Okay – fine. It's just, there must have been a *bit of* a power imbalance, knowing he could impact how you performed at university.'

Cat shook her head, annoyed. 'I'm not the victim here. I wanted him. The first time we had sex, it was me who started it. I kissed him. He was only showing me his office, and I kissed him.'

Laura rested a hand on the kitchen counter, inspecting Cat's face. 'But still – he had a choice. He could have walked away.'

Martin burst through the doors, carrying a stack of

empties. The women regarded him in silence as he placed them down on the kitchen worktop. 'I see, I see – I'm the only one around here working, as usual,' he said as he bus-tled out again.

Cat took a drag on her cigarette. She really did need to stop smoking again, save the money. 'I lied, Laura. James saw us together and I made up some panicked bullshit about Daniel coercing me into an affair. Got him so fucking angry he com-plained to Daniel's boss. And even though I made it clear to the university that everything was consensual, Daniel's still going to lose his job. I'm the one in the wrong here. What the fuck was I thinking?'

Laura put a hand on the small of her back as Cat flicked ash onto the saucer she was using as an ashtray. 'Gosh – it sounds complicated. Is there anything you can do to straighten things out?'

'Daniel asked me to deny we ever had sex. But it would mean going back to his boss and saying I basically *invented* an affair. Maybe it's the right thing to do. But surely they'd kick me out for being some kind of weird fantasist.'

'So, as it stands, the university have the truth. Nothing more?' Laura said.

Cat nodded.

'It sounds like Daniel must have known he'd be in trouble if he had sex with you. Yet he went ahead and did it anyway.'

Cat let the words settle and, for the first time, her body seemed to absorb their truth. It was a glorious moment of respite from days of twisting guilt. She'd given the university the truth, nothing more. It wasn't her duty to extricate Daniel at the cost of her own education. Yes, she'd lied to James. But really it was Daniel who set things in motion, by leading her to a bar instead of an interview room.

Cat had never quite been able to separate the adult Daniel from the boy of her memories, from the hope he represented, the feeling of potential sparked by his company. A student and a lecturer. Sex at an admissions interview. Could these things be right, simply because Cat had wanted them? She'd never considered Daniel's responsibilities as a member of the teaching staff – he'd undoubtedly wished her well, supporting and encouraging her. But she'd placed herself at his feet and he'd let her. He'd let her love him, knowing they could never be together.

Chapter 35

Louis Richardson had presented voluntary redundancy as a way out. At first, Daniel was enraged: he and Cat had been two consenting adults, their relationship predating his employment at the university, so surely exempt from its policies.

'I don't see why I can't hold my head up high and fight this nonsense,' he'd barked at Richardson. 'These are completely unique circumstances.'

The Dean had sighed, leaning back in his chair. 'It's your decision. But if it goes to the disciplinary committee, I can't protect you. Things like this terrify them – they have a habit of ending in nasty media coverage.'

'I've done nothing wrong!'

'Maybe not. But think how it looks on paper, Daniel – you were supposed to be interviewing the woman and you end up having extramarital sex. If you're formally reprimanded, you might find it awfully difficult getting another job. In your shoes, I'd leave before the investigation concludes. Everyone knows history enrolments are declining – your departure could look entirely natural.'

'There was nothing exploitative about our relationship. Nothing untoward at all.'

'But she's a student, Daniel. And you're a lecturer. There's always going to be a perception of imbalance.'

Daniel had shaken his head. He'd worked at the university for five years now and the only other complaint about him had come from a fantasist who believed the entire teaching staff were deliberately suppressing her grades.

He tried to secure allies, to speak with a couple of trusted colleagues who he felt sure would agree he'd been wronged and share his outrage. But after a couple of days of embarrassed exchanges, of these so-called friends suddenly remembering meetings they urgently had to get to, he accepted he'd made a mess of things. He filled out the relevant forms. HR sent him an agreement to sign. He cleared his desk, keeping the boxes of journals and research notes concealed in the boot of his car. Soon, the twenty thousand would be in his account.

But what to tell Elizabeth? He'd vowed to do it this weekend, but time was slipping by. Saturday was filled with the usual chores: entertaining the twins while Elizabeth did the weekly shop, several loads of laundry, plus the interminable tidying away of toys. The next day, they went for lunch at her parents, then took the kids to the seafront.

Sunday night, he bathed the twins, then cooked pasta while Elizabeth read them their story and got them settled into bed.

Finally, his wife came into the sitting room and flopped down onto the sofa. They were done for the night, off-duty at last. He brought her dinner in on a tray and they ate, listening to Kendra chatter to herself on the baby monitor. He had to tell Elizabeth. This should be the moment.

'I wanted to run something past you,' he said.

She turned to him. Without her make-up on, she looked

truly exhausted and he couldn't help feeling a surge of guilt. How tirelessly she worked. And she never complained, not even at the height of the pandemic when she often worked entire shifts at the hospital without eating or using the toilet.

'They're cost-cutting at work and they've opened up a voluntary redundancy scheme. It sounds a bit radical, but I was thinking of applying and using the money to finance a year working on the book.'

Elizabeth smiled lightly, but was too tired to be truly interested.

'It might give us more flexibility, save a bit on childcare costs,' he quickly offered. 'Lockdown made me realise just how much I enjoy being with them.'

She raised an eyebrow. 'I guess that could work.'

He was getting away with it; it didn't seem like she was going to probe the decision. He felt the strangest mix of guilt and elation. 'We could just put them in for half-days at nursery rather than full. I could use the mornings to research, pick them up in the afternoon, then do the writing in the evenings when they're in bed.'

Elizabeth nodded. 'If you felt able to work under those circumstances, then it could be good for the twins, having a bit more time at home.'

'I think I'd enjoy it – and it would be nice for all of us. I'll do it, I'll put an application in.' His mind was racing ahead. He didn't have to let on that he'd already agreed to leave his post immediately. Over the next few months, he could head to the library, start getting his research notes in order. He was almost shaking with excitement at just how perfectly this was all working out.

He felt strangely giddy as he took their empty plates into the kitchen. He'd managed to turn an unjust situation with the potential to destroy his career and family into an exciting new opportunity. He *would* work on his book over the coming months. He remembered the fire of enthusiasm when he first conceived the idea, filled with indignation about the dearth of accessible histories of the civil rights movement. How Cat had encouraged him. He felt a deep sadness in knowing that he'd never again talk it through with her, or feel her keen interest as he mapped out the remainder of his chapters. He had to be still for a moment as he rode out the skewering sensation of loss.

She'd betrayed him. She would have denied the affair, said anything he wanted, if he'd left his wife for her, Daniel was certain of it. It was all very well taking the high ground, refusing to lie, but really she'd been piqued at it ending. She'd punished Daniel for trying to do the right thing and preserve his marriage, for making sure his kids grew up in a two-parent home.

At least now there wouldn't be the possibility of him relenting, turning to her for solace in a moment of weakness. She'd been an addiction, the narcotic bliss of her turning him away from everything that was precious in his life. He'd known he was behaving badly, but it had felt so impossibly good.

He remembered the triumph he'd felt when she'd become his girlfriend back at college, how intrinsically linked it was to a feeling of power. Power to define his own future. He'd felt the shadow of those feelings each and every time they were together. No one had believed in him quite like she did. Lately, there had been moments – pinpricks of light – when he could imagine the versions of himself Cat daydreamed into being, and for brief seconds he was there with her.

He was on *Newsnight*, wittily demolishing government policy in an expensive suit. He was signing copies of his *Sunday Times* best-selling book, agreeing good-humouredly to selfies with people in the queue. He had it all in these happy visions – purpose, achievements, drive. He pictured himself together with Cat, lazy Sunday mornings in bed, analysing the papers. The electricity of their thoughts connecting. The sex. The fervour.

He put the kettle on, readied his and Elizabeth's cups. These were fantasies. And yet they were casting a shadow on everything he had, turning pride in his home, in his status as an academic, to dust.

Chapter 36

Eight weeks it had been since Bernice's last drink. She'd like to think she was beyond slipping now, but knew she'd likely always crave it, perhaps spending the rest of her life falling just short of being happy. It didn't help that her benefits still hadn't been paid, that she'd had to go to the food bank and be handed a few boxes of cereal and tins of soup by a very churchy-looking woman who probably shopped at Waitrose. She'd nicked loo roll from Martin's a couple of times, and her guilt about this was a constant burn in her chest.

But today she wouldn't let any of this show, because Cat had invited her for coffee at the home she shared with James. Bernice couldn't remember the last time she'd set foot in the house, but as she took her boots off on the mat in the hall, she felt the same apprehensive feeling. What kind of man put a cream carpet in his hallway? It seemed so unnecessarily fussy, designed to put people on edge the moment they stepped inside.

The carpet spread into the living room, which looked as though it belonged in a magazine spread. There was a fake fireplace, with two potted ferns on top and not a speck of dust to be seen. The only messy area was the long dining table at the far end, which was covered in books. Clearly Cat's domain.

'Sit down! Sit down!' James was smiling widely, but Bernice knew he was never really glad to see her.

She sat in a dark green armchair and folded her hands in her lap.

'I hear congratulations are in order.' James sat on the sofa.

'Huh?'

'Your new job.'

'Oh, that.' Martin was paying her to clean for an hour each morning. Cash in hand too, which was decent of him. It wasn't much, but it covered some food and the three cigarettes a day she was allowing herself. She reminded herself to be polite and gave James a smile.

'All right, Mum?' Cat stepped into the room, hair wet from the shower. 'I'm making a coffee, want one?'

'That would be lovely, darling, thank you.'

Both Bernice and James stiffened again the moment Cat was gone. Bernice was aware of a persistent ticking from the gold-framed clock on the wall. It made her nerves jangle and she fidgeted in her seat. She must make more of an effort to like this man, he provided a lovely home for Cat, and he did seem to dote on her.

'Cat'll be back at university soon,' she offered.

James nodded. 'She's navigated the situation with that Daniel Simmonds fellow rather well. I assume she told you about him?'

James knew that Cat was studying alongside her boyfriend from before? Bernice found herself surprised by this; none of the men she knew would have tolerated such a thing. But these so-called modern men were different, she supposed.

'It sickens me, the thought of him manipulating her.' James appeared to be talking to himself. The disgust in his voice unnerved Bernice, she hadn't marked him down as the kind of chap who'd have a problem with mixed-race couples.

'Oh, it wasn't like that.' Bernice gave him a sympathetic smile.

'What do you mean?'

She was a little taken aback by the intensity of his stare. 'Young love, wasn't it?'

'So, you *do* know about him?'

Bernice laughed. 'Well, I could hardly not know, could I? The chap was always in and out of our house.'

James leaned forward in his seat. His face was white, sickly, but his eyes had a feverish gleam. 'Hang on – you're saying they knew each other back when Cat was still living with you?'

Bernice felt a wave of dread. There was something fierce rippling beneath James's skin. It reminded her of Terry, the very calm voice he'd use before a row, tripping her up with questions that never had a right answer.

'Here we go.' Cat breezed into the room, placing a cup on the small table next to Bernice's chair. She saw James's face and straightened.

'Daniel was your *boyfriend*? You never thought to mention that?' His voice was still so calm.

Cat was silent, clutching her own cup.

Bernice looked at James. His eyes were radiating anger, and for the first time she thought him capable of hitting her daughter. 'It was all a very long time ago,' she offered. 'Cat was little more than a kiddie.'

Cat turned to face Bernice, her eyes wide with terror. 'What have you been telling him?'

'Never mind that, look at me.' James remained sitting, but he spat the words. Instinctively, Bernice stood up, positioning herself next to her daughter.

'You better go, Mum.'

'Let me help, darling, I—'

'Go! Please. It's okay.'

Bernice scuttled into the hallway, tears snaking down her nose as she stumbled around putting her boots back on. She was realising now the scale of the mistake she had made. But she couldn't have known. *How could she have known?*

As Cat stood in the centre of the room, eyes locked on James, she thought to herself how ordered these past few weeks have been, how *pleasant*. She'd started to feel fresh appreciation for the calm he brought to her life, once she'd decided there wouldn't be any harm in staying a little longer.

She placed her cup down on the table. 'Yes, we were girl-friend and boyfriend. But we were seventeen, it doesn't have a bearing on—'

'Of course it does.' James stood up. Some part of Cat registered surprise that his face looked more angry than hurt. 'It changes everything. You weren't manipulated. You've been screwing your ex. That throws a whole different light on everything.'

'James—' She reached for him, but he brushed her hand away.

'I've been so stupid.' He was shaking his head, his eyes wild. 'After everything I've done for you.'

Cat was unexpectedly wounded. Their relationship hadn't been entirely one-way, she reminded herself. She'd tried her best to make him happy, had fucked him frequently and inventively, trotted along to the tedious parties and family Christmases that were so important to him.

'What's he like in bed?' James's face was contorted, ugly and mean.

'I'm not going to answer that,' Cat said.

'How often did you sleep together?'

Cat shook her head. 'It doesn't matter.'

James took a step closer, put a hand on her shoulder as he brought his face right up against hers. 'I can't believe you'd do this to me. I've done everything for you. If it wasn't for me, you'd still be living in that same shithole with your mum.'

Cat didn't have to tolerate this. She tried removing his hand, but he seized her by the wrist. They tussled for a moment.

James was half crying, half growling with rage. 'You were a nothing, a nobody.'

Cat froze. The derision on James's face. He believed it. All these years – *a nothing, a nobody*. She could feel the kernel of resistance, glowing in her middle. She'd done well at university so far. She was capable. She didn't have to be her mother; she didn't have to live the life people expected of her.

'You're nothing but a common whore,' he spat.

She freed her arms and delivered a swift shove that made James lose his balance and fall down to the floor. She heard him take a sharp intake of breath, but for a moment he didn't move. An excruciating silence filled the room. *Common whore.* Cat was shocked, not by the words, but by the sudden realisation that she'd known, maybe for years, that this was how he viewed her. Why hadn't she embraced that truth and let herself see their relationship for what it really was? This contempt was so much worse than anything she'd done.

James propped himself up on his elbows and let out a bitter laugh. 'You're no better than your parents. No better than the yobbos that drink at that godawful bar.'

She kicked him in the ribs, as hard as she could, recoiling as pain shot through her foot. 'I might be common, but at least I'm not a complete cunt!' she yelled.

She drew herself back, ready to kick again, stopping herself only at the very last moment. A hundred memories of her father's face, of the way he towered over her mother, flooded in and sickened her. This was Terry's way; it didn't have to be hers. Trembling, she stepped backwards, almost tripping over the sofa.

James was curled up on the floor, wincing, his breathing ragged. She covered her face with her hands, but James's terrible words were still echoing inside her mind. She could picture herself falling upon him, pummelling his face with her fists. He deserved it.

But she would not be this person. She rejected the primal call of her DNA, refused to believe in fate. She took a few deep breaths and left the room.

'Cat!' His voice was different now. Desperate.

On some level, Cat knew that he would forgive her if she showed remorse. More than anything, he'd want to believe she'd loved him all along, that Cat was a victim and Daniel a predator. But all this was meaningless now that an alternative history was rising up in Cat's mind. *Common whore.* How different her memories looked now.

Her fags and purse were on the hallway table. She snatched them up and she ran from that house as if it were on fire.

Chapter 37

It was an unusually warm September day, and Cat walked for hours, out of the town through country lanes now opulent with foliage, branches overhanging the road creating tunnels of green. She didn't cry. Most of the time, she didn't even think, she simply felt compelled to move, to expend her rage before it poisoned her.

Her mother called, leaving a stilted voicemail asking Cat to call back because she didn't have the credit to keep ringing, but Cat didn't feel able to speak to her just yet. It wasn't that Bernice had done anything intentionally bad; she'd been entirely unaware of Cat's deceptions, so it wasn't fair to expect her to know the right or wrong things to say. But nonetheless Cat felt sharp waves of irritation. How typical of Bernice to be there at the moment of unravelling.

She walked until her legs were almost trembling from the unaccustomed exercise, until she'd smoked every last cigarette in her packet. Gradually, she became calm enough to think of the future, heading back into the town to buy more fags and a can of Coke from the newsagent's, then wandering into the churchyard and taking a seat on a bench. She was sitting to one side of a memorial garden, a small area where poppies and wildflowers grew with uncultivated abandon. It was a place where townsfolk scattered the ashes of their loved ones and in the far corner Cat saw another woman, maybe a little older than her, sitting in quiet contemplation.

She couldn't go back to the house. This wasn't an overreaction or dramatic gesture, an impulse that would fade after a night's sleep. She knew, quite certainly, that she'd never live with James again. It seemed so reprehensible to have been with him for so long, playing a part. That he harboured a sense of superiority wasn't a surprise, but it made their entire history feel coldly transactional. They'd taken what they needed from one another, while believing they were in some way doing the other person a favour. How had it lasted so long? And what damage had it done?

With an ache, Cat remembered a languid Sunday morning near the beginning, resting her head on James's toned chest, feeling a strange combination of joy and intimidation at the spacious master bedroom, the crispness of the pale-blue bed linen, the very fact of the en-suite bathroom. What relief these new surroundings had brought her; how wonderful it had felt to believe that life was becoming less tenuous, that happiness might once again become easy, as it had been with Daniel.

She had started talking about the Iraq War, enraged by what she'd read the day previously about generous reconstruction contracts being parcelled out to American firms.

'Yeah, but the Iraqis are free now.' James had run a finger along her spine as he spoke.

'Free to watch their country being asset-stripped.'

'But surely they're better off than they were under

Saddam?' He'd sounded animated, but there hadn't been any real emotion behind it – he'd been deploying the same techniques he used at dinner parties to make conversations sound more lively than they really were.

Cat had taken a breath, ready to articulate the many thoughts she had on the war's fabricated premise. For days, she'd been turning over in her mind the responsibilities that ought to fall on self-styled liberators, and how these obligations might be codified in international law. But she realised James lacked the capacity to follow. He'd try. But his comments, the questions he'd ask to try to mask his growing boredom, would only serve to irritate her. He was no Daniel.

And it had struck Cat, at the tender age of twenty-three, that the choices in front of her were different from what she'd first believed them to be. This wasn't destined to be a great love, a relationship that saw her sharing every part of herself. But at that point in her life, giving it up would have meant a return to her old bedroom, to walls coated in thick black mould, to Bernice parked on the sofa in her dressing-gown. Did she *have* to love James? Cat had asked herself. She could see how easy it would be to satisfy him. Could she not enjoy the life he offered, even though he might never understand how to make her happy?

Cat looked back on that Sunday and the pact she'd made with true sadness. How very different her life might have been, had she walked away at that moment. Pretences had corroded her from the inside out.

Closing her eyes, she remembered driving her foot into James while he'd been defenceless, on the floor. For a few moments, she'd felt completely out of control. Just like her father. Bile burned the back of her throat. *Common whore.* James had wanted to hurt her. The hatred in his eyes had been astonishing. She could live in his house, but she had to play by his rules, be who he wanted her to be. He deserved the kick after that. But then, didn't her father always have reasons for every violent act? Terry was always *provoked*, afterwards sounding regretful, not at his own actions, but at the slight delivered by the other party, the misstep that occasioned his violence. Perhaps Cat was more like him than she ever realised. Perhaps the rage inside her would swell with each passing year, until one day, she wouldn't be appalled at delivering a kick, she'd be proud.

No. She knew she could be better than that.

Cat ended up at Martin's. She wasn't supposed to know that the sofa in his office, a small room next to the cellar, doubled as a bed on those nights when Martin couldn't face going home to Miriam, his wife. It was her best option for tonight, or just until she found a place she could afford to rent. She wouldn't be able to stand Bernice's fussing if she were to go to her bedsit, and she'd vowed never to ask Terry for help.

Thankfully, it was Martin, not Laura behind the bar. 'Hello. To what do we owe the pleasure?' His face was lit with such delight at seeing her, it caught Cat in the throat.

After closing time, when it was just the two of them, smoking at the bar, Cat didn't quite confide in Martin. Although she felt no shame at admitting her relationship was over, she'd never feel able to tell another person about the scene in the living room. 'James and I are splitting up. I just need a place to stay for a couple of nights while I sort somewhere to live.'

'You're more than welcome to that natty old couch – I might even have a blanket somewhere.' He paused. 'I must say, I'm not entirely surprised.'

'Why's that?'

'There's a fire in you, Cat.'

Cat winced.

'James didn't know what he had,' Martin said, and something in his eyes made Cat feel embarrassed.

She stubbed out her cigarette. 'It's just time to move on.'

'What will you do?'

She shrugged. She didn't feel able to speak of her ambitions to stand for Parliament. She wasn't ready to be glib about it, to joke and treat it as though it wasn't serious. Strangely, the dream had become less abstract throughout the course of the day. She could picture herself putting in hours of unglamorous work; she felt ready for the effort of it, ready to challenge herself. Something about giving up the en-suite bathroom had made her less afraid of failure.

'I must say, I'm a little envious at the idea of leaving things behind. Starting again with a clear slate.' Martin raised his arms in a stretch and Cat saw a corner of his shirt work its way free from his waistband.

'Still fantasising about your overseas bar?' she asked.

'It doesn't have to be a fantasy.'

Cat looked at him. There was a question in his eyes, along with a deep and affecting fear. Today had changed her in a multitude of different ways, making her notice things she hadn't previously taken the trouble to see. But, right now, she didn't want to look at Martin and see fragility. If anything, she wanted half an hour of their usual sarcastic banter. She was too exhausted for anything else. 'Well, if you're going to start looking at a nice little taverna somewhere in the Med, you better move quickly. Before Brexit fucks everything up.'

'It could be a fresh start for both of us.' He was still looking at her far too intently. The hope in his eyes was so palpable, Cat couldn't help feeling repulsed by it.

She faked a small chuckle. 'Believe it or not, but I was hoping university might lead to something other than bar work.'

'How does proprietor sound? I think of you as more of a business partner, anyway.'

Cat tried to picture it. She'd seen the way holidaymakers threw their money around, and Brits always tended to gravitate to places owned by other Brits. As an idea, it sounded profitable. Homeless, with a budget that was barely going to cover a tiny studio flat, could she really afford to spurn such an opportunity?

She lit a new cigarette, even though she'd smoked so incessantly throughout the day that she felt a little sick. 'I'll think about it.'

'We're both so bored of this town. And Miriam would be glad to see the back of me. Why not take a gamble? I wouldn't expect ... There wouldn't be any funny business, you know that, right?' His eyes still had that questioning look.

'I should hope not, you're far too old for that sort of thing.'

'And Laura would have to make her own way. I wouldn't be bringing her out with me to sleep with a succession of sunburned, pot-bellied tourists.'

'Surely things aren't that bad?'

'I can't even begin to fathom that girl. I suppose you've heard; there's a rumour she's been at it with your father.'

'How utterly disgusting.'

'But why, Cat? That's what I can't understand. What is she trying to do?'

Cat shrugged. It had been a long day and she wasn't sure she could navigate a conversation about Laura with Martin, even though she knew the rumours wouldn't be anything more than gossipy speculation. More than anything, Cat needed to get some sleep, then work out what she was going to do next.

Chapter 38

Every in-breath felt like a knife. James could hardly bear to touch his fingers to his ribs to check on the swelling. Cracked, probably. It had been hours since Cat left the house. At first, he imagined she'd take a brisk, angry walk, then burst back through the door in time for lunch. He stayed where he was, crumpled on the floor, so that when she returned, she'd be confronted by her own brutality. He pictured her begging for forgiveness and planned to flinch when she approached him. 'You behaved like an animal,' he'd say. It wasn't retribution he was after; it would be for her own good – making her face up to the degenerate aspects of her personality. Only he understood her; had the ability to soothe her into a better version of herself.

But she hadn't returned all afternoon. James had eased himself up from the floor and taken a couple of codeine tablets, heated some soup. He kept checking his phone, but she didn't get in touch. Anyone else would be frantic with worry, desperate to explain themselves, pleading for forgiveness. Could it be that she'd gone to Daniel? That she could be in bed with him somewhere while James was in pain, fretting about her whereabouts?

His mind played an endless loop of imagined intimacies. Cat naked, hair fanning out beneath her. Daniel taking her from behind, or worse, on top looking into her eyes. Rage coursed through James's body as he remembered his easy acceptance of the lunchtime bar shifts that inexplicably went on until five in the afternoon. The nights she claimed to be in the library until it closed. He'd opened up his home to her. She'd had the best of everything, at his expense, and she'd treated him with contempt. Filthy skank. Believing that a tight little arse gave her the right to keep taking from him. He'd never known such entitlement.

James felt all this, and still wanted her. But he wanted her cowed, submissive. She had to realise, once and for all, that good things could be taken away. He wanted to see the fear of losing her home reverberating through her eyes. Only then would he know she was his. They could go on. The fact that he still loved her, still needed her, was an impossible cruelty, but he knew he'd never find anyone as beautiful as she was.

Dinner time came and went. He relented and tried calling, but she didn't answer. Even if she'd run into Daniel's arms, even if that had been the plan all along, it would have been basic decency to check that James was okay, to ensure he wasn't badly injured by her kick. He'd been reading up on broken ribs and in most cases there was nothing doctors could do, but sometimes a broken rib could puncture a lung. *He* might have a punctured lung, for all she knew and cared. How could she be sure she hadn't left him dying on the carpet? Selfish, selfish whore! His mother was right when she used to tell him *a girl like that is always going to go back to what she knows.* He should have cast her out years ago. Sent her off to get impregnated by some thug with a council flat.

As he eased himself into his bed that night, he felt gripped by cold fingers of desolation. Angry as he was, he couldn't ignore the fact that his need of her was absolute. To see her was to desire her. To live alongside her energy, her sharpness, made any other kind of life impossible.

All night he lay awake, terrified that she might creep in while he was sleeping and retrieve her things, erasing herself from his life forever. For so many years, he'd told himself she needed him, but really, she'd always be the stronger of the two. There was a part of her – the most majestic part, if he was honest – that was wholly indomitable. He saw it, even if sometimes she didn't.

It wasn't until mid-morning the following day that he heard her key in the lock. He was drinking his coffee in the living room and quickly shifted into a reclining position as he heard her come inside.

'Cat?'

She stepped into the room, clasping her hands in front of her. Yesterday's clothes and tangled hair.

'I thought you were going into the office today.' She remained in the doorway, gripping the frame tightly, her eyes wide. More than anything, James wanted to wrap her in his arms and reassure them both that everything was going to be all right. But if they were ever to pick up the pieces of their relationship, he had to make sure she was suitably ashamed.

'I had to call in sick. I think my ribs are broken,' he whispered.

She inhaled sharply. 'I should just pack a few things. I'll do that quickly now.'

'I need an X-ray,' he called out. 'I've been waiting for you to come back. I thought you'd help me get to the hospital. I can't drive myself.'

She turned back around, eyes uncertain, as if she was afraid of *him*. 'Is there someone I can call? Your mum—'

'I don't want anyone to know what happened.'

A flush spread across her neck. She opened her mouth to say something, but stuttered, clearly unsure what to do.

'Mum would insist on calling the police,' he said.

Cat looked down at the carpet. Took another deep breath. 'Maybe you ought to,' she replied. There was no sarcasm in her voice, none of the false bravado he'd become so familiar with over the years. A searing pain went through his middle as he recognised that she really meant it. Cat no longer cared, wasn't desperately trying to salvage everything she had. Where was she going to go? She'd have to squeeze into Bernice's place. Eat dinners from a can. Back to where she came from. She should be begging him for forgiveness, surely? *Unless.*

'You're going to him, aren't you? That man, that lecturer you've been shagging.'

He stood up, ribs forgotten.

'No. Listen, I'll get my things another time,' Cat said. And she ran, away from him, out into the street, like he was some sort of ogre, rather than the man who'd loved her so selflessly for years and years.

Chapter 39

Against all odds, Bernice was now on her second shift at the petrol station on the edge of town. They'd provided her with two green polo shirts, plus a fleece, which made her clothing situation less desperate. The supervisor, Alex, had turned out to be a lovely lady who took the trouble to say a few kind words about how quickly Bernice got the hang of everything. 'Most of the nippers we get in here are flummoxed by the coffee machine,' she'd said, with a smile that made Bernice feel wonderfully included, as though there might not be anything to worry about after all.

This afternoon, she was on stock, which she preferred to the tills. She was quick, no one could take that away from her, breaking open new boxes and filling from the back in immaculate rows. There was something strangely satisfying about blasting her way through a stock trolley, leaving full, tidy shelves in her wake.

Cat had promised to visit her later in the week. Bernice would splurge some of her cleaning money on fish and chips and they could have a proper girly night. She didn't want to jinx it, but she sensed she was now forgiven for her awful blunder. Cat hadn't come out and said it yet, but leaving

James was perhaps one of the best things she ever did. Bernice felt excited on her daughter's behalf.

The only blight on this new week had to do with Laura. She'd seemed such a nice girl, lending Bernice the five hundred that had tided her over, sharing her secret delight about the baby in her belly. It had felt natural to start thinking of the girl as a friend. At first, she refused to believe Fat Al's stories about her slutting around with Martin's regulars. Laura wasn't that kind of girl at all, she was classy, clean. But then one lunchtime she heard Terry laughing with a couple of his workmates. 'Yeah, these posh tarts can't help themselves. Dribbling at the mouth and between the legs, she was.'

It was like someone had reached into Bernice's chest and gripped her heart. She wasn't silly enough to hope for anything where Terry was concerned. From time to time, they'd cuddle up in bed for old times' sake. He sought Bernice out whenever he was feeling lonely, misunderstood or angry. Having a little taste of the early days together would do them both some good, but before she knew it, he'd be zipping up his flies and hurrying away. He wouldn't even give her so much as a hello the next time he saw her.

What had Laura been thinking? Terry was a handsome devil for sure, but Bernice couldn't help but feel disappointed by the girl's behaviour. She'd thought they were friends, and you really shouldn't go around shagging your friend's exes – it was one of those unwritten rules. There couldn't be any more of their nice chats now. Bernice was going to have to get on and pay back that money as soon as she could – she didn't like the idea of owing Laura, not when she was putting out for Terry. Cat was going to go apeshit when she heard about their goings-on.

'New job?'

Bernice looked up from the row of biscuits she was replenishing and saw James. He was wearing a light grey suit with a face mask in the exact same shade, but his eyes looked raw and wild with misery.

She tried to smile. 'Yep. Fallen on my feet. How about you, love? How are you holding up?'

He gave a quick shrug of his shoulders. The poor boy looked as though he might burst into tears at any moment, and Bernice felt her chest swelling with compassion. He'd not been able to understand just how wrong he was for Cat, so it was only natural he should feel the loss of her deeply.

'Try to think of it as a new start, love.' She broke open a cardboard box filled with tubs of cakes, not wanting to get caught slacking.

James snorted. There was something angry in it, which Bernice really didn't like. She was reminded of that feeling she always used to have, that the politeness was an act, that James was masquerading as something different from what he really was.

'I know it's tough, but this could be the making of Cat.' Bernice was shocked she had the nerve to say such a thing out loud. She smiled, to show that she didn't mean any harm by it.

James's eyes hardened. 'What do you mean by that?'

'You took good care of her, love. But I think she knows she's got to start fending for herself.'

James was silent for a few moments. He was standing rather too close to her, and when he spoke again, it was in a whisper.

'I'm the one who's been looking after her all these years. Your accident was the thing that stopped her from *fending for herself*, she gave up everything to look after you.'

Bernice swallowed, carrying on with her stacking. There was something cold in his voice and she found that she no longer felt sorry for him. He was probably right – but what a spiteful thing to say. She started piling up tubs of mini flapjacks, labels at the front, keeping the row nice and straight.

'She never talks about that time,' James continued. 'It's like she has to block it out, it's too hard for her to even think about. Only eighteen. Just think what it must have done to her. She might never fully recover from a traumatic experience like that.'

'I—' It was true. Bernice had always known it was true. She had failed her daughter, sabotaged her chances of success. Her hands shook as she tried to open the next box. She could sense James's eyes on her, could feel dislike rippling off him and wanted to cover her ears so that she didn't have to hear whatever he said next.

He sighed. 'We'll get past this, me and Cat.'

There was the ring of the bell. The lad on the till needed backup. Bernice pushed her stock trolley to one side, ready to go and help out.

James took hold of her arm. 'If you really care about her, you'll leave her alone. The damage will never heal if she keeps getting pulled into your little dramas.'

It felt as though Bernice had been punched in the stomach. She opened her mouth to speak, but no words came out, she just stood there like a gaping fish.

'I don't mean to be unkind,' James added. 'But I've lived with Cat for a long time. I understand her pretty well.'

The bell rang for a second time and Bernice hurried over to the front of the shop. There were around five or so people in the queue and she had to make a fancy coffee with whipped cream for the first chap she served. She was trying hard not to shake, aware of James inching up the queue. Thankfully, the lad served him, so she didn't have to speak with him again.

Once the queue had been taken care of, Bernice went back to her trolley and tried to run through everything she'd covered off in her therapy sessions. She breathed. She reassured herself that Cat was strong, that James only saw the version of her that suited him best. It's what people did, picking and choosing what they wanted to believe about their loved ones; weaving fairy tales that made them into heroes.

Unbidden came the memories of her daughter, curled up in the hospital visitor chair trying to read. Her face had been drained of colour as she tried questioning the doctors doing their rounds. It hadn't been any life for a teenager. And to think – four years of it – it would have felt like a lifetime at that tender age.

But dwelling on the past was a harmful habit, and one of the most dangerous where Bernice was concerned. Instead, she tried to imagine the lovely night she and Cat would have. Vinegary chips. The two of them sat on Bernice's bed, watching a bit of telly with the ashtray between them. Cat would tell her all about her studies. And Bernice would ask her about that politics business she'd set her sights on. Their lives didn't have to stay ruined. They could both become happier people.

Chapter 40

It had been almost a fortnight since the break-up with James; Cat was still sleeping in Martin's office, picking up a few extra shifts at weekends because Laura had suddenly quit and enrolled on a teacher-training course. Term had resumed for Cat too, so she took her showers in the university gym and studied in the library until late most nights. It was the kind of precarious existence she'd always feared.

She'd worked hard at trying to enjoy her life with James precisely because she'd known what poverty felt like, how it made the things you wanted to build for yourself feel impossible and exhausting. As a child, she'd had to wear her coat indoors in the winter and her mum would send her round to the neighbours, to borrow an egg or a couple of slices of bread. She'd been aware, even then, that what she was really doing was begging, that she was supposed to offer profuse thanks for every grudging kindness.

She couldn't blame herself for having taken the easy route when James presented it to her in all its air-freshened glory. It seemed so very materialistic to place such a high value on his clean, ordered home, but anyone who'd shared her upbringing would understand the lure of the washing machine, of the boiler whirring away on dark evenings, of walls that were freshly painted and not damp to the touch. James had made her feel seen, at a time when everyone else in her life was writing her off, assuming that becoming a small-town barmaid was a good fate for someone like her.

What a surprise it was to discover a kind of pride in getting by, even when the pleasant trimmings of her life had been taken away. Martin's sofa wasn't the most comfortable and she was starting to have the rumpled look of someone living out of bags – but she still felt a strange confidence in the future. Things didn't *feel* like they had when she was a child, mortified by every classroom snub, by people noticing things about her that didn't quite fit. Now she felt as though anyone who would judge her harshly wasn't worthy of her respect, their opinions didn't matter to her. She would never again make unseemly compromises or try to take shortcuts for the sake of comfort and ease.

She was due to visit her mother that evening. She'd seen her a handful of times since the row at James's. On the first morning, Bernice had shrieked in surprise, arriving to clean the club and finding Cat curled up asleep in the office. She'd been apologetic, and Cat had waved it away, declaring herself pleased to be out of the relationship with James, but refusing to have any kind of heart-to-heart. She simply wasn't ready to answer well-meaning questions, not while she was still trying to make sense of things.

Since then, most mornings she'd left before her mother's arrival. Bernice had invited Cat to move in with her, suggesting that they could sleep at opposite ends of her double bed.

Cat had been unsure – at Martin's she was at least able to barricade herself behind the office door, to put her earplugs in and read without anyone fussing over her. But taking stock of how her life was now, she started to feel that moving in with her mother would be the best thing to do.

She wouldn't have to squander her loan and scholarship payments on rent. A return to her roots didn't have to be a bad thing. It didn't matter if she lived in a grubby bedsit, she'd no longer be defined by such things. She had the highest grade average of her cohort, was a scholarship recipient – these were the kind of achievements she should be using to measure her worth. She wanted to be an advocate for the poor, so perhaps it was exactly right that she should live among them again, be part of the community she hoped to mobilise in the future.

Moving in with her mother would be going above and beyond the odd cup of tea and chat that Bernice said was all she needed. As well as helping with the rent, Cat would be able to keep a proper eye on her, intervening whenever she sensed she was lonely or the urge to have a drink was particularly strong.

When the train pulled into Petersfield, Cat walked to the Grove, a relatively new estate of densely packed high-rise flats. The housing association had transferred Bernice here shortly after Cat moved in with James. It struck Cat that this coincided precisely with the return to hard drinking. How foolish she'd been not to notice it back then, to resent her mother for undoing years of hard work and physiotherapy. She hadn't had Cat to keep her company at home, so she sought out company in clubs and bars. Cat had never considered her own actions to be a factor, but it seemed so obvious now.

A large group of teenagers were bouncing a ball against one of the walls. 'Give us a fag?'

Cat smiled and shook her head. An upbeat pop hit was blasting out from an open window. *Home*, Cat thought to herself. *This is going to be my home now.*

Bernice lived on the second floor. There was no response when Cat knocked on the door, but she had a key and Bernice had warned her she might be held up if there was a queue at the chippie.

Inside, the curtains were drawn, but through the gloom, Cat saw that her mother was curled up asleep on the bed. Beside her, on the floor, was a small cluster of empty bottles. *Fuck*. She was back to that, then. After doing so well for weeks now. She must have slept through work, would most likely be fired.

If Cat had just given Bernice a bit more of her time, if she'd reassured her that the argument with James wasn't her fault, she might have had the strength not to give in. But now they were back here – resuming the cycle of humiliation and anger.

Cat threw the curtains open and approached the bed. 'Wakey wakey!' The smell of booze and vomit was overpowering. On the floor, alongside the bottles, were dark patches of what looked like coffee grounds. 'Mum?'

Her mother's face was grey; the mouth was open and coated in that same sticky brown substance. It was all over the pillow too, crusted in her hair. Was it *blood*?

'Mum?'

Bernice was on her side, her legs under the sheet. Her eyes were closed, but not tightly, Cat could see the smallest slither of white beneath the lashes. Slowly, heart thudding, Cat laid a hand on her mother's arm. It was cold.

Chapter 41

As the days passed, James took comfort in the fact that Cat hadn't yet collected all of her belongings. She'd snuck back and taken her laptop and all the books from the dining-room table at some point, but her wardrobe had only been half emptied and her shampoo still sat on the shelf in the bathroom. Signs she might still intend to return.

After a couple of days of silence, he'd messaged her. *I didn't contact the police, you know I wasn't serious about that, right? I hope you're okay. I worry about you.*

She didn't respond, and he found himself regretting his tone. He sounded wheedling, a long way from the confident provider he wanted to be. God, he missed her. The feral energy, animating her face. Spanning his hands around her narrow waist, so slender he felt as though he could snap her spine in a single motion. Walking down the street with her, watching her tiny bottom, her long legs, register on the faces of everyone they passed. The grudging respect directed at him, the aphrodisiac of envy. How could she simply be gone from his life, after so many years together? He'd told no one about their fight. On the phone to his mother, he spoke of 'us' and 'we' as though their lives were going on as before. Why endure his mother's pity, his father's jovial laughter, when this was just a blip?

James changed tack. *Can you please let me know when you intend to pick up your stuff?* His stomach lurched as he pressed send. He hadn't wanted to sound aggressive, but she couldn't go on avoiding him. He had to see her so they could finally reckon with everything that had gone wrong and start rebuilding their lives.

His most treasured memories, those he would take out and examine whenever he was feeling down, all featured Cat. He remembered his brother's wedding. The way she'd made all those banker types trip over their words. His father sidling over and asking her for a dance, looking crushed when she refused because her feet hurt.

Their final trip, before this university business started, had been to Amsterdam and she'd taken him to a sex show, telling him it was a cultural experience. How scandalised and impressed his colleagues had been when he'd told them.

His phone beeped. *Sorry it's taken me so long. I can come tonight if convenient?*

He paced between the living room and kitchen, waiting for her to arrive. He had to get this right, had to make her understand he knew what was best for them both. It was hurt pride that was keeping her away, he was sure of it. Her ego wouldn't let her backtrack, even though she must be struggling to make ends meet.

At last, the ring of the doorbell.

'Cat, come in.' Her hair was up in a ponytail and she was wearing jeans with a maroon hoodie. She was holding herself awkwardly, her shoulders hunched, and she seemed reluctant to meet his eye.

Was it wrong to feel the warmth of hope fan out through his body at how dimished she seemed? She missed him. She was suffering without him.

She stood in the hallway, looking at the floor without making any move to take her trainers off, almost as though she expected to have a bag of belongings shoved at her. He ached with sadness for both of them, pained that after all this time she thought him capable of treating her in such a way.

'Would you like something to drink?' he offered.

She shook her head.

'Cat—' He put a hand on her shoulder, but she flinched. He drew his hand back and they both stood there, uncertain. 'Where have you been staying?'

'Martin's.'

'You've been sleeping in that dingy club?' He couldn't quite mask the outrage in his voice. She was acting like he was some sort of ogre, as though being around him was worse than squatting in a filthy, smoky bar.

'At first. But he made me sleep at his house from last week.'

James looked at her, awaiting further explanation. Surely, she hadn't shacked up with *Martin*? He'd known all along that the grubby old man was besotted with her.

Cat swallowed. 'My mum died. I thought she was doing so well, but she went on a drinking binge. I can't really understand—'

He gathered her up, wrapping her in his arms, feeling her frame judder with the effort of holding back tears. 'Oh Cat, I always worried about this day. You should have called me.'

She didn't respond. As they stood there in silence, James realised that this moment was precisely what he was built for. She could push him away. And, Christ, she really had been putting the effort into doing so over these past few weeks. But no one knew her like he did. No one was better placed to help her heal.

'Let me make you a nice mug of hot chocolate,' he said after a suitable pause. He held her by the shoulders, looking her in the eye, and he felt an understanding pass between them. She was ready to abandon whatever misguided notions had been keeping them apart. She was home.

He steered her into the living room, opting not to worry about her trainers still being on. And she obeyed. He was finally back in control.

As they sat next to one another on the sofa, the scene of so many amicable nights eating their dinner on trays, watching the news, or a film at the weekend, Cat told James about finding her mother. It surprised her, that she should be so willing to speak of it. But she found that each time she told the story, spoke of the bloody vomit, the chill of her mother's skin, the minutes that passed before she dialled 999 and was stumped, unsure whether to ask for the police or an ambulance – each time she spoke of these things, it was as though tiny fragments of pain were released into the ether. Indeed, she found she could hardly bear *not* talking about it. More than once, Martin's wife had politely abandoned conversations halfway, a disturbed expression on her face. But other people's discomfort seemed so irrelevant that Cat couldn't bring herself to stop.

James put his arm around her, and it felt so good simply

to be held, to have the comfort of a warm, living body next to hers. The familiar scent of his aftershave, of his hair products, acted as an anchor when the past few days had been so utterly dislocating.

'She was cold,' Cat said. 'So cold. I can hardly describe it, but I know what people mean now when they use the term "deathly cold".'

James squeezed her shoulders.

'She was doing so well – with not drinking. I really don't understand what went wrong. There must have been something. Something I wasn't seeing. I've been so bloody preoccupied. I wanted to do well this term. I ended up *rationing* my time with her, just like before.'

'She was an addict. You mustn't blame yourself.'

'But she didn't have anyone else. It was my job to keep an eye on her. How could I let essays become more important than my mother?'

James pressed his lips together, saying nothing.

'It was vanity. I wanted to see myself in a certain way. I liked the glory of the marks. I got a kick out of being the mature student outperforming the younger ones.'

James stroked her arm. She realised that a tiny part of her was hoping he would disagree. She wanted more than anything to create a story in which she wasn't a neglectful bystander, watching her mother drink herself to death. But the truth was, a few small interventions might have made all the difference. Why had she made Bernice wait for the girly night she seemed so excited about? Cat could have rearranged things, could have gone there on the Monday instead of making her mother wait until Thursday.

'What are you going to do now?' James asked.

'I don't know. The hospital has only just released her body. I've got to organise the cremation. And then there's her flat to clear out. I haven't been able to face going back there.' As she said this, she had a guilty hope that James might intervene. He was free from all obligations to her, but she was desperate to be told that of course she didn't have to return to the place where she'd discovered her mother's corpse.

She imagined James, bin bags in hand, bagging everything up so that Cat didn't have to look at belongings that could only feed her distress. She couldn't face the bedding, stained with her mother's vomit, with blood. She didn't want to be the one to gather up the bottles from the floor.

'I was thinking more long-term,' James said.

'I'm taking things one day at a time. I don't have the capacity to think more than a few days ahead at the moment.'

'I guess that means you'll take a break from university?'

'I don't know.'

James took a deep breath and placed a hand on her knee. 'There wouldn't be any shame in asking for a deferment. Not after what you've been through.'

Cat put a hand to her temple. The truth was, she couldn't imagine walking back inside the lecture theatre. Couldn't imagine finding the calm focus needed to plan an essay.

'I just can't stop thinking that university has bought us such terrible bad luck,' James said. 'I'm so sorry it wasn't the new start you wanted it to be.'

Cat felt a tugging sensation in her chest. She wanted to be angry, and she had every right to be. Her enrolling at university was wholly unconnected with her mother's death. That

James should make the tiniest hint to the contrary made her skin prickle with resentment. *And yet.* That tugging sensation. It was guilt.

Her mother had been a binge drinker for decades, true. How easy it would be to put this fact on a pedestal. To venerate it; return to it for reassurance again and again. Bernice's alcoholism allowed Cat to conceal from herself just how ungenerous she'd been. Oh, that twisting feeling of a recognised lie. The temptation to turn away, not to see her own culpability. She could imagine herself telling the story of her mother's demise years from now, and it could be a simple narrative, a sad tale of a lack of restraint that eventually proved fatal. But what of the moments Cat could have given her mother? How many cups of tea would it have taken? She'd never know. It could have been as little as one extra visit a month. And she'd never know.

'Come home,' James said tenderly. His eyes were serious. There was something about the purity of his face, his cleanliness, the well-groomed order of him, that made Cat want to weep over everything she'd lost. 'Come home,' he said again. 'I won't ask anything of you. You can take your time. Heal.'

Cat swallowed. How certain she'd been that leaving him was the right thing to do. But she'd learned to distrust certainty.

'We'll take a trip,' James continued. 'When the quarantine restrictions ease off. We can go anywhere you want. You said about Australia before. We should take three weeks. Give you a chance to recharge yourself.'

'But – I haven't decided anything yet. I've got essays to hand in—'

'Come home, Cat. This is where you belong. I'll take good care of you.'

Chapter 42

When Laura followed Cat into Bernice's flat, her hands instinctively covered her belly. There was an eerie density to the air, a kind of fug that combined unemptied ashtrays, damp clothes and vomit. It felt to Laura like she was walking into an intrinsically private space, that being here was stripping away any remaining dignity Bernice possessed. They were in a room mostly taken up by a double bed, the sheets still rumpled and covered by what looked like excrement.

Laura retched and Cat whipped her head around, looking at her with dead eyes. 'It's blood. She had a bleeding stomach ulcer.'

Laura rested an arm against the wall, trying to steady her breathing and prevent further retching. 'My god, Cat, I'm so sorry. Is that what killed her?'

'Maybe. Her blood alcohol levels were so high that it could have been her heart. The post-mortem was inconclusive. Not that it matters.'

The flatness of Cat's tone was disconcerting, but Laura knew her well enough now not to be riled by it. Feigning scorn, or indifference, was simply what Cat did. The longer

Laura had known her, the more deeply she believed that there were in fact oceans of feeling beneath that fierce exterior.

Laura couldn't help thinking of Bernice's collapse in Martin's toilets; of all the times she served her alcohol since. Bernice must have been in constant pain with an ulcerated stomach. Was there anything Laura could have done differently, anything that would have made a difference? She could feel herself wanting to dwell on the question, so she once again laid her hands over her abdomen. Honouring her atonement pledges felt wrong sometimes, as though she might be doing imperceptible harm to the being inside of her. She needed to suffer; it's what she owed to the parents of the young man she'd killed. Yet she wanted her child to know only happiness. The two things seemed so completely irreconcilable.

Cat threw open the windows, then reached into her rucksack to retrieve a roll of bin bags and two sets of rubber gloves. 'Right. Better get started.'

'What would you like me to do?' Laura asked.

A tiny muscle at the base of Cat's throat twitched. 'Would you mind bagging up the bedding? I don't think I can—'

Laura touched her on the shoulder. 'Of course.' She put the gloves on and immediately set to stripping the bed, stuffing the sheet and duvet into bags, focusing intently on the task to give Cat what privacy the narrow space afforded. It seemed so absurd to be here, chucking out Bernice's belongings. Just three weeks ago, Laura had met her for coffee. She'd seemed healthy, excited about Laura's pregnancy, reminiscing about how enormous she'd been when pregnant with Cat. She'd refused to talk about her miscarriages, the stillbirth. 'Won't do you any good thinking about morbid things like that, darling,' she'd said. Never had Laura encountered anyone so generous, with such a capacity to be happy for others.

Then, a fortnight ago, Laura's father had led Cat into the family home, her movements slow and dazed. There'd been angry whispers between her parents, while Cat kept saying over and over that she was happy to go on sleeping at the club.

'Her mother's died,' she heard her father say. And when she'd looked at Cat, Laura saw that she did indeed look orphaned, as though she was lost in some unfathomable way. She'd embraced her, and Cat had let herself be held.

Laura wiped her eyes with her sleeve. 'Okay. That's the bedding done. Shall I make a start on the bathroom?'

Cat was strangely still, her back to Laura, inspecting a pair of narrow blue jeans. 'All right. But don't throw stuff away for the sake of it. Keep anything unopened.'

Cat couldn't let go of the jeans, her own jeans, washed and carefully ironed; they'd been folded and placed on the chest of drawers. Her mother must have been planning on returning them, a thought which left Cat strangely discombobulated. Before drinking herself into a final stupor, she'd ironed Cat's jeans.

She wished James had offered to pitch in, so that Laura didn't have to see this place. Cat had moved back in with James, feeling strangely numb when he fussed over her, preparing her breakfast, insisting she rest. She'd told him she wasn't sure whether her return would be permanent, but the idea of going on as before, sheltering from the world in his vanilla-fragranced rooms, didn't feel quite so terrible any more.

It was a base, perverse instinct that had led her to accept Laura's offer of help. Laura had been pushing Cat to do more for her mother, so why not show her how Bernice really lived? Make her confront the ugliness, the utter lack of romance to be had from empty fridges and third-hand furniture. But now that Laura was here – cracking on with the job, to be fair – Cat felt as though she'd once again been disloyal. The congealed blood was so personal, as were the bottles, the final, fatal bottles. Bringing Laura here was exposing her mother to yet another humiliation. Bernice no longer had the option to keep anything private, to curate what other people saw. Cat had to keep perfectly still, or she'd start crying again.

Laura came out of the bathroom, placing another full bin bag by the door. 'Cat, are you all right? We can do this another time, if you need a break.'

Cat sank down on one edge of Bernice's stripped-down bed, closing her eyes.

Laura sat down next to her. 'She was so proud of you. You know that, right?'

Cat reached for her mother's cigarette packet, still half-full, sitting on the bedside table. She lit one, knowing Bernice wouldn't want them to go to waste.

'Is there anything I can do to help with the funeral?' Laura asked.

'It's going to be a cremation, family only.' Which in truth meant it was just going to be Cat and James. She'd called her father, asking him to come. She detested doing it, but felt very strongly that Bernice would want him there. 'Not my place,' he'd said. And none of Cat's pressing would change his mind.

Perhaps she shouldn't have been surprised, but she was

desperate for her father to acknowledge that the three of them had once been a family, even if it had been a long time ago. By acting as though Bernice's life had no connection with his, like she was inconsequential to him, he was once again dishonouring her. For a moment, Cat considered telling Laura some of this, but she couldn't bring herself to do it. Speaking her humiliations had always served to strengthen them, to somehow add to their power. Better simply to take a drag of her cigarette and seethe in silence.

Laura touched her arm. 'Okay. Well, if you think of anything, let me know.'

'How come you quit Martin's?' Cat managed to ask. Further talk of her mother might unmoor her completely; she needed to change the subject.

Laura adjusted her ponytail, looking at the wall opposite. 'I'm actually pregnant.'

Cat was about to congratulate her, it was reflexive, but then she remembered the lockdown spent with Roger, rumours of Laura and other customers, including Cat's own father.

'I haven't told my parents,' Laura continued. 'Bernice was the only other person who knew, actually. She was lovely about it.'

'Is the father . . . Do you want them involved?'

Laura shook her head.

'That's tough,' Cat said.

Laura swallowed, her eyes darting across the room. 'Right, better get back to the bathroom.'

Cat felt a flicker of curiosity, so unexpected and yet such a welcome contrast to the persistent sadness. She reached out, placing her hand on Laura's wrist. 'Who *is* the father?'

Laura's eyes filled with tears, but she said nothing.

'Did Mum know?'

'She didn't.'

'Do *you* know?'

Laura's face became very red. 'Cat, please—'

'It's not *my* dad, is it?'

Laura took a deep breath, looking wildly around the room.

Cat knew she was being unkind, but now the idea had occurred to her, she needed an answer. She stood up and extinguished her cigarette in her mother's ashtray, then turned back to Laura, placing her hands on her shoulders. 'It's okay,' she said. 'I'm just sad for you, that you'd even consider . . .'

Laura started to shake. The woman was pregnant, Cat reminded herself, she ought not to upset her.

'It's all right.' Tentatively, Cat hugged her friend.

She expected that they would move on. That Laura would briskly resume cleaning, or opt to leave. Instead, Laura started to cry, a desperate sobbing that brought sudden ice to Cat's veins. She knew this kind of guttural, wrenching cry. It punctuated far too many childhood memories, speaking of violence, of degradation. She remembered her mother crumpled on the kitchen floor. Remembered the bleeding nose, the black eyes that Bernice had never successfully covered with make-up. She just knew – with sickening certainty – that her father was behind it.

She cradled Laura's head, letting her expend her grief. Tears and snot soaking into the fabric of Cat's top. Several times, Cat wondered whether she ought to say anything. Much as she wanted to comfort, she lacked that natural understanding of how best to do it, holding herself stiffly as she waited for the crying to pass.

After, as Laura straightened up and tucked her hair behind her ears, Cat framed a question in her most gentle voice. 'What did he do? You can tell me.'

Laura shook her head. 'I should have said no, been more clear. I tried . . . '

'He *forced* you?'

The expression on Laura's face was so raw, so grief-stricken, that Cat felt a moment of perfect connection. How strange that she should look at snobby little Laura from school and recognise her suffering on such an instinctual level. It was all because of Bernice, and the pain Cat had witnessed every day of her childhood. As a younger woman, she chose to scorn her mother's wretchedness, weaving a narrative that somehow made everything Bernice's own fault. Here was an opportunity to do better, to atone in some small way.

'I didn't resist forcefully enough,' Laura said. 'I was frightened and it kind of paralysed me. I know how that must sound. But I just *couldn't* move, Cat. I couldn't.'

Cat conjured up her father's form. He was tall like her, but muscular from years of shouldering building materials. Whatever he wanted, he took. 'The utter cunt,' she said.

Laura wiped her eyes. 'I could have handled things differently. If I fought harder . . . maybe he misunderstood . . . '

Cat stood up and placed her hands either side of Laura's face. 'It was *not* your fault. Listen to me. He's a brute and what you're describing is rape. You should press charges. Make him pay.'

Laura laughed bitterly. 'It wouldn't stick though, would

it? Even if it went to court, they'd rip me to shreds. I've not exactly been celibate lately – can you imagine the fun they'd have with the whole Roger situation?'

As infuriating as it was, Cat had to acknowledge the truth of this. It would be a simple matter of Laura's word against her father's, with no real prospect of success. But Cat wasn't about to let him get away with it. She welcomed the indignation. It enraged her that gentle people like her mother, like Laura, had been made to suffer, while her violent, selfish father took any pleasure he wanted without repercussions.

And how Terry had manipulated Cat, inviting her to join him, to share in his derision, heaping yet further layers of humiliation onto Bernice as she nursed the bruised ribs, the split lips and ended pregnancies. Cat would think of something, a creative revenge, not just for Laura, but for her mother too. Already, her mind was racing ahead. She could blackmail him. For some reason, he seemed to value his marriage to Rhiannon more than any of his previous relationships. Cat could shake him down, make him pay out, a kind of alimony for a baby he could never know might be his. But, above all, she needed to make him suffer. He *must* feel some of the pain that he had so wantonly been spreading around.

Chapter 43

Her GP wouldn't give her sleeping tablets, even though Cat tried to depict for her the crushing misery of each wakeful night. Long stretches thinking of her mother, running through all the times she'd been needlessly dismissive or cruel. She'd never be able to apologise for these moments, and in the night they'd rise up, seeking to imprint themselves on her memory with sudden, painful heat. By day, it left her forgetful, her vision colonised by floating spots of purple and green.

What her doctor did prescribe was antidepressants, which confused Cat, because surely the pain of bereavement was a rite of passage. The only way to honour her mother was to let the guilt, the indignation, the sheer aching *absence*, inhabit her body. To not dismiss, or argue away, but to live alongside the beating pulse of these feelings, even if it meant she was always on the verge of falling to the floor.

James urged her to take the pills. He was taking good care of her; she couldn't dispute it. He cooked all the classics: toad in the hole, shepherd's pie, roast dinners – none of his usual health food muck. He didn't press social events or visits, limiting himself to wistful mentions of colleagues that were having people over. But in spite of the hours and hours of quiet rest, Cat still didn't feel able to analyse her grief dispassionately, she couldn't make it mean anything. And that's what she needed: meaning, the only thing that could lift her out of this strange, dispossessed state. It was as though she was waiting for insights to come rushing in, to wake up one morning with a clear understanding of what she needed to do, the kind of life she should live, if she was to stop feeling like a terrible person.

She'd already missed three weeks of lectures and an essay hand-in. She felt conflicted about university, the alternate futures she'd imagined for herself seemed so laughable now, selfish dreams that had blinded her to her mother's loneliness. The things Cat had loved – studying, reading, analysing and composing arguments – were now partnered with a sense of futility. Who cared about social cohesion during the Industrial Revolution? What purpose could one more essay on Hitler's rise to power possibly serve? Cat had hoped education would equip her to make a difference, but it felt like what she'd really done was cloister herself away from the pain and deprivation of real life.

'There's no shame in not continuing,' James had said more than once. But Cat wasn't sure he was right, she was too confused, too immersed in her own grief to understand what she really felt about anything.

So, it was with a strange absence of purpose that she took the train into Portsmouth one Wednesday afternoon. In her bag was a letter from her GP explaining that she was recently bereaved and struggling with insomnia and depression. By handing it to the administrators, she'd at least prevent herself being automatically removed from the course.

She had a small hope that walking through the city, among the grand university buildings, might provide some clarity. She remembered how she felt when she'd come along to the open day the previous year, the defiant spirit within her insisting she could find a meaningful path. The feeling that she was living in a landmark time, when politics was becoming ever more polarised and hate was going unchallenged. She looked back and admired herself for believing that there might just be something she could do about it. She didn't feel like that now.

As she left the administrative centre, she heard her name. It was her classmate Sophia, hurrying over, wearing a buttercup yellow trench coat over jeans, hair up in her usual untidy bun. 'Where have you been? I've been worried. I can't believe after all this time, I don't have your number.'

'My mum died.'

Sophia's eyes darted around, the most painful look of embarrassment on her face.

'It's okay,' Cat said. 'I'm not expecting you to say anything.'

'I can't even imagine . . .'

'No.'

'But you're back to class now?'

Cat shook her head. 'I'm not sure what I'm going to do, to be honest.'

'Come and have a coffee with me.' Sophia gripped her arm. 'I've missed you. Seminars are so flat without you there.'

Because there wasn't anywhere else she needed to be, Cat allowed the girl to lead her to a nearby Costa, where she ordered a panini and slice of cake to go with her syrupy latte. The place was full of students and she and Sophia managed to nab the very last table.

'You *have* to come back,' Sophia said, as Cat bit into the panini, scalding her mouth on the molten cheese.

'I'm forty years old. What use is a degree going to be? I mean, I've enjoyed my time here, but I've been pretending it represents this massive new start. Things don't work like that.'

Sophia looked momentarily wounded. 'But you're gifted. You can't waste it.'

A few weeks ago, Cat would have felt a surge of resentment at a teenager daring to comment on her life. She'd perhaps launch into a diatribe about the intrinsic unevenness of opportunity. Of the class system that made people like Cat the bartenders, and people like James the comfortably-off middle managers of the world. But not today, today she felt only weariness.

'Anyway, forty's not old,' Sophia continued. 'You're not even at the halfway mark, according to current life expectancies. You might find that you're drawing on your degree for the *next* forty years. Surely that's worth it?'

Cat smiled, brandishing her fag packet. 'You forget, I like my ciggies.'

Sophia looked uncertain for a moment, then frowned. 'I really don't get that about you. What intelligent person *smokes?*'

Cat shrugged. 'I think you're underestimating how scrumptious they are.'

Sophia sighed and shook her head.

Something about her classmate's apparent consternation made Cat feel as though she was being ridiculous. It wasn't just the fags. She felt as though she'd become a parody somehow, a stock character in a play: the bitter older woman. It gave her a jolt.

There hadn't been a moment when she'd chosen this role. Looking back over the years, it felt as though every moment of frustration, every time she was spoken down to at the bar, or paraded around by James, eager for his friends' approval and attention – each of these small moments added a caustic edge to her personality. It sounded so absurd to have allowed such petty things to get the better of her, to allow irritations and annoyances to guide her behaviour.

She rested her elbows on the table. 'Anyway, how are you getting on?'

Sophia leaned in. 'You know that Daniel Simmonds, like, abruptly disappeared, right? They said he was moving on, but didn't say where to.'

Cat said nothing.

Sophia looked at her. 'You two were, like, friends?'

'We were.' It struck Cat that in this moment in her life, Daniel was the person she most wanted to talk to. The only way out of her grief might be to sit with him in the canteen, forecasting what might happen in the US elections, or unpicking how various media outlets were covering China. Even now, she couldn't quite rid herself of the sense that when Daniel left for Oxford all those years ago, he'd taken a tiny part of her with him. She'd been incomplete, an atrophied version of herself ever since.

She swallowed. They'd never reconnect. Not after what she'd done. If she wanted to recover the hope and ambition he embodied for her, she'd have to find her own way. She'd met plenty of intelligent people over the last year. Surely, if she tried, really made an effort to get to know them and tease out their opinions, she might at least feel glimmers of connection?

She returned Sophia's gaze and smiled. 'Do you know what you want to do after you graduate?'

Chapter 44

Terry was the first to arrive at the club that Sunday. Martin rose to greet him, leaving his fag burning in the ashtray while he popped behind the bar to fix Terry's pint. Fella was always a little jumpy around him. Made Terry chuckle sometimes.

'Heard a rumour you put the place on the market,' Terry said.

Martin's eyes went wide. 'Yes. Well. Not getting any younger. Just exploring a few options for retirement.'

'Might make an offer. Always liked the idea of my own pub.' They were making a song and dance about another lockdown being on the way; if that was the case, it'd probably drive the price right down.

At that point, Cat walked in. She was a fine-looking lass, Terry couldn't dispute it, but she always seemed so bloody determined to appear rough as fuck, with her battered old trainers, hair scraped back, wearing one of those godawful surgical mask things. Couldn't be more different from his Rhiannon; she always got herself up like a princess, she did. Drove him mad when they were heading out together and he had to wait for her to finish mucking about with all her potions and fake eyelashes. Worth it though. Girl was a jewel, had his mates grinding their teeth with envy.

Cat slowed her approach. 'What are you doing here?'

'That's no way to talk to your old man,' Terry said. But he realised she was looking at Martin.

'Thought you might need a bit of moral support,' the old duffer said. 'Didn't like the idea of you being here on your lonesome.'

Cat raised an eyebrow at that, and hopped up on a bar stool, lighting a fag. 'I want to talk to you,' she said to Terry.

She looked over at Martin, who mumbled something about going to the cellar and cleaning the pipes. Pussy-whipped, he was. If it had been Terry, he would have twisted Cat's arm behind her back and reminded her who paid her wages. Maybe give it a few months and he'd be doing just that. If he bought the place, he'd soon put a stop to her backchat.

'You going to ask me how the cremation went?' Cat asked.

Terry took a long draught from his pint. 'Nope.'

She snorted. And for a moment Terry felt a pang at the waste of it. Such a pretty girl – clever, too – but she always took such pains to be unpleasant. Not a bloody clue where she got it from. Old Bern was a whiner and a pest, but there was none of this snark about her.

Cat exhaled smoke and fixed him with a look of complete loathing. 'Does Rhiannon know about you and Laura?' she asked.

Terry felt a prickle of unease. 'Keep your nose out of things that don't concern you.'

'You're a rapist.'

'Wash your fucking mouth out.'

'It'll cost you three grand, if you want me to be quiet. I know you can afford it. And, by the way, that's how much the funeral cost, thanks for asking.'

'You unhinged like your mother?'

Cat rested an elbow on the bar and smiled. It gave him the creeps. 'I rigged a camera on the top shelf. We thought Moira had been helping herself to the spirits. Wanted to gather evidence. Had a bit of a surprise when I watched the footage. There's no sound, but anyone can see Laura's unwilling. You forced her. It was rape.'

Terry sipped his pint, buying a few moments to think. *Could* it be true? His daughter could be a cunning little shit, but chances were, if she had such a recording, she wouldn't have been able to resist playing it to him. Yes. He was certain. She'd have shown him she had the goods before asking for money. The other slut had most probably been running her mouth, that was all.

'Nice try, love. But you ain't got nothing.' He folded his arms. Already, he was thinking of the fruities, wondering where Tom and Al were at; he didn't fancy any more of this nonsense.

'Three thousand pounds,' she said. 'Or Rhiannon gets to watch it.'

'You leave Rhiannon out of this.'

He saw the uncertainty on her face and couldn't help smiling. Who did the little madam think she was? Living with that posh bloke was giving her ideas. Tragic really. But with an attitude like that, if he did go ahead and buy the place, he'd tell her to fuck right off, replace her with a juicy eighteen-year-old.

Terry chuckled to himself as he pulled a twenty out of his pocket. 'I'll have some coins for the machines.'

A loud crack and he tumbled from the bar stool, landing heavily on his side. Pain shot through his temple, his right eye. Fuck! For a moment, he wasn't sure he could see. But then her face. Standing over him. Shrieking her head off about not letting him get away with something or another. She was holding the ashtray. Cunt had only clobbered him over the head with it.

Just as he understood what was happening, she was on top of him. Howling as she drove a flimsy little punch to his jaw. He rolled over and pinned her down. Drove his head into her face. 'Behave yourself!' he yelled.

She was still shrieking. Her face a mess of blood, she gurgled and coughed as she flailed her arms and legs, desperate to land a blow. It was an ugly sight. But Terry was buggered if he was going to feel guilty. He felt strangely calm as he stood and took a step backwards, rubbing his temple. He was going to have one hell of a shiner.

The ashtray was on the floor beside them. A heavy, glass affair. If she had stronger arms, the bitch could have cracked his skull. Idly, he wondered whether that's perhaps what she'd wanted. Her mother's child. Crazy, gobby bitch. Mouthful of broken teeth was her getting away lightly. If she had any sense, she'd take this as a lesson. Lord knows what had sparked this righteous little escapade. What did she care what he got up to?

He dusted himself off, picking up the twenty that had fallen to the floor. Cat was quiet now, but he could hear her ragged breathing. She pulled herself up onto all fours, spitting blood onto the carpet.

Fuck it, he'd move on to The Bell, enjoy a pint in peace. Calmly he drained the remainders of his drink and turned to leave.

'What in God's name . . .'

Martin was back. Charging towards him he was, but then he thought better of it, slowing his approach as Terry faced him full on.

'What have you done to her?'

Terry shrugged and walked on by.

Cat stayed on her knees, conducting an audit of her mouth with her tongue. Three, four broken teeth. Searing pain. But part of her was jubilant. She was finally done with her father. Never again would she worry about his antics, the light they cast on her. Never again would she search for a glimmer of respect that he just wasn't capable of feeling. They were done. For years, she'd concealed a hope that one day he might be proud, that he might admire her for being so very different from his other children. Her unexpected act of violence seemed to have purged it from her body. She felt elated, liberated from her own past.

'Cat?' Martin was crouching down next to her. 'My god, your face. Do we need to get you to a hospital?'

She wiped her eyes, shook her head and laughed. It was an ugly sound, distorted by her battered mouth. At that moment, Fat Al and Tommy Grainger arrived. Their conversation stopped the minute they saw her.

'Dearest daddy felt the need to headbutt me,' Cat said, flashing what must be a gruesome smile.

They were frozen in horror. It struck Cat with sudden

poignancy that this might be the one thing they couldn't forgive. Terry had licence to knock his wives around as he pleased, but laying a finger on Cat was different. Cat belonged to *them*, to all the punters. She saw in Tommy and Al's eyes that Terry had misjudged, overstepped, there was none of the grudging respect offered up when he battered some bloke who looked at Rhiannon the wrong way.

'Let's get some ice on that.'

Martin steered her into the kitchen, where he wrapped a handful of ice with a grubby tea towel. As she took it from him and pressed it to her tender jaw, her eyes watered with gratitude.

'I've seen a lovely little bar up for grabs in Majorca,' Martin whispered. 'This pandemic business has pushed the price right down.'

Cat put a hand on his arm. If he'd raised the possibility a day or so ago, then perhaps she'd have grasped at the opportunity to escape. But it was clear to her now that she had to reckon with who she was, had to finish what she'd started the previous summer, when she first decided she should try to get her degree.

'You should go,' she said. 'Be a lovely change for you.'

Martin fixed her with a sad stare. Almost as though he knew that their time together was drawing to a close. 'You're a very special woman, Cat.'

Chapter 45

'I've come to give you a lift home.'

Cat could tell Laura was trying her hardest not to react to the mess of her face. But she wasn't doing a very good job of it; she looked hunched, bracing herself for bad news, a startled look in her eyes. She appeared indisputably pregnant now, and Cat found it hard to believe that neither of Laura's parents had noticed.

She was still in the kitchen, forty minutes into what should have been her shift. She'd replaced the ice in the tea towel several times and her face was stinging cold, her lips throbbed and a strange kind of ache was transmitting itself from where her teeth used to be. She'd been smoking continually, which probably hadn't helped the situation – the ashtray next to her was filled with bloodstained butts.

But despite the pain, she felt wonderfully unburdened. How strange that a violent assault should be the thing to make her feel free. She could no longer go on believing that, in his way, her father loved her. And it was only now that she realised how desperately she'd been yearning for his attention, all these years. It was shocking – perhaps she really ought to feel upset, but she had the glorious certainty that he'd never be able to humiliate her again. Nor would she care about the assumptions people might make about her, being the daughter of such a thug.

'Are you okay? Maybe we should get you checked out at the hospital,' Laura said.

Cat smiled. 'Actually, you know what I want more than anything? A walk. Let's take a stroll around the lake.'

It was a bright spring day and as they approached the town's lake, they could hear the excited shrieks of toddlers in the playground. It seemed every passing dog walker was arrested by the sight of Cat's face, something that riled Laura more than it did Cat.

'I can't believe your own father would . . . '

'Only time he played father was when he wanted to upset Bernice.' She'd come out with such bitter statements before, but there'd always been a splinter of hope, a secret belief that Terry knew she was special.

'But to *hit* you?'

'Well, to be fair, I hit him first.'

Laura's breath caught. 'Not because of what we were talking about the other day?'

'Kind of. Although it's not as noble as it sounds. I was trying to blackmail him – I thought you deserved some of his money. And when he didn't fall for it, I saw red. He raped you, Laura. He shouldn't get away with it.'

'Oh Cat. You didn't have to do that.'

'Don't feel sorry for me. It was something I needed to get out of my system.'

'But your teeth . . . '

'It's not the end of the world.'

Once they were halfway around the lake, they took a seat on one of the benches by the water's edge. A small group of ducks swam up expectantly, then slowly dispersed when no food was forthcoming.

'I'm buying a house,' Laura said. 'A two-bedder on that new estate by the Esso garage. The money I got from the divorce just about covers it, but I'll have to rent out the spare room to cover bills.'

'That's great news,' Cat said.

'I was wondering whether you might be interested? I'd like to share with someone I know. I could keep the rent low, in exchange for helping out with the housework – there'll be a lot of it, when the baby's born.' Laura looked out across the water, her body still.

Cat was caught off guard. 'That's really kind of you. But I'm back with James now.'

'You are?' Laura turned to face her, clearly surprised. 'I wasn't sure whether that was just a temporary thing. While you were grieving.'

Cat smiled in response. She didn't know how she could explain the soothing effect of familiarity, how the idea of change felt exhausting. It seemed that if she tried hard enough, she could imagine herself into a graduation gown, into a career, but she couldn't see herself abandoning that house. A house that had never been her home, that seemed to rebuke her somehow with its cream carpeting and gleaming kitchen tiles. Recognising this made her feel suddenly frightened, and she tried to shift her thoughts away. The agony of her mouth was a useful distraction.

Laura looked at her. 'I know you're dealing with a lot right now, but you should know how proud Bernice was of you for daring to make a change.'

'What do you mean?'

'Well, she just kept bringing it up – how you were studying now because you didn't get to when you were younger. She looked so happy every time she spoke about it.'

Cat swallowed. Some reflex within her prepared to dismiss the comment, to bat it away, but she was spellbound. Laura couldn't possibly know how desperate she was for every single word, for this echo of Bernice's voice.

'She knew you had it tough.' Laura's eyes were wide as she said this.

Cat could see that Laura was afraid to go on, waiting for Cat to say something cutting, or to erupt with an angry outburst. Instead, she took hold of Laura's hand and squeezed it. Was this what friendship was? She couldn't say she took pleasure in Laura's company exactly, yet being with her sometimes made Cat feel as though she was recognising herself for the first time.

Laura continued. 'She was in awe of you. Because you weren't defeated. You hoped for more and were prepared to work for it.'

They were silent after that. A light wind rippled across the water, rustling the leaves of the oak trees behind them. Fighting tears, Cat thought of all the things Bernice hadn't known. The lie she'd told James, painting Daniel as some kind of predator to avoid being thrown out. The times she'd found being with her mother so *hard*. For so long, the lack of an education had been a kind of excuse, it had been so easy to blame everything she disliked about herself on the accident and her mother. It had stopped her from really reckoning with herself, with putting in the effort required to change. Was it too late to try again? To forge ahead with her studies and keep trying – striving – to become the version of herself she used to dream of?

After Laura dropped her at the bottom of her road, Cat looked at her phone and saw an increasingly desperate string of messages from James. *I phoned the club, and Martin said you weren't there!!!* the last of these read.

He met her in the hallway. His face was pink and he was just about to say something when he noticed her damaged mouth. For a moment, he looked aghast, then he swallowed and met her eye with a look of calculated spite. 'Were you with him? Did he do that?'

Cat closed her eyes. Surely, James wasn't alluding to Daniel?

'It was Dad.' As she said it, Cat relived the moment, her father's snarling face inches from her own, the ease with which he rendered her immobile.

Was that a flicker of relief on James's face? His eyes seemed to soften. 'Christ. What a thug. Where have you been? I've been frantic.'

He hadn't asked her how she was. This wasn't the kind of thing that Cat would usually notice, but it felt significant that he hadn't.

'I went for a walk with Laura. I wanted some fresh air.'

'With your face looking like that?'

Cat sighed. 'James, calm down. It's *my* face.'

He approached her, placing his hands lightly on either side

of her jaw, inspecting the damage more carefully. Perhaps it was weakness that made Cat want to be held. Her body ached for it, but she didn't feel it was right to ask. Her eyes began to water. She wanted to describe the impotent rage that had made her pick up the ashtray. The hatred in her father's eyes as he got ready to bring his skull crashing down onto her mouth.

Until that point, she'd been expecting a different response from Terry. Recognition. Respect. But they were entirely absent and realising that was intoxicating. She wanted to describe the euphoria she felt as she understood there could be no reconciliation. She was free of her father. Her whole adult life, he'd been a shadowy presence, lurking within her most deep-seated and unspoken fears. She was destined to be just like him – that's what James believed, and she'd believed it too. It had always been there. And now it was gone.

James kissed her forehead, placed a hand lightly on her back to steer her into the living room. 'We'll get you an emergency appointment tomorrow, see about tooth implants. I'll pay.' He sat down on the sofa, and Cat sank down next to him.

'Not tomorrow. I've got an exam.' The talk with Laura, hearing about Bernice's misplaced pride, had made her determined to try to salvage the university semester. Tomorrow's exam was on Mao's China, and although Cat had missed the last few classes, there was a chance she might be able to cherry-pick her questions and focus on areas she'd covered.

James sighed. 'Cat, bless you, but you can't walk around like that. You'll end up with an infection if you don't get it seen to.'

Cat shrugged. She was feeling genuinely relaxed about the

situation until she saw the cold fury in his eyes. 'James, I can't miss the exam because I need to book a dental appointment. That's ludicrous.'

'This isn't a joke, you look—'

'Like what?' Cat stood up from the sofa and faced him.

He turned his head to one side, refusing to look at her. 'Please, let's just get you fixed.'

'I look like some council-estate skank, is that what you meant to say?'

He snorted. 'I'm not playing this game, Cat.'

She balled her hands into fists. How close she'd come to retreating back into their old life. It had been so easy. But she couldn't persist in being *James's Cat*, a person she'd never much liked or respected.

'I'll get my things,' she said.

James began his profuse apologies the moment she started packing, following her around the bedroom as she quickly bundled her clothes into carrier bags. 'Cat, come on. You're overreacting. You can't make me into the bad guy for wanting to fix your mouth.'

Cat shook her head. Her own certainty had taken her by surprise, but she knew she had to do this now, embrace this moment of bravery and take a definitive step towards the life she wanted.

'I've done so much for you. No one else would have taken you back after you'd shagged around.'

Cat stopped listening and focused on the task in hand. There was Laura's offer of a room. For now, it seemed like the perfect solution. She hurried. It wasn't as though James's pleas – later tears – failed to move her. She was just painfully aware that they'd *done* this, the cycles of anger and reconciliation never served to bring them any closer together. She had the euphoric sense that she was stepping outside of all that now. It was the only way to be free.

Epilogue

Cat and Adele had set their stand up in Petersfield's town centre, just off the square where the market was already doing a brisk trade. They'd laid out literature on a small table draped in a European Union flag, and behind them were banners for the campaign to re-join the EU, a movement that had slowly built momentum over the previous year.

In Cat's final year as a student, Adele had been something of a mentor, welcoming Cat into the local Labour Party and signing her up to help at their events. The older woman had long grey hair and dressed in flowing skirts and kaftan tops. When they worked as a pair, they looked so unthreatening, but over the past few months, they'd been jeered at many times, the occasional glob of spit landing at their feet.

Adele was an expert in starting conversations. Every hostile 'British jobs for British people' jibe was met with calm, open questioning. She never told people they were wrong, she asked them *why* they felt a particular way, and was often deeply absorbed in conversation within minutes. 'We're here to listen, not to set people straight,' she'd told Cat.

And, working these events with a more experienced activist, was slowly teaching Cat to keep her own frustrations in check, to resist the impulse to go in with a hard challenge, but rather to search for the tiniest slither of common ground.

'Should I have worn something different?' Cat asked, looking down at her shorts. This was only the second event she'd done in her hometown, and she felt strangely self-conscious.

'Of course not. It's already baking,' Adele said. 'And I've said before, there's no need to dress up, you just have to be yourself at these things.'

The nice weather drew people into the town centre, and the streets were soon alive with shopping couples, with friends strolling along, sipping iced coffee. Laura stopped by with little Reuben in his pushchair. He broke into a grin when he saw Cat, waving his dimpled little arms, then reaching out, asking to be picked up.

Cat unclipped him and swooped him up into the air, prompting a shriek of glee. She had fully expected to want to move out of Laura's place after Reuben was born, but found that with earplugs, she generally got the sleep she needed. In those first early weeks, she really earned her keep, doing endless rounds of washing, preparing meals for an exhausted Laura. She was able to finally free herself from the idea that Laura pitied her and could now enjoy a friendship based on mutual support. The first time Reuben laughed at her, a raucous, unaffected chuckle, Cat had let herself become smitten. These people were her family now.

It was later in the afternoon, when the white heat of midday was finally abating, replaced with a golden glow, that she saw Daniel. Cat froze. He was wearing shorts and flip-flops, smiling as he walked hand in hand with a stocky blonde. *His wife.* She was wearing a pink sundress paired with sensible, tan sandals and her hair was straightened into a severe bob. How ordinary she looked. Their children walked a couple of paces in front, repeatedly turning back to talk to their parents. They were on the other side of the road, heading down the high street. There was every chance he might not see her. *What was he doing here, anyway?*

He turned and their eyes locked. His lips sprang apart and he quickly looked away. His steps faltered, but only slightly. His wife hadn't noticed, was still talking, and on they went, this happy little unit.

Cat exhaled. These last few years had seen a string of euphoric firsts. Leaving James. Finding real friendship with Laura. Being in proximity to a small child and not hating it. Graduating with a first and taking a low-paid but rewarding job as a political researcher while she worked on her master's. There was so much to be proud of, but every time her thoughts turned to Daniel, something inside her snapped shut. If she let herself think of him, of how they'd treated one another, everything was spoiled.

'Fucking joke this is.'

She looked up and saw a heavily tattooed young man regarding the stand. She smiled at him. 'What makes you say that?'

She was just finishing her conversation with that same man ten minutes later, the two of them laughingly agreeing to disagree, when she became aware of Daniel, waiting nearby. This time, he was alone.

'Daniel.' She swallowed, clasping her hands in front of her.

'Look at you,' he said, gesturing to the stand. She wasn't sure what she expected, but his friendly tone was hard to bear.

'Where's your family?' She felt strangely off balance, there was a trembling sensation in her legs.

'They've walked on. We're here for a day out. Lunch and a walk around the lake. I can't stay long, I'm supposed to be getting us drinks. I just wanted to say hello, I guess.'

'How's your book coming along?' It was the first thing she could think to ask. She was so desperate to convey friendship.

Daniel shifted his weight from foot to foot. 'It kind of stalled. I actually got offered another job, all online, no commute.'

'That's great.' Her body still hadn't recovered from the shock of seeing him, but her mind was racing. This might be the very last time. There was so much she wanted to say, so much she needed him to understand.

'Urgh. Communists,' a thin, well-dressed woman sniped as she walked past.

Cat edged away from the stand. She saw a nearby bench become free, but if she suggested sitting down, Daniel might flee.

'I'm sorry we left things as we did,' she said.

Daniel raised an eyebrow.

'There must have been a way, something I could have said to straighten everything out. Not recanted, but ... I don't know. Maybe I should have just been honest with James in the first place.'

Daniel opened his mouth, then closed it. He looked over his shoulder, then back at Cat. 'I know I ought to regret what happened between us,' he said in a low voice. 'But I can't.'

Cat stared at him. She'd expected anger, not this.

Daniel exhaled sharply, his features strangely squeezed. 'I know you're going to do great things,' he said.

With that, he turned and hurried off down the high street. Cat watched him go, thinking of all the times she'd touched him, believing some unspoken force was passing between them. Had it been real? Perhaps. She knew she'd never feel that way again. But she didn't need to. Piece by piece, she was constructing a life that she was proud to inhabit. It was all she ever wanted.

Acknowledgements

Thank you to everyone at Dialogue Books for being such indefatigable champions of untold stories, with special thanks to Millie Seaward, Emily Moran and Amy Baxter, plus copy editor Jade Craddock. It's been my privilege to work with not one, but two talented editors – Sharmaine Lovegrove and Maisie Lawrence – and I've been incredibly grateful for their brilliant insights and suggestions.

Special thanks to my agent Cara Lee Simpson for her encouragement and sound editorial advice. And to Kalika Sands for the generous and careful critiques provided throughout multiple drafts.

I'd like to also thank Paul Burston for opening so many doors for me with my first book through his great work with the Polari Salon and Polari Prize.

Finally, a huge thank you to my family, for everything.

Bringing a book from manuscript to what you are reading is a team effort.

Dialogue Books would like to thank everyone at Little, Brown who helped to publish *Ungrateful* in the UK.

Editorial
Sharmaine Lovegrove
Maisie Lawrence
Amy Baxter

Contracts
Anniina Vuori

Sales
Caitriona Row
Lucy Howkins
Lucy Hine
Hannah Methuen
Dominic Smith

Design
Duncan Spilling

Production
Narges Nojoumi

Publicity
Millie Seaward

Marketing
Emily Moran

Copy Editor
Jade Craddock

Proofreader
Jane Donovan